'McAuley is one of the best'  *nt*

'Few writers conjure futures as convincingly as McAuley' *Guardian*

'McAuley is part of a spearhead of writers who for pure imagination, hipness, vision and fun have made Britain the Memphis Sun Records of SF' *Mail on Sunday*

'He subtly explores what makes us human' *BBC Focus*

PAUL McAULEY

EVENING'S EMPIRES

Copyright © Paul McAuley 2013
All rights reserved

The right of Paul McAuley to be identified as the author
of this work has been asserted by him in accordance
with the Copyright, Designs and Patents Act 1988.

First published in Great Britain in 2013 by Gollancz
An imprint of the Orion Publishing Group
Orion House, 5 Upper St Martin's Lane, London WC2H 9EA
An Hachette UK Company

This edition published in Great Britain in 2014 by Gollancz

1 3 5 7 9 10 8 6 4 2

A CIP catalogue record for this book
is available from the British Library

ISBN 978 0 575 10081 7

Typeset at The Spartan Press Ltd,
Lymington, Hants

Printed and bound by CPI Group (UK) Ltd,
Croydon, CR0 4YY

The Orion Publishing Group's policy is to use papers
that are natural, renewable and recyclable products and
made from wood grown in sustainable forests. The logging
and manufacturing processes are expected to conform
to the environmental regulations of the country of origin.

www.unlikelyworlds.blogspot.com
www.orionbooks.co.uk
www.gollancz.co.uk

To Georgina,
and to Jon Courtenay Grimwood

'In good times magicians are laughed at. They're a luxury of the spoiled wealthy few. But in bad times people sell their souls for magic cures and buy perpetual-motion machines to power their war rockets.'

Fritz Leiber, *Poor Superman*

'No thought can perish.'

Edgar Allan Poe, *The Power of Words*

PART ONE
CHILDHOOD'S END

1

It was a remote and unremarkable C-type asteroid, a dark, dust-bound rock pile with a big dent smacked into its equator by some ancient impact. There were thousands like it in the Belt. Hundreds of thousands. It was mostly known by its original name, 207061 Themba, the name it had been given when it had been discovered in the long ago. It lacked significant deposits of metals or rare earths, and its eccentric orbit, skirting the outer edge of the Belt, didn't bring it within easy reach of any centres of civilisation. Even so, it had been touched by human history.

About a thousand years ago, for instance, towards the end of the Great Expansion, someone had seeded it with a dynamic ecology of vacuum organisms. Its undulating intercrater plains were mantled with pavements of crustose species; briar patches of tangled wires spread across the floors of many of its craters; tall spindly things a little like sunflowers stood on wrinkle ridges and crater walls. A cluster of sunflowers up on the rim of a large circular crater stirred now, the dishes of their solar collectors turning eastward as the horizon dropped away from the sun. Boulders scattered across the upper slopes of the crater threw long shadows. Sunlight starred the needle point caps of a cluster of silvery spires and gleaming streaks shot down their tapering flanks as darkness drained away, shrank to overlapping pools cast around their footings.

One spire near the edge of the little crowd had been painted black. A small movement twinkled at its base. A door dilating, a circle of weak yellow light framing a human shadow. The only inhabitant of these ruins, of this ordinary rock, stepping out into another day of silence and exile.

It was forty-two days after Gajananvihari Pilot had woken in a crippled lifepod on the cold hillside of the crater's inner slope, one hundred and seventy-four days after he had escaped from the hijack of *Pabuji's Gift*. He'd been aimed at the first of a chain of waypoints that would help him reach Tannhauser Gate, had been sinking into the deep sleep of hibernation, when the motor of his lifepod had suffered a near-catastrophic failure and lost most of its reaction mass. The lifepod's little mind had recalculated its options, used the waypoint to change course and establish a minimum-energy trajectory to Themba.

Repair mites had patched up the motor while the lifepod was in transit, but the asteroid was a long way from anywhere else. Hari was grievously short of reaction mass, and couldn't call for help because the outer belt lacked a general commons, and a distress signal might attract the attention of the hijackers or some other villainous crew. Besides, he'd been taught to distrust everyone but his family. His father, his two brothers, Agrata. All most likely dead now. Murdered, as he would have been murdered if he hadn't escaped.

He was nineteen years old, alone for the first time in his life.

He'd channelled his grief and anger into a single-minded determination to save himself. He'd synched his internal clock to Themba's fourteen-hour day, established a strict routine. Waking just before dawn, drinking a protein shake while examining the latest products of the maker and checking his comms (picking up only the ticking of distant beacons; no general traffic, no threats or warnings from the hijackers). Hauling on his pressure suit and leaving his cosy little nest in the spire, climbing a friction track laid down by the spire builders, following it over the crater's rim and through sunflower thickets to the plains beyond.

That day, like every other day, Hari paused at the far side of the sunflowers and used his pressure suit's radar and optical systems to survey each quarter of the visible sky. As usual, the p-suit's eidolon manifested beside him. A shadowy sketch of a slim young woman in a white one-piece bodysuit and an unlikely bubble helmet, her eyes smudged hollows in which faint stars twinkled.

'There appears to be nothing out there,' she said.

'Nothing but stars and planets and moons and rocks,' Hari said. 'Garden habitats. Various kinds of human civilisation. *Pabuji's Gift*, if the hijackers didn't destroy her.'

'No ships. No immediate danger.'

4

'No hope of rescue, either.'

It was more or less the same exchange they had every day. Like most QIs, the eidolon wasn't fully conscious. Her conversations were shaped by decision trees and phatic responses.

She said, as she'd said many times before, 'You will survive this, Gajananvihari. I have great faith in your resourcefulness and resolve.'

'Don't forget anger, suit.'

'Anger has no utility, Gajananvihari.'

'Anger is an energy. Anger feeds my resolve. Anger keeps me going.'

Hari was staring at a faint, fuzzy star above the western horizon. Jackson's Reef, where *Pabuji's Gift* had been hijacked. More than seventy million kilometres distant. He studied it every day, to renew his determination to escape and have his revenge on the criminals who'd murdered his family and stolen their ship and destroyed his life, and to search for the spark of a fusion motor. *Pabuji's Gift* or some other ship, come looking for him.

But that day, like every other day, there was no spark, no ship.

The floor, the surface of the asteroid, sloped away in every direction to the irregular circle of the horizon, still and quiet under the black sky. Vacuum-organism pavements stretched everywhere, patchwork blankets of big, irregular polygons in various shades of red or brown or black, outlined by pale necrotic borders where neighbouring species strove to overgrow each other, punctuated by the slumped bowls of small craters, spatters of debris, scattered boulders. Everything untagged, unaugmented, unadorned by overlays or indices. Naked. Unmapped. Hari had learned to read the contours and patterns of the landscape, but still felt a faint hum of caution when he set out across the surface. He was an intruder in this vast emptiness. A ghost in the desert of the real.

He moved with a sliding shuffle in the negligible gravity, using ski sticks to keep his balance while tethers whipped from his waist, gecko-pads at their tips slapping against the rock-hard surface of the vacuum-organism pavement, retracting, whipping out again. The eidolon drifted beside him. Hari had been born and raised in microgravity – *Pabuji's Gift* was thrifty with reaction mass and spent most of its time coasting in free fall – but he wasn't used to unbounded spaces and found it hard to keep a sense of orientation in the rolling landscape. Everything was either too far away or too close. Sometimes he seemed to be climbing a wall; sometimes he seemed to be descending a near-vertical ramp, moving faster and faster, feeling that he was about to fall away into the sky. Fall, and keep falling for ever. Then he'd stop and catch his breath before setting off again.

Jupiter's brilliant star rose in the east, chasing the sun towards zenith. Themba was small, with an average diameter of just six kilometres. Even at Hari's cautious pace, it was easy to outwalk the day.

His bright yellow p-suit was tanned to the hips with inground dust, and dust had worked into its joints, stiffening the left knee, limiting the rotation of the right shoulder. It had already reached the limits of self-repair. Hari hadn't been able to print new parts or adapt spares scavenged from the antique p-suits of Themba's dead, but he was determined to keep working until he had finished refuelling the lifepod.

That day, like every day, he prospected for beads of water-ice, amino acids, and polycylic aromatics extruded by the lobes and ruffles of the vacuum-organism pavements. He swept up the beads with an extension tool and dumped them into a bag hung from his waist; when the bag was full, he sealed it and headed towards a patch of vacuum organism he'd infected with a virus from the lifepod's library. This was a dark red crustose species with pillowy lobes at its margins which, after the virus had reprogrammed its metabolism, had begun to accumulate organic precursors and elements that the lifepod's hybrid motor could use to synthesise reaction mass. Clusters of flaky crystals glittered with green sparks in the beam of the p-suit's black-light lamp; Hari swept them up into a fresh bag. It was his second harvest from this patch, one of the first he'd turned. Synthesis was slow in the freezing vacuum, but he had over six hectares in production now. Pretty soon he'd have enough reaction mass to reach the nearest settlement, a trip of three hundred days or so. A long stretch in hibernation, but not impossible . . .

It was his only real hope of escaping Themba. Any ships the spire builders might have possessed were long gone, taken as trophies of war or claimed by scavengers, and the rock's most recent inhabitant, an ascetic hermit who had died long before Hari's arrival, must have hitched a ride to it with someone who'd traded the favour for good karma. Hari had searched long and hard in and around the spires and the crater, had probed permanent shadows in scores of crevasses and pits, but had found no trace of a lifepod or gig.

He moved on to another patch of modified vacuum organism, and another. Spiralling outward, skirting a huge boulder socketed in a fat collar of vacuum-organism growth, climbing a wrinkle ridge, passing the slim black rectangle of the monolith set on top. A sect of philosopher-monks had planted them on asteroids across the Belt during the Great Expansion. They were different sizes, but all possessed the same proportions – 1:4:9 – and anyone who touched the black mirrors of their faces elicited a radio squeal aimed at the core of the galaxy. Some thought that it brought good luck, to touch a monolith. Others believed that their stuttering pulses might one day alert some vast, cool, implacably hostile intelligence, which was why only a few survived intact, usually on remote and untenanted rocks.

Themba's monolith was four times Hari's height. Jupiter's bright star hung above it. As usual, he gave it a wide berth. If he set it off, the hijackers or some wandering dacoit ship might detect the signal, would know at once that Themba was inhabited.

Sometimes, though, he was tempted to step up to the monolith and set his gloved hand against its black face and trigger its here-I-am squeal. Sometimes he hoped the hijackers would track him down. He had no defence against them except for a few simple traps and tricks, they'd almost certainly capture or kill him, but one way or another it would put an end to the torment and uncertainty of his exile. And perhaps he'd be able to take some of them with him before he was overwhelmed. He pictured them jerking in nets. Impaled by spikes. He pictured himself slashing at a horde of faceless figures with an incandescent energy beam. He pictured himself attacking them with fists and feet. He hadn't been able to take part in the fight to save the ship. He swore that he wouldn't miss his chance next time.

Early in his exile, still raw with grief and fear, he'd told the eidolon about these fantasies. 'Agrata should have given me weapons,' he'd said. 'Drones. Bomblets. A gauss rifle or a reaction pistol.'

'Agrata didn't want you to fight,' the eidolon had said. 'She wanted you to survive.'

She sometimes said something unexpected. Something that made Hari think. He'd thought about that remark for a long time, and it had strengthened his resolve to escape from Themba and reach Tannhauser Gate. But in spite of trying to fill his hours and days with routine and work and meticulous planning, he was sometimes overcome by a tremendous raging despair at the cosmic injustice of what had happened to him, to his family. At how their future had been smashed, how he'd been left dazed, stranded in the wreckage. The awful details of the hijack lurked at the edge of his mind like one of the insanity memes that the True Empire had deployed against its enemies. A monstrous presence haunting the service levels of his mind, an ancient and insane bot raving against the limits of its protocols.

Anger was an energy, all right. If he wasn't careful, it would consume him.

At last he had collected his daily quota of beads, and headed home. Scooting in a straight line towards the crater, sunflowers suddenly bristling at the top of a long crest. Their black dishes were aimed west now, where the sun hung a handspan above the crater's floor. Hari found the friction track and followed it towards the cluster of spires at the bottom of the slope. ·

Once, the spire builders had spread across more than a third of the main belt, with outposts in the outer belt and the Hildas and Trojan groups, but like most clades it had overreached itself, splintering into sects that had fought bitter battles over minor differences in doctrine. The spire builders on Themba had been wiped out when their home had been struck by drones that shredded into expanding clouds of needles seconds before impact, perforating the spires and their unfortunate inhabitants. Centuries later, the ascetic hermit had settled there. He had removed the bodies of the spire builders and buried them in a common grave, carved a pocket habitat from the maze of little rooms in the base of one spire, pressurised it, and lit and warmed it using power drawn from the black paint he'd sprayed on its riddled skin. And then he'd stripped out another spire, and begun to decorate the interior of its shell with intricate murals that combined scenes and incidents from obscure poems, songs and stories with visions of a marriage between the physical world and the human mind.

The hermit had been working on one of these murals when he had returned to the Wheel. Although, being an ascetic, he would not have thought of his death in that way. There were no heavens or hells, according to them, no cycles of reincarnation. Hari had found him on a net strung between two I-beams, a shrivelled mummy kneeling in his pressure suit, his paint wand still clutched in his gloved hand.

According to a book that Hari had found in the shelter, the hermit's name had been Kinson Ib Kana, and he had died twenty-eight years ago. Or at least, that was the last time he had opened the book. Hari had learned little else. Kinson Ib Kana's p-suit was as dead as its owner, and like all followers of his faith he lacked a bios. Hari didn't know why he'd settled on Themba, where he had come from, whether he had any family, or how old he'd been when he'd died.

He had wrapped Kinson Ib Kana's leathery corpse in its parti-coloured robe and laid it on the ground beyond the spires and covered it with rocks taken from the margins of the big cairn that marked the common grave of the spire builders. He stopped there now, and with the eidolon standing shadowlike at his back paid his respects to the dead man and told him about his day, then shuffled across the dusty slope to the blunt cone of his lifepod. He tipped the reaction-mass makings into the maw of its motor, skimmed down the slope to the spires, and cycled through the airlock into the pocket habitat. He stripped off his p-suit, tumbled his harvest of water-ice, amino acids and aromatics into the hopper of the hermit's maker. Shat, scrubbed himself clean, ate the ration of paste and pellets extruded by the maker, worked for a while on a dart thrower, read a story in the ascetic's book, and at last wrapped himself in the narrow hammock strung between two struts and told the lights to fade.

Another day gone. As always, he fell asleep while thinking about what he would do once he reached civilisation. He was supposed to make his way to Tannhauser Gate and, with the help of his family's broker, contact the hijackers and offer to trade Dr Gagarian's head for the release of any hostages, and the ship. But he was late, so very late, and it was highly probable that only he had survived. Agrata had said as much. His father's viron had been erased; she had lost contact with his brothers and their bioses had fallen silent. It was possible that the hijackers had taken her alive, but when he'd left her, when he'd been shot out of the ship in the lifepod, she had been getting ready to fight them to the death. He'd get to Tannhauser Gate, he'd try to negotiate with the hijackers, but if there were no survivors, if they didn't want to give up the ship, he'd crack open the files cached in Dr Gagarian's head and sell them. He'd mine old databases, locate a trove of ancient treasures in the outer dark, and convince some freebooter to enter into a partnership and make his fortune. He'd pull off a coup in a city bourse, become the bodyguard of some rich trader and save her life, work ten or twenty years in the docks, do everything and anything he could to raise enough funds to hire a gang of reivers and track down the people who had murdered his family and wrecked his life. And then, oh then, he would have his revenge . . .

Another day passed, and another. Early one morning, he woke to find the eidolon bending over him, the twin stars of her eyes gleaming above the sketch of her smile.

'I have news, Gajananvihari! I have good news! It is Agrata! It is Agrata Konwas! She is alive! And I have a message from her!'

2

In the long ago, in their motherland on Earth, Gajananvihari Pilot's family would have been called kabadiwallahs. Junk peddlers. They located derelict gardens and settlements, salvaged machines that could be refurbished or repurposed, isolated and cultured novel vacuum organisms and biologics, concentrated and refined rare earths and metals. They burrowed through the remains of grand schemes abandoned in place or wrecked by war. They ransacked homes and public spaces. They were not sentimental about their work. They were grateful to the dead, but did not try to appease them. The dead no longer had any claim over what they'd left behind, no longer needed it.

There were thousands of derelict settlements, gardens and habitats in the Belt, tens of thousands of abandoned way stations, refuges, supply dumps, observatories, quarries, strip mines, and refineries, but salvage was not an easy way of making a living. Most of the ruins whose orbits brought them close to the remaining cities and settlements had been stripped out long ago; those so far untouched traced distant or eccentric paths, and were often laced with lethal traps and unexpected dangers.

Forty years before Hari had been quickened, his mother, Mullai, had succumbed to a rogue prion that had infected her while she had been cataloguing the feral biosphere of an ancient garden, and converted her brain to tangles of pseudo-organic fibrils. His father, Aakash, after surviving radiation poisoning, six different cancers, and injuries caused by two serious accidents, had passed over fifteen years later, and migrated into a viron. And then Mullai and Aakash's first son, Rakesh, had been killed when he was caught up in riots sparked by one of the end-time cults.

This was several years after the Bright Moment, when everyone everywhere, awake or asleep, baseliner or posthuman, had been struck by the same brief vision: a man on a bicycle turning to look at the viewer as he glided away into a flare of light. It was generally agreed that this vision had been caused or created by an ancient gene wizard, Sri Hong-Owen. At the beginning of the Great Expansion she had left the Solar System in a ship fashioned from a fragment of one of Saturn's moons, and after a troubled voyage of more than fifteen hundred years had arrived in the middle of a war between colonists over control of Fomalhaut's gas-giant planet Cthuga, whose core was rumoured to be inhabited by a vast and ancient intelligence. Sri Hong-Owen's ship had plunged into Cthuga, and twenty years later something strange and wonderful had happened in the depths of the gas giant. Something that had kindled the Bright Moment.

Hundreds of sects, cults, and circles of magicians, hieratics, tele-othetics, psychomancers and idiolaters had sprung up in its wake, like crystals condensing out of a shocked supersaturated solution. They believed that human history had been abruptly and utterly transformed, that the Bright Moment was the harbinger of a final reckoning in which only the elect would be saved, that it was a magical solution to the problems that oppressed their worlds: the static hierarchies that governed them; the centuries-long, belt-wide economic recession; reliance on ancient, half-understood machines and technologies; the lack of new political and philosophical ideas. Some broke away from established religions; others were founded by charismatic self-styled prophets or revelators. Some were violently aggressive; others manifested an ethereal spirituality. Some believed that the Bright Moment commemorated the vastening of an ascended god created by the fusion of Sri Hong-Owen's mind with Cthuga's alien intelligence, foreshadowing an age in which all of humanity would enter a new state of being; others preached that it was a sign that something inhuman and inimical had intruded into the universe, the beginning of a final war between good and evil. They squabbled over minor and major points of doctrine and interpretation, accused each other of heresy and apostasy, and fissioned into a bewildering variety of squabbling schismatic sects.

Only a few survived the first decade after the Bright Moment. Most were short-lived: brief, bright candles consumed by the fever-frenzy of their faith. Some imploded when their leaders were assassinated or arrested; some destroyed themselves in mass suicides, believing that death at an auspicious hour would allow them to ascend into the new heaven created by Sri Hong-Owen, or to create new heavens of their own; some were overthrown when they went to war against the governments and polis of their cities and settlements.

Rakesh was caught up in one of these insurrections. He was negotiating the sale of salvaged machinery in New Shetland when a radical cult, the Exaltation of the Free Mind, began to attack posthumans, accusing them of using memes implanted during the Bright Moment to control the thoughts and actions of baseliners. Riots broke out across the city; Rakesh was killed while trying to reach the elevators to the docks.

Hari was quickened soon afterwards, cloned from Rakesh's gene library. His childhood was tinted by the death of his predecessor and his father's forthright hatred of the Exaltation of the Free Mind and the rest of the end-time cults. According to him, they threatened to create an age of superstition and unreason worse than the tyranny of the True Empire. He was particularly exercised by claims that the Bright Moment was a miracle that circumvented or violated natural laws: an intervention by a supernatural deity that stood outside the ordinary flow of events and could not be parsed by the ordinary human mind. The Bright Moment's challenge to our world-picture should stimulate our curiosity, Aakash said, not close it down. It was a question of epistemology, not eschatology.

Hari loved talking with his father, loved stepping through the translation frame into the viron where Aakash had made his home after he had passed over. It mirrored the desert homeland of one of the Pilot family's ancestors, on Earth. The blue and starless sky, dominated by the platinum coin of the sun. Red rocks and red sand studded with vegetation, stretching towards a flat horizon. Rugged cliffs rooted in talus slopes, a narrow path winding through boulder fields to the tall cave mouth where Aakash met his visitors. A magical place where even time was different. Sometimes Hari would emerge from the viron and discover that hours or days had flown by, out in the real world.

Sometimes he and his father would sit on slabs of warm sandstone outside the cave while they talked; sometimes they wandered through the desert. The old man bare-chested in a crisp white dhoti, stocky, broad-shouldered, a head shorter than Hari. His searching gaze and gentle voice. One hand combing the snowy flood of his beard while he anatomised some arcane nugget of philosophy or history.

Because Aakash believed that everything was connected to everything else, that every detail in the world's vast tapestry was significant, his conversations tended to veer in sudden and unexpected directions or lose themselves in digressions about the culture of ancient universities, the chemistry and manufacture of the oil paints used by Renaissance masters, the intractable problem of qualia, or some other topic suggested by what appeared to be random association. He'd always been like this, Agrata said, but his tendency to ramble far from his starting point had become more pronounced after he'd passed. He was no longer anchored to common clock time in his viron, and could extemporise for hours on any subject that caught and held his interest.

As Hari and his father followed long meandering paths through the desert, windows would pop open to illustrate a point Aakash was making, diagrams would scribble across the sand, equations would ink themselves across the screen of the sky. The pocket universe of the viron was contiguous with Aakash's thoughts, an extension of his mind, but its detailed, self-consistent landscape was also interesting in its own right. An expression of an ancient, alien logic. Ripples of sand formed ridged cells like those Hari's tongue could parse on the roof of his mouth. Little crescent dunes were patched here and there, none higher than his knees. Scatterings of stones. Gravel pans. Interlocking circles of thorny bushes. Palisades of spiny paddles. Lizards darting across bare rock like small green lightnings. Small birds flicking between clumps of vegetation or hovering on a blur of wings as they inserted their hypodermic beaks into flowers. Larger birds tracing patient circles high above. All of this generated from rules that mimicked a place long ago lost under ice, on Earth.

As Hari grew older, his conversations with his father increasingly turned to the influence of cults on the politics of the surviving cities and settlements of the Belt and Mars and the moons of the outer planets, the personalities and backgrounds of key players, how various scenarios might be gamed, whether attempts to begin a dialogue with certain powers on Earth were useful or foolish, rumours about the suppression of philosophical explorations and research into the cause and nature of the Bright Moment, and so on, and so forth.

Nabhomani, who after Rakesh's death had taken charge of negotiations with politicians and officials in the cities and settlements visited by the ship, said that the old man had retreated into a fantasy world of conspiracies and hypotheses because he no longer had any traction or influence outside the little world of his ship. That was why he wouldn't allow Hari to explore any of *Pabuji's Gift*'s ports of call, Nabhomani said. Not because Hari wasn't old enough to take care of himself, but because Aakash didn't want him exposed to inconvenient truths.

Agrata, as usual, took Aakash's side. The last of the original crew, tirelessly loyal, she had been on the ship ever since it had been refurbished and relaunched. She said that everything had been thrown into hazard by the shock of the Bright Moment. Old certainties were crumbling, political alliances were shifting, the influence of the end-time cults was spreading in strange and unpredictable ways.

'We must do our best to understand these changes if we are to survive,' she said.

'And this obsession with the Bright Moment?' Nabhomani said. 'How will that help us survive?'

'Aakash hopes to keep a little light of reason alive in a growing sea of darkness. I see no harm in it.'

'You can't reason with people whose beliefs are based on unreason,' Nabhomani said. 'I should know. I must deal with them at every port.'

Nabhoj, as usual, wouldn't be drawn into these arguments. He had a ship to run.

Nabhomani and Nabhoj were clones of Aakash, physically identical but with very different personalities. Nabhomani was affable, convivial, rakish, dressed in a vivid motley of fashions picked up from the cities and settlements he visited, loved gossip, and possessed a sharp eye for the affectations and foolishness of others. Nabhoj was a phlegmatic technician who rarely socialised with the passengers, and could sulk for days if he lost an argument about how best to solve a problem encountered during salvage work. Once, when Hari had been helping him try to free a recalcitrant pressure-hose coupling, he'd fetched a diamond knife and methodically hacked the coupling to a cloud of splinters. And then the fit had passed, and he'd given Hari one of his rare smiles and told him that although it wasn't a standard procedure it had solved the problem quite neatly.

Hari was schooled in every aspect of the family trade by Agrata and his two brothers, received a patchwork education in philosophical truths and methods from his father and various travelling scholars, and played with the children of passengers and specialists in the many disused volumes of his family's ship. It was a ring ship, *Pabuji's Gift*, a broad ribbon caught in a circle five hundred metres across, with a twist

15

that turned it into the single continuous surface of a Möbius strip. The ship's motor hung from a web of tethers and spars at the centre of the ring; its hull was studded with the cubes and domes that contained workshops, utility bays, power units, an industrial maker, and the giant centrifuges, light chromatographs, and cultures of half-life nematodes and tailored bacteria; its interior was partitioned into cargo holds, garages for gigs and the big machines used in salvage work, and the lifesystem. Much of this space was unused. The ship could support more than a thousand people, but even when Hari's father had been alive it had never carried more than a tenth of that number.

Hari and the children of passengers and specialist crews had the run of the empty cargo holds, habitats and modules, the mazes of ducts and serviceways. A world parallel to the world of the adults, with a social structure equally complicated, possessing its own traditions and myths, rivalries and challenges, fads and fashions. Endless games of tig on one voyage; hide-and-seek on another. One year, Hari organised flyball matches inside a cylinder turfed with halflife grass; when interest in that began to wane, he divided the children into troops that fought each other for possession of tagged locations scattered through the ship.

He was fifteen then. Tall and slender, glossy black hair done up in corn rows woven with glass beads. Even though every adult – everyone over the age of twenty – still seemed impossibly old, adulthood was no longer mysterious and unattainable, but a condition he was advancing towards day by day. He knew that he would soon have to give up childish games and shoulder his share of the family's work. He was beginning to understand the limits of his life, beginning to realise how small his world really was, how little it counted in the grand scheme of things.

And then he fell in love for the first time.

Her name was Sora Exodus Adel. A passenger travelling with her brother and her mother between Tannhauser Gate (where *Pabuji's Gift* had unloaded most of the salvage from her last job) and Trantor (where she would unload the rest). Sora was a year older than Hari, languidly elegant, too old for the kind of games that Hari felt he was too old for now.

He couldn't tell Sora how he felt. He and his brothers were not allowed to have what Agrata called intimate relations with any of the passengers or specialists. Nabhoj was partnered to the ship; Nabhomani told Hari outrageous stories about debauchery with women and men he met during his negotiations in cities and settlements, promised to let Hari have a taste of the good life when Hari was at last allowed to go ashore. Hari could admire Sora Exodus Adel from a distance, engage in a little light banter, no more than that. Better to avoid her altogether, he thought. Find some work he could vanish into until the ship docked at Trantor and Sora disembarked. Then one of the other passengers, Jyotirmoy Hala, came up with a plan to put on a dance performance based on one of the stories about the parochial god from whom the ship had taken its name.

Jyotirmoy was three years older than Hari, the only child of two philosophers who were studying the topology of the space-time distortions around the seraphs, and expected their son to take up their work. Jyotirmoy did not argue with his parents. He simply refused to listen to them. He spent a dozen hours a day practising dance and the art of gesture. The only way to be good at something, he told Hari, was to let it take over your life. To dedicate yourself to it. You had to practise an elevation or a gesture over and over until you had it right. Or at least, until you stopped making obvious mistakes. And then you could get down to the serious work. Then you could think about making something new.

Agrata approved of Jyotirmoy's idea, and Hari found himself helping to put a troupe selected from the younger passengers, including Sora, through twenty days of rehearsals. Jyotirmoy plotted the choreography, chose the music from the ship's library, and supervised the design and manufacture of costumes and masks; Hari spent as much time as he could with Sora. He learned that she and her brother had been born on Mars but for most of their lives had been travelling with their mother, a musician who played ancient symphonies using an orchestra thing controlled by the play of her hands through columns of light. Sora maintained the orchestra thing; her brother organised events and arranged travel. She liked the gypsy life, she said, but she wouldn't work for her mother for ever: she'd settle down eventually, design gardens, and raise children. She and Hari talked about the places she had visited, the people who lived there. Admirers of her mother's work. Collaborators. Other artists. Hari was still young enough to believe that the world was sensitive to his emotions and moods, that everyone was a player in the drama of his life. It gave him an odd, lonesome feeling to think of Sora leaving the ship, travelling on without him to places he'd never see, the precious time they had together dwindling to an anecdote, a memory.

Sora said that she found it odd that Hari had never gone ashore at any of the cities and settlements *Pabuji's Gift* had visited, said that his life and his family were very strange.

'Really?'

'You don't see it because you don't know anything else,' Sora said. 'But in all the cities and settlements I've visited, all the ships I've travelled on, I've never before met someone like you.'

'We're just ordinary people, trying to get by.'

'Don't you think it's the tiniest bit weird, being born after your parents died?'

Hari loved Sora's bold, straightforward manner. Her candid gaze. She had a way, while talking, of running a hand through the cloud of her hair and twisting a clump of it in her fingers and turning it to and fro, as if trying to tune into stray thoughts. She had long, dexterous fingers. Her fingernails were tinted dark green, with mica flecks.

Hari said, 'My father passed over. He isn't exactly dead.'

'What's the difference?'

'You could ask him.'

'He is like a ghost. A haunt who manifests himself in the drones and manikins. Can he really operate several of them at once?'

'Of course. He assigns their addresses to temporary sub-selves, and reintegrates when he has finished.'

'You think that is ordinary?'

He loved the little uptick in the corner of her smile. A sly little warp, a playful complicity. There were five different shades of gold in her eyes.

He said, 'It's just what he does.'

Sora said, 'Many of the passengers are scared of him.'

'Are you scared?'

'Of course not. Well, just a tiny bit. Actually, Agrata scares me more. I don't think she likes me.'

'Agrata can be . . . abrupt, I suppose. It's hard to know what she likes and doesn't like, but I bet she'd like you, once she got to know you.'

'That's sweet of you, Hari.'

Hari loved Sora's small kindnesses, her unaffected sophistication, was jealous when she paid attention to anyone else, envious of the easy way Jyotirmoy talked with her about details of the performance, of the way the two of them hung close together, studying sketches for costumes, watching recordings of rehearsals, discussing staging and the movements of performers, where they should start and where they should come to rest, and half a hundred other things whose significance Hari barely understood. For the first time, he saw himself as others might see him. An outsider. An awkward, peculiar kid who knew everything about his ship and his family's trade, and almost nothing about anything that really mattered.

But when Jyotirmoy at last led his crew into the hollow sphere of the stage, with the adult passengers hung all around its perimeter, Hari dissolved into his role and the gestalt of the performance. Costumed in fluttering silks, faces painted white, lips tinted black, eyes emphasised by red and gold make-up, he and the other players flitted through the web of ratlines and perches, through washes of light and music, like the little birds in Aakash's viron. Breaking into freefall dances, freezing in tableaux when one of the principals performed a solo part. Jyotirmoy played Pabuji; Hari played Pabuji's friend, the snake god Gogaji; Sora played Gogaji's bride and Pabuji's niece, Kelam; Sora's brother, Jubilee, played Ravana the Demon King, from whom Pabuji stole the she-camels he gave as a wedding present to Gogaji and Kelam; the other children doubled as wedding guests and the camels.

Hari inhabited the intricate sequence of his role with a kind of exalted serenity. Every move, every pose, sprang from memories laid down in his bios and muscles during the painstaking rehearsals, a single thread in the weave of the whole. Coming together, spinning apart. His concentration broke only once. Moving out of the dance in which he and Sora mirrored each other's gestures and poses in an expression of joyful fidelity, he overshot the perch where he would rest in shadow while Pabuji, with comically elaborate caution, stalked the she-camels. Jyotirmoy caught his arm and halted and turned him, and their gazes met. A strange moment of doubling, seeing Jyotirmoy's concern flash in Pabuji's mask. And then Hari was in the correct position, and Pabuji soared away into a cone of light, and Hari was caught up again in the flow of the dance and the unfolding dream logic of the story, waking at the end of it, dazed and happy and exhausted, to the audience's applause.

At the party after the performance, still wearing Gagaji's green tunic and trousers, Hari dared to ask Sora if she wanted to see his favourite place on the ship, a diamond composite blister where you could switch off all the lights and lose yourself in the rapture of the starry dark. And was amazed, even though he'd so often imagined floating in the small intimate space with her, her warmth, her touch, when she smiled and said why not? It was as if he still inhabited the dream reality of the play. Anything seemed possible. But when they started across the crowded space Agrata materialised out of the throng and told Hari that Sora's mother wanted to congratulate him on his performance. And Agrata's look told Hari that she knew. She knew all about his plan, his private fantasy.

He submitted, of course. He didn't know what else to do. Following Agrata, smiling and nodding while Sora's mother talked, hardly hearing what she said to him or what he said to her, Sora somewhere else in the big, crowded, noisy volume, the moment lost. And that was that. The next day, *Pabuji's Gift* docked at Trantor, unloaded its cargo of refined rare earths, let off a few passengers, took on a few more. Sora and her family were among those who disembarked. And Jyotirmoy vanished. Abandoned his parents and jumped ship.

Agrata didn't say anything about Jyotirmoy's defection or Hari's unrequited love for Sora, but one day, during a discussion about re-configuring passenger accommodation, she began to talk about the early days of the ship.

'There wasn't much to it,' she said. 'Just two modules powered and pressurised, one for crew, one for the farm that fed the crew. A handful of gigs, most of them still in need of complete overhaul. Very little in the way of equipment. Your father refurbished it himself, with the help of a small crew he recruited from people who answered a note he'd posted in the commons. We were idealists, but we were not day-dreamers or utopians. We knew what was possible and what was not. We were practical. We made plans and we worked together to make those plans possible. We were all like your father, in short. As he was then.'

'He changed, and you didn't,' Hari said.

'I've told you this many times before, I know. Yes, he changed. There were just ten of us, when the ship set out on its maiden voyage. Nominally, we were a collective, but Aakash was in charge. A bene-volent despot who ruled by charisma and an intimidating intellect. No one could argue with him because he had an answer to every question, every objection. I remember when he tried to introduce democracy to our little crew. One of his enthusiasms. He had so many, in those days.

It was part of his charm, and bled off his excess energy. Like most of them, democracy did not last, but it was fun while it did. Now we're all bound by custom. Even your father. We do things in a certain way because that's the way we do things.'

They were sitting in the omphalos, at the heart of the passengers' quarters. Pale walls of architectural weave wrapped around an open cylindrical core lightly webbed by walkways and ziplines. The architectural weave knotted at various levels into platforms, like the one on which Hari and Agrata sat, or thickened into suites of rooms. Only a few people were about. Hari usually liked the drowsy peace of the omphalos, but now it seemed to close in on him like a helmet filled with stale rebreathed air.

He said, 'I'd like to take this ship to new places. Places people don't go any more. To Neptune's Trojans. To the Centaurs, and the scattered disc. To the Kuiper belt. There are all kinds of places out there, places no one has visited for centuries. Who knows what we might find?'

Agrata said, 'You want to shake things up.'

'Why not?'

'Yes, why not? The family needs to be challenged if it is to stay strong. But I don't think you're telling me what you want to do,' Agrata said. 'I think you're really telling me what you don't want to do.'

'You think I should do what I'm told. Even though I think it's wrong.'

'Rakesh once said more or less the same thing. He was about your age, as I recall.'

'I suppose we've all done the same things or wanted the same things,' Hari said.

Sometimes he felt that every thought, every idea, was an echo of the thoughts and ideas of his brothers and his father. That everything that happened to him had already happened to them. That there were no new stories.

Agrata studied him. She was more than a century old, and because she lacked every trace of vanity, and because it gave her authority with the passengers, she let her age show. Her face was creased and lined; her skin was freckled with pale spots where viral treatment had removed incipient carcinomas; her coarse grey hair was brushed back from her forehead and braided into a long rope coiled at her back.

She said, 'You feel sorry for yourself. Hard done by.'

'Rakesh didn't have to deal with Aakash's fantasies about the Bright Moment and the cults and all the rest.'

'Now you sound like Nabhomani.'

'Perhaps Nabhomani is right.'

'You should talk to your father about your ideas. Argue with him. Start to take the initiative. The worst that can happen is that he won't listen to you.'

Hari tried his best. And at first Aakash seemed to take note of his comments. At least, he did not dismiss them immediately.

'You've been taking advice from the old woman,' he said.

Hari admitted it.

His father was amused. 'We've been together a long time. She knows how I think; I know how she thinks. She believes that I can't change. What about you?'

They were sitting cross-legged on a slab of warm sandstone at the entrance to the cave, in the shadow of the cliffs.

Hari said, 'I think you want what you think is best for the ship.'

'A diplomat's answer. Maybe you're learning something. I want what's best for you, too. You may not think it, but I do. You'll see how it all works out.'

How it worked out, a little over a year after Hari started to push back against his father's ideas, after he had for the first time left the ship to observe how Nabhomani negotiated with officials on Sugar Mountain and had, not very seriously and for only a few hours, run away, Aakash announced that the family would suspend its salvage work for a while. They were going to try a new direction, he said. They were going to help a very good friend of his complete his research into the nature of the Bright Moment.

Some fifty days later, *Pabuji's Gift* reached Ceres and the tick-tock philosopher Dr Gagarian came aboard, and everything changed.

3

The pressure suit's eidolon possessed a childlike naivety. Usually, her unaffected optimism and innocence was charming. Playful. But sometimes, as when Hari tried to explain the hijackers' subterfuge, why he knew that Agrata wasn't really Agrata, it seemed like wilful obstinacy, a capricious refusal to acknowledge unpalatable facts.

He was working while he talked to her, inside the spire that the ascetic hermit, Kinson Ib Kana, had hollowed out and decorated with murals. Checking his traps, greasing pawls and ratchets, making sure that lines were strung tight, bladders containing his special chemical mix hadn't hardened off, and nets were packed just so. Working as steadily as he could, despite tremors in his fingers and the soup of mercury and molten poison cooking in his bowels.

'I've known her all my life,' he told the eidolon. 'We talked every day. And the person I talked to isn't that person.'

'Did she give the wrong answers to your questions?'

The eidolon was perched on the intersection of two crossbeams. Her eyes gleaming in the shadows.

'Not at all. She knew everything. They'd done their research. But Agrata – the real Agrata – wouldn't have tried to answer those questions.'

No, she would have told him to stop being so silly. She would have told him to be sensible. That was one of her favourite words. Sensible. Also trust, pride, loyalty, duty. Hari desperately wanted it to be Agrata come to rescue him, to take him home, but he knew that it was his duty to keep Dr Gagarian's head safe and reach Tannhauser Gate and begin negotiations with the hijackers. It was his duty to make sure that his heart did not overrule his judgement.

'I suppose there is a small chance that Agrata might be a prisoner.

Saying whatever the hijackers tell her to say because they are holding hostages they have promised to hurt of kill if she does not cooperate. But I don't think she is a prisoner,' Hari said, and felt a freezing pinch in his heart again. 'I think she's a djinn, probably generated from her bios. It is a good copy, but not quite good enough.'

He was trying to quantify an instinctive feeling of wrongness, searching for an explanation of something deeper than reason. Because what is the mass of a feeling? What is its wavelength, its position on the electromagnetic spectrum?

'But if it's really the hijackers,' the eidolon said, 'why would they want to talk to you? Why would they warn you that they were coming here?'

Hari had to remind himself that this artless simplicity was a feature of her mindscape, not a bug.

'They spotted the lifepod, and knew I was here. And they also knew that they were within range of the lifepod's radar. They knew I would know they were approaching Themba. So they tried to convince me that I was going to be rescued rather than be captured or killed. Because if they stayed silent, I would know at once that I was in danger.'

Hari had finished checking the alignment of the last of the traps; now he pushed off towards the floor. Picts flared as he dropped past murals, wrapping him in momentary sensations of colour and movement, triggering fleeting emotions he couldn't quite name. Strange cousins of wonder and awe and agape. Nostalgia for things he'd never seen or experienced. A profound and disorientating déjà vu. He hoped the murals would distract his enemies. If they did, he'd build a shrine to honour the memory of Kinson Ib Kana.

He hit the floor, swaying as his boots stuck and waist tethers shot out and anchored him, and the eidolon appeared at his side, saying, 'Isn't that why you made all this? Because you knew you were in danger?'

Hari watched the glow of the murals die back into darkness. Scattered lamps shone out of the shadows around him. He could see the wires and rigging of the traps around the hatch, told himself that he could see them because he knew where to look. Told himself that even if the hijackers spotted them, they would think they were part of the spire's internal construction.

Now he knew that they were coming for him, he was excited and scared. Excited because he would soon have a chance to confront them. Scared because he might fail. This was this, as Professor Aluthgamage

24

had liked to say. There were a trillion trillion trillion alternate versions of the universe, a trillion trillion trillion realities, but this was the only one Hari inhabited, the only one he knew. And his only defence against his enemies was a handful of childish tricks and traps built from junk.

'I wasn't one hundred per cent certain that they would find me,' he said. 'I hoped that they wouldn't. I really did. But it made sense to prepare a little welcoming party just in case. And besides, it kept me busy. It passed the time.'

The eidolon shrugged. An unsettlingly human gesture. 'You will look foolish if you are wrong, and catch Agrata in your traps.'

'I will be dead if I'm right, and don't do anything.'

Hari ducked out of the hatch at the base of the spire, and shuffled across the dusty ground towards the lifepod. Jupiter was following the sun down towards the western horizon. The spark of the hijacker's ship hung high above. It was one of the brightest stars in the sky now. It would reach Themba in a little under three hours.

The eidolon drifted beside him, saying, 'Are you are planning to escape? I thought that the lifepod lacked sufficient reaction mass.'

'I have another use for it,' Hari said.

He reached into the hard-code matrix of the lifepod, reconfigured its proximity and navigation protocols, and began to write the first of two short command strings. He'd been working for ten minutes when the eidolon spoke. Saying that Agrata wanted to talk to him again.

'She says she will be with you soon. She says she looks forward to embracing you and telling you everything.'

'Don't reply,' Hari said. 'The hijackers are wondering what I'm doing. Let them.'

'I'm scared, Gajananvihari.'

'Me too.'

'I'm scared that you may be right. And if you are right, if the ship is piloted by the hijackers, if they are trying to fool you with a copy of Agrata, shouldn't you reply? Otherwise, they will realise that you know that she is not who she claims to be.'

It was a good point.

Hari thought for a moment, then told the eidolon to open the channel. At once, Agrata's face appeared in a small window. It looked exactly like her. Her grey hair brushed back from her forehead. The wrinkles at the corners of her eyes deepening when she smiled and asked him what he was doing.

'Packing up.'

'There's nothing you need in that little capsule.'

The hijackers were watching him. Of course they were.

He stepped on his anger and fear and said, 'I'm salvaging a few things.'

'You have kept the head safe?'

'As I told you.'

'You should retrieve it now. So we can leave as soon as possible.'

'Remember how I used to play hide-and-seek? Me and the other children. We'd switch off our bioses and scatter, and the person appointed seeker would have to find the rest. Every person the seeker found had to help him until only one person – the winner – was left undiscovered. I wasn't much use at being a seeker, but I was very good at hiding.'

There was a pause. Agrata – no, not Agrata, it was some kind of djinn, a puppet manipulated by his enemies – was still smiling, but more than ever her face seemed like a mask. At last, she said, 'This isn't a game.'

'I managed to stay hidden for a whole day, once. Long after the game was supposed to end. The others searched and searched but they couldn't find me. They were so angry when I came out of hiding. So were you, because you thought I'd come to some harm.'

'I'm not angry. I am pleased that you stayed hidden and kept the head safe. And I am pleased to have found you alive and well.'

'I'm good at hiding. And I'm good at hiding things, too. You won't ever find it without me.'

He wanted the hijackers to know that if they killed him they would have a hard time tracking down Dr Gagarian's head.

Another pause, not so long this time.

'I'm not surprised that you're scared, Gajananvihari. It must have been a terrible trial, hiding on this lonely rock, wondering if anyone would ever come to rescue you. Well, here I am. Ready to take you back to the ship. Where you'll be given a hero's welcome.'

No one in Hari's family would have said *take you back to the ship*. They would have said, *bring you home*.

He said, 'Will you let me become a pilot?'

'You can be anything you want to be, Gajananvihari.'

'We'll make a fresh start.'

'Of course.'

'Head into the outer dark and have all kinds of adventures.'

'Anything you want. Perhaps you could fetch Dr Gagarian's head now. It would save so much time.'

'I have to go. Finish shutting things down.'

'I will see you very soon.'

'Yes,' Hari said and cut the connection.

'It was her,' the eidolon said. 'Wasn't it?'

'No. No, it wasn't.'

'Are you all right, Gajananvihari?'

Hari blinked and sniffed and swallowed. 'Shut up and let me finish this work.'

'I don't understand what you're doing.'

'It's another surprise.'

Hari finished writing the command strings, ran a simulation. It would have to do. He closed down the interface and shuffled away to a safe distance and initiated the lifepod's ground-effect routine. Dust blew straight out all around it and it rose up several metres and settled back, balanced on the faint breath of its motor.

'I don't suppose you'll tell me why you are wasting reaction mass,' the eidolon said.

'I decided that I need a distraction,' Hari said.

This was the tricky part. Themba's gravity was very shallow; escape velocity was just twenty kilometres per hour. An untethered person could bounce into a long, low suborbital lob using only the power of their leg muscles. The lifepod see-sawed on minuscule variations in thrust, and it took thirty minutes to walk it down the slope into the deep shadows at the bases of the spires, and position it in the small space between three of the tallest. One of them was the spire that Kinson Ib Kana had hollowed out – the spire Hari had filled with traps.

'They are almost certainly watching you,' the eidolon said.

'I know.'

'It is not a good hiding place.'

'I'm not trying to hide it,' Hari said.

The lifepod settled in a brief squall of dust. The spires reared above, their tops burning with raw sunlight.

'They will be able to see its infrared footprint,' the eidolon said.

'You really don't know what I'm doing, do you?'

'Perhaps it is good that I do not. In case they hack me.'

Hari hadn't thought of that. He said, 'Tell me at once if they try.'

'I may not be able to detect it,' the eidolon said.

'You may have been hacked already. Is that what you are telling me?'

'How does anyone know who they really are?'

Hari was back inside the hollow spire, checking the zipline he'd strung across a short gap to one of the spire's neighbours, when the eidolon appeared right in front of him.

'You asked me to tell you when the ship made its final burn,' she said. 'It's doing it now.'

Hari levered himself halfway out of the hole he'd cut in the triple skin of the spire, hanging on to the taut cable of the zipline as he twisted to look straight up at the black sky. His helmet visor placed green brackets around the ship's brilliant star. A block of flickering figures showed changes in delta vee and distance. It was close enough to ping its registry, now: one of the gigs from *Pabuji's Gift*, *Little Helper*. It was spiralling in to match Themba's orbital velocity, sinking towards the western horizon. Hari believed that it would touch down as soon as it was out of sight, or drop a search party riding scooters or broomsticks. But he didn't even have that long.

'Uh-oh,' the eidolon said.

'What? What is it?'

'I'm not sure.'

'Give me your best guess.'

'Incoming.'

'Incoming what?'

'I don't know. Small. Fast. Here.'

There was a flash of light far below, beyond the shadows that drowned the spires' footings. A plume of dust shot up, rising above the sharp tips of the spires, a kilometre tall, two, three. Its top glowing in sunlight, beginning to evert into complex sheets and folds, its base lifting away from a fresh crater where something small and bright jiggled with frantic energy. Hari leaned out further, clinging to the zipline, used his visor's zoom facility, saw a tangle of wires knitting itself into the shape of a man. A man-shaped drone.

It stood up, half-collapsed, rose again. It was five metres tall, and very thin. The red dot burning in the centre of its small cylindrical head turned towards Hari, who flinched away. Then it leapt. A long and graceful parabola aimed at the spire where he perched.

Hari's mouth was flooded with the taste of burnt plastic. Gauzy lights shimmered in his left eye, he felt a sudden hot pressure behind it, and something fell away from him.

It was the eidolon, arrowing past the spires, colliding with the drone, vanishing. The machine froze, rigid as a statue, hit the side of the spire and rebounded, soaring away, striking the upper part of the crater's slope amidst flying sheets of dust and disappearing beyond the sunflowers at the top of the rim wall.

For a moment, nothing moved but ropes and threads of dust falling out of the giant plume, glowing golden-brown in the level, late-afternoon sunlight. Then the eidolon was suddenly beside Hari, sitting at the lip of the round opening in the spire's silvery skin, saying, 'Did you see? Did you? Did you see?'

'I saw it. I'm not sure what it was.'

Hari was still watching the top of the rim wall, half-expecting the drone to come bounding back like some demented conjuror's trick.

'I neutralised it. Did you see? I am weaponised. I didn't know until I needed to know.'

'Is it dead?'

'It is neutralised.'

'If you could force it to work for me it would be a useful weapon.'

'I stripped out its protocols. Erased them. I don't know how to put them back.'

Hari studied the eidolon. The sparks of her eyes glimmering in the ghostly sketch of her face. 'What else can you do?'

'I don't know! Isn't that amazing?'

'Could you protect me from the hijackers, when they come? Could you disable their suits, disable their weapons?'

'Yes. No. Maybe. I don't know.' The eidolon paused, then said, 'Agrata wants to talk to you again.'

'Tell her to come find me.'

4

The long, slow paths that *Pabuji's Gift* traced between cities and settlements and the distant and obscure ruins where Hari's family searched for salvage sometimes attracted itinerant philosophers who needed seclusion and tranquillity to concentrate on their studies. One of them, Professor Ari Aluthgamage, was developing a taxonomic scheme that classified hinge points in history by type and significance and would eventually, according to her, frame an objective assessment of claims by end-timers that the Bright Moment had jolted history on to a new path and opened up previously inaccessible possibilities. She entertained Hari with stories about obscure pivotal moments in the long ago, and tried to teach him something of quantum philosophy; he learned that he really wasn't much good at grasping the mathematics that described the architecture of the various possible species of multiverse – quilted, inflationary, cyclic, landscape, holographic, and so on – but never forgot one of the professor's analogies. The multiverse, she said, was like an old library whose shelves were packed with books arranged by a cataloguing system that ranked them according to similarity, each book containing within its covers a story that varied only slightly from the stories of its immediate neighbours, but by increasing degrees from those of increasingly distant books. Yet even books whose covers were jammed together, whose contents differed by just a single letter, were discrete and self-contained entities. No information could cross from one to the other.

There are billions of possible histories, Professor Aluthgamage told Hari, but ours is the only one we can experience, the only one whose existence is beyond doubt. This is this.

Although the underlying mathematics were dauntingly complex, it was easy to imagine how histories could diverge at the whim of the assassin's bullet or bomb, because of a general's decision, or a chance meeting, or the accidental death of a philosopher, before she came into her full power. Professor Aluthgamage told Hari about refinements of the old argument about whether the influence of one person was more important than the political situation in which they were embedded. It took her two minutes to teach him an ancient rhyme about a nail, a shoe, a horse, and a battle and a kingdom lost; two days to explain its context.

She was especially interested in the many hinge-points in the long life of the gene wizard Sri Hong-Owen, and was anatomising the possible histories that they might have generated in other universes. Hari knew most of the story already. His father often talked about Sri Hong-Owen, how she'd grown up in a small town in the ruined rainforests of Greater Brazil, developed weapons that had helped to defeat the Outer city states of the moons of Jupiter and Saturn, and synthesised new wonders based on techniques harvested from the Outers' knowledge bases; how she'd used those techniques to create hundreds of orbital gardens, a significant contribution to the peaceful expansion of human civilisation into every part of the Solar System, before lighting out for Fomalhaut with a crew of strange children she'd tailored from her own genome, and so on, and so forth.

'Surely all that matters is what she became, not what she was,' Hari told Professor Aluthgamage. 'And we have no idea what she became because we aren't capable of understanding it.'

He'd had enough of history for one day, and had long ago learned that testing his teacher's patience with impertinent and contrarian assertions was an effective way of ending a seemingly interminable lecture or lesson. But Professor Aluthgamage was one of those philosophers who thrived on dissent.

'The Bright Moment is merely the climax of a long chain of hinge points. Sri Hong-Owen could not have reached that final step without travelling through its many predecessors. And any point in that chain is no more or less important than any other. Everything we do has a consequence, Gajananvihari,' she said, and proceeded to expound upon a long list of examples.

Professor Aluthgamage spent many hours discussing her work with Hari's father, but after she left the ship Hari never learned if she ever completed her taxonomic analysis of other histories. Probably not. The various philosophers who travelled on *Pabuji's Gift* usually valued the chase far more than the prize.

Like the rest of his family, Hari preferred to deal with practical problems. Fixing malfunctioning machinery, devising work-arounds and short cuts, overcoming constraints imposed by lack of time or slender resources. By the age of eighteen he had worked in every part of the ship and on every aspect of the family trade, and was developing plans to explore the outer reaches of the Solar System and discover long-forgotten settlements. He correlated information mined from obscure and debased databases, borrowed time on the ship's navigation system to plot the orbits of distant kobolds and model multibody trajectories that optimised expenditure of reaction mass and time. He believed that he was mapping out a new future for his family, and was grievously upset and dismayed when his father told him that he must set aside his plans and become a full-time assistant to the ship's latest guest, Dr Gagarian.

Dr Gagarian was a tall skinny tick-tock person some three hundred years old. His jointed carapace of black fibrogen resembled an ambulatory pressure suit or an animated man-sized insect; his major organs had been replaced by machine equivalents; his brain was laced with neural nets that formed a kind of shadow mind that stored his every thought and reaction; his eyes were dull white stones in a leathery inexpressive face. A remote, forbidding figure. Inhuman, barely mammalian. In an age where there was very little philosophical investigation, and most of that was theoretical, he was an incredibly rare beast: an experimental physicist. For the past twenty years, he and his small crew of collaborators had been attempting to identify, measure and define changes in the fine grain of space-time caused by the passing of the Bright Moment. *Pabuji's Gift*, whose exploration of remote ruins often took it far from the background noise of human civilisation, was an ideal platform for his latest experiments, and its store of ancient machines and the debris of half a hundred clades and cultures provided useful components for his experiment apparatus.

Nabhomani believed that Dr Gagarian was a charlatan. A magician disguised as a philosopher, consumed by a fantasy of mastering secret powers. Nabhoj and Agrata had little time for Dr Gagarian's experiments, either. But Aakash was convinced that the tick-tock philosopher and his collaborators were engaged on a hugely important project.

'We are able to make a living from mining the past because so many of the old technologies have been forgotten,' he told Hari. 'Baseliners have given up on philosophy, and posthuman clades prefer theory to application. We live in an age that cannibalises its past because it has lost faith in its future. But with our help, Dr Gagarian and his friends will change that. We will be at the root of a great new flowering of practical philosophy. Think of what we will be able to do, once we master the principles that created the Bright Moment! New kinds of communication devices. Unlimited computational capacity within the metrical frame of space-time. New technologies, Hari. New technologies and new ideas.'

'Will we be rich?' Hari said.

'Everyone will be enriched,' Aakash said. 'That's the important thing. Everyone will benefit, and everyone will be enriched '

A year after Dr Gagarian came aboard, *Pabuji's Gift* dropped off the last of its other passengers and gave itself over entirely to his research. Running silent and dark for days at a time, every system powered down, while Dr Gagarian attempted to make delicate measurements involving teleportation of entangled virtual particles, or created high-energy Planck-scale entities and analysed their decay. Cruising above the plane of the ecliptic, where the planets and most asteroids traced their orbits, dropping off autonomous probes that when linked together would form a long-baseline interferometer.

Hari's family had abandoned their salvage work, were surviving on reserves of credit that had been greatly depleted by purchase of components and raw materials essential to Dr Gagarian's experiments. They were indentured to the tick-tock philosopher's research and their father's monomania.

Hari had little interest in or understanding of the ideas that were being tested, but he discovered that he liked solving the challenges of assembling and deploying the experimental apparatus. Using the ship's big maker to fabricate some components, sourcing the rest from the ship's stores, he constructed probes and detectors designed by one of Dr Gagarian's collaborators, the partner of the Pilot family's broker at Tannhauser Gate, and spent hours in vacuum and freefall, setting up experimental rigs on the hull or at the ends of tow lines kilometres long. It was difficult and sometimes dangerous work, but Dr Gagarian was sparing with his praise and, although he spent many hours discussing his theories and results with Aakash, he had no time for Hari's naive questions.

'There's no point trying to explain my work to someone who knows so little that he doesn't even know what he doesn't know,' he once said.

According to Aakash, Dr Gagarian was attempting to solve two important problems. First, why the signal that had triggered the Bright Moment had affected everyone, awake or asleep, baseline or post-human, in the same way. And second, why it had shown no measurable attenuation. The gravitational force between two bodies was inversely proportional to the square of the distance between them. The intensity of sunlight falling on a planet was inversely proportional to the square of the planet's distance from the sun: Venus, twice as far from the sun as Mercury, received a quarter of Mercury's insolation. The density of the flux of any energetic or physical force was necessarily diluted as it radiated outward and the area of its wavefront expanded. But the wavefront of the Bright Moment, originating from a point source twenty-five light years distant, had maintained the same intensity as it crossed the Solar System. If light had possessed the same property, the sky would have been white-hot with the radiation of every star in the Milky Way, and of all the galaxies inside the light-horizon. For that reason, Aakash said, the Bright Moment could not continue to maintain the same intensity as it continued to expand into the infinite universe, because it would require infinite energy to do so. At some point it would attenuate, or perhaps pop like an over-inflated balloon. But over relatively short distances, its wavefront seemed to be able to expand while maintaining its flux density at a constant value.

Dr Gagarian believed that the Bright Moment had propagated as a jitter or wave in the ocean of the Higgs field, a relic of the Big Bang that permeated the entire universe and offered resistance to particles when they accelerated or decelerated. The masses of the various kinds of fundamental sub-atomic particles were defined by the way they interacted with the Higgs field; particles which moved through vacuum at a constant speed, like photons, were massless because the Higgs field didn't affect them. It was possible to manipulate the value of the Higgs field in a volume of space, Aakash told Hari, but only at temperatures equivalent to those of the universe immediately after the Big Bang.

'Such temperatures, a trillion degrees or so, can be created in high-energy particle colliders, but only change the value of the Higgs field on a microscopic scale, and only for a very short time. Also, it would oscillate as wildly as in the first instant of creation, before the universe cooled below the critical temperature at which those oscillations condensed into a non-zero value. It would not be possible to impose a signal on it. However, the contemporary Higgs field is not completely frozen,' Aakash said. 'It fluctuates about its non-zero value. I'm sure you know why.'

Hari thought hard, then said, 'Because the universe hasn't yet cooled down to absolute zero.'

'Exactly. The fluctuations are usually minuscule, random, and universal. But Dr Gagarian's long-baseline experiments have acquired evidence for traces left by local, non-random changes. He believes that the carrier wave for the Bright Moment may have been hidden somewhere in that microscopic jitter. Created by manipulating the spin-0 particles that make up the Higgs field, perhaps. Encoded in dimensions folded into loops smaller than any fundamental particle . . . It appears to conflict with special relativity, which requires the Higgs field to be everywhere uniform, but if that can be resolved – *once* it is resolved – it will change everything.'

It was a grand vision, but seemed impossibly distant. There was always more work to be done. Measurements to be refined, ideas to be tested and retested. We must be patient, Aakash told his family. We must take the long view.

A year passed, Dr Gagarian's second aboard *Pabuji's Gift*. They put in at Porto Jeffre to purchase consumables, and elements required for fabrication of components of Dr Gagarian's probes, and resumed their cruise above the plane of the ecliptic. But the family's credit lines were almost exhausted, and Nabhomani and Nabhoj were growing mutinous. At last, Aakash and Dr Gagarian agreed to suspend their work for a short while, and *Pabuji's Gift* headed out to search for salvage in a distant and long-abandoned garden, Jackson's Reef.

5

Hari had retreated to a hiding place high up in the hollow spire, braced in the angle where three spars met in absolute shadow beside the exit hole and its zipline. He was draped in camo fabric that absorbed his p-suit's infrared and electromagnetic signatures, and had set up decoys at various levels – man-shaped balloons kept inflated and heated by simple resistor circuits. They wouldn't fool anyone for more than a couple of seconds, but he hoped that be enough time to spring his traps. The nets and the darts, the deadfall and all the rest.

He wished for what must have been the hundredth time that the hermit's maker had possessed templates for firearms or energy rifles. He had managed to persuade it to extrude simple weapons – darts, throwing knives, shuriken – but right now he would have traded all of them for a basic kinetic handgun.

Feeds from cameras on top of various spires gave him overlapping views of the crater. The gleam of friction tracks laid across dun ground, running between wiry tangles of vacuum organisms. Bootprints every-where. The rock field of the cairn. The grave of Kinson Ib Kana. The small crater blasted by the drone's descent. It was close to sunset, and the cluster of spires threw long shadows towards the rim wall.

Let his enemies come. Let them step into his trap. Let them come now. Let this be over. Let this be over.

Then the camera feeds vanished all at once and a patch of wall at the base of the spire glowed red and white and blew out in a transient caul of vapour and dust. The last reserves of Hari's confidence vanished. He'd set most of his traps around the entrance to the spire, hadn't thought of this obvious move. Two pressure-suited figures stepped through the circular gap. At once, the murals and picts sprang into life

36

and Hari's traps fired. Spring-loaded tubes shot ceramic darts at the entrance; nets woven from fullerene thread spun towards the floor, propelled by tiny canisters of carbon dioxide; the lower part of the hollow space was filled with a storm of metallic flakes designed to confuse radar and other imaging systems. A moment later, squibs of reaction mass ignited and the deadfall, a tall narrow box fabricated from fullerene sheets and packed with rock dust, guillotined down.

The nets and darts missed the intruders. One waved the broad beam of an infrared laser through the floating flakes, shrivelling them; the other released a crowd of tiny drones that rose up in spiralling search patterns. A moment later, the murals and picts went out.

Someone was trying to talk to Hari on the common channel. A woman's voice, calling to him, telling him to surrender. The balloon decoys began to pop one by one as the drones discovered them.

'It's over,' the woman said. 'Come out now.'

Less than a minute had passed since the intruders had stepped into the spire, and Hari was down to his last trick. He activated the first of the command strings he'd written into the lifepod's control system, and set off strings of flashbang explosives. As they filled the hollow spire with sharp stutters of lightning and blew open bladders containing his special mix of chemicals, he shrugged off the camo fabric and grabbed the grips of the zipline pulley and kicked off as hard as he could.

He flew out of the spire into an expanding dust storm. Above, he could just make out the spark of the lifepod's motor, powering away into the sky.

The wall of the neighbouring spire loomed out of the dust. A moment later Hari shot through the hole he'd cut in it, crashed into layers of expanded foam that killed most of his momentum, and struck the far wall with a solid thump. As he drifted backwards through collapsing sheets of foam, he let go of the zipline pulley and ripped a ceramic throwing knife from the velcro patch on his left hip. Caught the edge of the hole, severed the zipline, and hung there, listening to the harsh engine of his breath.

A fierce light flared high overhead, glowing through the fog of falling dust. The shadows of the spires slanted through it, fading as the flare-light dimmed.

The eidolon appeared beside Hari. Saying, 'You blew up the lifepod.'

'Something like that.'

'Your distraction.'

'To cover my escape from the spire. And if they think I tried and failed to flee Themba, they may not come looking for me.'

'They may not have noticed it,' the eidolon said, and showed him an infrared image. It was the spire, glowing with the ghost heat of chemical reaction. At the base, two small figures shone brightly, caught in awkward attitudes, unmoving.

Hari floated down through falling dust into the absolute darkness around the bases of the spires and found his way to the far side of the hollow spire. His helmet light showed that the hole the two intruders had blown in the wall was filled with a grotesque bulge of black stuff, like an organ spilling from a wound. A small portion of the foam generated when the two chemicals had been explosively mixed, expanding to fill the spire from top to bottom and hardening almost at once.

He pulled up the infrared view again. The intruders were still caught in the same positions. One crouching, the other sprawled face-down. When Hari called to them on the common channel, a woman answered, saying she'd kill him when she got free.

'What's your name?'

'I am the arm and hand.'

'Whose arm and hand?'

'My own, now. You killed my sister. The foam damaged her lifepack. Did something to her rebreather. Have you ever heard someone dying of anoxia? Listened to their breathing get faster and faster? Listened to it stop? We would have saved you, boy. Those were our instructions. Find you. If you were dead, bring back your body. If you were alive, bring you back safe and sound. But you killed my sister, and I'm going to strike you down by my own arm, my own hand.'

'You should keep still,' Hari said. Nabhomani had taught him how to control his voice; he sounded a lot calmer than he felt. 'Don't struggle. The foam is an excellent insulator, so your suit won't be able to exhaust your waste heat. If you struggle, you'll die of heatstroke.'

The woman cursed him and his ancestors, cursed all the children he would never have after she had finished with him. She was very imaginative, but her breathing soon became laboured and she fell silent.

Hari asked her again who she worked for.

'I don't have to tell you anything.'

'Deel Fertita and the others were friends of yours, weren't they?'

The woman didn't reply.

Hari said, 'Who paid them? Who paid you?'

Silence.

'Your employer has my ship and my family. I have Dr Gagarian's head. That's what this is about, isn't it? Dr Gagarian's head, and the files it contains. That's why you were looking for me. Well, you found me, and I'm ready to make a deal. I want to negotiate with your employer. If you tell me how I can contact them, I'll free you.'

'That's the best you can do?'

'It's a good deal. If things work out, everyone will get what they want. You, me, your boss, my family.'

Another silence. Hari let it stretch. Let her think about the way out she'd been offered.

At last, the woman said, 'You aren't in a position to help your family. All you can do is decide whether or not you want to save yourself. And the only way you can do that is by cutting me free and giving me the tick-tock's head. Do that, do it right now, and I'll let you live.'

She would be able to free herself when the foam cooled and began to lose its integrity, but Hari wasn't about to tell her that. He said, 'It seems to me that you aren't in a position to threaten me.'

'Do you really think we were the only ones looking for you? As soon as we found you, boy, we called our sisters. They're on their way, and you aren't going anywhere. We came down on a broomstick that went into orbit as soon as we hopped off, and it won't return unless I call it. And your lifepod blew up when you tried to put it out of harm's way.'

'Is that what you think you saw?' Hari said.

'You don't have any way of getting off this rock,' the woman said. 'We'll wait here, you and I, until my sisters arrive. And when they do, you'll spend the last hours of your life wishing you'd surrendered the head when I asked you to.'

'I'll only give it up when your boss agrees to free my family.'

The infrared image showed that the woman was gripping a laser wand in her right hand. It was jammed against the breastplate of her p-suit, and she was trying to twist back and forth in the coffining foam, trying to open a space so that she could use the wand to cut herself free.

She said, 'What if I told you that you can't help your family because they're dead? As dead as my sister.'

Blood beat in Hari's head. The monster stirred in the shadows.

'Prove it,' he said.

'There it is,' the woman said. 'There's the problem with the way you're trying to play this. You won't believe anything I say, and I don't care if you cut me free or not. If you don't do it, my sisters will. But I'll give you one more chance to do things my way. Cut me free, and then fetch the tick-tock's head from its hiding place and lay it at my feet. That's the best deal I can offer. The only deal you're going to get.'

Hari decided to call her bluff. 'I can't walk away from my family. But I can walk away from you. In fact, that's exactly what I'm going to do. I'm going to take the gig you stole and leave you to strangle in your own waste heat.'

'That's what I thought,' the woman said, and there was a red flash and something struck Hari and knocked him backwards. He flew a long way, bounced once, twice, ground and sky wheeling past, and smashed into a clump of dark red wires and was caught there, dazed and breathless. After a little while, the p-suit's eidolon bent over him, asking him if he was all right, if he could remember his name, if he could at least talk.

'She blew herself up,' Hari said stupidly.

His head sang, and when he began to extract himself from the wires he discovered that he couldn't move his left arm. Downslope, the spires stood quiet and still under the black sky.

'I sustained no significant damage,' the eidolon said, 'but I'm afraid that the humerus of your left arm is fractured. I have numbed and set it, but it will require further medical attention.'

'I'm all right,' Hari said.

'I would have prevented her if I could,' the eidolon said.

'It was my mistake. I thought I could talk to her. I thought I could make a deal.'

'She tried to kill you by killing herself. Why would she do that?'

'Because she was a fanatic. Because she was no ordinary dacoit.'

The eidolon was silent for a few moments, as if processing this. Then she said, 'What will you do now?'

'I can't stay here. I have to assume that she was telling the truth. That her sisters are on their way.'

'How can you leave? The gig is still in orbit. And so is the broomstick that the woman and her sister used to reach the surface. I will try to command it to return, but I cannot guarantee that it will listen to me.'

'I have a better idea,' Hari said. He used his bios to send a brief command string, and pointed out the brief flicker of motor exhaust to the eidolon.

'That is not the gig,' the eidolon said. 'I would know if you were flying the gig by wire.'

'It's the lifepod.'

'You destroyed the lifepod.'

'It flared off a couple of hundred grams of reaction mass through a safety valve, and ignited it with a brief pulse of its motor. As if it had been fatally damaged when I tried to escape. We'll use it to reach the gig.'

'Do you think you can outrun her sisters?'

'I'm going to try,' Hari said.

6

Jackson's Reef was a froth of bubble habitats wrapped around a shaped sliver of rock some ten kilometres long. Half its volume was ravaged, open to vacuum; the rest had devolved to low-diversity, low-energy ecosystems dominated by tough, slow-growing chlorophytes, blue-green algae, and archaebacteria. There were hundreds of similar bodies within the Belt and beyond; Jackson's Reef was distinguished from all the others by its eccentric, long-period orbit.

It had once been the centre of the Golden Mean, a kingdom of gardens and settlements in the outer belt that had flourished several centuries before the rise of the True Empire. When they'd been deposed by a vicious civil war, the last members of its ruling family had hastily converted their capital city into a multigeneration starship and aimed it at 61 Cygni, but its mass drivers had failed before it could acquire solar escape velocity. It had become trapped in a cometary orbit with a period of more than six hundred years, taking it out above the plane of the ecliptic and across the Kuiper belt to the edge of the Oort Cloud before swinging back towards the sun. Its original inhabitants were either dead or long gone by the time it first returned to the Belt. A crew of rovers laid claim to it, tried and failed to revive its ruined biomes, abandoned the project. And now it was returning to the Belt for the second time, and Nabhomani and Nabhoj had devised a plan to strip out salvageable machinery and artefacts, and mine what was left of its ecosystem for useful biologics and unique genomes.

Aakash surprised Hari and his brothers by making only token objections. But really, Nabhomani's and Nabhoj's case was more or less airtight. The family had spent more than two years collaborating with Dr Gagarian, they were low on credit and the consumables required to make up for inefficiencies in the ship's recycling systems, and their current course, cruising above the plane of the ecliptic, meant that they were well placed to reach Jackson's Reef with a minimal change in delta vee.

While four specialists recruited by the family's broker in Tannhauser Gate zipped towards *Pabuji's Gift* in a bottle rocket, Hari and his brothers readied the gigs and bots, prepped refineries, separation tanks and mass chromatographs, grew up bacterial cultures and suspensions of halflife nematodes, surveyed the reef using a swarm of fast flyby drones, and planned a schedule of work. Dr Gagarian kept to himself, analysing the results of his experiments and keeping watch on his chain of detectors. It was a busy, pleasant time.

The specialists arrived, unpacked their equipment, familiarised themselves with *Pabuji's Gift*'s systems. The ship was making its final approach to the reef, and Hari was in one of the storage bays, sourcing a replacement for a failed component in the motor of one of the gigs, when a brief tremor set tools and small machines and machine parts rocking and chiming in their racks. The link between Hari's bios and the ship's commons fell over. For the first time in his life, he couldn't talk to anyone else. And then he discovered that the bay's hatch had locked itself.

He thought at first that it was one of Nabhomani's stupid pranks. His brother had locked him in, and now he had to figure out how to escape. He tried and failed to force the hatch to respond to his commands, tried and failed to dig into the security shell that had sprung up around its stubborn little mind. Shouting at it was equally useless, although it relieved the sudden hot pressure of his anger. He swam up and down the storage racks, looking for another way out and failing to find it, came back to the hatch, studied its mechanism, went to search for a couple of tools.

He was dismantling the hydraulic latch when the hatch's clamshell halves parted with a juddering groan, seizing up before they were fully open, and someone in a red pressure suit eeled through the narrow gap.

It was Agrata. Her helmet hung on one hip, a fat cryoflask hung on the other. She gripped Hari's hands in hers and drew him close and asked him if he was all right.

'What happened?'

The old woman's grim, haunted gaze frightened him. She smelled strongly of smoke.

'We have been hijacked,' she said, and told him that one of the members of the specialist crew had sabotaged the ship's comms system and its mind, picted a clip showing a storm of sparks sweeping out from the reef: sleds ridden by hijackers, a small fleet of drones and bots. They had swarmed through cargo hatches and airlocks, Agrata said, securing the ship module by module, hunting down its occupants. Aakash's viron had been infected by djinns and erased; she hadn't been able to contact Nabhomani and Nabhoj. Their bioses were down. She believed that they were dead, that she and Hari were the last of the family. They had lost control of the ship and were outnumbered and outgunned.

Shock blanked Hari's mind. He asked several stupid questions. Who had locked him in? Why did she think that Nabhomani and Nabhoj were dead? How had they died? Where was Dr Gagarian?

Agrata gave him a stern and tender look that pierced him through and through. 'You have to be ready to do a hard thing,' she said.

Something was caught in Hari's throat. 'You want to surrender.'

'I want you to follow me.'

The four-way junction outside was hazed by drifting layers of smoke. The pungent odour made Hari sneeze. He recoiled against the frame of the hatch, clung there, saw a body floating overhead. It was one of the specialists, a thin pale man named Odd Samuelson. Slowly turning, arms and legs askew, a dark patch of blood seeping across the chest of his blue suit liner. One of the maintenance bots hung close by. It was dead too.

'Let's go,' Agrata said, and they arrowed through ripples of smoke and dove through a hatch into the long corridor that ran parallel to the hold where Hari assembled Dr Gagarian's experimental apparatus. In the airlock at the far end, Agrata fastened her helmet and helped Hari pull on and check the systems of an unfamiliar pressure suit that popped and creaked as it adjusted to fit him. Its eidolon greeted him and cheerfully asked what he would like to do today. He ordered her to be quiet with absent-minded curtness. There was the quick vibration of pumps, a brief flash of mist as moisture condensed from the last of the air, and the external hatch opened to raw vacuum and sunlight.

He chased Agrata around the ship's ring. They flew from shadow to shadow as if playing a game of tig, pausing, looking all around, moving on. One of the storage bays was venting a plume of vapour, but otherwise everything looked absolutely normal. Sunlight glared on the sides of modules, on stretches of hull. Hari's blank shock was beginning to be coloured by fear and excitement. He saw the irregular shape of the reef beyond the twist in the ring and the tower of the command and control module, then realised that something was wrong with the tower – its skin was punctured and torn open in several places and a cloud of debris was expanding away from it . . .

Agrata grabbed his arm and pulled him into a scuttle hole. A hatch slammed shut, lights came on, air hissed as the lock pressurised. Agrata told Hari to keep his suit sealed, and he followed her out into a small, red-lit, spherical space he'd never seen before: rows of small flatscreen panels set amongst quilted padding; three acceleration couches jutting from the walls.

It was the old emergency bridge, according to Agrata. She shucked her helmet, stuck a gloved hand in a slot in the wall, twisted something. A square hatch slid open beside her and she turned to Hari and told him that it gave access to a lifepod, told what he had to do.

He refused, shocked and dismayed.

'You want to fight the hijackers,' Agrata said. 'But it wouldn't do any good. The security systems fell over. We were unable to implement internal defence protocols or activate the reaction cannon. We lost control of manikins and bots and drones. Your father is gone. I believe that Nabhoj and Nabhomani are gone, too. The ship is lost. Pay attention! You have to reach Tannhauser Gate. This lifepod will get you there, but it will take more than two hundred days – you'll have to spend most of the trip in hibernation. When you arrive, you'll contact our broker and his partner. Rember Wole and Worden Hanburanaman. No, don't ask questions. There's no time. You will also take this with you.'

She unhooked the insulated flask, told Hari what was inside.

'We were lucky. Lucky that you were working in a place where you could be isolated from the lighting. Lucky that I found Deel Fertita before she could finish cutting off Dr Gagarian's head.'

'She was doing what? Why?'

Deel Fertita was a proteome specialist, one of the people the family's broker had recruited to help the family strip Jackson's Reef.

'Deel Fertita and the others were in league with the hijackers. They sabotaged the security and comms systems, infected your father's viron and the ship's mind with djinns. And Deel Fertita killed Dr Gagarian, and I killed her before she killed me,' Agrata said flatly: a blunt statement of fact. 'I killed her, and then I finished what she'd been doing. One thing is clear. Dr Gagarian's head is valuable to the hijackers. Its files must contain something they or their employer badly

45

want. You will take it, use it to bargain for the freedom of anyone left alive. And for the ship.'

'What about you?'

Hari found it difficult to get the words past the obstruction in his throat.

'The lifepod can carry only one person,' Agrata said, 'and it is the only one still active, because it isn't connected to the commons. Aakash installed it when the ship was refurbished. A last-ditch measure for an emergency he hoped would never come. But here it is, and here we are. Don't worry about me, Gajananvihari. I am a hundred and twelve years old. I was born in Thrale, Mars, and left as soon as I could. I worked for a biotech merchant in Iron Mountain. Learned enough to start my own export business. Lost everything, wrote librettos for two operas, made enough to start my life over. I have visited all of the major cities in the Belt. I have been to Earth. I have been partnered three times. I had two children. My son died in an accident more than seventy years ago, but my daughter is still alive, and I have three grandchildren, and five great-grandchildren. One of my granddaughters is the mayor of Thrale. Another is a famous composer of aeolian symphonies. I have had a long life, Gajananvihari. A good life. I'll keep the hijackers distracted for as long as I can, and if I die it will be with few regrets. You will get to Tannhauser Gate and find Rember Wole and Worden Hanburanaman. Rember will help you get in contact with the hijackers and negotiate the return of the ship. Worden will help you understand Dr Gagarian's work, and how to carry it forward.'

'What if the hijackers won't talk to me?'

'They'll want to talk because of who you are, and because you have what they want. You'll understand everything when you get to Tann-hauser Gate.'

Agrata gave Hari a card that would allow him to draw on the credit the ship had deposited in Tannhauser Gate's bourse.

'I know that I am asking a hard thing of you,' she said. 'But you are the only one who can do this. There it is.'

There it was. No chance to make a last glorious stand, or fight the leader of the hijackers in hand-to-hand combat. Instead, ignominious flight, exile from everything he knew and loved, and an impossible mission.

'I won't disappoint you,' he said.

'I know,' Agrata said.

7

Hari landed the lifepod by remote control and walked out across the surface of Themba for the last time. The sun had set and he navigated by enhanced starlight. Reviewing the brief conversation with the hijacker over and again as he crossed grainy, monochrome vacuum-organism pavements. Trying to work out where he'd gone wrong, what he should have said.

'I failed them,' he told the eidolon. 'I failed my family. I screwed up. It was a simple transaction. Her freedom in exchange for the answer to a single question. It should have been an easy sale. Absolutely straight-forward. But I failed.'

'You told me that she was a fanatic,' the eidolon said. 'It is my understanding that such people are not amenable to reason.'

'Nabhomani would have persuaded her. He told me that you start making a sale when the customer turns you down. You have to make them want what you're selling. You have to lead them to the decision. That's what I failed to do.'

'She was willing to pay with her life, and yours,' the eidolon said. 'Even if she had been dealing with someone who possessed superior negotiating skills, it would not have changed the logic of the situation.'

'You don't really understand people,' Hari said.

But as he walked on, examining his conversation with the hijacker from every angle, he couldn't see how it could have ended up at a different place. The ruthless logic of self-sacrifice scared him. It would make another encounter with the hijackers extremely risky, but he knew he had to find them, had to talk to them. He had get off Themba and reach Tannhauser Gate, and Rember Wole and Worden Hanbur-anaman. He had to save Agrata and his brothers, if they still lived. He had to negotiate their return, and the return of the ship. And he still wanted revenge. Now more than ever.

He wished he knew why the hijackers wanted the head. Something Dr Gagarian knew. Something he had discovered. Something to do with the traces left by the Bright Moment. He should have paid more attention to the tick-tock philosopher's work.

The lifepod had landed some way beyond the slim rectangle of the monolith, squatting at the centre of a circle of scabbed char. Hari shuffled due south from the monolith to a small, shallow crater packed with tangles of fine wire. The eidolon watched as he knelt at the edge of the crater, tangled threads gleaming shocking scarlet in the beam of his helmet lamp, and pulled from its pit of loose dust a cryoflask wrapped in radar-absorbent cloth.

He carried it to the lifepod and wriggled inside, acquired his destination, pressed the big red button that floated in the virtual keyboard. Twenty minutes later, he was climbing into the airlock of *Little Helper*.

The gig was a stack of three spherical modules of diminishing size. A simple, sturdy design. The smallest module housed the lifesystem; the one in the middle was an unpressurised cargo hold; the largest contained the motor, fission batteries, and tanks of air, water, and reaction mass. The gig slowly revolved about its long axis as it swung around Themba's battered sphere, with the lifepod's blunt cone nosed into the open hatch of the cargo hold.

The two hijackers hadn't bothered to change the security profile. Hari worked up a course, ignited the motor. Themba's lopsided profile shrank into the starry black. Dwindling to a fleck, a faint point, gone.

For several days, *Little Helper* fell sunwards on a free-fall trajectory, heading for a waypoint that would slingshot it towards the outer edge of the main belt and Tannhauser Gate. Then attitude thrusters ringed around the joint between its motor and equipment hold modules popped and stuttered, aiming it towards a new destination, and its motor ignited and kept burning.

Hari had discovered that he was being followed.

PART TWO

MAROONED OFF
VESTA

1

The pursuer came trolling out of the outer dark at a steady 0.1g. *Easy Does It*, the largest of *Pabuji's Gift*'s gigs. When Hari had first spotted it, it had been more than fifty million kilometres away. Twenty days later it had closed half that distance, and was still coming on.

Hari had given up on Tannhauser Gate. It was a long way around the outer edge of the main belt, and *Easy Does It* would catch him long before he reached it. Instead, he'd altered course, driving *Little Helper* towards a waypoint on the far side of the 3:1 Kirkwood gap.

Easy Does It altered its course, too. Hari made no attempt to contact his pursuers. Opening a channel risked infection by the same species of djinn that had compromised the comms of *Pabuji's Gift*. His pursuers didn't attempt to contact him directly, either, but soon after they matched his new course the eidolon reported persistent attempts to locate and utilise open ports in *Little Helper*'s comms, and Hari was forced to shut everything down. The gig running dark and silent as it crossed the Kirkwood gap, falling towards the waypoint.

The prominent gap, one of several swept clean by orbital resonance with Jupiter, divided the Belt into two unequal halves: the populous main belt, close to Mars, and the more diffuse outer belt and its outlying clusters. More than ten thousand gardens and habitats constructed from materials mined from rocks and comets orbited within the main belt; there were more than a million and a half rocks with a diameter of more than a kilometre. A few, like Vesta and Pallas and Hygiea, had diameters of several hundred kilometres; Ceres was almost a thousand kilometres across. There were cratered rubble-piles blanketed in deep layers of dust and debris. There were mountains of nickel-iron, stony mountains of pyroxene, olivine and feldspar. There were rocks rich in tarry carbonaceous tars, clays, and water ice. Some orbited in loose groups, or in more closely associated families of fragments created by catastrophic shatterings of parent bodies, but most traced solitary paths, separated by an average distance twice that between the Earth and the Moon, everything moving, everything constantly changing its position relative to everything else.

Little Helper closed on the waypoint and swung through its steep gravity well, changing course and gaining velocity, racing towards Vesta and its artificial moon, Fei Shen. It was an old trading city, Fei Shen. *Pabuji's Gift* had visited it several times after Hari had been born. There would be people who knew his family and their ship, people who might help him.

Easy Does It swung past the waypoint, too.

Hari made his plans, unmade them, remade them. He read in Kinson Ib Kana's book. It was a slim black slab that woke when he tapped its surface three times. There was no index, no method of making any kind of input or connection to whatever spark of intelligence it possessed. Each time he woke it, it displayed a random sample of unadorned, unaugmented text, usually an aphorism or a brief verse or a praise song:

I shall not coil my tangled hair
But let it hang free
And when I bathe
I shall splash water all around
But never wet my hair.

And:

Secrets are safest in the mind of a wise man.

And:

On the seashore of endless worlds the children meet with shouts and dances.

They lingered for ten minutes or for an hour or more before they faded and were replaced by another random sample. Hari supposed that he was meant to study them and unpack and contemplate every possible meaning; instead, he short-circuited the process by switching off the book with three quick taps and switching it on again. Tap tap tap, tap tap tap. On/off, on/off, on/off. Skipping through poems and songs and sayings until the book presented him with something more substantial. Stories about the long ago, before human beings had quit the shelter of Earth's skies; stories about the Age of Expansion or the True Empire; stories about dream worlds, or worlds of other stars.

Some were as long and intricate as any saga. The story of a Martian paladin's quest during the rise of the True Empire, for instance. The Trues had conquered Ceres, the Koronis Emirates, and half a hundred lesser kingdoms and republics, and as they began to probe the defences of Mars the Czarina dispatched twenty of her paladins to search for the armill of one of her ancestors, which was believed to augment the wisdom of its wearer and control secret caches of powerful weapons and squads of shellback troopers from the long ago.

After adventures in the deserts and mountains of the red planet, fighting bandits, dust ghouls, and rogue gene wizards and their monstrous offspring, the paladin was riding through the trackless forests of the Hellas Basin when she discovered a circular lake with a slim, bone-white tower rising from its centre. As she approached the slender bridge that arched between shore and tower, another rider came out of the trees and challenged her: a rogue paladin whose armour, like hers, had lost its devices and beacons to battle-damage and sandstorms. They drew their vorpal blades and spurred their chargers and flew headlong into combat. Their chargers bit and mauled each other and collapsed; the paladins fought on into the night. Sparks and flames from their clashing blades lit up the lake and the tower, and the red rain of their blood speckled the stones of the shore. Both were grievously wounded, but neither would yield. At last, the paladin dispatched her enemy with a killing thrust, but when she wrenched off his helmet she discovered that he was her own brother. As she wept over his body a man dressed in black furs appeared. He gathered her into his arms and carried her across the bridge, into the tower. She glimpsed the armill, a slim platinum bracelet set on a bolster inside a crystal reliquary; then its guardian carried her down a spiral stair to a basement room, stripped off her damaged armour, and lowered her into the casket of an ancient medical engine.

When the paladin woke, she was hungry and thirsty, and very weak. The room was dark, the stairs were blocked by rubble, her armour was gone. After she clawed her way out, she discovered that the tower was in ruins. There was no sign of the reliquary and its guardian, and the lake was dry and the forest all around was a wasteland of ash and charred stumps.

She had been asleep for a century. Mars had fallen to the Trues. The Czarina and her family were long dead; her battalions and her ships were destroyed or scattered. The last paladin dug up the grave of the brother she had killed, put on his armour, and went out into the world and waged a long and terrible war against the conquerors of Mars. She was a fierce and relentless enemy, driven by remorse and guilt. She killed everyone who pursued her, including five suzerains, and raised an army of brigands and sacked the ancient capital. But nothing could atone for the mortal sin that had derailed her quest. When she and the tattered remnant of her army were at last cornered in the Labyrinth of the Night by five squadrons of elite shock troopers, she died with her dead brother's name on her lips.

Hari's broken arm healed, aided by scaffolding laid down by mites that the gig's medical kit injected into his bloodstream, and he built up its strength by careful exercise. Vesta grew from a point of light to a small lopsided disc, one half illuminated by direct sunlight, the other in shadow. And then, just after *Little Helper* had begun the manoeuvre that would insert it into orbit around the little world, the interface with its motor blazed with overload and failure alarms, and the reaction chamber flamed out.

Hari's first thought was that it was sabotage. That his pursuers had managed to find an open, unsecured port and slip in a djinn or transmit a command string that had executed some kind of fail-safe procedure. But a quick inspection revealed that the motor hadn't simply shut down: it was badly damaged. The feeds to the reaction chamber were out of alignment and its ceramic casing was cracked.

He pulled up recent footage of *Easy Does It*, looking for a flare or sudden spark that would betray the launch of some kind of drone, but it turned out that the hijackers had been more subtle than that. Just after he had initiated the insertion burn sequence, the faint star of the pursuing gig had begun to flicker with coherent, high-energy pulses from a maser.

'They needed to get in range,' he told the eidolon, 'but they didn't need to get too close because it didn't require much energy to do the damage. The maser's frequency lock-stepped with the ignition pulses in the reaction chamber, and ramped them up uncontrollably and chaotically.'

The eidolon, dressed in a simple white jumpsuit, a white cap fitted close to her shaven skull, sat cross-legged in the air like one of the saints of the long ago. She said, '*Easy Does It* is still moving faster than we are. I calculate that it will catch up with us long before the repair mites can fix the motor.'

'Yes. And meanwhile the window for orbital insertion is closing.'

It had the grim logic of one of the old stories in which heroes fail to overcome the iron laws imposed by their gods.

'I'm sorry, Gajananvihari,' the eidolon said. 'I see no alternative to surrender.'

'I have another idea,' Hari said.

2

Details began to resolve in and around Vesta's half-disc. Its sun lamps were a chain of bright stars tilted around its equator. The enormous crater stamped into its south pole was aimed towards the sun – it was summer, there, the middle of a year-long perpetual day. The rounded peak of the mountain at its centre punched through the atmosphere, its flanks and the smashed terrain around it partly obscured by a fragmented girdle of wispy clouds.

Little Helper was falling free, unable to reduce its velocity and make a direct or orbital rendezvous with Vesta's little moon and the city of Fei Shen. Behind it, *Easy Does It* came on inexorably. It would close on *Little Helper* a few hours after both gigs had passed the asteroid.

Hari wasn't going to be aboard when that happened.

He pulled on his pressure suit and passed through the airlock, clambered around the sharp curve of the lifesystem's sphere, swung into the lifepod and shut its hatch. The crash couch adjusted around him and his bios synched with the lifepod's systems. A gentle puff from the lifepod's attitude jets sent it drifting away from the gig; then, at a distance of two kilometres, its motor lit up.

Little Helper dwindled into the black sky. The lifepod curved inwards, decelerating, falling down Vesta's gravity well. Hari had been planning to swing *Little Helper* around Vesta in an elliptical orbit that would take it close to the edge of the atmosphere and then back out towards Fei Shen, but the lifepod didn't have enough reaction mass to complete the manoeuvre. There was only one place it could reach before Hari's pursuers caught up with it.

The lifepod's motor cut off. He was committed now. He couldn't risk opening the comms and contacting Fei Shen's traffic control because his pursuers might piggyback the transmission and hack into the life-pod's control system. He had to assume that he was being tracked.

Vesta flattened into a landscape stamped with craters, raked with grooves and ridges. Hari saw fleets of giant dunes rippling across inter-crater plains. He saw three craters of diminishing size stacked one on top of the other like a cross-section of *Little Helper*, slanted away from the equator. He saw a circular crater capped with a broken dome two kilometres across. He saw the sharp fleck of the little moon, the rock on which Fei Shen perched, rise above the horizon, hopelessly beyond reach.

He made the final adjustments to the lifepod's trim, and then it hit the outer edge of Vesta's atmosphere and was enveloped in a shell of shock-heated gas, sullen red brightening to shocking pinks and oranges. Heat pulsed through the lifepod. Hari sweated inside his pressure suit, crushed into the crash couch by the brutal force of deceleration, shaken by a drilling vibration. The optical feeds showed only flowing glare. And then there was a long moment of free fall and the burning envelope around the lifepod died back and he saw that it was dropping towards a rumpled landscape.

A curved ridge flew past, the rim wall of a crater. Another ridge came up from the horizon. Hari closed his eyes, an ancient hardwired reflex. Crash balloons inflated with a sharp crack. Cased in twelve tough spheres, the lifepod struck the crest of the ridge, spun through the air and bounced across a garden of thorny plants spread across the crater's floor, shedding momentum with every impact. Inside, in the grip of the crash couch's holster, Hari was jarred and inverted and thrown from side to side. Every bounce a crunching wham! crash! followed by a moment of soaring grace, then wham! crash! again.

He was unconscious long before the lifepod's lumpy parcel struck a terraced cliff at the far side of the crater and rebounded and came to rest in the middle of a run-out of tumbled boulders. And woke to find himself marching with a stiff bounding gait across a gently rumpled plain. The sun hung just above the horizon behind him and a single lamp burned high in the dark blue sky, so that he walked at the apex of a double shadow.

The cryoflask containing Dr Gagarian's head was hooked to the belt of his p-suit and bumped his left hip with every other step.

He slowed by degrees, came to a halt close to a spatter of rocks flung from a small impact crater. According to the p-suit's eidolon, he was in the low northern latitudes, some twenty-two kilometres north-east of the crash site. He had been walking for more than six hours. His breathing was laboured and his legs ached. His whole body hurt, in fact, bruised and battered by the hard landing. The pain was a remote, not unpleasant throb, pushed away by something the p-suit had given him.

'Talk to me,' he said. 'Tell me what you did.'

The eidolon appeared beside him, a sketch in light and shadow, the two stars of her eyes level with his. She said, 'You were unconscious. I could not wake you. And because our pursuers must have tracked our descent I decided it would be best to put some distance between us and the lifepod as soon as possible.'

'The authorities in Fei Shen would have tracked it, too. I was relying on them to rescue me.'

Hari was angry at the eidolon's presumption, humiliated at the thought of being turned into a meat puppet. And he'd lost the lifepod, his last link with his family's ship . . .

The eidolon apologised for her presumption, picted a map. 'You require replenishment of power and other supplies, and a place to rest. There is a shelter seventeen point four kilometres away. It will supply everything you need.'

'Is that where I was heading before I woke up?'

'You were walking straight towards it.'

'This shelter, does it have a direct link to Fei Shen?'

'I believe so.'

'You have it all figured out.'

'I am trying my best to be of service.'

'Don't ever help me again unless I ask for your help. Is that clear?'

'Yes.'

'Good. Now let's find this shelter.'

Hari walked on. Using craters as waypoints, comparing them with the eidolon's map, trying to keep to the line she had drawn to the shelter. He discovered that he was not afraid. He was determined to survive this. He would not give up his life easily: dying would mean that he had failed his family. He had survived a hijack and a kidnap attempt and a spaceship crash. He would survive a short stroll across the surface of Vesta.

The sun set inside a kind of shell of hard, pinkish light that slowly faded out of the darkening sky. The lamp swung overhead and another rose ahead of Hari, followed by Vesta's moon, a pale splinter of bone with a tiny diamond glinting off-centre: the city of Fei Shen, tantalising, unreachable.

Hari set a rhythm, walking for twenty minutes, resting for ten, squatting on his haunches, sipping water, moving on. The dusty plain was punctuated by small craters, thickets of wiry grey plants, stray boulders, rippling aprons of black sand. It reminded Hari of his father's viron. He would not have been surprised to see the old man walking towards him, opening windows in the air, preparing a campaign to recapture his ship.

But this ashy desert was still and silent, and there was no trace of habitation. No structures, no roads or paths or tracks. The Free People of Fei Shen, Vesta's self-appointed guardians, did not allow any permanent settlements on the surface. They'd once been Martians, the Free People. A gypsy race of environmental engineers and gene wizards living off the land, travelling in caravans of construction machinery, mobile soil factories and greenhouses. Descendants of a Gaian cult, they believed that the mother goddess of Earth was merely one aspect of a deity who had quickened and spread life into every possible niche: every living thing, from archaebacteria to human beings, was part of that divine presence. When Trues had gone to war against Mars, some of the Free People had gone underground, preserving their genome libraries, while the rest had gone up and out. Riding ships in slow, low-energy paths, spreading through the forgotten places of the Belt, colonising and repairing abandoned gardens, settling on un-inhabited rocks and seeding their surfaces with vacuum organisms, burrowing into them and creating gardens in tunnels and voids. A great and holy work that would end only when every rock in the Belt, every moon of the outer planets, every kobold in the Kuiper belt, had been quickened with some kind of life.

Vesta was their holiest shrine. Their great cathedral, their omphalos. An alliance of baseliners from Earth and Jupiter's moons had begun to terraform it a thousand years ago. A superstring injected into its core had deepened its gravity well; sun lamps and fusion engines had raised its surface temperature and pumped heat into its frozen regolith; engineers had mined and released carbon dioxide, nitrogen, and argon. Boreal forests and bogs planted inside craters, and dense blooms of cyanobacteria in meltwater lakes, had fixed most of the carbon dioxide and raised the partial pressure of oxygen. The atmospheric pressure had

59

stabilised at a little over two hundred millibars at zero elevation point. Tweaked animals had been introduced. Once, the little world had been the hunting grounds of True suzerains; now, it was a curated wilderness. No one was supposed to land there without permission. Hari hoped to be arrested for trespass, so that he could escape his pursuers and explain his predicament.

Vesta's deepened gravity, 0.2 g, was twice the maximum acceleration of *Pabuji's Gift*. Even with the help of the p-suit's pseudomusculature, Hari found it hard going. He walked and rested, walked and rested. His legs grew heavy, his feet slow and uncertain. His perspective narrowed to the ground ahead. To the next step, and the next. The hiss of air in his helmet. The thump of blood in his head.

Vesta's rotation period was short, less than six hours. The lamps and the moon chased each other to the western horizon and the sky brightened above a crescent of hills directly ahead. As the sun rose, Hari climbed a long slope that ended in a crest of shattered stone. The bowl of the crater stretched away below, filled edge to edge with a dense forest, obscured here and there by streamers of mist. A far-off gleam of water.

The eidolon glimmered beside Hari. 'You could walk around it,' she said.

Hari checked the map. The shelter was two klicks beyond the far side of the crater. If he circumnavigated the crater's rim it would more than triple the distance, and the terrain was cut by blocky upthrusts and crevasses that would be difficult to negotiate.

'Best to keep going forward,' he said, and crabbed down a run-out slope that pushed a long ridge into the forest. Trees closed in on either side; their canopy closed up overhead. There seemed to be just two species. Tall dark green pines forming long rows in every direction, punctuated by stands of even taller vacuum-organism trees, their slim black columns topped with filmy parasols supported by delicate arching ribs. The parasols meshed like the clockwork of vast and unfathomable mechanisms, and the tips of their ribs divided into fingerlike projections that swelled and spurted misty jets of carbon dioxide and water vapour drawn from frozen reservoirs deep underground.

It was a strange, spooky place. Shadows slowly shifted as the sun tracked across the sky. Vacuum-organism trees moaned and whistled. When a low ridge of pockmarked basalt cut across Hari's path he scrambled to the top and saw a mirror-smooth plane stretching away, gleaming with a steely sheen in the level light of the setting sun. A lamp was rising to the east, blurred by a stretch of thin mist.

He had reached the shore of the lake at the centre of the crater. Strange to see so much water, enough to drown *Pabuji's Gift* and a hundred ships like her. Strange to see it lying there flat, submitting to gravity.

Hari followed the ridge clockwise around the lake. The sun set; a second lamp rose. The ridge grew broader, descended to a swampy delta of sluggish streams braided between low islands and stretches of reeds. On the far side, a giant monolith stood on a kind of platform or apron of bare rock, taller than the ragged fringe of pine trees behind it. Hari waded through muddy water, scrambled over folds of basalt overgrown with shaggy black moss. He was more than halfway across when a ragged chorus of high-pitched hooting started up, drifting across the delta from the trees behind the monolith.

The eidolon brightened in front of him. 'Be careful,' she said.

'What is it?'

She flung out an arm, pointing towards stooped figures emerging from shadows under the trees. Small, barrel-chested, bandy-legged, clad only in dark pelts. Human eyes gleaming under ridged brows. A species of man-ape derived from the human genome, according to Hari's bios, with an enhanced lung capacity and tweaked haemoglobin.

There were twenty, thirty, forty of them. Advancing past the monolith to the edge of the apron of rock, stamping, slapping their hands over their heads, raising their heads and pant-hooting. Hari, pleased by this exuberant greeting, waved and ploughed on through knee-deep water.

'Incoming,' the eidolon said.

A reticle popped up in the visor of Hari's helmet, tracking a small object falling towards him. He sidestepped it, but more projectiles were dropping out of the sky. Most splashed into the water around him, but one banged into the chestplate of his p-suit and dropped at his feet. He stooped, felt around in the muddy water, scooped it up. An obsidian cobble, flaked into a point at one end.

A stone struck his shoulder. A stone glanced off his helmet. He felt the impact through the padding.

The man-apes were capering in front of the monolith. Feet slapped rock. Long arms swung, flinging stones in high arcs.

'We should have gone around the crater, not across,' the eidolon said.

'It's too late to go back,' Hari said.

A volley of stones fell around him. His helmet was struck again, hard enough to stun him for a moment. Several man-apes had climbed to the tops of the trees to one side of the monolith. Silhouetted against the deep indigo sky, gripping branches with prehensile toes, they shrieked and hooted and beat the drums of their chests with their fists. Around the base of the monolith, man-apes thrashed broken branches over their heads or ran up to the edge of the apron and flung stones and retreated. One, a head taller than the others, broad-shouldered, pelt streaked with silver, splashed into the water and advanced towards Hari with uncompromising determination.

Hari stood his ground and switched on his helmet lamp, aimed its beam at this imposing challenger. The man-ape squinted against the glare, black lips twisted back from stout incisors, then beat his chest and stamped his feet, spraying water and mud, shrieking defiance, coming on.

'I am frightened,' the eidolon said.

'Strobe the lamp and give me a siren,' Hari said.

The big man-ape reeled back as lightning stuttered and the siren howled. Hari laughed, gripped by an atavistic exhilaration. He beat his chestplate, roared, sloshed forward.

The man-ape stared at Hari, then looked up at the sky and turned and scampered back to the shore, pausing to glance back before following the others into the darkness under the trees. Hari had almost reached the apron of bare rock around the towering monolith when a shadow fell across him. He looked up, saw a teardrop-shaped craft dropping out of the sky. The common channel lit, and a high clear voice speaking Portuga told him to stay exactly where he was.

3

Hari's cell was a self-contained egg of glass and plastic scarcely larger than the lifepod, hung from the overhead of a white-tiled tube. A spigot supplied distilled water. Food was extruded from a patch in the cell's floor: variations on dole yeast and edible plastic, no worse than the stuff supplied by the ascetic hermit's maker on Themba.

Identical cells dwindled away on either side, spaced at regular intervals. Those nearest Hari's were empty; the occupants of more distant cells did not respond to any of the questions he shaped with his hands. No doubt they were all rock-huggers who didn't know shiptalk.

At irregular intervals an eidolon brightened in the air outside the tall oval window and interrogated Hari about the hijack, his escape from his would-be captors on Themba, the pursuit that had brought him to Vesta. It refused to tell him when he would be released, what had happened to his pressure suit and Dr Gagarian's head, if his pursuers had docked at Fei Shen. It told him that an investigation into his misdemeanours was under way, interrogated him about the story he had told the commissars who had arrested him for landing without permission on Vesta.

During the first session, Hari had explained that he was on an urgent mission to save his family, and must be released at once. 'Before my pursuers forced me to change course, I was heading to Tannhauser Gate. My family has a broker there. Rember Wole. He'll vouch for me.'

Hari had only met the broker once. Four years ago, the last time *Pabuji's Gift* had docked at Tannhauser Gate. Rember Wole, a tall man with a cloud of black hair and a grave manner, had come aboard, Hari had been introduced to him, they'd had a brief, inconsequential conversation. He didn't really know the man, and he'd never met his

63

partner, Worden Hanburanaman, but he was certain that they would help them. Why else would he have been aimed at Tannhauser Gate?

'Contact Rember Wole,' he told the eidolon. 'Talk to him. Talk to his partner, Worden Hanburanaman. They will confirm my identity: Gajananvihari Pilot, the son of Aakash Pilot, the true heir to the salvage ship *Pabuji's Gift*.'

But when the eidolon returned the next day, it told Hari that it had been unable to speak with either Rember Wole or Worden Hanburanaman.

'Let me try,' Hari said. 'They'll talk to me.'

'Unfortunately, Rember Wole and Worden Hanburanaman are dead,' the eidolon said.

Hari felt a freezing plunge of shock, asked the usual stupid questions about when and where and how. The eidolon told him that the two men had disappeared on the day that *Pabuji's Gift* had been hijacked, and their bodies had been found three days later.

'The murderer or murderers have not been identified,' it said. 'I am sorry for your loss.'

'I know who killed them. Or at least, I know why they were killed. It is connected to the hijack of my family's ship,' Hari said.

But the eidolon refused to allow him to talk to Tannhauser Gate's police, and vanished when he demanded to be allowed to speak to someone with real authority. It wouldn't talk about the murders the next time it appeared outside the window of the cell, began to ask random questions about Hari's story as if nothing had changed.

But everything had changed. Hari had been given a mission. Reach Tannhauser Gate; find Rember Wole and Worden Hanburanaman. *Rember will help you get in contact with the hijackers and negotiate the return of the ship. Worden will help you understand Dr Gagarian's work, and how to carry it forward.* He still had to contact the hijackers, still had to negotiate with them, but there was no longer anyone to help him. He was on his own, pursued by a powerful, highly organised enemy.

He told himself that despair and self-pity were selfish and pointless indulgences. He told himself that he still had what his enemies wanted. He still had leverage. He was in prison, but that was part of his plan. Eventually the Free People would realise who he was, and release him. Perhaps they would even help him.

He tried to empty his mind with mediation. He sat cross-legged and chanted a mantra he had found in Kinson Ib Kana's book. *All things shall be well and all manner of things shall be well.* He exercised, strengthening the muscles in his legs and arms and back. The gravity well of Fei Shen's small rock had been deepened, like Vesta's. Hari needed to build up his strength. He did sit-ups and press-ups. He did squat thrusts. He did pull-ups, when he was strong enough. Wedging his fingers against the top of the frame of the cell's window, lifting and lowering himself until the muscles in his arms and shoulders liquified. And he slept, sank away into hours of blissful oblivion. He exercised and he meditated, but most of the time he slept.

One day, he was woken by a ragged percussion that immediately reminded him of the ape-men on Vesta. It was the other prisoners, drumming on the walls of their cells as two commissars walked down the long white tube. The commissars halted outside Hari's cell, and before he could frame a question the base dilated and he dropped straight down and landed in a breathless sprawl at their feet.

Hari and the commissars rode an elevator up a transparent shaft to the so-called new section of the city, walked through a sunlit forest of screw pines and birches and tree ferns. Aakash had taught Hari the basics of architectural geomancy, using his viron as an exemplar. Showing him how a rich patchwork of spaces could be created by clever landscaping, subtle transitions, and the choices provided by networks of intersecting paths. How framing vistas and blending the borders of the viron into its backdrop made its small footprint seem much larger than it really was, how shade and the white noise of falling water encouraged restful contemplation, how open sky and contoured paths that restricted sightlines and revealed views from different angles encouraged exploration, and so on and so forth. Hari knew that the forest biome, the perspectives of its green aisles, ladders of sunlight leaning between trees, was meticulously constructed to induce a sense of oceanic peace, and he could appreciate the intimidating beauty of the glade where one of the Free People's matriarchs, Ma Sakitei, was waiting for him. A flawless carpet of scarlet and maroon turf spread within a circle of trees and flowering rhododendrons, copper and gold butterflies tumbling through subaqueous light, a small brown bird perched on a low branch, trilling a lovely, liquid song. The product of centuries of patient, masterful skill. A statement of strength and will no less powerful than an iron throne flanked by ranks of shuttered myrmidons.

Ma Sakitei sat zazen-style on a handwoven mat in the centre of the glade. An old woman less than half Hari's height, white hair as tightly curled as airsheep wool, dressed in a plain tunic cinched at the waist by a broad belt hung with pouches and tools. Butterflies circled her, landed on her hands, clung to her cheek or to the corners of her eyes. Tiny sparks of information that pinged Hari's bios but were, to him, unreadable. Green thoughts in a green shade.

The matriarch dismissed the commissars and asked Hari to sit with her, asked him to tell his story. As if he hadn't already told it a dozen times, and been questioned about every aspect of it. He spoke plainly and concisely, without any trace of anger or self-pity. Nabhomani had taught him that those with power over others were not moved by crude attempts to manipulate their emotions. It implied weakness, and powerful people despised weakness. It was always best to keep your story simple and straightforward, without qualifications or justifications or special pleading.

There was a long pause after he finished. The bird sang on with inexhaustible invention, as if it was singing the world into being, moment to moment to moment. Bright packets of information fluttered by. Hari believed that most of Ma Sakitei's attention was focused on these little messengers. As far as she was concerned, he was a trivial problem, a blip in the calm flow of the days and years of tending this forest biome and the wild forests and deserts of Vesta. Yet his life turned on the hinge-point of her decision.

At last, she said, 'Usually, we prosecute trespassers. Two of your fellow prisoners, for instance, are traders in biologics who attempted to plunder Vesta's ecosystems.'

'I had no choice. My ship was badly damaged.'

'You could have allowed your pursuers to capture you.'

'I have been given an important mission. I will not give it up so easily. I would like to thank you,' Hari said, 'for rescuing me.'

'We did not rescue you,' Ma Sakitei said. 'We arrested you before you could harm the man-apes. They were created by Trues, who used to hunt them with spears and take their heads as trophies. We believe that it is our duty to care for them as best we can, to atone for all that has been done to them in the past. We do not allow anyone to interfere with them.'

Hari apologised and said that he had meant the man-apes no harm, had only been trying to drive them off after they had attacked him.

'They attacked you because you trespassed on their territory,' Ma Sakitei said.

Nabhomani had taught Hari that, even when negotiating from a position of strength, it was important to control your emotions. Pride gave you confidence and motivated you to maximise outcomes and build strong relationships, but you should never let it tip over into arrogance and conceit, or use it to humble or belittle other people. And sometimes, if you overreached yourself during negotiations, if the other side uncovered a transgression or exposed an attempt to deceive or trick them, it was necessary to swallow your pride, express guilt and contrition, and accept responsibility for your actions. It was necessary to expose your throat to the teeth of your opponents, and hope for mercy.

Exposing his throat now, Hari said, 'I realise that I have made some foolish mistakes. I hope I can learn from them.'

'I hope you do,' Ma Sakitei said. 'Tell me about the head you were carrying. The head of the tick-tock philosopher, Dr Gagarian. Why do your pursuers think it so valuable?'

'They didn't tell me. I assume it has something to with his research into the Bright Moment.'

'With the files locked inside his head.'

'Yes.'

'Can you open them?'

'No. That's why I was heading towards Tannhauser Gate.'

'Where your family's broker lived.'

'He and his partner were supposed to help me.'

'And they were murdered.'

'That's what your commissars told me.'

'It seems that your pursuers have a long reach. That they are no ordinary dacoits.'

'I'm not sure what they are,' Hari said. 'I do know that I would surrender the head at once, if I could be certain they would give me my family's ship and any of my family who might still be alive.'

'But they were all killed during the hijack. Only you are left alive.'

'I think so.'

Hari was amazed that he could speak so calmly about his dead.

'Your pursuers tell a somewhat different story,' Ma Sakitei said.

'You have spoken to them? They're here?'

'They passed through cis-Vestan space and rendezvoused with your ship and continued onwards. But we have spoken to them. They claim to be specialists hired by your family. They say that you murdered Dr Gagarian and stole his head, then murdered two of their companions who gave chase. They say that they are attempting to bring you to justice.'

'Did they also tell you that they hijacked my family's ship? That they wiped my father's viron, and murdered my brothers and the woman who raised me?'

'We are not your enemy,' Ma Sakitei said. 'We are merely trying to establish whether your story is true.'

Hari apologised. He was ashamed of his loss of self-control, scared that he'd compromised any chance that the Free People would help him.

A butterfly landed on Ma Sakitei's hand, perching on the web between thumb and forefinger. She lifted it to the level of her eyes and studied it for a moment, and then it fluttered away.

'Your pursuers asked us to render you up to them,' she said. 'You, and the head of the tick-tock philosopher. We refused. First, because they deployed a weapon inside the volume of space that we control. Second, because we are minded to grant you refugee status.'

Hari began to thank her, fell silent when she held up a hand.

'We cannot confirm many of the details of your story,' she said, 'but your DNA profile confirms that you are the son of Aakash Pilot, and the nephew of Tamonash Pilot. We were able to compare your profile with theirs because both have done business with us in the past. Both have been good friends to us.'

'Tamonash Pilot?'

'The free trader.'

'He is my uncle?'

'You do not know him?'

'I have never met him,' Hari said.

No one in his family had ever mentioned that his father had a brother. That he had an uncle . . .

Ma Sakitei threw a small file – the requirements and qualifications for refugee status – to Hari's bios, and told him to study it.

'We are an open city,' she said. 'We provide a peaceful, neutral environment where trade and business flourish. But when it comes to maintaining order we are vigilant, and swift to punish any who exploit or abuse our hospitality. And we do not takes sides in disputes and vendettas outwith our sphere of influence. While you remain here, you will make no attempt to contact your pursuers, or anyone able to negotiate with them on your behalf. If you seek justice or revenge you must look elsewhere.'

'I will.'

A butterfly landed on Ma Sakitei's cheek. She closed her eyes and said, 'Were you ever employed as a librarian or an archivist by your family?'

'My father maintained our records.'

'I see. Perhaps you worked as a courier.'

'I have been trained in most aspects of running a ship. And I helped Dr Gagarian construct the machines he used in his experiments.'

The butterfly flicked into the air. Ma Sakitei opened her eyes.

'Everyone in Fei Shen must pay for their time,' she said. 'Even refugees. You will be able to obtain a little credit here. Enough to support you for a short time, not enough to buy passage elsewhere. You will need to find work, sooner or later. When you do, come and talk to me again.'

'I will,' Hari said again.

But he'd already decided that he wanted to leave Fei Shen as soon as possible. He'd reach out to Dr Gagarian's colleagues for help. He'd work his passage if he couldn't buy it. He'd smuggle himself aboard a ship if he had no other choice . . .

He said, 'May I ask one more favour? You have taken custody of my pressure suit and Dr Gagarian's head. Also a book that's important to me. I would like them back.'

'You may have the head and the book, but we cannot allow the pressure suit to enter the city. Its eidolon confessed to us that it is weaponised.'

'It is naive, and often does not know what it is saying.'

'Nevertheless, your suit will be stored at the docks until you leave the city. Fare well, Gajananvihari Pilot. When we meet again, we will discuss how you can repay our hospitality.'

4

Dressed in leggings and a plain jerkin issued by the commissars, the cryoflask that contained Dr Gagarian's head slung over one shoulder, Kinson Ib Kana's book in his pocket, Hari walked out into Fei Shen. It was as scary-strange as his first foray across the surface of Themba. His bios couldn't handshake with the antique protocols of the city's commons, so everything he encountered – the wide corridors (called avenues), the buildings, street furniture, bots, drones, avatars, people – was naked and unreadable. Alien and mysterious, thrilling and terrifying.

Fei Shen, the flying mountain, sometimes called Wufen Shan, the Fifth Sacred Mountain, sometimes First New Shanghai, was an old city. Earth's Pacific Community had built it inside an impact crater at the prow of a small, wedge-shaped asteroid some fifteen hundred years ago, in the early years of the Great Expansion. At the height of the True Empire, it had been shifted into orbit around Vesta to serve as a platform for crews tending the ongoing terraforming project, and as an interchange for highborn Trues on their way to Vesta's hunting grounds. It had been largely untouched by the wars that had brought down the Trues; the Free People had demolished the palace inside the tent of the new section and replaced it with a gardened forest, but had changed little else.

The Pacific Community had used Fei Shen as a centre for trade with the gardens and settlements of the Belt, and now it was a trade centre again, although much diminished. There was a bazaar that sold half-life carpets in every colour and pattern and texture, another that sold vacuum organisms, genetic templates, and facsimiles of animals and birds from the long ago, from legends and sagas, and from the single extrasolar world that possessed its own biosphere. One avenue was dedicated to the repair and refurbishment of gardens and other enclosed biomes. Two more were crowded with life-extension parlours and chop shops advertising every kind of tweak and augmentation, many related to exotic forms of sexual intercourse.

Because he couldn't call up a map or a helpful eidolon, Hari had to ask a passer-by to direct him to the city's bourse. It was in the ground level of the big rotunda at the hub of the starburst of avenues, beneath the apex of the city's dome. Inside, individuals and gossipy little groups of baseliners, avatars and eidolons studying empty air (no doubt packed with picts, sims and windows that Hari's bios was unable to detect) were scattered across the bare, white, circular floor. As he looked around, a pale-skinned man drifted over and said, 'I know you. The kid who crashed on Vesta, with dacoits in hot pursuit. More fun than I ever expect to see in my humble life. I'm Gabriel. Gabriel Daza. One of the proctors. I know, I look far too young to be a proctor. That's because I *am* young. But I'm also a proctor. The son, grandson, and great-grandson of proctors. Whether you're here to buy or sell, I can help.'

'My ship has credit on deposit with the bourse at Tannhauser Gate,' Hari said. 'I need to access it.'

Gabriel Daza studied him. His sharp, clever face was framed by the high collar of his white, silver-trimmed tunic. 'You aren't connected to the commons,' he said.

'I need to fix that. But first I need to be able to draw on my ship's credit.'

'You have a tag, an embedded licence, some other form of a guarantee?'

'A card,' Hari said, and took it out.

It was a small rectangle of plastic that displayed a pict of *Pabuji's Gift* slowly rotating against the star smoke of the Milky Way.

'Fabulously old-fashioned, but I can make it work,' Gabriel Daza said. 'You understand the terms?'

'Perhaps you could explain them.'

'Of course. You lack connectivity. You are purchasing a limited credit line, drawing on a reciprocal arrangement between Fei Shen and Tannhauser Gate. The fees for the arrangement and the exchange rate are fixed; so is the amount available. Penalties apply if your guarantee misrepresents the amount of credit deposited, if there is a legal challenge to the transaction by a third party, and so on and so forth. Do you want to hear the penalties? There are an awful lot of them.'

'My ship's credit is good.'

'No one ever wants to read the fine print,' Gabriel Daza said. 'Let's confirm your identity.'

A drone dropped from the high ceiling and verified the card's qubit watermark and confirmed that Hari's DNA profile matched the profile embedded in its memory; Gabriel Daza opened a window so that Hari could check the credit available to him, and the services he could buy. It seemed to be a useful amount, but the young proctor explained that the city had suffered a recent bout of what he called stagflation. The credit line, with its alluring rows of zeroes, would purchase no more than two hundred hours' residency.

'That's at ordinary rates, of course,' the young proctor said. 'You're paying the refugee surcharge, so you have less than fifty hours. After that, unless you find a way of earning your keep, the city owns you.'

Hari did his best to hide his dismay. 'Does the surcharge apply to everything I buy?'

'Only to consumables. Per diem quanta of air, power, water, use of the commons . . . Speaking of which, I recommend the Almond Pit, on the Avenue of the Elevation of the Mind. Tell Rong Che that Gabriel sent you. She'll give you a good price for a trait that will let you access basic functions.'

'I have a set of files I need to open. Would she be able to break their encryption?'

'She could certainly try. The head doctors in Fei Shen draw on centuries of tradition, and Rong Che is the best of them all.'

Hari thanked the young proctor, asked if he had enough credit to pay for data searches.

'The city's databases are open access,' Gabriel Daza said. 'After you get yourself fixed up at the Pit, you'll be able to ask anything you like.'

'But I'll have to pay the surcharge.'

'That's true.'

'So it would be cheaper to have you do it for me.'

'I see that you are a quick study.'

Hari explained that he was searching for one of his relatives, Tamonash Pilot. 'I believe he traded with the Free People, or had some other business with them. And he may be living in Ophir.'

Aakash had been born in Ophir, had refurbished *Pabuji's Gift* in its docks.

'I would also want to send messages to Ophir, Chavez Labyrinth, and Greater Brazil,' Hari said. He wanted to find out if Dr Gagarian's colleagues, Salx Minnot Flores, Ivanova Galchan and Ioni Robles Nguini, were still alive. He wanted to ask them for help.

'Sending a message to anyone on Earth is a problem,' Gabriel Daza said. 'The cost of negotiating its security would exceed your credit. Also, the Free People have a long-running dispute with several nations, including Greater Brazil. You would have to contact your friend via back channels. More expense.'

'But you can send messages to Ophir and Chavez Labyrinth,' Hari said.

'Of course. I can do everything for the special price of eight hours fifty minutes.'

'How much do I already owe you?'

'For accessing your ship's credit record? One hour ten. It's the standard fee.'

'Take the hour and ten minutes. I'll do the other things myself.'

'It will cost you far more.'

'Or I could ask your colleagues for a better deal.'

'You won't find a better deal, but rather than waste your time I'm prepared to reduce the price further. Let's say six hours thirty.'

'Let's say a round six hours.'

'For the query and the message?'

'For the query and the message, and for access to my credit.'

'I have already put myself out,' Gabriel Daza said.

'I don't think so, since you charged me the standard fee.'

'Six hours it is, all in. And I'm giving my time away.'

Because the proctor had agreed so readily Hari suspected that it wasn't much of a bargain, but he didn't intend to stay in the city long enough to exhaust his credit. He had places to go and people to see.

Gabriel Daza's attention went away for a few moments; then he told Hari that Tamonash Pilot, a trader from Ophir, had purchased samples of rare vacuum organisms from a scavenger more than three years ago. Before that, he'd been involved in a transaction with the Free People of Fei Shen and their cousins in Tivoli Wrecks, a reef that orbited between Earth and Mars.

73

'Does the scavenger live here?' Hari said.

'She is away on business. I won't charge you for that information, by the way,' Gabriel Daza said. 'Do you want to contact this long-lost relative?'

'I'd like to confirm that he is still living in Ophir. And send those messages.'

Gabriel Daza called up three djinns, gave one a query about Tamonash Pilot, gave the others Hari's messages to Salx Minnot Flores and Ivanova Galchan.

'It might take a little while,' the proctor said. 'Signal lag and security protocols and so on. Especially security protocols. Business would be so much easier if cities and settlements trusted each other. Best come back tomorrow.'

Hari asked where transients stayed, in Fei Shen; Gabriel Daza told him that there were caravanserais in the parkland at the city's edge.

'Any that have room will take you in. Fees are fixed, so don't waste your time trying to muscle anyone into accepting less.'

'Would I find ships' crews there?'

'Of course. But if you are hoping to work your passage you'll find thin pickings. The city is no longer the hub it once was.'

'I am thinking of reivers.'

'You want to become one?'

'I want to hire one.'

'Good luck with that.'

'"Hire" is the wrong word for the arrangement I have in mind, perhaps. "Go into partnership" might be better.'

'Again, good luck with that. The city doesn't allow reivers to dock here.'

'Reivers have been known to become traders when it suits them. And vice versa. If you know of anyone who sometimes works on the dark side, it will be worth your while to introduce me.'

'I doubt that,' Gabriel Daza said. 'But perhaps I can ask around.'

'I have one more question,' Hari said. 'Is there anyone in the city who deals in salvage?'

'If this is about your lifepod, I believe the city has claimed it. You landed on Vesta without permission. Not the best idea.'

'I was forced to land because I was attacked,' Hari said. 'The lifepod is my family's property, and I need to sell it as soon as possible. Can I contest the city's appropriation of my property?'

'You could. If you don't mind risking your refugee status.'

'Perhaps someone else would like to try, then. I'll be happy to sell my claim to them.'

'I think you have a better chance of finding a reiver.'

'Is the city's government bound by the same laws as its citizens?'

Gabriel Daza said that it was.

'And are those laws and their interpretation ever disputed?'

Gabriel Daza allowed that the city's codex was neither infallible nor static.

Hari smiled. 'Find me someone willing to buy my claim on the lifepod, and I'll give you five per cent of the price.'

'Fifteen would be more realistic.' Gabriel Daza was smiling too. They were both having fun. 'Given the difficulty of finding someone who loves unusual and high-risk ventures.'

After some equitable to and fro they settled on eight per cent.

'You are no innocent in this game,' Gabriel Daza said.

'I had good teachers,' Hari said, and felt the familiar ache of loss and loneliness.

When they parted, Gabriel Daza reminded Hari to pay a visit to the Almond Pit, but it was late in the day and Hari was tired, and decided that he could manage without access to the commons for one night.He had managed for far longer on Themba, after all, and believed that he was beginning to make sense of the city. He was making progress. He felt, for the first time since the hijack, an unqualified happiness.

The caravanserais were scattered through a belt of parkland that girdled the edge of the city. Some were defined by posts or lines of black stones; others were enclosed by flowering hedges or low walls. Hari chose one whose wall was decorated with fierce faces with red and gold skin, staring eyes, and elaborate headdresses: representations of the gods of his distant ancestors. He hoped that he might have something in common with the people who lodged there.

The place was run by three androgyne neuters, sometimes known as the painted men or the weird women. Altered by surgery and genetic and cosmetic therapy, their traditions stretched back to an early post-humanist sect. Once upon a time, they had ruled half a hundred gardens and rocks in the Belt but, like so many others, their principality had fallen to the True Empire. Now the last remnants of their clade recruited children from refugees and poor or fallen families, and ran hostels and caravanserais for transients, or scratched a parlous existence by using an ancient school of stochastic mathematics to make predictions about the future.

Hari took a bath, standing under a shower and scrubbing himself with a long-handled brush before climbing into the hot black water inside the big tub. He sat on a wooden ledge, submerged to his chin, and gossiped with the old man who shared the bath with him, a free trader from Porto Jeffre. The old man asked all kinds of impertinent questions, as did the other guests during the communal meal. Hari was famous, it seemed, in the city's small compass. He showed them Kinson Ib Kana's book, explained what it was and how it had fallen into his hands, asked if anyone knew how he could find the family and friends of the dead man who had saved his life.

One of the guests told Hari about a group of ascetics she'd met on Ceres; another said that she'd once traded with Nabhomani and was sorry to hear of his death; a third declared that dacoits had been getting too bold lately, and something should be done about them.

A big man sitting back in the shadows, wrapped in some kind of cloak like a warrior out of some saga of the long ago, said, 'How do you know these hijackers were dacoits?'

'They behaved like dacoits. I don't know if that's what they really are or where they came from,' Hari said. 'Not yet.'

The old man from Porto Jeffre said dacoits were getting bolder because cities and settlements and gardens lacked the resources or inclination to deal with them, and the focus of the conversation moved away from Hari as people argued about which city was the most powerful and which the most permissive, discussed rumours about the resurgence of the black fleets and distant gardens and settlements that had fallen under the control of dacoits, or were secretly encouraging them to attack rivals, or told anecdotes about run-ins with over-zealous security and customs officials.

By now, the dimming chandelier lights had guttered out. It was night outside the city, too. Beyond the dome's shadow-web of diamond composite panes, Vesta's lopsided crescent gleamed amongst shoals of stars that washed across the black sky. Later, lying on a hard pallet on the hard ground, his head pillowed on the cryoflask, all alone amongst strangers in a strange land, Hari comforted himself with the small hope that he had taken the first step on the long road to his revenge, and fell asleep in the middle of a fantasy of leading a small fleet of reivers against a nest of dacoits and capturing their leader and putting him to the question, and discovering who was behind the hijack, and making a great and good crusade against them.

5

When Hari returned to the bourse the next morning Gabriel Daza told him that he hadn't yet found anyone interested in salvage rights for the lifepod and gig. 'But give me a little time. These are delicate matters.'

'What about our other business?'

'You haven't been to the Almond Pit.'

'It's next on my list. What do you have for me?'

Gabriel Daza looked at something to one side of Hari and said, 'There's good news and bad. Which would you like to hear first?'

'Tell me about Salx Minnot Flores and Ivanova Galchan. Have they replied to my messages?'

'That's the bad news. I haven't heard anything from Ivanova Galchan, and the message to Salx Minnot Flores attracted the attention of the police in Ophir. After I established my credentials, I had a brief exchange with one of them. According to her, Salx Minnot Flores was murdered.'

The shock was slighter than that Hari had felt at the news of Rember Wole's death and his partner's disappearance. Hari supposed that he had been expecting the worst.

He said, 'The police officer, did she say who killed Salx Minnot Flores, or when it happened?'

'No. But she did ask to speak to you. I hope I haven't got you into trouble,' Gabriel Daza said.

'I've been in trouble for some time,' Hari said. 'What about my query?'

'That's the good news. Your relative is still resident in Ophir. A trader in biologics, widowed, with two daughters. Alive, as far as I know.'

Hari thanked Gabriel Daza for his help; the young proctor reminded

Hari to mention his name when he visited the Almond Pit, said that he hoped they would meet again soon.

Outside, a column of men and women were marching in solemn procession along the road that circled the big building, watched by a handful of spectators. They were all more or less baseline, the marchers, all stripped to the waist. Heads shaven, wearing only sandals and baggy white trousers. Their arms held out before them, a bouquet of drooping wires clasped in each hand, their backs striped with slick red threads and the waistbands of their trousers soaked in red, they shuffled behind a pair of clerics in sun-yellow robes and a single drummer who beat a slow and simple heartbeat rhythm on the kettle drum hung at his belly. Boom-*boom*. Boom-*boom*. Boom-*boom*.

As Hari watched, the procession halted, the drum fell silent, the two clerics sang a brief prayer and shook their hands above their heads, and the marchers crossed their arms smartly over their chests so that the handles of their flails smacked against their shoulders and wires tipped with razor taglets struck their backs, raking flesh and drawing fresh blood. The clerics pressed their hands together and touched their foreheads with their fingertips, the drum started beating again, and the marchers moved forward, blank faces glazed with sweat, eyes fixed on infinity. Small children in white tunics followed them, brushing the avenue's half-life grass with strips of cloth, mopping up spatters of holy blood.

'You won't find what you're looking for there,' someone said.

Hari turned, saw a man twice his height smiling down at him: the man who had asked him about dacoits last night, in the caravanserai. The leathery folds that fell around him weren't a cloak, Hari realised, but wings that stretched from shoulders to hips. Within a second, the catalogue in his bios had matched the man to a posthuman clade that lived in the Republic of Arden, a garden in the main belt's outer edge.

The Ardenist told Hari that the marchers were a sect particular to Fei Shen.

'Exculpationists who believe that shedding blood will help to bring about the birth of a new age. They process through the city every seventh day, and after they've flayed themselves raw their clerics sing about the end times. The usual stuff: a great and holy war, the righteous inheriting the universe, everyone else damned to eternal torment. They're castrated, the clerics. Very pure voices. And their songs are very lovely. Very lovely, and so very wrong. I'm Rav,' the Ardenist said, placing his right hand on a bare, broad chest slashed with the pale ridges of old scars. 'It isn't my real name, but you wouldn't be able to begin to pronounce that. You of course need no introduction. The youngblood who wants to track down the people who hijacked his family's ship. Well, I'm the man who can help you.'

'Are you a reiver?'

Rav spread his arms and wings wide. 'Do I look like a reiver?'

'As a matter of fact—'

'I'm no more than a humble artisan who travels the Belt in search of honest work. Exactly like you and your family. And we have something else in common. Something that you'll definitely be interested in. There's a tearoom close by. Let's talk there. I'll explain our connection, and tell you how I can help you get your ship back.'

'I have business elsewhere. But we can talk along the way, if you like.'

'Those charlatans in the Avenue of the Elevation of the Mind can just about manage to implant mundane traits and recover childhood memories, but they won't be able to get inside Dr Gagarian's head.'

Rav's smile displayed a pair of impressive incisors capped with silver. Hari didn't like that smile. It was altogether too knowing.

'You're thinking, how did he do that?' the Ardenist said. 'Is he a magician? Can he read my mind? Well, I can, just a little. You base-liners broadcast reactions and intentions through posture and pupil dilation, blood flow in skin capillaries . . . You have some training in guarding your thoughts, youngblood, and it might work with other baseliners, but as far as I'm concerned you're so leaky that I can't help picking up tells. But how I know about the head, that's nothing but basic physics and a little deduction. If you don't want people to know what's inside that cryoflask, you should use better shielding. A basic pair of X-ray spex was all I needed to see that you are carrying the head of a tick-tock person. And according to the story you told last night, the people who hijacked your family's ship murdered its only passenger. Dr Gagarian, a tick-tock philosopher. The hijackers wanted something hidden in his files, they killed him, they cut off his head . . . And you managed to escape with it, and ever since you've been wondering what it contains. Why those hijackers want it so badly. How you can exchange it for your family, your ship. You see? Nothing to it.'

'Several people have already tried to take it from me,' Hari said. 'And at least two of them are dead.'

Rav's smile widened a notch. His grass-green eyes had the slit pupils of a predator. His mop of golden curls was bushed up by a white rag knotted over one ear. 'I can see that we're going to have fun together. And I also see that you don't have access to the city's commons yet – otherwise you would have checked my status. I can fix that for you, free of charge.'

'That's why I need to see a head doctor,' Hari said

But he knew it sounded weak. He was fairly certain that the Ardenist was going to try to sell him something he didn't want or need, but what harm could talking do? And he might learn something. He didn't know enough. He knew almost nothing, really. He didn't even know what he needed to know.

Rav told him that there was no need to pay a head doctor to get his bios tweaked. 'It's a little scam to bleed the city's visitors. Easy enough to bypass if you have the ways and means. I'll introduce you to someone who'll fix you up free of charge, and then we'll talk about our common interests, and how we can help each other.'

She was a small, slight woman not much older than Hari, the sleeves of her oversized quilted jacket cuffed back to her elbows. She yawned when Rav started to explain who Hari was and how he had ended up in Fei Shen, said every transient had some kind of bad-luck story and none of them were very interesting.

'Use this, kid,' she told Hari, and threw a package at him.

His bios caught it, ran it through a sandbox to check for hidden djinns, implemented the simple trait it contained. Layers of information settled through him. Map and phone functions, a ticker that showed the slow, steady unravelling of his store of credit. The hours left before he had to go to work for the city, or find a way of leaving it.

He thanked the woman (her tag was a wireframe cube that contained a clear blue flame and no readable information, not even her name); she shrugged inside her jacket.

This was in a dark little shop where thick, heavy True lifebooks, bound in metal or manskin or shimmering polymers, were chained to wooden presses. A single volume was spreadeagled on a lectern, its broad pages spread wider than the span of Hari's arms and printed with double columns of elegant handwritten script as black as the outer dark. Intricate and colourful illustrations framed the tall initial letters of the first words of every paragraph, and at the top of the right-hand page a woman with a burning gaze and bright yellow hair looked out of a window, talking about something that no doubt had been important in the long ago, when she had been alive.

The teashop was next door, an open-air terrace two storeys up, overlooking a hutong crowded with stalls selling flotsam and jetsam from the long ago. Rav and Hari settled on cushions at the edge of the terrace, Hari with a cup of smoky gunpowder tea, Rav with a glass of hot water into which he crushed acid yellow berries, releasing a sharp pungent odour and giving the water a urinous tint. Hari's tweaked bios revealed schools of tags glittering above the stalls, explicating the function and provenance of every item. Machines, machine parts. Antique costumes. The glass catafalque of an ancient surgical bot. Frayed battle colours. Cases of trait rings. A flock of dead microsats. A p-suit helmet with a slit visor and a pinlight crest, reputed to have been owned by the Champion of the Tharsis Protectorate . . .

'I wouldn't be surprised to find trinkets excavated by your family down there,' Rav said.

Hari blushed: it was exactly what he'd been thinking. 'You tailor algorithms to revive old machines,' he said, reading the information off Rav's tag. 'Is that what we have in common – salvage?'

'That's what I do for a living, but that isn't why I came here to find you. Dig deeper. Begin at the beginning. Where was I quickened?'

'That I already knew,' Hari said. 'The Republic of Arden. My family had some business there, years ago.'

'Before the Bright Moment, no doubt. Before my people took a wrong turn.'

'You had a civil war . . .'

'Now we're getting to it,' Rav said. 'We were philosophers once upon a time, mostly interested in the fine structure of universes. Theoretical work, mostly. And then the elders became infected with bad ideas about the nature of the Bright Moment, and joined up with an end-time cult, the Saints. That's when we had ourselves that civil war. I was on the losing side.'

'And you think that these Saints have something to do with the hijack of my family's ship,' Hari said.

'Their leader, Levi, took his name from the leader of another, much older cult. He took many of his ideas from it, too. A mixture of philosophy and frank mysticism. He plans to vasten himself and his followers, just as Sri Hong-Owen vastened herself. He wants to become

82

a god. He believes that the Bright Moment contains instructions on how that can be done. The elders of my people think that, too. The Saints have recruited a number of philosophers to their cause, and are reputed to have kidnapped others. And Dr Gagarian and his associates were working on the nature of the Bright Moment . . .'

'It's an interesting theory,' Hari said. 'But do you have any hard evidence that these Saints had anything to do with the hijack?'

'Even if they didn't, I'd still like to find out what your late tick-tock philosopher discovered. Most of my friends were killed in the civil war. The rest of us fled into exile, where we've been plotting to overthrow the elders and pitch out the Saints ever since. The problem is, we are each of us individualists,' Rav said. 'It's our nature. When we hunt, we like to hunt alone. We need a strong idea to unite us. Preferably something that will disprove the nonsense championed by the elders and the Saints.'

'Can you open Dr Gagarian's files?'

Rav inhaled the steam rising from his infusion, then gulped it down with a sudden swift motion. Hari wouldn't have been surprised if the Ardenist had crushed the glass in his fist and chewed down the fragments; like Nabhomani, he had the restless, barely contained energies of someone easily bored, who'd do something shocking for the instant reaction, to challenge himself or other people.

What he did instead was curl his long, pointed red tongue inside the glass and lick the slurry of berry pulp from the bottom. 'Although I have many talents,' he said, 'the ability to break tick-tock encryption isn't one of them. But I know someone who can.'

'Here, in Fei Shen?'

'That would be convenient, wouldn't it? No, she doesn't live here, but I have a ship, I can take you to her . . . Ah, now I really do have your interest. More than anything else, I think, you want to get off this rock. I don't blame you. Fei Shen is a good place to do business, but the Free People extract a high price for their hospitality. You want a ticket out; I have a ship. You have the tick-tock philosopher's head, we both want to find out what's inside it, and I know someone who can help us with that . . . It all works out very neatly, don't you think?'

'I think I need to think about it,' Hari said.

'I understand. We're both exiles. And when you're an exile, well, not to put your trust in anyone; that is the Law. I've already helped you tweak your bios – it was nothing, no need to thank me for it, and I'll give you something else for free, too. To show my good intentions. To prove that I can help you. Meet me this evening at the caravanserai, and we'll visit a friend of mine.'

'Why would I want to do that?'

'Because you're curious. Because you have enough sense to realise I can help you.' Rav stood, quick and fluid, smiled down at Hari. 'Oh, and because my friend has some information about the location of your family's ship.'

6

As he crossed Fei Shen, navigating the starburst of its avenues and the ladders of narrow hutongs that linked them, Hari used his new trait to access the city's commons. He tried and failed to contact the p-suit's eidolon, and after a little thought set up a room in the freespace quarter and equipped it with a model of *Pabuji's Gift* and a message point: if the eidolon was searching for him, she'd find that sooner or later. Then he checked the records of the city's docks, and discovered that a ship registered to Rav, of the True Sons of the Republic of Arden, had put in fifteen days ago. So that much was true: Rav could help him escape from Fei Shen. And then there was his claim that one of his friends knew the current location of *Pabuji's Gift* . . .

Hari didn't trust the Ardenist, but he knew that he couldn't walk away from his offer of help. It was possible – it seemed to be the best possibility – that Rav was honest but crazy. Posthumans were prone to extremes of pareidolia. They heard whispering voices in the radio pulses of Jupiter or Saturn. They saw patterns in sunspot activity that predicted the future, connections between past and present that hinted at vast and malign secret histories. Rav blamed his exile on an end-time cult, the Saints, so it wouldn't be surprising if he saw traces of their conspiracies everywhere, including the hijack of *Pabuji's Gift*. But it was more likely, Hari thought, that Rav's interest in him was purely mercenary: that he saw the chance to make a profit from exploiting the secrets locked inside Dr Gagarian's head. It was even possible that the Ardenist was working for the hijackers, or was hoping to make some kind of deal with them.

Nabhomani had taught Hari that if someone makes an offer that seems too good to be true, nine times out of ten it *is* too good to be true.

A lure, bait for some kind of scam or deception. Trash talk masquerading as the truth. But you don't dismiss it out of hand, Nabhomani had said. You examine it from every angle and investigate the person who made the offer, and if it turns out that it might be of value, you use what you've learned to make a counter-offer.

Hari definitely needed to learn more about Rav: to find out whether he was mad or bad. Or mad *and* bad. And he needed to learn all he could about the files in Dr Gagarian's head, too. Even if Rav was right, even if an ordinary head doctor couldn't crack the tick-tock's encryption, he could at least find out if anyone else had tried.

The Avenue of the Elevation of the Mind was quiet and shabby. It reminded Hari of the unused sections of the ship, of abandoned settlements and installations. The poignant dilapidation of things that had lost meaning and purpose, their slow decay unwatched, unmarked. More than half the buildings on either side of its broad strip of half-life grass were shuttered; most of the rest housed workshops that repaired and refurbished bots. Hari found the Almond Pit at one end of a short arcade of head shops, but walked past it because he didn't quite trust Gabriel Daza, and didn't want to incur a debt by accepting his recommendation.

Most of the other head shops had eidolons posted outside. They targeted Hari as he went by, drifting after him, getting in his face, conjuring windows, trying to port fliers to his bios, bragging about the prowess of their owners and warning him about the dishonest claims of rivals, making extravagant promises about boosting intelligence, information processing and theory-of-mind skills, removing or recovering memories, enhancing sexual pleasure and aesthetic appreciation, implanting traits . . . A small comet-tail of especially persistent eidolons followed him down the avenue, and at last he ducked into a place that lacked any kind of advertisement to shake them off.

Steps led down to a small, square, dimly lit room. Its walls were hung with swags and folds of pinkish-grey fabric. More fabric bulged from the ceiling. It was blessedly quiet, and shielded from the city's cloud; the sole piece of furniture was a kind of attenuated crash couch that hung above the floor with no visible means of support.

The proprietor, Eli Yong according to her tag, materialised from the shadows behind the floating couch. She was a small, neat woman dressed in leggings and a knee-length smock. Her shaved scalp was tattooed with spidery words or symbols in a language Hari's bios didn't recognise; her eyes were masked by tinted goggles.

'You're the boy who crashed on Vesta.'

'I suppose I am.'

'And I suppose you want me to fix that black-market trait,' Eli Yong said. 'You purchased it from some free trader who told you it would work as well as the official version, and now you've come to your senses.'

'I was wondering if you could open files stored in a tick-tock's head,' Hari said.

'The head you're carrying in that flask, I assume.'

'It's the only head I possess.'

'Apart from your own.'

'I think I know what's inside my own head. I came here because I need to find out what's inside the tick-tock's.'

'If everyone knew their own head, I would be out of business,' Eli Yong said. 'As for the tick-tock's, to open that you'll need to find another tick-tock. I'm the best head doctor in Fei Shen, but even I won't be able to get at its files And if anyone else here promises they can, they'll be lying. Tick-tock encryption is famously gnarly.'

'So I've been told. But even if you can't open the files, could you determine whether or not anyone else has tried to look inside?'

The head doctor was silent for a moment, staring at Hari through her tinted goggles. He was beginning to wonder if he'd insulted or upset her when she surprised him with a quick smile.

'Why not?' she said, and waved away his question about a fee. 'I'll do it for fun. I've never interrogated a tick-tock's head before.'

Hari shrugged the cryoflask from his shoulder, asked if he should take out the head. He assumed that Eli Yong would plug it into some kind of arcane apparatus. Probes guided by laser-painted grids, the hum and crackle of mysterious energies . . .

'I've already scanned it,' the head doctor said.

A pict appeared in the air above the couch's slim rectangle: a head clad in smooth black skin that slowly became transparent, revealing the articulation of the lower jaw and tombstone rows of teeth, the balls of the eyes, the cloudy jelly of the brain. There were cylindrical and rectangular modules and beaded strings embedded everywhere in the brain's hemispheres, and the whole was wrapped in a thin shroud woven from fine, intricately tangled threads and filaments.

Eli Yong brushed the air with long white fingers; the view zoomed in. 'Someone inserted a probe behind his eye,' she said. 'There.'

The pict of the head enlarged, and a single thread was suddenly painted with bright scarlet light. It curved around the ball of the right eye, entered the brain through a notched aperture at the back of the socket, and traced a path towards the rear of the brain's left hemisphere.

'They tried to hide it by running it parallel to the optic nerve,' the head doctor said. 'Very sly, but not sly enough. It terminates at this false gyrus, close to the parietal lobe. That's where most traits and files are accessed and controlled by the subject's consciousness, because it plays an important role in integrating sensory input and visuospatial processing. It's where the brain deals with symbology, too. Mathematics, reading, writing. See how the thread frays into dense, short branches where it terminates? It's a parasensory patch. It looks like they attempted to induce a memory dump by directly stimulating the connections between brain and neural net.'

Hari said, 'Can you tell who did this?'

'You're wondering if the commissars tried to get at the files stored in the head while you were in prison,' Eli Yong said.

'Were they successful?'

Hari's mouth was dry. If the Free People had unlocked the secrets inside Dr Gagarian's head, he would lose any advantage he might have had over the hijackers.

The head doctor did not reply at once. She seemed to withdraw into herself, standing silent and still. At last, she said in a faint, faraway whisper, 'I'm almost inside.'

Hari could see his face reflected in the amber lenses of her goggles, and suddenly had a weird sense of doubling, of looking at the head doctor and looking at himself looking at her. A high note keened in his ears. An exquisite pain pierced his left eye . . .

Then, with a violent snap, he was back inside his head. His entire body ached, as if it had been gripped by an all-over cramp, and he was lying on his back, looking up at the bulges of pinkish-grey fabric that covered the ceiling. Realising, with a serene, floating detachment, that it was supposed to resemble the inside of a brain. Something had happened, but he didn't know what it was. He pushed to his feet, dizzy and light-headed. The pict was fading out of the air and Eli Yong leaned over against the couch, fists planted on its surface, head bowed. After a few moments, she shuddered all over and looked up at Hari. Her pale face was slick with sweat. The lenses of her goggles were silvery mirrors.

'Go,' she said. Her voice was harsh and angry. 'Go now!'

'What happened? What did you do?'

'A djinn. It sent a copy after me. Put up quite a fight before my security destroyed it.'

Hari immediately thought of the p-suit's eidolon. He said, 'It was protecting Dr Gagarian's files.'

'Dr Gagarian? Oh, you mean the head. Someone tried to open the files, as I showed you, but they couldn't break the encryption.' Eli Yong straightened and took a deep, shuddering breath. 'You need to find a tick-tock. And you need to go. *I* need you to go. It knows about me, it's probing my security for weak spots . . .'

The head doctor stepped backwards, dissolving into the shadows that filled the rear of the little room, and something thrust towards Hari, a feral face with parchment skin stretched over its muzzle and high cheekbones, huge burning eyes fixed on him.

'Go!' it roared. 'Go now!'

The apparition was a ridiculous cliché, but its voice was laden with subsonic harmonics that assaulted Hari's sympathetic nervous system with exquisite accuracy. Seized with sudden unreasoning panic, he grabbed the cryoflask and ran, blundering up the steps into shockingly bright chandelier light and scattering an ambush of eidolons.

7

A three-wheeled cargo bot hooted as it swerved to avoid Hari. He slowed and stopped, breathless, half-expecting to see the feral apparition generated by Eli Yong's security system floating after him. Apart from the cargo bot, the broad corridor, the avenue, was empty. But as he walked on Hari had the disquieting feeling that the head doctor was somehow following him. A quiet presence at his back, immediately behind his head. It took an effort not to look around.

He walked a long way around the city, through hutongs, across avenues. Trying to process what had happened, trying to fit it into what he already knew. Dr Gagarian's head was protected by a djinn, that much seemed clear. Eli Yong had triggered it, and no doubt the commissars had also triggered it, when they had attempted to access the tick-tock's files. He was certain, now, that the head had been returned to him only after the commissars had tried and failed to crack its encryption, that he had been released from prison as bait for the hijackers or any friends and allies they might have in the city. He remembered how the p-suit's eidolon had attacked the hijacker's drone, wondered if she really had been weaponised, or if she had been ridden by the djinn. Dr Gagarian's head had been hidden more than ten kilometres away from the spires, but perhaps the djinn had a long reach. Or perhaps it had made a copy of itself and inserted it into his p-suit . . .

Thinking about all of this, Hari ate a small meal of sprouting mung beans and steamed fermented tofu at a stall in the Avenue of the Menagerie of Worlds. Behind the triple-paned window of a neighbouring shop, transparent cryoflasks containing miniature silicon-based biomes stood amongst fuming blocks of nitrogen snow. In another, blobjects tinted with bright primary colours pulsed in bubbling aquarium tanks. A parade of equally exotic people passed by, bit-players in his story, heroes of their own mysterious lives. Hari sipped from his tumbler of grey, sticky-sweet fruit juice. One thing was clear. He needed to talk to Rav again.

When Hari returned to the caravanserai, he found the Ardenist deep in conversation with Taqi Koothvar, one of the neuters who ran the place. They sat cross-legged on a rug, sharing a smokebubble: Rav hunched in the cowl of his wings; the neuter, a plump, cheerful person dressed in a red silk shirt and shimmering gold trousers. The two of them looking at Hari as he came across the compound.

Taqi Koothvar blew out a riffle of smoke, handed the mouthpiece to Rav, and told Hari that yo was pleased to hear that he had found someone who could help him.

'I haven't made up my mind about that yet,' Hari said.

'Yet here you are, and here I am,' Rav said. 'How did it go at the head shop, by the way?'

'Have you been tracking me?'

Hari's first thought was that some tiny djinn had been hidden inside the trait that Rav's friend had given him. His second was that if he'd taken up Eli Yong's offer to overwrite the trait with the official version, he wouldn't have been able to trust the replacement, either . . .

'It's a small city,' Rav said. 'Everyone breathes the same air, drinks the same water. Did you learn anything useful? The chances are so vanishingly slight I don't know why I bother to ask the question, but I'm prepared to be amazed.'

'Not as much as I hoped, but more than I expected,' Hari said, meeting the Ardenist's grass-green gaze.

The water in the smokebubble rattled and frothed as Rav drew on the mouthpiece. He said, his voice tight, pinched, 'What you choose to tell me is up to you. As for me, I'm always ready to share useful information with my partners.'

'We aren't in any way partners,' Hari said. 'And besides, I'm sure you already know everything you need to know.'

Rav smiled and blew a smoke ring, then blew a second smaller ring that, rotating counterclockwise, passed through the first.

'Let me have a taste of that,' Hari said.

'Here's a youngblood who thinks he's fully fledged,' Rav told Taqi Koothvar.

'This is a tweaked strain of kif,' Taqi Koothvar told Hari. 'It isn't meant for baseline humans.'

'The passengers brought all kinds of drugs aboard our ship,' Hari said. 'Baseliner, posthuman, it's all the same to me.'

He wanted to show them that he wasn't an innocent tourist, prove that he had knocked about and knew something about the worlds and their illict pleasures. He'd never before tried kif, a drug rumoured to be as old as the human species, but he had several times drunk mildly psychotrophic teas, and had once experienced a long, strange, highly detailed hallucination under the influence of an ephedrine mimic allegedly derived from the cerebrospinal fluid of a posthuman clade, the Quick, that had left the Solar System before the rise of the True Empire.

The neuter shrugged, handed him the mouthpiece. Yo's blue-black hair was teased into a kind of disordered wave and yo's face painted white, with black pigment staining yo's eye sockets and lips. It was impossible to tell if yo had once been a man or a woman. Elements of both combined in yo to make something else.

'Knock yourself out,' yo said.

Hari sucked up cool, mentholated smoke that numbed his mouth. He felt it percolate through the inverted trees of his lungs, felt as if Fei Shen's gravity had flattened out.

Rav took the mouthpiece from him and said, 'Don't huff too much. We have work to do.'

'You said a friend of yours knows where my family's ship is,' Hari said. The free-floating feeling emboldened him.

'It's his news. He should tell you.'

'Well, take me to him.'

'If you're staying another night,' Taqi Koothvar told Hari, 'you should eat before you leave. The evening meal is included in our fee.'

Hari was still buzzing from his hit of smoke as he followed Rav through the dusky parkland. His brain seemed to have expanded, separating and disconnecting his thoughts, and everything around him was saturated with arcane significance. The piping call of a night bird. Pale paths scribbled around shadowy stands of trees. Mounds of mosses glowing in pastel shades as if dabbed by a child's thumb. Fireflies tracing bright signatures through black air . . .

He tried his best to hide his delight in these wonders, but then the path bent around a stand of tall conifers and he was confronted by a magnolia in full bloom, its flowers glowing like a flock of moons, and he couldn't suppress his cry of delight.

Rav laughed. 'You really are high.'

'Perhaps just a little. Where is this friend of yours, anyway?'

'We're almost there.'

The path dipped into a little garden where patches of white gravel were raked around stands of bamboo and ragged chunks of black iron. At the far side, Rav hunched into the tent of his wings and ducked under an arch of roughly dressed stone blocks. Hari followed, came out on to a circle of grass that rimmed a pool of cold, faintly sulphurous water. Beneath the surface, a chain of lights dropped towards distant shadows. When Hari leaned out to study their dim vanishing point, Rav put a hand on his shoulder to steady him.

'No need to go swimming,' he said. 'My friend's right here.'

Ferny platelets of ice rocked on gelid waves as an undulating man-shape rose to the surface and pushed to the edge of the pool. A human face looked up at Hari, large, liquid black eyes, a flattened nose with pinched nostrils. Two lengths of scarlet scarf floated out behind, external gills composed of pseudo-cellular nanotech, half-obscuring a sleek, sinuous body. The legs were fused, and fringed with long fins that met at a broad point where the feet should have been.

Rav made the introductions. His friend, Vazy Klushtsev, was the ambassador for the Ten Thousand Collectives of Europa.

'It is in fact twelve thousand five hundred and thirty-three at this moment, not counting the Old Deep Ones,' Vazy said. 'But ten thousand is a good round number and suggests a certain romance.'

Hari asked him how he and Rav had first met.

'The youngblood wants a measure of my reputation,' Rav said. 'Be kind.'

'I tell the truth, which is kind enough to you. I knew our friend first when I worked in the Office of External Affairs,' Vazy told Hari. 'On Europa we have a city from the long ago, when our ancestors had not yet learned to breathe water as well as air. It connects the surface with the world-ocean; visitors live there. Rav helped to fix part of its environmental conditioning system.'

'It was clever enough to have gone insane,' Rav said, 'but not clever enough to know that it had.'

'We became friends then,' Vazy said, 'and we are friends still. We talk, whenever he comes to Fei Shen, and he tells me about places he has visited, people he has seen. Part of my work is to gather such intelligence.'

'You're a spy,' Hari said to Rav.

He and Rav were sprawled on cushions at the water's edge. He had splashed icy water on his face, and felt a little less spacey.

'I prefer to think of myself as a trusted source of information,' Rav said.

'Such things are unfortunately necessary in these debased times,' Vazy said.

They were an old clade, the Europans, inhabiting bubble-biomes tethered or adrift in the world-ocean under the icy shell of Jupiter's fourth-largest moon. Their economy was based on the ancient system of tradable reputation once shared by the cities and settlements of the outer system; Vazy told Hari that when he returned home at the end of the twelve-year span of his appointment, he would have accumulated enough kudos to found his own collective. Meanwhile, he helped to negotiate trade deals and treaties, and represented the interests of the Ten Thousand Collectives at conclaves and conferences. Face-to-face meetings and discussions were increasingly important because the remnants of the system-wide commons was haunted by djinns and trust in avatars and other virtual representations had been undermined by fakes and finger puppets deployed by unscrupulous governments and individuals.

'Once, you gave your word, and it was enough,' Vazy said. 'A handshake, a kiss – the same thing as a contract. Because to renege on an agreement was shameful. A loss of kudos. Now, who cares about kudos? Where is there trust amongst peoples? There are bandits, I don't need to tell you about them. There are gangs that infiltrate governments of cities and settlements and loot their reserves of consumables and credit. Sell off essentials. They underbid on contracts, this is a new thing. They take control of a city by flattering some senile or docile ruling family, or by bribing it, and they sell off its assets and run up debts and contract out the labour of its citizens at a bargain price. Strip out everything of value and move on. They prey on the small places now, remote and marginal cities unable to put up resistance, but if things do not change they will soon be asset-stripping places like Fei Shen. Because who is to stop them? Once there was consensus, unity. A shared culture. Now there is only mistrust and dissent.'

Vazy reminded Hari of garrulous old scholars who'd bought passage on *Pabuji's Gift*. Custodians of outmoded and half-forgotten doctrines who venerated a personal golden age because they didn't understand the present and feared the future, who had an opinion about every topic and a repertoire of anecdotes and mordant observations, who always had to have the last word.

'I had several dealings with your father when I was working with the office of external affairs,' Vazy told Hari. He leaned against the pool's rim, his chin resting on his folded arms. 'He was of the old school. A man of his word, very much so. I was sorry to hear of it, when he passed over. And sorry also to hear of your family's recent bad luck.'

'I am told you may have some good news about my family,' Hari said. 'Or at least, about our ship.'

The Europan's large eyes were blanked by semitranslucent membranes for a few seconds. 'Your father and this tick-tock, Dr Gagarian, were working on the physics of the Bright Moment with several like-minded philosophers. Including a former Europan, recently deceased.'

'Ivanova Galchan,' Hari said, with a dropping feeling. 'Do you know how she died?'

'It seems that she disappeared on the day your family's ship was hijacked. Her body was found many days afterwards, in a remote part of the aquatic quarter of her adopted home, Chavez Labyrinth. There were signs that she had been tortured. The city police are searching for the murderer, so far without success. It is a big, busy place, Chavez Labyrinth. More than a hundred ships passed through its docks in the time between her disappearance and the discovery of her body. Her former collective was notified, but her remains have not been repatriated. It seems that she entered into a multiple partnership, and her partners chose to commit her remains to the biome of her adopted home. Nevertheless, she was born on Europa, and her death diminishes us all,' Vazy said. 'And that is why I have an interest in the connection between her death and the hijack of your ship.'

'I think you should tell him what you found, before he bursts with impatience,' Rav said.

'We maintain a good traffic control system around Jupiter,' Vazy said. 'It is very old, very powerful. And necessary, for Jupiter is the broom of the system. Many things approaching the Sun from the outer reaches are swept into his gravity well. And many ships steal from his angular momentum to throw themselves further outward. The traffic system watches for comets and rocks, and also tracks ships. And one of them, it was your family's ship.'

Hari said, 'At Jupiter? When? Where is it now?'

'It passed through one hundred and fifty-two days ago,' Vazy said. 'It was flying under a new name and registry, but our traffic system recognised it in any case.'

The Europan opened a window that showed *Pabuji's Gift*'s twisted ring in sharp silhouette against the white swirls of Jupiter's equatorial band. It hadn't made orbit around Jupiter or any of his moons, Vazy said, and threw up a rotating glyph showing the ship's track through the Jupiter system and its changes in delta vee. Instead, like many other ships transiting through the system, it had used a gravity-assist man-oeuvre to gain velocity and bend its course outward. Towards Saturn, which was presently on the same side of the sun as Jupiter.

'Here's an interesting fact,' Rav said. 'The Saints own a wheel habitat that orbits Saturn. That's where Levi lives.'

'Many others live there too,' Vazy said. 'Including the seraphs.'

'But only the Saints would be interested in the research of Dr Gagarian and his friends,' Rav said.

Hari couldn't look away from the image of his family's ship. Wondering if any of his family were still alive, wondering who was piloting it, where it was now.

Vazy told him that it had long since passed beyond the volume monitored by Jupiter's traffic control system. 'Still, I hope it is useful, the information. I give it to help you and your family out of friendship. And in the hope that you might return the favour, should you find anything about the death of Ivanova Galchan.'

'Vazy is a good person,' Rav told Hari, 'but he has one weakness. His sentimentality.'

'Lucky for you I have this so-called weakness,' Vazy said. 'You are a very long way from the definition of a "good person", but for senti-mental reasons I still consider you my friend.'

Hari thanked him, and the Europan talked briefly with Rav about people and places Hari didn't know, then wished Hari luck and said that he hoped they would meet again in happier circumstances. 'Please give your father my regards, if it is ever possible.'

Coming back through the luminous park, Hari pulled up the charges for sending messages to the Saturn system. They were startlingly exorbitant. Even if he managed to trade his rights to the lifepod, he would be able to afford only a few minutes' access to the commons of any of the cities and settlements of Saturn's moons.

He said, 'We should go there. Right now.'

'It's a long old trip,' Rav said. 'And what would you do, when you arrived?'

'Take back my ship, of course. Free my family.'

'If they are alive.'

'Take back the ship and have my revenge, if they are dead.'

'Take it back by force, against an unknown number of opponents? I'm good, but not quite that good.'

'What about your friends?'

'It's the Republic they want to liberate, not your ship. We need to find out what the hijackers want, to begin with,' Rav said. 'Find out what's inside Dr Gagarian's head, find out why they want it, what they want to do with it. Once we know that, we can work out what to do next. There's no point plunging into a cloud in the hope that some tasty morsel is hiding inside it. If you want to track something down, you must first learn its habits—'

'What is it?'

Rav had stopped, was looking all around. 'Someone is following us,' he said, and ran full tilt at a tree and scrambled up its trunk, vanishing inside a shadowy cloud of leaves that suddenly shattered as he launched himself into the air. And twisted sideways, wings folding, and tumbled head over heels into a dense stand of bushes.

As Hari started towards him, Rav thrashed out of the bushes, clutching a bouquet of red flowers to his chest. Falling to his knees, looking at Hari, his mouth working, holding out the flowers like a suitor in a dance.

'Run,' he said. 'Run while you can.'

Something struck Hari's chest. A red flower had sprung up from his jerkin. No, it was the fletching of a dart, similar to the darts with which the ship's security bots were armed. Hari pulled it out and showed it to Rav, but the Ardenist was sprawled under the cowl of his wings, and the world was swaying wildly. Hari lost his balance and sat down hard, and everything swung around him and fell away.

8

Hari's father hung in the air above a circular pool of water that reflected with absolute fidelity the argosy of white clouds that sailed the blue sky. His bare feet, toes pointing down like a sadhu in an ancient pict, almost touched their reflection. All around, the stony desolation of the desert. And now Aakash Pilot revolved and looked at Hari and told him that he could walk out across the water. All he needed was faith. Believe in me, his father said. Trust me. Everything follows from the first step.

But Hari, standing on a slab of rock at the edge of the pool, somehow regressed to age four and dressed in pantaloons and a vest as blue as the sky and decorated with six-pointed silver stars, was too scared to take that step. Hot and slick with embarrassment and shame and fear. Fear of failure. Fear of falling. His father was explaining the physics of his viron, but he spoke in a mumbling whisper and it was difficult to hear what he was saying, and something was stalking through the desert, shaking it with huge, regular footfalls. The pool's mirror shattered. Rocks jumped and rolled. And Hari was on his back, looking up at clouds and sky, trying to tell his father that it wasn't his fault he had fallen . . .

Drums. The sharp pulse of a headache behind his eyes, filling his head, crowding out thought. His blood beating in his ears. The pitter-patter of small drums rapped by fingertips, echoing in a large open space.

Hari tried and failed to open his eyes. He tried and failed to move his hands, his arms.

His head felt as if it had been pierced by razor-edged skewers and then kicked down every corridor of the ship by a manic crew of futzball players. He scarcely noticed the tight feeling in his shoulders and back and buttocks, the cold damp air on his skin. He was naked, hanging naked somewhere, arms stretched up above his head. He could hear the drums. Water dripping into water.

He tried to speak, but his mouth was sealed. Tried again, using the back of his throat and his nasal cavity, shaping words that were mostly vowels. 'Uh mmm ah? Oo ah u?'

No one answered. And with a swooning falling feeling that gripped him from fingertips to feet Hari realised who his captors must be. Somehow, the hijackers had infiltrated the city and made their move. They'd avoided the trap set by Ma Sakitei, the trap for which Hari had been bait, and now he was in their power, aboard *Easy Does It* or some other ship (which must be accelerating, because there was a definite sense of up and down), or somewhere else far, far away. Beyond Jupiter. Orbiting Saturn, or even further out. Beyond any hope of rescue.

'He's ready,' a woman said.

Something wet was swiped across Hari's forehead and cheeks. A brief cold spray on his eyelids dissolved the glue that had held them closed, fingers pried them open. He saw a shadowy figure withdrawing, saw a flock of small shapes move in.

He was hung vertically on some kind of board, glued there like a specimen, naked and vulnerable. A swarm of drones hung in front of his face, little white balls slung under the blurred halos of tiny rotors. He couldn't turn his head because it was glued to the board. His arms were glued above his head. His legs were glued together. When he tried to blink he discovered that his eyelids, once glued shut, were now glued open.

He used his peripheral vision to look around. A distant overhead speckled with bright stars. Small islands scattered across a black flood, low and flat and covered in white moss, long tendrils floating out from their edges. He was raised up at the centre of one of these islands. And it was cold, so cold that his breath plumed from his nostrils and his naked skin felt tight and frozen.

The little drones began to flash stuttering patterns of light. A constellation of novas exploding in his face. Pain pulsed: jagged screeches of tearing metal. Cold hummed in his ears. The insistent pitter-patter of the drums prickled across his flanks. Pale mosses tasted like icy grit; black water like burnt plastic. Synaesthesia cross-wiring his senses until everything went blank and for a moment he hung in the still centre of silent and absolute whiteness before sight and hearing, touch, taste and smell, returned.

Figures moved beyond the stuttering stars of the drones. Four, five, six of them. Two appeared to be children. They were dressed in long white coats and their faces were masked with luminous green dots and dashes and swirls, and they carried poles topped with swaying bouquets of skulls. The skulls were hung from coloured threads strung through holes drilled in their bony caps, and painted with the same luminous patterns as the faces of the pole-bearers, who stepped forward one after the other, planting their burdens in the soft ground and stepping back and clasping their hands before their chests and beginning to sing. A polyphonic chant founded on the insistent patter of the drums, slowly building and falling away and building again.

The lights of the drones began to pulse in time to the pulse of the chant. The luminous patterns painted on the skulls and on the faces of the celebrants of this strange ceremony were pulsing too. And with each throbbing beat Hari's sense of self expanded outward. Dissolving by steady increments into the pulsing chant, the pulsing patterns of light. He felt questing intelligences drift past his unknotting thoughts, felt them sink into the substrate of his mind . . .

And then, all at once, everything stopped. The chant broke off in the middle of a phrase; the beat of the drums was suspended; the patterns of light winked out and the drones fell out of the air. Hari's senses, abruptly unconstrained, expanded like gas escaping from a punctured p-suit. He saw the module entire, like a transparent model of itself. He saw a city stretching away above it, and realised with a quick sharp stab of hope that he must still be in Fei Shen. He could see the radial pattern of its avenues and the outlines of its buildings, a honeycomb of virtual rooms and spaces. And in one of those rooms the ghost of the p-suit's eidolon turned to him and asked him why he had taken so long to get in touch.

Help me, he said. And with a falling feeling he was back in his body, hung naked on the board. Something was picking its way through the twilight towards him. It was inhumanly tall and thin and radiated a fell menace, but he could not move, could not shut his eyes, could not look away. He could only watch, heart banging in his chest, sweat pricking over his entire body, as it grew closer. Then a pale translucent figure leaned past him and swept up the fallen drones. It turned and smiled at him, a sly, shrewd, familiar smile, then spun and hurled the drones into the twilight beyond the skull-laden poles. Someone screamed, a sharp cry of rage and fear that echoed off the overhead. The figure smiled at Hari again, and faded into the dark air like a sketch erasing itself.

The patterns painted on the skulls were likewise fading. People in white coats sprawled on the mossy ground, eyes rolled back, faces contorted in rigid grimaces as they twitched and fitted and at last passed into something like sleep. One was the proctor, Gabriel Daza. Two more were Free People.

Hari hung there a long time. Shivering, passing in and out of consciousness. His eyes dry stones. At last, he glimpsed a movement far off in the scatter of pale islands: a low and narrow boat gliding across the water, poled by two upright figures. As it drew nearer, he recognised Rav and the neuter Taqi Koothvar. He tried to call out, but his mouth was still glued shut.

The boat nosed through the fringe of moss at the island's edge and Rav sprang ashore and cantered towards Hari, telling him everything would be fine. Behind him, Taqi Koothvar's anxious expression betrayed the lie.

9

Rav and Taqi Koothvar lowered the board to which Hari was fastened, found a canister of spray, and used it to dissolve the glue. Hari sat up, moving slowly and carefully. His back felt as if it had been flayed. His shoulders and arms ached stiffly. His hands throbbed as blood began to circulate in them again.

While Rav moved from pole to pole, methodically crushing the skulls hung from them, Taqi Koothvar used a cloth wetted with spray to remove the glue that sealed Hari's mouth and held his eyes open, wiped green stuff from his face, and pasted several patches on his chest that eased his pain and turned the world as soft as a daydream.

Taqi Koothvar helped Hari to stand and walk about. His former captors were still unconscious or asleep, sprawled in their white coats. They were skull feeders, according to Rav. An antique cult that practised a peculiar form of amortality.

'They infect themselves with mites that construct molecular archives in the bones of their skulls, and record every moment of their lives. They feed the skulls of their ancestors with infusions necessary for the survival and operation of these archives, and every skull,' Rav said, mashing one between his hands with a dry, snapping crunch, 'is plugged into a network via patterns of tweaked bacteria, so that they can communicate with each other and with their keepers.'

'They painted the same stuff on you,' Taqi Koothvar told Hari.

'They were trying to link your bios with their network,' Rav said.

'I know one of them,' Hari said. 'He approached me when I visited the bourse, helped me gain access to my family's credit, made inquiries on my behalf. He pointed me towards a head clinic, too. I suppose that if I had followed his advice I would have been taken here directly. Instead, they kidnapped me.'

'This one is different,' Taqi Koothvar said. 'Also, she is dead.'

The neuter was standing over a slender woman dressed in a black, close-fitting bodysuit, sprawled face down on moss tinted by her blood. She had been pierced many times in the back and head. When Taqi Koothvar and Rav turned her over, Hari recognised her at once. Her hair was cut close to her skull and dyed white, but her pale, angular face was the spit of Deel Fertita's, the proteome specialist who, according to Agrata, had murdered Dr Gagarian.

There are many of us, one of the hijackers had told Hari, on Themba. Many sisters.

Hari told Rav and Taqi Koothvar who she was. 'She must have followed these . . . What did you call them?'

'Skull feeders,' Rav said. 'It looks like she tried to sneak up on them, and something sneaked up on her instead.'

Hari remembered the face of the translucent figure. His father's face, his father's sly smile.

He said, 'There was a djinn. It took control of the skull-feeders' drones and threw them at the woman and killed her.'

Rav said, 'This was while the skull feeders were opening you up, or while they were trying to unlock the tick-tock's head?'

Hari tried to focus through the drowsy haze of Taqi Koothvar's patches. 'They got inside my head, and everything stopped. The song they were singing, the drums, the lights. I saw the eidolon. The eidolon of my p-suit. I saw that woman, too. She looked like a demon. Like she was made out of knives. And then the djinn appeared.'

'You reached out to this eidolon, or it reached out to you,' Rav said. 'It penetrated the skull feeders' network, and sent a djinn to help you.'

'It claims that it has been weaponised,' Hari said.

Kinson Ib Kana's book and the flask containing Dr Gagarian's head lay next to the dead woman. Rav stooped and picked them up, then plucked something else from the moss and showed it to Hari. A slim, silvery drone the length of his little finger.

'Is this one of the skull feeders' drones?'

'They were smaller,' Hari said. 'Like little white balls.'

Rav thought for a moment, weighing the drone in his palm.

'I think I know what went down here,' he said. 'The skull feeders wanted to get inside the tick-tock's head. They tried and failed to unlock it, and then they opened you up, looking for a key or a code. And while they were busy with you, the hijacker took her chance and knocked them out. She probably used this drone to attack their network. Their minds were linked together. When the network went down, so did they. That gave you the chance to contact your p-suit, its eidolon dealt with the hijacker, and then it called me. That's how we found you. Someone or something sent me the coordinates of this place. Have I got it right or have I got it right?'

'More or less.' Hari remembered the eidolon, turning towards him in the virtual room. But she hadn't thrown the skull feeders' drones at the hijacker. The djinn had scooped them up. The djinn with the face of his father . . .

'You have some serious protection, youngblood,' Rav said. 'I shall have to mind my manners.'

'How long has it been?' Hari said. 'How long since they took me?'

'A night and a day,' Rav said. 'We have to get off this rock before the commissars find out what happened here.'

'It was self-defence,' Taqi Koothvar said.

'The commissars might not see it like that,' Rav said. 'Especially as two of the skull feeders are their bosses.'

Taqi Koothvar helped Hari into a white coat and sat him in the middle of the little boat. He clutched the flask and the book to his chest while the neuter and Rav poled through channels of black water, between the pale islands.

They beached the boat at the entrance to the flooded chamber and walked down a long corridor lit by dabs of sharp blue phosphorescence, its stone walls everywhere carved with diagrams and crude drawings and epithets in languages long forgotten. Taqi Koothvar pointed to runes carved at the bases of the walls. Made by rats, yo said. The floor was thick with dust that formed little drifts and dunes, marked with footprints and the tracks of animals. A disabled bot lay on its back, a human-shaped shell of corroded plastic, memory clay inside its skull gone to white dust that seeped from empty eye sockets. Hari felt the age of the city, the crushing weight of its history.

They reached an intersection and turned left, following a narrow, steeply sloping passage. Presently, Hari's bios registered Fei Shen's commons, and soon afterwards the three of them emerged through a small hatch into one of the hutongs that ran between the avenues, this one lined with single-storey flat-roofed modules – buildings, homes – painted in bright primary colours. Taqi Koothvar led Hari and Rav to the station, and they rode a capsule that dropped them through the core of Fei Shen's rock to the docks on the far side. Rav was impatient to get away, but Hari insisted on retrieving his p-suit.

In the airy hub of the public storerooms, a slender bot checked Hari's ID, stalked away down one of the corridors, and returned some five minutes later, pushing a wheeled frame in which the scuffed, dust-stained p-suit hung like a flayed trophy.

The eidolon drifted behind the bot, unseen by any but Hari.

Rav and Hari settled their bills for use of the city's services, and Rav slung the p-suit over his shoulder and picked up the helmet and started towards the exit, followed by Hari and Taqi Koothvar, and the eidolon. They hadn't gone more than ten steps when the bot called out. Hari turned, expected to see a posse of commissars hurrying towards them, or a flock of drones vectoring in with weapon-pods everted. In the screen set in the bot's chest, Ma Sakitei smiled at him.

'You are leaving. I am sorry to see it.'

Hari thanked her for her help and hospitality. He felt a freezing apprehension, wondered if she knew about the skull feeders, if she was a friend or sympathiser.

'We feel somewhat used,' Ma Sakitei said.

'I didn't mean to bring trouble here.'

'We think you knew exactly what you were doing.'

'I won't forget your kindness.'

'May we give you some advice?'

'Of course.'

'You believe the Ardenist can help you. You are wrong.'

'Have I broken any laws?' Rav said.

'We don't know,' Ma Sakitei said. 'Have you?'

'I owe this city nothing,' Rav said. 'The youngblood owes nothing. We are free to go.'

'There is no need to leave,' Ma Sakitei told Hari. 'Your enemies cannot touch you here. And we can help you find out who they are. We can help you in many ways.'

'You told me to look for justice elsewhere,' Hari said. 'That's what I'm doing.'

'We have been investigating your story, and the circumstances of the hijack of your family's ship,' Ma Sakitei said. 'We can be useful to you, if you let us. And you can help us.'

Hari said, 'What did you find?'

And Rav stepped up and struck the bot's cluster of sensors with the tips of his fingers, once, twice. It froze in mid-gesture, and its screen went dark.

'She's trying to delay you until the commissars get here,' Rav told Hari. 'Time to go.'

In other parts of the large space bots turned from conversations with their clients, stepped forward from niches. Ma Sakitei's face floated in their chest-screens. Her voice called Hari's name in an overlapping chorus.

'Run,' Rav said.

They ran. Hari in his borrowed white coat, the cryoflask slung over his shoulder, Taqi Koothvar in yo's bright silks, Rav forbiddingly tall and massive, shouldering past a bot when it tried to intercept Hari, sending it spinning away.

At the jetty to Rav's ship, Hari told Taqi Koothvar that he needed one last favour, asked if yo would witness an agreement between him and Rav.

'What agreement is this?' Rav said.

Hari took a breath and said, 'That in exchange for the help you have given me in the past, and for whatever help you may give me in the future, you will receive a share in any profits realisable on the research of Dr Gagarian, those profits to be divided equally between you, any surviving members of my family, including myself, and any living relatives of Dr Gagarian.'

He had composed this on the short ride to the docks, and hoped that Nabhomani would have approved.

Rav laughed. 'You traders probably tried to monetise the cosmic egg before it hatched. Suppose I don't agree? Will you refuse to come with me?'

'I want to make sure you get your fair share. Especially if you survive this and I don't. Will you swear to uphold the agreement?'

Rav shrugged with a leathery rustle. 'Why not?'

'I so swear,' Hari told Taqi Koothvar.

'And I so witness,' the neuter said.

Rav said, 'Are we done?'

Hari asked Taqi Koothvar if yo would be all right.

'Of course. I have done no more than help one of my guests.'

'I meant the skull feeders.'

'I doubt that they would want to draw attention to themselves and their crimes. And my people are not without resources. We ruled an empire once.' Taqi Koothvar paused, then said, 'Give me your hands.'

The neuter's grip was hot and surprisingly strong. Yo looked into Hari's eyes and after a moment yo's warm brown gaze went out of focus and yo said, 'When people go looking for something, Gajananvihari Pilot, they often find something else.'

'Is that one of your predictions,' Rav said, 'or a scrap of folk wisdom?'

Taqi Koothvar let go of Hari's hands and smoothed the blue-black wave of yo's hair with an elegant gesture. 'It is what it is.'

'Any words of advice for me?' Rav said.

Taqi Koothvar smiled. 'Would you listen to them?'

'Good point,' Rav said, and pushed Hari forward, and then they were running again, bounding towards the ship.

PART THREE

THE CAVES
OF STEEL

PART THREE

1

Rav claimed that his ship, *Brighter Than Creation's Dark*, was named after an ancient blasphemy. He also said that he'd won it in a dice game while riding the elevator from Phobos down to the surface of Mars, and that he'd had to dispatch three reivers who'd been hired by the unlucky former owner to stop him taking possession of his prize. It was an old design: a froth of spherical pods, all different sizes, clustered around a motor and utility shaft. Rav and his son lived in the largest pod, a mostly empty, unpartitioned volume with padded walls; the others were used to store cargo or accommodate passengers.

Ardenists were exclusively male. They quickened their sons from templates derived from artificial recombinations of their own genome and that of a temporary or permanent partner, and treated them as bonded servants. Rav's nameless son was a slight, austere person about Hari's size who deferred completely to his father and had been arrested in prepubescence. he would not achieve maturity until Rav died. Whenever Hari tried to talk to him, he'd shrug and turn away. Hunch into himself, as if trying to minimise the space he occupied. He hardly ever spoke, and when he did he always glanced at his father for permission. Saying once that he did not need to be thanked for carrying out his usual tasks. Saying another time that he was older than Hari thought he was, and could take care of himself.

'Oh, he's old, all right,' Rav said. 'A lot older than you, youngblood. But he still has a lot to learn. I worry, sometimes, that he isn't bright enough or tough enough to survive on his own after I'm gone.'

The ship cut a long chord across the inner belt, swinging past a single waypoint, a tiny uninhabited rubble pile crushed down to a sphere by the string injected into its centre to deepen its gravity well. Part of an ancient network constructed by Trues, using technology stolen from one of the posthuman clades they had conquered, to facilitate travel throughout the Belt.

Plugged into the ship's mind, Hari watched the insignificant fleck of the waypoint brighten and swell into a tiny crescent that rushed at the ship and swung beneath its keel. The rigid patterns of the stars swung too, as the ship gained a fraction of the waypoint's orbital energy from the slingshot encounter, increasing its velocity and altering its trajectory. Heading for the world-city Ophir, the Caves of Steel.

It had been Rav's idea to go to Ophir. Hari had wanted to light out for Tannhauser Gate, to find out all he could about Deel Fertita and the murders of Rember Wole and Worden Hanburanaman, and to attempt to make contact with the hijackers through one of the agents who arbitrated ransom deals for hostages, ships and cargoes seized by dacoit crews. And if the hijackers refused to talk to him, or demanded a price he couldn't pay, he would round up a crew of reivers willing to chase after *Pabuji's Gift* and take her back by main force.

But Rav had other plans. Tannhauser Gate was presently on the far side of the sun, he said; Ophir was much closer. A diversion that would cost them only a few days. Hari could make himself known to his uncle, who might be able to give him all the help he needed. He could investigate the murder of Salx Minnot Flores. And Rav knew a tick-tock matriarch who lived in Ophir. If she couldn't crack open Dr Gagarian's files and find out what they contained, he said, no one could.

Hari suspected that the Ardenist's interest in his plight would end once he had a copy of Dr Gagarian's research, but knew that there was no point trying to argue with him. It was Rav's ship, after all. For the first time in his life, Hari was a passenger.

Even with the gravity-assist manoeuvre, it took fifteen days to reach Ophir. Hari read a long story he found in Kinson Ib Kana's book, a tragic saga about a bloody civil war between scions of a True suzerain who decided to hand over power to his youngest daughter. Rav examined what was left of the drone he'd taken from the dead woman, Deel Fertita's sister, and determined that it had been purchased in Fei Shen and modified with black-market combat algorithms. The woman's genome, read off a skin scraping, didn't yield a match on any of the databases he was able to consult, but that wasn't surprising.

'Most cities and settlements keep the records of their citizens locked, and public catalogues of felons and fanatics are partial and corrupted.

She isn't on any of the watch lists, and neither are any of her close relatives, but that doesn't mean she isn't a Saint. She could be a fresh recruit. A clean skin. Or someone operating in deep cover.'

Hari knew that it would be a waste of time to point out that the dead woman and her sisters were most likely dacoits. Most of the stories Rav told about his adventures and escapades were either exaggerations or outright fabrications, but his obsession with the Saints seemed genuine. One of the first things he'd done, after they'd left Fei Shen, was show Hari a saga he'd obtained from a disaffected member of the cult, depicting the mythic origins of its leader, Levi. A rarity that only a few outsiders had seen. Essential background information for their joint mission.

According to the saga, Levi had been born in a remote agricultural garden inhabited by a humble sect, the Congregation of the Children of the True Christ, whose ancestors had quit Earth more than a thousand years ago. They herded skysheep and tended orchards and platform farms. They cultivated vacuum organisms on the small rock which the garden orbited. They had no makers, no QIs or virons. They maintained the ancient machineries that regulated the ecosystem of their garden and repaired their handbuilt pressure suits and scooters, but otherwise rejected every kind of technology.

Levi's parents were sheep herders. He was their only child. Until the age of fourteen, he had lived an unremarkable life in the free-fall orchards and farms of his home. And then the wavefront of the Bright Moment passed through the Solar System. The inhabitants of the Congregation's garden, no more than two hundred souls, were badly traumatised by its brief universal vision. There were outbreaks of panic and hysteria. Two men killed themselves; another murdered his wife and child, then swam out of an airlock into vacuum.

The elders told the Congregation that the vision was yet another false miracle in an age of false miracles and prophets put up by the Great Enemy to tempt people from the True Way. These things had happened before, and would happen again. The Great Enemy worked through cursed technology created by posthumans who believed themselves little gods. He worked through the seraphs. He worked through the weaknesses of otherwise blameless men and women. We must all stand firm, the elders said. We must know and understand that even though the Great Enemy frightens and tempts us with visions sent directly into our minds, as the Christ was tempted in the desert, those visions are false. Our souls will remain unsullied as long as our faith remains strong, and our faith will be strengthened by our refusal to be tempted.

Every so often a ship visited the garden to trade essential goods and machine parts for the exquisite rugs that the Congregation's children wove on hand looms. When it returned, a couple of hundred days after the Bright Moment, its captain, the only outsider allowed into the garden, told the elders that the vision had been experienced by every living human being in the Solar System, and its origin had been discovered in ancient files on Earth: a pict of the father of an ancient gene wizard, Sri Hong-Owen. The Bright Moment, the captain said, was a signal created when she had fused with entities in the atmosphere of Fomalhaut's only gas-giant planet, and had undergone a transformation similar to the vastening of the seraphs.

The elders seized on this story and made it their own. They told the Congregation that Sri Hong-Owen had dared to believe that she could challenge the Creator. She had tried to vasten herself using evil technology derived from a Godless alien intelligence, and she had been punished for her hubris. The Bright Moment was a warning: a glimpse of her headlong rush into the arms of the Great Enemy, who had likewise rebelled, and had been expelled from Heaven. The Christ, in the image of her father, had tried to save her, and she had refused to be saved, and because of her pride she had been cast out of His light into perpetual darkness.

Levi thought differently. He had always been an independent and wayward child. He had been beaten by his parents many times, had been publicly flogged for challenging the elders. But he refused to stop asking questions because he knew that unexamined faith was worthless. Belief was weakened and compromised if its tenets were never challenged; interpretations of holy writ must be tested and retested until every flaw had been exposed and corrected.

Slowly, he began to formulate his own exegesis of the Bright Moment. The QIs that had vastened themselves into seraphs had never been anything other than machines, but Sri Hong-Owen had once been human. If she had become something like a seraph, it would be no ordinary seraph, and her vastening would be no ordinary vastening. And even though it had required the intervention of some kind of alien intelligence, it could still be a holy act proceeding from the will of the Creator. After all, the entire universe was holy, because everything in it had once been enclosed within the cosmic point quickened by the Creator. Time and space, light and matter, stars, planets, human beings – even, why not, the alien intelligence in the gas giant orbiting Fomalhaut. It was entirely possible, Levi thought, that the Bright Moment was a vision of an apotheosis rather than a fall from grace. The equivalent of an ascension to Heaven by someone yet living, as achieved by certain saints of the long ago.

He tried to discuss his ideas with his friends, and one of them immediately denounced him to the elders. He was accused of subversion, flogged, and sentenced to spend a hundred days in a hut hung close to the roof of the garden, to think about his sins and to pray for forgiveness.

After the elaborate dance sequence depicting his trial and punishment, the saga cut to an image of Levi clad in a holy nimbus as he knelt in prayer at the edge of the little world. In one direction was everything he knew and loved: a sea of green islands floating at various depths around the sunlamp at the centre of the garden. In the other was the stark inhospitality of the outer dark, visible through the long slit of a window set in the rind of water-ice and foamed fullerene that protected the garden from solar and cosmic radiation, and from strikes by flecks of debris too small to trigger the attention of the anti-collision guns.

The elders expected Levi to meditate on the contrast between his own insignificant life and the inhuman scale of the universe. The billions of stars and planets of the Milky Way, the billions of galaxies beyond. A cosmic hymn to the Creator's power. Instead, Levi was increasingly troubled by thoughts of the cruelty, waste and stupidity of human history. The world was fallen, and those in it could be redeemed only by the blood sacrifice of the Christ, but almost four thousand years later human history was still far from the path of the righteous. One day, he was visited by a terrifying revelation. He saw that the Bright Moment was a sign that the universe had reconfigured itself to accommodate the possibility of vastenings of human beings; a small window of hope which those who possessed true faith could widen into a new golden age. They would share in the miracle it symbolised, sweep away false idols, from posthumans to seraphs, and raise themselves into a state of grace.

Levi knew what he must do. He understood the great burden that had been laid upon him and he prayed that he would prove himself worthy. He received no answer, but knew that he could not do anything other than that which he had been born to do.

The saga showed him returning to the Congregation, and preaching, and everyone falling at his feet in wonder and amazement before rising and uniting in a final dance sequence. 'What actually happened,' Rav told Hari, 'was that he came back from exile, pretended that he'd seen the error of his ways, and secretly recruited four of his closest friends. They armed themselves with agricultural implements. At the next meeting, he stood up and told the Congregation about his vision. His friends killed two elders who tried to stop him, and subdued everyone else, and he preached for a day and a night. He told the Congregation that they were God's chosen messengers. He told them that they were Saints. Those who refused to join him were killed. And when the freighter that traded with the garden next put in, Levi and his Saints captured it and voyaged out into the Belt to begin their so-called holy work.'

Levi had taken his name from an earlier prophet, the leader of a cult that had called themselves Ghosts. They'd tried to take control of the settlements and cities on Saturn's moons; Sri Hong-Owen had helped to defeat them. Later, they had established a colony in the asteroid belt of the star beta Hydrus, and had attempted seize Fomalhaut's gas-giant planet, Cthuga. And once again, Sri Hong-Owen had been involved in their defeat. The original Levi had claimed that a message from his future self would change the human history; his followers had called themselves Ghosts because they believed that they were living in a history that was provisional, soon to be rewritten. The leader of the Saints claimed that he was the true incarnation of the Ghosts' leader, that his incarnation was only possible because the past had been changed by Sri Hong-Owen's Becoming, and that he and his followers were the vanguard of a utopian era in which all true believers would be vastened as the seraphs and Sri Hong-Owen had been vastened, and each would become the totipotent deity of their own universe.

'I sometimes wonder,' Rav said, 'if Sri Hong-Owen would be amused or appalled to discover that she's the inspiration for a bad copy of the cult she twice defeated.'

The Saints had established schools in most of the major cities in the Belt, and offered to teach anyone willing to listen the secrets that Levi had unpicked from the Bright Moment. Students were offered free audits, and then were asked to pay for counselling sessions that would raise them, degree by degree, towards true enlightenment. Levi had proven adept at flattering iconoclasts, had wooed and won the Old Ones of the Republic of Arden, and had caused a schism in the Koronis Emirates. One of its scions had given him a wheel garden, and his disciples had moved it outward, into orbit around Saturn.

That was where Levi was now, Rav said, planning some kind of assault on the seraphs. Many end-time cults believed the seraphs could provide direct vastening of baseliner minds, but the Saints' approach was more pragmatic than most.

'They are training adepts who will enter the information horizons of seraphs, vasten, and use their new superhuman powers to usher in Levi's utopia. Peace and harmony and universal brotherhood, and so on. The precursor to a final battle in which the Saints' enemies will be defeated and the Saints will be vastened into their individual versions of heaven. The usual end-timer utopian cant, dressed up in pseudo-scientific drivel. My guess is that they found out about the research of your Dr Gagarian and think that it could help them breach the seraphs' defences.'

Hari said, 'I should let them know that I am willing to exchange Dr Gagarian's head for the ship, and any hostages they hold.'

'You want to trade with them.'

'If they are the hijackers.'

'You want to talk to Levi.'

Rav was amused.

'If I can find someone who will pass my message to him,' Hari said, 'he will want to talk to me.'

'And you'll do what? Ask him if he ordered the hijack? Do you think he'd admit it? No,' Rav said, 'Before we do anything else, we must find out what's in those files. When we know that, we'll know what the Saints want. And then we'll be able to use it against them.'

Aakash would have been able to discuss the scientism of the Saints with Rav; Nabhomani would have matched Rav's unlikely yarns of his exploits with equally unlikely yarns of his own; even Nabhoj would have been able to talk about Rav's ship, its systems, its capabilities. Hari, lacking their experience and knowledge, listened patiently to the Ardenist's stories about Levi and the Saints, his vague, grandiose fantasies about uniting the exiled Ardenists and leading them in a crusade to take back the Republic. Agrata had taught Hari that if you

117

allowed people to talk they often revealed their true selves; he learnt that Rav was conceited, brilliant, vain, capricious, resourceful, a scholar of history (which he called human foolishness) and arcane mathematics, insightful about everyone but himself. Although he didn't treat Hari with the rough contempt he showed towards his son, it was clear that he didn't think they were equal partners in what he called their joint enterprise. As far as he was concerned, the files in Dr Gagarian's head were a means to an end. Something he could use to unite the exiled Ardenists against their old enemy, if he was telling the truth. Something he could steal and sell if he wasn't.

Rav had helped to save Hari's life, he was a useful ally, and there was, after all, a small chance that the Saints really had been behind the hijack. The Saints, or some other crew of end-time fanatics. But Hari didn't trust the Ardenist, and made his own plans about what he would do when he reached Ophir.

He talked to the p-suit's eidolon, asked her about the skull feeders and the hijacker and the djinn. She claimed to know nothing about it. 'You told me to call your friend and tell him where you were,' she said. 'And that's what I did. Was that the right thing to do?'

'Of course,' Hari said.

'I wish I could have done more.'

'I wish I knew what you are capable of doing.'

He was thinking of the djinn that the head doctor, Eli Yong, had woken when she'd tried to look inside Dr Gagarian's head. Later, it had attacked the woman who had infiltrated the lair of the skull feeders, probably because she had also tried to open the head.

Rav was wrong, he thought. I'm not the one with serious protection. It's Dr Gagarian's head. And it has an agenda of its own . . .

He borrowed time on the ship's comms, searching for and failing to find evidence for the final destination of *Pabuji's Gift*, and exchanging messages with his uncle, Tamonash, who offered to assist in any way he could.

'We are family, Gajananvihari,' he said in one message. 'And that is the beginning and end of everything.'

Rav, who made no secret about listening to these exchanges, said that this sentimental assertion was about the only thing Hari should believe, as far as his uncle was concerned.

'There are all kinds of traps in this sorry universe,' he said, 'but families are the hardest to escape.'

'If we can't trust our families, who can we trust?' Hari said.

'If you want to survive this, youngblood, don't put your trust in anyone.'

'Not even in you?'

'If I were you? I wouldn't even trust myself.'

2

Hari followed Rav out of the booming elevator they'd ridden down from the docks and for a moment thought he saw his father standing in the bustle and flow of the dispersing passengers. A stocky old man with the familiar hawkish profile and bristling white eyebrows, but clean-shaven, dressed in a long black jacket elaborately embroidered with gold thread, black pyjama trousers. Smiling now, holding out his hands, saying, 'Nephew! Gajananvihari! How good it is to meet you at last! I am Tamonash. Welcome to Down Town. Welcome to Ophir.'

Tamonash Pilot, Hari's uncle, his father's younger brother, was about the same age now as Aakash had been when he'd passed over. He told Hari that he and Rav could stay in the family compound for as long as they liked, said that he would try to help in any way he could, but feared that it wouldn't amount to much. He and Aakash had fallen out years before Hari had been born, during the refurbishment of *Pabuji's Gift*. He had paid little attention to his brother's career after that, Tamonash said, knew nothing about Aakash's interest in the Bright Moment and his partnership with Dr Gagarian, and regretted that he had far less influence with the authorities than he deserved. Times were hard. Scoundrels prospered at the expense of honest, hard-working people.

'I will of course do all I can to help you find the villains who hijacked your ship and gave my brother the true death,' he said. 'But I must warn you that it will not amount to much. I am an honest businessman. I have never dealt with dacoits or reivers, and have no experience in ransoming hostages or hijacked goods. And as you can see, while I have every hope that my prospects will soon improve, at the moment I am grievously short of credit.'

Tamonash's partner had died more than twenty years ago; his

daughter and her family had emigrated to Earth. He lived alone, in a big room in the old family compound on the floor of Ophir's largest chamber, a little way beyond the shadow cast by the chandelier city, Down Town. The place was half-ruined. Hari swept decades of detritus and dust from the small room Tamonash gave him, draped the mattress over the sill of one of the unglazed slit ports in a futile attempt to get rid of a strong odour of mould.

The room was at the top of a slim tower, with a view across the overgrown gardens of the compound towards the looming stalactite of Down Town. A cone of ring-shaped tiers spindled around a central core, the smallest at the top, beneath the overhead, the largest at the base, its edge ornamented with the villas and alcazars of the wealthy. When the Trues had constructed Ophir, they had hung Down Town and their palaces, bastions, and pleasure domes from the shell wrapped around the world city, high above a fantasy patchwork of parklands and wildernesses landscaped across its floor. Much later, after the fall of the True Empire, parts of the floor had been colonised, but anyone who was anyone lived aloft.

Tamonash told Hari that he had devoted his life to the elevation of his family, and with a kind of mordant relish described various business schemes which had foundered on bad luck, bad faith, betrayal by his partners, and astounding levels of corruption in the governments of Ophir and other cities. If he'd had no more than ordinary luck, if his business partners had been only averagely dishonest, Tamonash said, he would have made his fortune several times over, and be living in a villa at the edge of the lowest tier of Ophir. As it was, he had poured all that remained of his credit into selling novel vacuum organisms and rare biologics to Earth's governments.

Earth was beginning to open up to trade with Mars and the Belt, and Tamonash had won an early foothold in what, according to him, would soon be a vastly profitable market. His daughter and her family had recently moved to Cape Town, where they were cultivating contacts and contracts; he could put Hari's experience in the salvage business to good use, he said, dealing with prospectors and free traders in the Belt, locating and mining previously undiscovered sources, and so on. The Pilot family had fallen on hard times, but they had standards to maintain. It would not do to lose any degree of auqat, the measure of the respect of their neighbours and peers.

'Apni auqat mat bhool,' he told Hari. 'Don't forget where you belong. Don't do anything that would bring shame on you and your family.'

This was after Hari had contacted Ophir's police and asked to speak to someone about the woman, Angley Li, who had murdered Salx Minnot Flores. The officer who had taken his call told him that the inspector in charge of the investigation was unavailable, and cut short his explanation about the connection between the death of the philosopher and the hijack of *Pabuji's Gift*. Angley Li had killed herself rather than be arrested; she had been acting alone; the case was closed.

It was a political decision, according to Tamonash. The government of Ophir didn't have the resources or inclination to mount an investigation beyond their jurisdiction, so the murder had been given a narrative – rivalry between philosophers that had flared into violence – and folded away.

'Angley Li wasn't a philosopher,' Hari said. 'She was an assassin.'

He'd found images of her in Down Town's commons: the murder had created a small, transient sensation that had left traces in news and gossip nodes. Slim, pale-skinned, Angley Li was the identical twin of Deel Fertita, of the woman who had come after him in Fei Shen.

'I need to find out where she came from,' he told Tamonash. 'Where she lived, in Ophir. Who she talked to. Anything that might help me identify the hijackers.'

'I know someone in the Ministry of Justice. I will ask him to find out what he can, but I should warn you that these things take time,' Tamonash said, and launched into a lecture about the intractable bureaucracies that maintained the support systems and what was left of civil order in Ophir, and the intrigues and complex relationships of what he called the major players in the world city's politics.

'Be patient, Gajananvihari,' he said. 'Tread cautiously. You do not want to attract the attention of the wrong kind of people, or stir up trouble with the police. You will not advance your cause by being arrested, or by being expelled from Ophir.'

But Hari had no intention of taking Tamonash's advice. It was more than two hundred days since the hijack; he had not yet begun to negotiate the release of any survivors and the ship; assassins were chasing him from worldlet to worldlet. He didn't have time to cultivate patience. And he didn't believe that his uncle would be able to provide much in the way of practical assistance. Tamonash lacked credit, influence and useful connections, and it was clear that he was scared of what had happened to his brother's family in the outer dark, was scared that it might reach out to him, here in Ophir.

No, if he was going to track down the hijackers, Hari would have to rely on Rav, and this mysterious tick-tock matriarch. And he had a few ideas of his own, too.

The next day, he and Rav returned to Down Town. The Ardenist was heading out around Ophir, to petition the tick-tock matriarch; amongst other things, Hari wanted to transfer credit from Tannhauser Gate's bourse, find an ascetic and pass on the book of Kinson Ib Kana, and scope out the house of the murdered philosopher Salx Minnot Flores.

It was at the edge of one of Ophir's lower tiers, the house, a squat stone tower rising from a garden of flowering bushes and trees. Its circular ports were shattered and sooty, and part of one wall had collapsed: the assassin, Angloy Li, had set fire to it after she had tortured and killed Salx Minnot Flores. The security system of a neighbouring property had captured images of the assassin as she strolled away from the blaze, and the police had quickly tracked her to the docks, but when they had tried to arrest her she had blown herself up with explosives cached in the long bones of her legs, killing two officers outright and injuring half a dozen others.

Hari and Rav studied the ruins from the corridor – the street. There were rope-and-plank walkways strung between the big trees at the far edge of the garden. Hari imagined Salx Minnot Flores strolling there at the evening's dimming. Looking out across the panorama of the world city's floor while he grappled with some esoteric philosophical problem.

Rav pointed out a small drone that hung under a scorched tree, watching them. 'Now the police know we are interested,' he said.

'They already know,' Hari said. 'And don't care.'

'I could easily confuse that silly little machine if you want to explore the place,' Rav said, 'but what's the point? Anything useful will have been destroyed or confiscated.'

'I needed to see it,' Hari said. 'I needed to see where she had been, and what she did.'

'It wasn't elegant, but it was effective.'

'There was a desperate violence to it. The fire, her suicide. A kind of anger.'

Rav looked down at him. 'I believe that you are trembling on the edge of an insight.'

'Do the Saints have a history of violence?'

'They were born in violence. Baptised in blood. Could they have sanctioned something like this?' Rav said. 'Easily. All too easily.'

They rose to the jostle and buzz of the commercial tiers. Down Town had once been one of the centres of baseline philosophical research. Now it was a dense patchwork of rival religions, crowded with churches and temples, cathedrals and mosques, basilicas and tabernacles. Every day was a holy day for some congregation or assembly. Always some procession of monks, or ecstatics, or skyclad sadhus. Always some itinerant preacher proclaiming that the apocalypse was imminent, or had just happened, or could be prevented by a bonfire of the vanities or by petitioning the seraphs. Prayer drones roamed everywhere. Shops sold holy medals, prayer beads, relics, and tweaks supposedly leaked from the information horizons of seraphs. Shrines to gods and seraphs stood in recesses in walls, or under trees; many were equipped with traps that plunged unwary passers-by into brief but intense chiliastic visions. The second time Hari was snagged by one of these traps, Rav teased him so unmercifully that he called up a map to the nearest head shop and borrowed credit from Rav and purchased a trait for his bios that would give him immunity.

'It is the best,' the head doctor assured him, when Hari tried to negotiate a better price for the trait. 'Released yesterday. I guarantee that you will be fully protected for at least six days before the shrines work out how to break it.'

'What do I do then?'

'Come back to me and I will sell you a patch. The best, at the best price.'

The head doctor pointed Hari towards an ascetic hermit, reputedly the holiest man in the city. He lived in a tree, one of the big coral trees that shaded the broad boulevard that circled the edge of the highest and largest of Ophir's terraces. He had not touched the ground for more than forty years. He chewed the tree's alkaloid-rich seeds and leaves and spoke with gods and monsters. People made donations of food and water which he drew up in the same bucket he used to dispose of his wastes.

Hari and Rav stepped through circles of offerings and prayers spread around the tree. Hundreds of dip candles flickered in the green shade. Aromatic smoke curled from incense sticks jammed into the rough bark of its branches and trunk.

'You could leave the book here,' Rav said.

'I have to explain how I came by it,' Hari said. 'I have to explain my debt.'

He joined a small queue of penitents and, paid a fee to a steward, who explained that he could have exactly ten minutes in the holy presence, inclusive of the time it took to climb up to him.

'Those of true faith fly up the tree,' the steward said. 'Those who are merely curious find the way harder. So balance and harmony are achieved.'

'Do you also count the time it takes to climb back down?' Rav said.

'Of course not. But do not overstay your allotted time,' the steward said. 'Many want to see the master, and I control drones that will persuade you to leave more quickly than you thought possible.'

Another steward tried to sell to Hari a medal that would absorb the blessing of the hermit's holy presence. Rav was delighted by this, and told Hari to buy as many as possible. 'Think of the armour they'll make.'

Although there were ladders and ropeways strung up the tree's broad trunk it was a hard scramble in Ophir's deepened gravity. Hari was slick with sweat and his heart was jackhammering in his chest when he at last reached the crux between two high branches where the hermit sat cross-legged. A small man dressed in a multicoloured patchwork coat, black hair hanging in ringlets around his thin, calm face. His eyes were closed and he was chewing leaves, plucking them one after the other from a broken branch he held in one hand, milling them between strong yellow teeth and spitting out the pulp. He did not open his eyes or in any way acknowledge Hari's presence while Hari explained how the dead hermit Kinson Ib Kana had saved his life, a debt he hoped to pay by passing Kinson Ib Kana's book to one of his fellow ascetics.

After Hari had finished speaking, he became aware of the small sounds around him. Wind moving through the drifts of leaves and bright red flowers. The buzz of an erratic traffic of live drones that his bios identified as bees, the mingled noise of the city beyond. The hermit spat a dribble of green pulp and plucked another leaf and pushed it into his mouth. At last, a bell rang far below, signalling that Hari's time was up, and he set the book in a hollow near the hermit's feet and climbed down to the deck, the ground.

'Did you learn anything?' Rav said.

'Only that I am a fool,' Hari said. 'But it's done.'

'We should have bought medals,' Rav said. 'I know I'll regret it later.'

'I'm glad you find our quaint baseliner customs so amusing.'

As he and Rav picked their way through the litter of offerings and candles, Hari heard a scream of fright or rage high above and looked up and saw something small and dark smashing through the fans of leaves. Rav stepped forward, moving quickly but without haste, and plucked the falling book from the air and handed it to him.

Black letters on its white face:

Streams rise in many places and flow by many paths, but all at last reach the sea.

'I suppose it's some kind of answer,' Rav said, 'even if it isn't the one you wanted.'

Hari had no better luck with a group of ascetics he and Rav met at the train station: an old woman enveloped in an ankle-length patchwork coat, and her acolytes, young men and women in plain white shirts, chanting verses of an epic to the rhythm of small drums and finger cymbals and three droning electric guitars. They listened to Hari's story and the old woman examined the book with tender reverence, declaring at last that the person who had owned it had been very close to the great bliss of the void that was the goal of every ascetic.

'Perhaps he found it when he died. But if he did, he cannot tell us, and we can never know,' she said, and gave the book back to Hari.

'I was hoping that you could pass it on to his family, or to someone who knew him,' Hari said.

'We come into this world with nothing, and leave with nothing. We honour our dead by singing their songs, not by curating their relics,' the old woman said. She was a small plump woman, with a mass of dreadlocked white hair that framed her round, wrinkled face, and a gentle, kindly manner. 'You believe that Kinson Ib Kana saved your life. You could not thank him, since he is dead, so you rescued his treasury of songs and stories and proverbs and carried them out into the world. You hope to find a place where they can live again. But they already live, through you. And will continue to live, for as long as you read them. Is that such a great obligation?'

So Hari was stuck with the book. Rav caught a train, travelling halfway around Ophir to the palace of the tick-tock matriarch, who was, according to Rav, very old and very paranoid, and would need to be flattered and cajoled before she would consider seeing Hari and opening the files in Dr Gagarian's head. Less than an hour later, after a brief visit to Down Town's bourse to establish his credit line, after purchasing a black brocade jacket to wear over the leggings and long white shirt that his uncle's maker had tailored for him, and a hasty meal of cold pickled noodles at one of the many food stalls along the Great Promenade, Hari was sitting beside a pool of water in a sunlit square, composing a message to the school of the Saints.

3

The square was floored with real grass, green springy turf starred with small white flowers, and bordered on all sides by buildings of different heights and different architectural styles. The school of the Saints stood at one corner, a three-storey building faced with pinkish stone, ports blinded with white shutters. Hari imagined that people were studying him from behind those shutters, imagined a hurried conference about his message, communications with some higher authority . . .

Or perhaps they had dismissed the message out of hand, nothing to do with them. However it fell out, he would learn something about the Saints, about Rav.

He sat on the low wall that rimmed the pool. In its centre, a sculptural assembly of large, translucent blue cubes slowly shifted from one configuration to another. Water sluiced over the faces of the cubes and cascaded into the pool. Small white birds strutted and pecked and fluttered across the turf.

It was a lovely, peaceful place, warm in the sunlight that slanted between the flat roofs of the buildings and the overhead of the next tier. Hari felt a little anxious, wondering how the Saints would react to his message, but he was happy, too: happy to be out and about on his own, on an adventure, after the confines of Rav's ship.

After a while, he opened a window and the p-suit's eidolon leaned in and said that she had nothing to report.

'What about Rav's son?'

'He is asleep. He spends more time than I thought possible asleep.'

'And the honey trap?'

Hari had set up an advertisement on Down Town's commons, offering a reward for information leading to the arrest of any persons connected to the murder of Salx Minnot Flores. It contained a fake link that appeared to lead to his bios; he hoped that the hijackers would try to follow it, and leave clues that would enable him to track them down.

'No activity that I can detect,' the eidolon said. 'You appear to be waiting for someone.'

'I want to talk with the Saints. But it does not look like they want to talk with me.'

'I should be in Ophir,' the eidolon said. 'I cannot properly protect you from the ship.'

'I won't be here for much longer,' Hari said.

A man came out of one of the buildings and disappeared into another. A flock of small children chased each other out of one of the streets or corridors that intersected the square, and ran past the pool where Hari sat. Two paused to study him, but when he asked them if they knew the Saints they shook their heads and ran, laughing, after their friends. One of the white birds – they were doves – fluttered up to perch on an angled edge of the sculpture, fluttered away as the edge retracted into the restless blue mass. The sculpture rounded into a rough sphere and the sphere flattened into a fat pancake and the pancake grew into a tall spire. At last, a woman and two men stepped out of the deep-set doorway of the pink stone building and walked across the square towards Hari.

He stood up as they approached, his whole skin tingling with anticipation.

'Gajananvihari Pilot, I presume,' the woman said.

She wasn't much older than Hari, broad-hipped, dressed in a plain white jerkin and loose white trousers. Her name was Esme, according to her tag. An adept of the sixth elevation. Her companions, bare-chested and barefoot in white trousers, stood behind her, studying Hari with professional interest.

Hari tried to ignore them, thanked the woman for coming to talk to him.

'We can talk more comfortably in our house.'

'I am happy to talk here. Perhaps your friends could give us a little privacy. I assure you that I mean no harm.'

'Are you intimidated by them? Good. You're meant to be,' the woman, Esme, said. She had the mild, calm manner of someone who did not expect to be surprised by anything she encountered.

They sat on the rim of the pool. The two men stood a few metres away, arms folded over the muscular shields of their chests.

'Well,' Esme said, 'what do you want to sell to us?'

'If you know who I am, you know why I am here.'

'All I know is that you claim to have something we have been looking for. As we haven't lost anything, it must be something you want to sell.'

'I have the head of Dr Gagarian,' Hari said.

There was no change in the woman's expression, no flicker of recognition in her gaze.

'Perhaps I am talking to the wrong person,' Hari said.

'I'm the only one who will speak to you. Why should we want to buy this head?'

'I don't want to sell it. I want to exchange it. I haven't brought it with me,' Hari said. 'It's in a safe place. If you want to see it, I can take you there.'

He had deposited the cryoflask containing Dr Gagarian's head in the bonded store in the elevator terminus. Rav had said that it would be safer on his ship, had laughed when Hari said that he had decided to take his advice about trust.

'I think I understand,' Esme said. 'Was it a relative, or a friend?'

'My family, if they still live. And my family's ship.'

'People who join us do so of their own free will,' Esme said. 'It is their decision, made without any coercion or intimidation. Your family will have taken a vow of silence during the period of induction, but when that is over you can speak to them. I hope you will. But I should warn you that you will not be able to convince them that they are mistaken. Why? It is simple. They are not mistaken. They have chosen the right path.'

'My family did not become Saints,' Hari said. 'They were taken. Kidnapped. That is, if they were not killed. And our ship was taken, too. It was hijacked. That's why I'm here. To ransom any of my family who are still alive, and to take back our ship.'

Esme thought about that, then said, softly and sympathetically, 'I think you have made a mistake.'

Hari couldn't tell if she was genuinely puzzled or if she was bluffing, but he was determined to see this through. To set out his bait and see if the Saints came snuffling after it. If they did, he would be one step closer to his revenge; if not, then he would know that Rav was either deluded or could not be trusted, and he would have to go on alone, or throw in with his uncle. And he'd be sorry, because he'd grown fond of the big, boisterous, boastful Ardenist. But as Nabhomani had said many times, when it comes to business you have to harden your heart and do what needs to be done to close the deal.

'I don't know what an adept of the sixth elevation is,' Hari said to the Saint, Esme. 'What rank it is, in your crew. But if you're telling the truth, if you don't know why your superiors are interested in Dr Gagarian and his research, perhaps you could pass a message to them. Perhaps you could tell them that I want to talk to them. That I am ready to negotiate.'

'Are you a religious person, Gajananvihari Pilot?'

'Do I believe what you believe? No.'

'But do you belong to a particular faith or sect?'

'I was taught that the existence of the Universe does not require a first cause. And that its creation and everything in it can be explained by observation and deduction.'

Hari had a sudden sharp, piercing vision of his father walking in the desert viron, studying windows that he pulled out of the air.

'We celebrate the Bright Moment because it is a sign that something wonderful happened,' Esme said. 'Sri Hong-Owen Became something else, and the Bright Moment is an echo of her Becoming. An echo of a moment of transcendence. Of joy. And because it touched everyone, everyone contains the seed of that transcendence. And one day, when things change, when the crooked path is made straight, those seeds will grow into something wonderful. Philosophers cannot understand those seeds any more than they can understand how the Bright Moment touched everyone. They cannot understand how Sri Hong-Owen changed, or what she Became. They cannot understand how we will change, because it has nothing to do with the so-called fundamental truths about the universe "discovered" by philosophical investigation. Because this universe, this reality is nothing. It is an illusion. A veil over deeper and more meaningful realities. So why would we have any interest in anything your Dr Gagarian or his friends claim to have found out?'

'Does that mean you won't pass on my message?'

'I hope your search brings you peace,' Esme said, and stood up and walked off around the pool, followed by the two men.

Hari watched them cross the square and enter the pink house, then dipped up a handful of water and splashed it on his face.

After Hari had told him about the unsatisfactory confrontation with the Saints, Tamonash said, 'I suppose it was your friend's idea.'

'It was entirely mine,' Hari said. 'Rav didn't want to begin negotiations with the Saints until we had opened Dr Gagarian's files.'

'But you are not yet certain that the Saints are the guilty party.'

'That's why I made my offer. To see how they reacted.'

Hari and his uncle were talking over supper, at one end of the long room where Tamonash slept, ate, and did most of his business. One wall displayed a view of one of Earth's oceans, ragged scraps of ice drifting on blue water stretching under a pale blue sky towards a distant horizon where ice cliffs blinked in cold sunlight, a live feed off the coast of Europe, near the Pilot family's last home on Earth. A coast locked under the ice that, despite the best efforts of climate engineers to reverse the Long Twilight, still covered more than half of Earth's land surface.

Hari's father had sometimes shown him archive images from their family's long, long history. He remembered one in particular: a young man and a young woman in strange clothes standing rigid with pride beside some kind of primitive ground vehicle in a street of two-storey brick houses joined each to each and stepping down a steep corridor towards a simmering basin of brick and smoke. The man had been the first of the Pilot family to leave the mother country; the woman was his bride; the image had been captured so long ago that their family had yet to take up the name Pilot. More than two thousand years. All that history ground away by time, by ice that had marched north and south during the century of twilight imposed by seraphs at the end of the fall of the Empire of the True.

The ocean panorama tinted the air with shifting blue shadows; blue highlights glinted on the carapaces of the automata lined along the opposite wall. They were arranged by height, from squat domestic servants to a lithe, long-limbed racing strider with a basket saddle behind its tiny head. One of them especially interested Hari. A re-purposed battle bot, identical to those used on *Pabuji's Gift* for general maintenance on the hull and in the drive chambers. Otherwise, the room was mostly empty, apart from a bed shrouded by a muslin tent, and the chairs on which Hari and Tamonash sat, facing each other across a low table of beaten brass set on a pedestal of raw nickel-iron.

A myrmidon stood behind Tamonash's chair, slim and tall and alert, several pairs of red eyes burning under the leading edge of the sleek armour that hooded its head. Tamonash had hired it after Hari had contacted him and told him why he was heading towards Ophir.

'You are as headstrong as your father,' Tamonash said.

'I feel this is not a compliment,' Hari said.

Tamonash still had not explained the circumstances of the rift between himself and Hari's father, but it was clear that it was deep and bitter.

'You should not have talked to those fanatics,' Tamonash said. 'What if they decide to steal this head? To take it by force instead of bargaining with you.'

'I told them it was stored in a safe place, Uncle. So you have nothing to worry about.'

'Why would they believe you? And if they don't believe you, where would they look first?'

It was a good point. Hari apologised, said that he would contact the Saints at once, and offer to take them to the bonded store and show them the head.

'The damage is already done,' Tamonash said. 'You may do more, trying to undo it.'

Hari apologised again. They ate in silence for a while.

At last, Tamonash said, 'Perhaps you would like to tell me about your visit to the house of the dead philosopher.'

'Have you been spying on me, Uncle?'

'My contact in the Ministry of Justice tells me that the police started a file on you after you pestered them with impertinent questions about Flores' death. Your visit was noted.'

'I did nothing wrong.'

'The police may not agree.'

'I assume that you don't, either.'

'The hijackers want the files cached inside the tick-tock's head. Open them. Study them. Learn all you can about what you need to sell to get your family and your ship back.'

'The hijackers were interested in Salx Minnot Flores' work, too,' Hari said. 'That's why they had him killed. That's why I need to know what the police know about the woman who killed him. And why I need to find out all I can about his research.'

Tamonash leaned back in his chair and studied Hari over steepled fingertips. 'Yes, you are just like your father.'

'I'm doing this for him, and for my brothers, and Agrata. For my family, Uncle. My family, and yours.'

'You won't give up this foolish idea.'

'You know that I can't.'

'Then perhaps you should meet an acquaintance of mine. A business acquaintance. Mr D.V. Mussa, a free trader. I purchase vacuum organism strains from him, but he deals in many other things. I happened to talk to him today, and mentioned your predicament. And it turns out that Mr Mussa supplied Salx Minnot Flores with certain pieces of apparatus, and may know something about his research.'

Hari wanted to trust his uncle. He'd been raised to believe that no bond was stronger than blood on blood. That genes sing to genes, as his father liked to say. But although Tamonash lived like an eccentric recluse in the ruins of his family's compound and his family's history, he was a shrewd and manipulative businessman, and Hari suspected that he'd have to pay this free trader for information about Salx Minnot Flores, and Tamonash would take a cut. But he didn't care. He needed to know. He needed to know everything.

'I think I should meet this friend of yours as soon as possible,' he said.

Tamonash smiled. 'Can you contain your impatience until tomorrow?'

4

'Salx Minnot Flores was a regular customer of mine,' Mr D.V. Mussa told Hari, 'but I didn't pay much attention to his work. Frankly, I didn't think much of it. He was a little like one of those end-time cultists who examines images of the Bright Moment for hidden messages. More than a little.'

The philosopher had been trying to replicate the Bright Moment, according to Mr Mussa. The image it triggered.

'My avatar was not affected by his apparatus, of course, but he once showed me a clip he claimed to have transmitted into the visual centre of his own brain. A kind of jerky stick figure that was, apparently, the cue or seed that stimulated a more complex image. Baseline human memory is a construct, patched together from real memories, approximations, and stock images. Only part of it is true, and none of it is real. As with memory, so with his version of the Bright Moment. Or so Flores said.'

Mr D.V. Mussa was a tanky, an adherent of an old form of amortality that involved extracting the brain and essential parts of the organ-tree and maintaining them in amniotic fluid laced with mites and engineered bacteria. His avatar was a fist-sized glob of white light like a cut diamond with a dark cross in its centre: a nucleus or hive of microbots that could each act independently, or merge with as many of its neighbours as necessary to perform tasks involving gross manipulation of objects and materials. It slowly revolved as it hung in the air, casting swarms of fleeting stars across the floor and walls and overhead of the long room (it was night, on Earth, dark waves rolling across a dark sea, cloud-shadows scudding across a star-spattered sky).

Hari asked if the philosopher had ever talked about Dr Gagarian's work.

'I supplied him with components for his apparatus, and he told me about the progress of his work. That's as far as it went,' Mr Mussa said. 'I didn't know that he was collaborating with your Dr Gagarian until Tamonash told me about the hijack of your family's ship.'

They talked about the assistance that Hari's family had given to the tick-tock philosopher. Hari was careful not to reveal too much, parried the free trader's questions as best he could, and turned the conversation back to Salx Minnot Flores and his work.

Mr Mussa gave a portrait of a harmless obsessive who lived on the residue of a long-lost family business, was estranged from his partner and children, and had given himself entirely to his work.

'I'd see him in town,' Mr Mussa said. His avatar had a soft, mellifluous baritone voice. It sounded amused, indulgent. Like a parent recalling the harmless transgressions of a small child. 'Talking to street preachers and end-timers. Sometimes in quiet discussion, sometimes in fierce argument. Hard to tell, I would think to myself, which was the philosopher and which the fanatical cultist.'

Hari said, 'Did he ever talk with any of the Saints?'

'Not that I know of. You are thinking of the woman who killed him, of course. Who you think might have been a Saint. What did *they* have to say to you about that, by the way?'

Hari gave Tamonash a sharp look; Tamonash looked away.

'Your uncle mentioned your encounter,' Mr Mussa said, 'but I had already heard about it. I have, let us say, my sources.'

'In the Saints?'

'In the government. Someone like me, in the import/export business, benefits from friends who can influence decisions about the movement of goods, obtain answers to urgent questions, and so on. Friends who can do all kinds of favours, for the right price.'

There it was. The hook. Hari saw it plain and clear, but took it anyway.

'Perhaps your friends could help me find out a little more about Salx Minnot Flores' research.'

'Of course,' Mr Mussa said. 'Although you will have to cover certain expenses. Bribes, that kind of thing.'

Tamonash cleared his throat. 'There's a saying that Ophir has the best government and police that credit can buy. And it's absolutely true.'

❋

Hari shot Mr D.V. Mussa half the credit he'd transferred from the ship's account in Tannhauser Gate. The next day, Tamonash and the free trader took him to meet Chum Vahsny, the Under-Minister for External Traffic. She shook Hari's hand and introduced him to one of her secretaries, who listened to Hari's story with absent-minded politeness, took many notes, and told him that the under-minister would attempt to ask the police about progress regarding the investigation into the most regrettable death of the philosopher, and try to trace any relevant files.

Hari, who had been taught enough about negotiations to recognise the secretary's evasive tactics – answering questions not asked, countering direct questions with other questions, managing expectations with ambiguous promises – was convinced that the under-minister would do nothing of the kind. Two days passed. These things take time, Tamonash said. There were complex webs of checks and balances to be negotiated, protocols to be followed.

'On another matter, Mr D.V. Mussa tells me that he knows several tick-tock philosophers. Any one of them could open the files in Dr Gagarian's head.'

'Do they live here, in Ophir?'

'One lives in Gan 'Éden, which is presently just two days' travel away.'

'If Gun Ako Akoi is unsuccessful,' Hari said, 'I'll certainly consider it.'

'Why put your trust in strangers, Gajananvihari? We should keep this in the family.'

'With respect, Uncle, everyone is a stranger to me.'

Tamonash put on a credible display of wounded indignation. 'Your father and I had our differences, nephew. But that's ancient history. I hope things can be different between us.'

'I hope so too.'

Hari felt sorry for him, really: his petty scheming, his circumscribed life in the wreckage of his dreams.

'Mr Mussa also told me that he is making good progress,' Tamonash said. 'He hopes to talk with a senior police officer tomorrow. So if you could supply just a little more credit . . .'

Hari supplied it, although he was certain that it wouldn't buy him anything more than another pointless meeting with some official equipped with a sheaf of excuses and evasions.

He sat in his little room in the little tower, reading in Kinson Ib

Kana's book, his book now, watching the road from Down Town's elevator stack, waiting for Rav to return from his visit with the tick-tock matriarch Gun Ako Akoi. At night, he imagined an assassin sneaking across the ruined perimeter wall of the compound, a flickering shadow in a camo cloak, a knife gleaming in her teeth.

He trawled the cluttered wreckage of the compound's workshop, but found no weapons, and nothing that could be repurposed as a weapon.

He had Tamonash's maker print off a batch of shuriken, and practised throwing them at a target pinned to a tree at one end of the overgrown lawn. It wasn't easy: they flew in arcs instead of straight lines.

The Saint, Esme, didn't call, and he couldn't call her because it would show weakness.

He spoke to the p-suit's eidolon. She had nothing to report.

And then, late in the afternoon of the second day, Rav returned and told Hari that Gun Ako Akoi had agreed to meet him.

'Did she say that she can open the files?'

'She made Dr Gagarian what he is,' Rav said. 'If she can't unlock him, no one can. But there is something we must do for her, first. A small favour. A little task. Something you'll appreciate, what with being in the salvage trade. She covets a trinket she gave away long ago, and wants back. A fragment taken from a QI just before it vastened into a seraph. I've spent the past two days tracking it down. All we have to do now is get hold of it.'

'You want me to what? Negotiate a price with the owner?'

'Not exactly. The present owners of this trinket, the Masters of the Measureless Mind, are a gypsy sect who for some reason believe it to be a holy relic. They aren't about to sell it, so we'll have steal it instead,' Rav said. 'It should be simple enough. A little distraction, a little legerdemain, and hey presto! The trinket will fall into our hands.'

'Just like that,' Hari said.

'Why not? You baseliners see what you want to see. Everything follows from that.'

Hari told the Ardenist about Mr D.V. Mussa, and his visit with the under-minister. Trying to turn it into a joke about himself. Saying, 'I knew there was a good chance that I would be swindled, but fortunately I didn't have much to lose.'

'If you mean the credit you were able to transfer to Ophir's bourse, you're right. You won't need or miss it because as soon as Gun Ako Akoi cracks open the tick-tock's head we can be on our way. But what about the credit still on deposit in Tannhauser Gate?'

'There isn't much left. My father used most of it to fund Dr Gagarian's research.'

Rav fixed Hari with his lambent gaze and recited a string of numbers of increasing size, pausing after the last and then choosing one somewhere in the mid-range of the string, repeating it three times as if relishing the sound it made.

'It's nothing like that,' Hari said, trying to hide his dismay. Rav's guess had been scarily close.

'It isn't a fortune, but it's a useful little sum,' Rav said. 'It has heft. It has leverage. Don't worry. Unlike your uncle, I'm not interested in it. If I was, I would have taken it long ago. In addition to mind-reading, I'm adept at legerdemain, hypnotism, and illusions grand and small. Luckily for you, I'm on your side. Luckily for you, we have interests in common.'

Hari felt a prickling unease, wondering if Rav knew about his contact with the Saints.

He said, 'I don't mind losing a little credit. It repays my uncle's hospitality.'

'Such as it is.'

'But I am disappointed that I haven't been able to access Salx Minnot Flores' files.'

'He was a good friend of your father and Dr Gagarian, wasn't he? I'm sure he shared his secrets with them. So anything in his files will also be inside the tick-tock's head.'

'They talked freely with all their collaborators,' Hari said. 'But I can't be sure that their collaborators talked freely with them. And it isn't only his files. Mr Mussa told me that he had built something that duplicated the experience of the Bright Moment. It would be interesting, I think, to examine that.'

Hari watched Rav think about it.

'I suppose we might learn something,' the Ardenist said. 'Also, it would annoy your uncle. Let me see what I can do.'

He came back a few hours later, striding into the long room where Hari and Tamonash were sharing a frugal supper of dahl, chapatis and pickled vegetables, sitting down uninvited at the table.

'It's arranged,' he told Hari. 'The inspector in charge of the investigation will show you the dead philosopher's possessions first thing tomorrow morning.'

'Just like that?'

Rav shrugged. 'I'm a barbarian. I'm not interested in etiquette and formality. And neither, as it turns out, is our police inspector.'

'You do not have to live with the consequences of your actions,' Tamonash said. 'You barge in, cause trouble, and leave others to repair the damage.'

'And how was your way of doing things working out? There aren't any files,' Rav told Hari. 'No physical records were found in the house, and its mind had been destroyed. Salx Minnot Flores rented storage space in the commons, but that was wiped clean by a djinn. And there isn't much left of his experimental equipment, after the fire. But maybe you'll spot something useful.'

'And how much will this cost my nephew?' Tamonash said.

'A trifling bribe,' Rav said. 'Nothing like the credit you and your tanky friend have been bleeding from him.'

Tamonash drew himself up and said that he deeply resented the implication that he was profiting from helping his nephew.

'Oh, I've noticed that you have little liking for the truth,' Rav said.

He was vivid and vital, as if lit by the radiance of another, better world. Sitting on the floor with one leg crooked beneath the other, hands clasping his knee. Wings falling on either side of his bare, scarred torso, his silver-capped teeth gleaming in his easy smile, his green eyes flashing as the myrmidon behind Tamonash stirred.

'That's rented, isn't it?' Rav said.

'It is bonded to me, and completely under my control,' Tamonash said.

'Tell it to stand down, or you'll have to find the credit to repair it,' Rav said, and stood with a swift, fluid motion. 'Meet me at the elevators at first light, youngblood. And say goodbye to your uncle. We'll set out on our little adventure as soon as we've checked out the wreckage.'

That was before the message came. The message that came in the night, like an assassin.

5

After Hari's bios had checked the message for djinns and tried and failed to track its origin, after he had watched it with mounting dismay, after he had rewatched it with furious concentration, he rose from his bed and walked around and around his little room, trying to make sense of what he'd seen. He punched the wall, and the pain surprised him. The shock and the sting of it. He punched the wall again, and again, and felt calmer. He stood at the unglazed port. Cool air blowing across his face; cool flowstone pressing against his thighs. It was an hour before dawn. Everything in shades of grey. The sunstrip was a pearlescent ribbon running across the overhead from horizon to horizon. Down Town's tiers were defined by lights scattered amongst the buildings along their edges. A few lights were shuttling up and down the elevator stalk that connected it to the floor.

Hari saw all this without really seeing it. The hijackers had found him. They had reached out to him and shown him a nightmare. A crude threat meant to shock and intimidate him. And he was shocked. Shocked, appalled, angry. But he had to get past his shock and anger. He had to work out what he should do.

He stared out of the port. He paced around the room. At last he called Rav, who answered at once.

Hari said, 'The hijackers sent a message.'

'Are you sure it's from them?'

'Absolutely.'

'What did it say?'

'I have a confession to make. I talked to the Saints.'

'I know.'

'You know?'

141

'Always assume that I know everything, youngblood. You finally realised that the Saints were behind the hijack, and decided to approach them directly. You could have tried to send a message to their leaders, but you weren't sure how to go about it, and besides, your family are traders. You prefer to negotiate face to face. The Saints have a school in Down Town, and that's where you went while I was talking with Gun Ako Akoi. You thought that I was making a deal that would be to my advantage, so you decided to make a deal that would be to *your* advantage, by offering to exchange the tick-tock's head for your family and your ship. The Saints you talked to denied that they had anything to do with the hijack. And they were probably telling the truth. They're locals, recruiting for a cause they don't fully understand. But they contacted their superiors, the message went up the command chain, just as you hoped it would, and now you've received a reply. Am I right, or am I right?'

'You had someone follow me, didn't you? Or wait – you talked to the Saints too.'

'If I ever talk to any of the Saints, it wouldn't be a cosy little chat about mutual acquaintances. And I didn't have you followed. I worked it out from basic principles.'

'It must be nice, always being right,' Hari said.

'Actually, it's usually disappointing,' Rav said. 'Time and again, I hope people aren't going to do the obvious thing. Time and again, they let me down.'

'Although I'm still not entirely certain that it *was* the Saints,' Hari said. 'Despite the timing.'

'Who else would it be? You pushed them. They pushed back. I suppose they made some kind of threat or ultimatum. Because if they'd agreed to your terms, you would have taken that head straight to the school in Down Town.'

'Do you want to see the message, or do you want to assume that you already know what it is?'

'Show me. Isn't that why you called?'

Hari sent the short clip to Rav.

They watched it together.

It began without introduction or overture. Here was Nabhoj, naked, looking past the viewpoint with an uncertain expression, as if waiting for instruction. A stocky man with a small pot belly and curls of black hair on his chest. Standing in front of a wall of rough dark rock, shivering slightly as he spoke.

This time around, Hari felt a slow burn of sympathetic humiliation. Nabhoj was a quiet, serious man. Long on thought, short on words, as Nabhomani liked to say. Brooding in the tower of the command and control module like some ruined prince. Formidable. Minatory. And shy, this was something Hari had realised only recently, from the new perspective of his exile. Nabhoj had avoided ordinary human discourse as much as possible because he was shy. But now he was stripped of his dignity, a naked shivering forked creature with his black hair loose in lank strings about his shoulders. Halting, stumbling, as he recited what was clearly a prepared script. Licking his lips, once losing the thread of a sentence and starting over. Asking Hari to do the right thing. Telling him that he must forget about heroics and tricks. Telling him that he was responsible for the lives of everyone he held dear. That there was only one right thing to do; only one way that things would come out right.

'You should not have run to Ophir. There is no help for you there. The Ardenist cannot help you. Tamonash Pilot cannot help you. There is no safety in his house. Give up the head of Dr Gagarian. Deposit it in a safe place. You will be contacted again, and you will tell them where they can find the head. If you do that, they will let us go. You have my word on that, Gajananvihari. You know that I do not lie. You know how precious the truth is to me. And you know what they can do. Give up the head. Do it straight away. Do it—'

The abrupt ending of the clip was a blow to the heart.

Rav said, 'It raises several questions. The first and most important is this: was that really your brother?'

Hari said, 'I wondered about that too. The two women who tracked me down, on Themba, tried to trick me with an eidolon of Agrata. It's possible that this could be more of the same.'

'But you don't think so.'

'Agrata told me that she thought that Nabhoj had been killed by the hijackers. But she wasn't certain. She couldn't contact him, or Nabhomani. Their bioses were down. But she hadn't seen them. She hadn't seen their bodies . . .'

'It was clever, implying that others of your family are still alive. And the ending, that was also a nice touch. Melodramatic, but effective.'

'I have to assume that it was him. That he's alive. But don't worry, I am not going to do anything rash.'

'Except you already did. No need to apologise, by the way,' Rav said. 'I already factored it into my plans. And I have to admit that I'm disappointed that they responded with this cheap little threat. I was hoping that they would try to snatch you, force you to retrieve the head from the bonded store. Then we could have had some real fun.'

'They are trying to panic me. Trying to make me do something foolish. To give them what they want without talking to them, without negotiating. Well, I won't,' Hari said.

His anger was back. The unreasoning anger that had possessed him during his first days of exile on Themba. Prowling the basement of his mind. Hot and black and raw with grief and fear.

Rav said, 'Have you told your uncle about this?'

'Not yet.'

'His attempts to help you haven't amounted to much so far,' Rav said. 'Send him a message, or don't, but come and meet me right away. We'll take a quick look at the dead philosopher's stuff, and then we'll knock the dust of this rotten little town from our wings.'

6

The government store was a dimly lit grey cube cluttered with machines and furniture and racks and crates of sooty, scorched kibble. The stink of char sharp in the dry chill air. Everything tagged with dense blocks of police code.

The unsmiling police inspector explained that Salx Minnot Flores' possessions were being stored there because a complex dispute about the terms of his will had not yet been resolved, told Hari and Rav that they were welcome to look around but must not touch anything.

Rav leaned against the wall, picking at his teeth with a bamboo splinter, while Hari walked up and down. The breakfast he'd eaten at a hawker's cart sat heavily in his stomach. He found it hard to concentrate. He kept seeing moments from the hijackers' message. His brother, naked, pleading, humiliated.

There was a maker, racks of machine parts, assemblies of what might have been guns or telescopes, elaborate arrangements of mirrors. Some of it vaguely resembled the apparatus Hari had built for Dr Gagarian, but on a much smaller scale. All of it was broken and blistered and smoke-blackened. He couldn't begin to imagine what it had been designed to probe or measure.

There were crates of burned debris. Carbonised shards and slabs. Ashy fragments. There was a table of heat-warped, piebald artefacts that mites had been reconstructing, millimetre by millimetre, molecule by molecule, when the murder investigation had been abandoned.

'That doohickey inside the Faraday cage is faintly interesting,' Rav said. 'Looks very much like some kind of neural inducer.'

He pushed away from the wall and stalked past a stack of storage crates and pulled open the door of a wire-mesh booth.

The inspector reminded him that he was forbidden to touch anything. Rav ignored her, peering at the chair and the spidery apparatus hung over it, looking over his shoulder at Hari, saying that this looked very much like the kind of thing that would let you play with your own brain.

'I told you to leave the stuff alone,' the inspector said.

'And I decided to ignore you,' Rav said. 'We bribed you for access, so you have no way to back up your authority.'

'Think again,' the inspector said, and reached inside a slit in her scarlet uniform jacket.

'Don't be silly,' Rav said.

He held up her slug pistol, dangling from the little finger of his left hand by its trigger-guard, then leaned into the booth and made an adjustment to the spidery apparatus. There was a low, deep hum as something powered up.

The inspector said that he was in serious trouble.

Rav showed his teeth. 'Oh, and who are you going to tell?'

Hari said, 'Let me try it. Let me see what it does.'

'I think we should all try it,' Rav said, and hooked his claws in the mesh roof of the booth and peeled it back, then reached inside again.

The inspector started towards the Ardenist and there was a soundless flash of white light inside Hari's head. It consumed everything. Thought, sight, everything. And then he was back in the dim, cluttered cube.

The inspector had fallen to her knees. She pushed to her feet and glared up at Rav and told him to have intercourse with his grandmother.

'I never had a grandmother,' Rav said.

Hari said, 'I didn't see a stick figure.'

'Neither did I,' Rav said. 'Just the carrier wave.'

'The white light.'

'The white light.'

'Right in the middle of my head.'

'Right in the middle of everything.'

'You're meddling in things you do not understand,' the inspector said.

'Oh, I know exactly what I'm doing,' Rav said. 'And so did Salx Minnot Flores, as it turns out.'

○

'It wasn't much like the Bright Moment,' Hari said, as he and Rav walked towards the elevators to the docks.

'What would you know about the Bright Moment, youngblood?' Rav said.

'I've experienced simulations.'

'I very much doubt that they were much like the Bright Moment, either. But it was impressive, in a way. And it was only a prototype. I wonder what the final version could do. A machine built by a baseliner, capable of approximating a vision cast off by a posthuman intelligence at the moment of its vastening. Yes, I am impressed. How about you?'

'I was impressed too. And frightened.'

'Worth the price of admission, I think,' Rav said. 'And now we'll get Gun Ako Akoi to open up your tick-tock philosopher's head. We'll find out about the work of Dr Gagarian and the rest of that busy little crew, and then we'll offer it to the Saints.'

'Assuming the Saints sent that message,' Hari said.

He was almost certain that they had. He wanted to believe that they had. It would make everything so much simpler. But a small margin of doubt remained, because the hijackers had been so very careful to hide their identity.

'Of course it was the Saints,' Rav said. 'If you can't trust me, youngblood, at least try to believe that I know what I'm doing.'

It wasn't just Rav's size – his height and heft, the breadth of his wings – that made him so formidable. It wasn't just his talons and his teeth. It was his unassailable assurance. His bombproof self-confidence.

Hari said, 'I'll do my best.'

7

In the bonded store of Down Town's elevator terminal, in the close confines of a privacy module, a storekeeper with golden fur and a severe manner confirmed Hari's identity and accepted a fee that bit a sizeable chunk out of what remained of his credit. Less than two minutes later, a bot delivered the cryoflask that contained Dr Gagarian's head.

Outside, Rav watched as Hari examined the flask's seal. 'Few things are what they once were, in these debased times,' the Ardenist said, 'but you can still count on the integrity and discretion of the bonded stores. There's a story that one of the last of the True suzerains put his family in storage to save them from assassination. He was killed the next day, but the storekeepers fought and defeated the mercenaries who came after his family. Their descendants are still living in storage, waiting for someone to pay a redemption fee that's by now so astronomical that the entire Solar System wouldn't suffice as collateral.'

'You have a story for every occasion,' Hari said.

'You don't like my stories? They're better than any you'll find in that book of yours.'

'When it comes to business, I prefer plain facts to fantasies.'

It was something his father sometimes said whenever Nabhomani's reports of his negotiations and deals became especially florid.

'To put it plainly,' Rav said, 'not even I could figure out a way to look inside that head while it was in store.'

Hari paid a public maker to spin a kitbag, so that it wouldn't be immediately obvious that he was carrying the cryoflask, and he and Rav caught a car travelling west, or antispinward, along Ophir's equatorial railway. According to Rav, they were heading towards a religious festival where the sect which owned the trinket coveted by Gun Ako Akoi was presently camped.

The car ran at a leisurely fifty kilometres per hour along a track that clung to the overhead. Hari and Rav had it to themselves. They sat in the nose like kings of the world, sweeping through sector after sector, each separated from the next by a transparent bulkhead. A sea of white sand dunes. An intricate puzzle of lakes and forest. Thick, unbroken jungle. Old towns and palaces hung from the overhead; newer settlements were scattered across the floor. Banyan patches, strings of half-buried blockhouses, clumps of flimsy shacks circled by defensive walls, villages straggling around pele towers of various heights and degrees of ruin: remnants of the war games Trues had liked to play, great slaughters organised for the entertainment of jaded suzerains and optimates. One tower, at the centre of a craggy canyonland, was as big as a town, the concentric rings of defences around its base broken and pitted by the wounds of an ancient bombardment and overgrown by trees and a shawl of creepers from which a swirl of black birds rose as the car passed by high above, hurtling onwards around Ophir's great curve, above towers and villages and towns and fields and wilderness, above woods and fields, above stretches of deadland stripped to the fullerene strands of the world city's rind.

All of this was contained in a habitable deck or shell fifty kilometres in diameter, wrapped around the nickel-iron keel on which Ophir had been founded. A surface area of eight thousand square kilometres. The overhead was more than a kilometre high, and there was weather beneath it. Shoals of wispy clouds; a dark rainstorm. Vast perspectives were interrupted by enormous bulkheads of diamond-fullerene composite pierced here and there by ship-sized airlocks through which rail cars and ground traffic passed.

Once, the rock at the centre of Ophir's shell had been occupied by a single small, tented town and a scatter of vacuum-organism farms. And then the True Empire had absorbed it, and embarked on an insanely grand engineering project. Thousands of huge machines had processed primordial organic material mined from a score of comets, levelled the cratered terrain and covered it with densely woven layers of fullerene, and floated a shell a kilometre above this foundation, supported by bulkheads that divided the interior into a hundred segments, each landscaped with a different garden biome. A world city. A monument to the Trues' hubris.

It was the one of largest structures ever built in the Solar System, yet despite its adamantine foundations and bulkheads, and the deep layers of foamed fullerenes that formed the outer skin of its shell, it was hopelessly vulnerable. Its defence system of ablative lasers and swarms of bomblets and drones was sufficient to sweep and deflect debris from its orbital path, but offered no protection from a concerted attack.

The Trues had built Ophir as an act of ego and of defiance. To prove that they could; to prove that none of their enemies could challenge them. And their enemies had called it the City of the Caves of Steel because, like that ancient construction material, it was both massive and brittle. Collision with a single rock just a few tens of metres across would utterly destroy it. When the True Empire had at last fallen, the world city had been spared only because a small majority of post-humans could not countenance the murder of several hundred thousand citizens. Five hundred years later, the descendants of those citizens were still forbidden to travel beyond the shell of the city's overhead, and their numbers had been swollen by baseliners fleeing predatory dacoits and the capricious rule of posthuman clades. The magnificent folly of the True Empire had become a refuge and a prison.

Shortly after they'd passed through the fifth of the huge bulkheads, Rav pointed to threads of smoke bending up in the distance and said, 'The signature of the species.'

He opened a window linked to a feed from a police drone that was keeping watch on the source of the smoke: a small grid of crude huts roofed with bundles of reeds, standing on a square of elevated ground amongst a patchwork of flooded fields. Several of the huts were on fire, and little sparks snapped in the fields, defining opposing lines of battle. Men and women lay prone at the edge of a stand of tall reeds, or crouched behind one of the low embankments that defined the boundaries of fields, or ran in jerky zigzags across open ground.

Hari said, 'These are dacoits, attacking the village?'

'There are no dacoits in Ophir,' Rav said. 'This is a war between neighbouring tribes, killing each other over differences in ideology.'

The drone's viewpoint shifted, tracking a running man whose head suddenly burst in a puff of crimson, his body tumbling forward, collapsing in an awkward sprawl.

Rav said, 'True suzerains brought tribes of autochthons from Earth to Ophir, and used them to fight proxy wars. The Trues are long gone, but their proxies fight on. A century ago, one of your kind, a self-styled prophet who believed himself to be enlightened beyond all ordinary human measure, visited one of the autochthons' villages and tried to persuade its inhabitants to give up warfare. They killed him and his followers, and stuck their heads on poles. Much like the skull feeders, now I think of it.'

'Another of your stories,' Hari said.

'A true story. The proxies are proud of their prowess in combat, and fiercely jealous of the ancient rivalries and resentments that feed their little wars. They fight because it defines who they are.'

The viewpoint of the drone widened, giving a panoptic view of the little battlefield, then zoomed in on a low rise where three men stripped to the waist were pounding big kettle drums, and a woman naked beneath a cloak of green feathers was watching the battle through field glasses.

Hari thought of the drum which had preceded the flagellants as they had marched through Fei Shen.

'Someone knows a little about tactics,' Rav said. 'See the feint over there? They're drawing their enemy in by falling back, and then they'll strike from two sides. An old trick, but effective.'

He was watching the feed from the drone with a hungry interest. The slit pupils of his grass-green eyes were dilated. The sharp tip of his red tongue was nipped between his teeth.

'You're more like them than you like to think,' Hari said.

'We use combat – hand-to-hand combat, the noble art, nothing like the silly capering and random slaughter down there – to defeat those who are too vain or too stubborn to acknowledge that their theories have been displaced by new and better ideas. We fight to establish fundamental truths. The proxies fight over whether or not meat from a particular species of animal should be eaten, or on which day it should be eaten, or how it should be prepared. But I admit that I do rather admire them. They could certainly teach you a thing or two about revenge.'

Two lines of warriors ran at each other from either side of a flooded field, knees raised high as they splashed though the water towards each other, brandishing spears and spiked clubs. Just before they met, the rail car passed through a bulkhead and the feed snapped off.

Hari and Rav disembarked at the next station and rode the elevator to the village below. It was a small place. A handful of wooden houses strung along a paved road, with steeply pitched roofs woven from bundles of dried grasses. The ends of the beams that projected from the corners of the roofs were carved into the heads of fantastic creatures with red and gold scales, forked tongues flopping from long racks of sharp white teeth, and yellow eyes with slitted pupils glaring beneath ridged brows. Dragons, according to Rav.

'You can find them in the next sector. Trues hunted them. There are no large species left, just little ones about the length of my hand. They live under stones, mostly, and roast unwary birds.'

Beyond the last of the houses, the road ran through a big square gate cut into the bulkhead's gleaming cliff. Neither the road nor the houses – heaps of dumb, dead wood standing in gardens of uncertain taxonomies – were tagged. The villagers, dressed in yellow robes, engaged in enigmatic tasks in strip fields and open workshops, herding a flock of man-sized, long-necked birds, weren't tagged either.

People who lived outside towns usually lacked bioses, Rav said. 'Most of them are direct descendants of Trues or proxies. And this is a penitent community. They hope to atone for the sins of their ancestors by living humble lives of hard labour and prayer, and refuse connectivity and any technology that isn't powered by muscle or wind or water. Sounds noble, doesn't it? But the fact is, they're frauds. Hypocrites. Because the technology they scorn built Ophir and maintains the integrity of its biomes. Without it, without the machines that repair and maintain the world city's shell and regulate its atmospheric and hydrological cycles, the so-called wildernesses in which they live would soon die back to desert. And if a stray rock knocked a hole in their ceiling, what would they mend the hole with? The grass matting those old woman are weaving? No, they rely on other people to keep them safe and to keep their little world working.'

'You sound as if you have a grudge against them,' Hari said.

'Perhaps they remind me of my own people, who gave up reason for superstition. A friend left us a scooter at the gate; otherwise, we'd have to walk to the festival.'

'A friend?'

'You'll find that you have a lot in common,' Rav said. 'We'll eat before we set off. Good plans are founded in regular meals.'

They ate in the village commons, boiled rice mixed with flash-fried slivers of vegetables, shreds of dark meat that Hari left in his bowl. A boy he'd seen earlier, herding the big flightless birds, sat with him. A sturdy kid a couple of years younger than Hari, with long black hair and an eager, frank curiosity. His name was Nobita. He had lived all his life in the village, expected to grow old and die there, and was the happiest person Hari had ever met.

They spoke in Pinglish, the ancient lingua franca of Earth's Pacific Community; Nobita's native language, Nihongo, was so old and obscure that Hari's bios lacked the ability to translate it. The language of a proud and capable people who had built the first settlement on Earth's Moon, but had been assimilated into general Outer culture long ago, and had more or less vanished from Earth. Their native land was under ice, now, like so many others. This village was the last refuge of traditions more than four thousand years old.

Hari learned a little of the villagers' routine of work and prayer. He learned that the religious festival was a gathering of gypsy preachers and sects which endlessly circled the world-city, seeking to redeem the sins of their ancestors through holy and charitable works. They gathered at sacred places, and then broke up and moved on along their separate paths. Ascetics sometimes passed through the village, too, Nobita said.

'They can cause trouble. Although they claim to reject the world of things, they like pleasures that are forbidden to us. But they are good musicians, and so are we. I have learned several songs from them, and hope to learn more.'

Hari showed him the little book that had once belonged to the ascetic hermit Kinson Ib Kana. Nobita couldn't read the script, so Hari read out the fragment it randomly displayed. Nobita asked Hari to repeat it, then repeated it himself.

> I have walked the way for a hundred years
> And after a hundred more I will still be seeking
> The Unknown Bird.

'I have found some good stories in here, but I don't really understand or appreciate this kind of stuff,' Hari confessed. 'My family are practical. We like things to mean what they mean.'

'I was taught that you find the meaning in yourself, not the thing itself,' Nobita said. 'A small coin is nothing to a rich man, but means a meal and happiness to an indigent, or brings comfort to a grieving mother, because it was the last gift of a dead son.'

Hari explained that he'd found the book when he'd been marooned on a rock, after his family's ship had been stolen by bandits. 'I managed to escape, and met Rav, and now we're looking for the bandits. I have a treasure they want, and hope to trade it for the lives of my family. But first I have to find the key to unlock it.'

Nobita said that it sounded like one of the old stories from the long ago, when people everywhere had lived as his people lived now, under the sky of Earth. Stories of fierce bandits who oppressed villages, and heroes who gave up their lives to save ordinary people, or walked the land looking for adventure because they hoped to regain the honour they had lost because of some selfish action, or because they had loved someone they were forbidden to love.

'Rav would say that our stories haven't changed because we haven't changed,' Hari said. 'He claims to be different, but I think that he is like one of those old warrior-heroes. Or likes to think he is.'

Nobita looked across the room to where Rav was talking with several old men and women, then bent towards Hari and said quietly, 'Have you known him long?'

'Not really.'

'I have seen him before. When I was very young. He fought two others like him, in the forest. They used lightning against each other, and burned many trees. You can still see some of the dead places. He killed his enemies, but he was wounded, and rested here for several days. Yes, just like one of the old heroes.'

Hari was astonished. 'Why were they fighting?'

'He said that they were trying to steal something from him. Something he was taking to a powerful witch who lives in a sky-castle.'

'This witch. Was she called Gun Ako Akoi?'

'You know this story?'

'I think I am part of it,' Hari said.

The scooter was a small, bulbous vehicle with two pairs of fan motors and a double saddle. Hari sat behind Rav as the Ardenist took them out above the forest. Although the saddle cupped Hari like a hand, it didn't seem like a very secure perch, especially when Rav tilted left or right. Hari's hands sweated on the grips; his stomach performed airy gymnastics.

White paths threaded through the trees below, and there were clearings where clumps of ferns and banks of bushes with glossy leaves and big red flowers grew. Man-sized flightless birds like the ones in the village rooted about amongst the ferns. Rav dipped low, scattering several of them, and told Hari that they were fun to hunt.

'The yellow-robes eat their meat and their eggs, trade in their feathers and hides. They ride them, too.'

'I know.'

'I saw you talking with that kid. Learn anything interesting?'

'I found out that we both grew up in a small world, close to our families,' Hari said, wondering if Rav knew that he knew about the fight in the forest, and Rav's relationship with Gun Ako Akoi.

'The bulkheads polarise light, so that birds can detect them,' the Ardenist said. 'So they won't fly into them. In one section, autochthons paint patches of the bulkhead with a polymer that scrambles the polarised light back into its ordinary random orientation. Those patches look like holes, to birds, and those that try to fly through them are knocked senseless or killed outright, and are caught in nets that the autochthons spread at the bulkhead's base. They dance on high days and holidays in cloaks made from feathers, and wear tall headdresses of feathers too.'

'Like that woman we saw,' Hari said.

'She is from a different people,' Rav said. 'They keep herons birds who use their beaks to spear fish from shallow water. They eat fish caught by their herons, and pluck the flight feathers from the wings of the herons to stop them flying off, and dye them and make headdresses.'

'You know a lot about Ophir.'

'Oh, I lived here, once upon a time,' Rav said. 'I've lived in a lot of places, but I wouldn't call any of them home.'

While the Ardenist told several tall tales about the customs and ceremonies of the peoples who inhabited the wildernesses of the world city, Hari wondered how he had met Gun Ako Akoi, why he had been working for her, whether he still owed her a debt. But he wasn't ready to ask about it, not yet. He reckoned that it gave him an advantage, an edge, if Rav didn't know that he knew.

A narrow valley cut through the forest, the silvery thread of a swift, shallow river sewn into its crease. Rav and Hari turned to follow it, and the valley grew wider and the river meandered through lush meadows and at last emptied into a lake that stretched away to the horizon, its surface mirroring sunlight from a thousand restless points.

They turned again, following the shoreline. Pine trees crowded a steep slope that rose to a long ridge of bare black rock. Rav pointed to a road that ran along the shore of the lake, a congregation of tents: the festival. Then they swung away and rose towards a castle peak of rock. A solitary figure stood there, a young woman silhouetted against the light of the sunstrip, shading her eyes with a hand as she watched them sidle towards her.

8

The young woman, Riyya Lo Minnot, was the daughter of Salx Minnot Flores. Rav had traced her through the legal dispute over the philosopher's property. When he'd explained that he and Hari were looking for the people who had murdered her father, she had immediately offered her help.

'And now I'm beginning to regret it,' Riyya Lo Minnot said. 'It wasn't easy to get away at short notice. I was nearly caught.'

'But here you are, and here we are, ready to do what we need to do,' Rav said.

'How did it go at the store?' Riyya said.

Hari looked at Rav, making a connection. Rav smiled. 'I admit that I was given a little help when I reached out to that silly little police inspector,' he said, 'but you wouldn't have seen what you saw without me.'

'You saw the transmitter,' Riyya said.

She had a brisk, brittle manner, was dressed in a white shift belted with a broad black belt, black trousers, polished black boots. The uniform of Ophir's Climate Corps, according to Hari's bios. Her skin was pale and freckled; the fringe of her red hair was cut straight across her brow. Her bios was locked and displayed no personal data that Hari could access, not even a capsule bio.

'I saw it, and I woke it up,' Rav said. 'We were both impressed, weren't we, youngblood?'

'My father knew your father,' Hari told Riyya. 'I wish that he had told me more about the work they did together.'

'I wish that my father had never met Dr Gagarian,' Riyya said.

'You are both entangled in the failed ambitions of your fathers,' Rav said. 'But with my help there'll be a happy ending.'

'Some kind of ending, anyway,' Riyya said, and walked to the edge of the platform of bare rock and looked down at the encampment. 'I still think it would be better to wait until the festival breaks up and this gypsy sect is on the road. I can hit them with a fierce little rainstorm, you can swoop in while they're dealing with panicked draft animals and wagons bogged down in mud . . . Quick and clean and neat. If we're lucky, no one will notice the tweak in the weather.'

'We have to do it now,' Rav said. 'The bad guys know where we are, hostages have been threatened, tick tick tick. Besides, mounting a raid in the middle of the festival will cause more confusion, and will give us a better chance of making a clean escape. And it will be a lot more fun.'

'It means a bigger tweak. More chance that it will be noticed, more chance that someone will get hurt,' Riyya said.

'A little rain never hurt anyone,' Rav said.

'How little you know about rain,' Riyya said.

'I want to go in just after sunset,' Rav said. 'The darkness will add to the confusion. Does that give you enough time to cook up the weather?'

'It will have to be quick and dirty, but I can do it,' Riyya said.

'Dirty is good. Quick is even better. You and Hari should talk. Get to know one another. Bond, or whatever it is you baseliners do,' Rav said, and turned and took three quick strides to the edge of the drop and leaped into the air. He flared his wings as he fell, swooping down to the trees, catching hold of the top of a tall pine and clinging there with hands and feet as it whipped to and fro, then dropping out of sight.

Riyya looked at Hari and said, 'Is he always like this?'

'Rude, arrogant, and annoying? Pretty much.'

Riyya's smile was there and gone. 'How long have you known him?'

'Not long. I hardly know him at all.'

'You had better tell me everything, anyway.'

They sat on a flat shelf of rock with a view across the tree-clad slope that dropped to the sweep of glittering water. The sunstrip burned with golden light and a warm wind blew from the lake, carrying the clean odour of the pine trees and snatches of music from the tents strung along the edge of the water.

Riyya told Hari that Rav had explained about the hijack of *Pabuji's Gift*, and had sent her a copy of the message from the hijackers.

'It was cruel,' she said. 'We're dealing with dangerous and desperate people.'

'Absolutely.'

Hari saw Nabhoj, naked and pleading. He was embarrassed and angry, and trying his best not to show it. When Riyya asked if Dr Gagarian's head really was in his kitbag, he said, 'Rav told you everything, didn't he?'

'He gave me a full briefing. If that upsets you, take it up with him.'

There was a short silence. Hari realised that Riyya was also embarrassed. They had been thrown together by their losses and by Rav's scheming, were uncertain how to proceed. He asked her about her father; she said that she'd never been close to him.

'He joined the Climate Corps when he and my mother partnered, but he walked away from everything after the Bright Moment. From my mother, from the Corps. She was pregnant at the time. My mother. She was carrying me. She cut him off. Wouldn't talk to him. Hardly ever talked about him to me or to my brothers. He was a mystery to me, I wanted to know more about him, so two years ago, when I reached my majority, I contacted him. My mother didn't like it, but she couldn't stop me. We started to talk, my father and I, and he invited me to Ophir. I saw him six times, in all. Six times in two years. I was about to visit him again when what happened happened.' Riyya paused, then said, 'Rav told me that the woman who killed my father was a sister or clone of the woman who killed Dr Gagarian.'

'As were the two women who tried to catch me on Themba,' Hari said. 'One of them killed herself, like your father's assassin.'

Riyya nodded.

'Rav really did tell you everything, didn't he?'

'He was very candid.'

'Do you believe his theory that the hijackers are Saints?'

'Do you?'

'I'm coming around to the idea. Did your father ever mention the Saints? Did he feel threatened by them, or by any of the other cults?'

'My father was a gentle man,' Riyya said. 'Very clever, driven, but unworldly. My mother's family has deep roots in the Climate Corps. Most of them are philosophers and technicians. Practical, pragmatic. My father . . . After the Bright Moment, after he walked away from the Corps, he went to work for one of the trading families. He refurbished the lifesystems of several of their ships, and when he had earned enough credit he disappeared into his work on the Bright Moment. He wasn't interested in how it could be used, how to sell it. He was only interested in the problem, in how it had triggered the vision of the man on the bicycle. How it had put the same image in the heads of everyone alive. The same image, the same emotions.'

He had corresponded with other philosophers who had been working on the Bright Moment, Riyya said. That was how he had met Dr Gagarian. They'd known each other for more than twelve years, had stayed in contact after Dr Gagarian took up with Hari's family.

'I wouldn't say they were good friends, but they respected each other's work,' she said. 'And he was collaborating with Dr Gagarian and the others on those experiments. That was why it was such a shock, when Dr Gagarian cut him off.'

'When the ship was hijacked, you mean,' Hari said.

'No,' Riyya said, 'it was before that.'

It had been about two hundred days before the hijack, according to her. Before *Pabuji's Gift* had put in at Porto Jeffre. The tick-tock philosopher had stopped replying to Salx Minnot Flores' messages, had also cut all contact with Ioni Robles Nguini and Ivanova Galchan.

'The engineer in Tannhauser Gate, Worden Hanburanaman, stopped communicating with them too,' Riyya said. 'My father was very upset. He talked about travelling to Tannhauser Gate, to confront him.'

'I didn't know,' Hari said.

'You didn't know?'

'I didn't know. Really. I didn't talk much with Dr Gagarian. He gave me my instructions, I did whatever needed doing. He wasn't secretive, exactly, but he didn't have any small talk.'

But his father must have known, Hari thought. Aakash must have known that Dr Gagarian had stopped talking to his friends and collaborators. Had cut them out of the loop. His father must have known, and he'd never told him . . .

'My father thought that Dr Gagarian must have made a breakthrough,' Riyya said. 'That he'd discovered something important, and decided to keep it to himself.'

'I don't think so,' Hari said.

But he was wondering if that was why Aakash had agreed to break off the experimental work, and head out to Jackson's Reef.

Riyya said, 'My father and the others, Ioni Robles Nguini and Ivanova Galchan, pooled their data and spent a lot of time trying to work out what Dr Gagarian might have discovered. I don't think they had much success. And my father had his own work, of course. He threw himself into that. And then he was killed. Then that woman killed him.'

There was a brief silence. Riyya was staring out towards the lake, but Hari was certain that she was looking at something else. Her hair was tucked behind the pale shells of her ears. It was the colour of raw copper. A stray lock fluttered in the wind.

She said, 'For a long time, I thought Dr Gagarian had something to do with it. That he'd paid reivers to eliminate anyone who knew about his work. I had all kind of mad fantasies about revenge. And then Rav contacted me, and told me about the hijack of your family's ship.'

'I'm going to find out who did it,' Hari said. 'Who hijacked the ship, and killed everyone else. It's all connected.'

'He was so very close,' Riyya said. 'So very close to completing his work. I saw what he could do. It was the second time we met, the first time I visited his house.'

'Rav switched on the apparatus in the store,' Hari said. 'I saw a white flash. A white light right in the middle of my head.'

'That was an early prototype,' Riyya said. 'I saw a man riding a bicycle into a flare of light. Riding along, and vanishing. Dissolving into light. Have you ever been caught by one of those rogue shrines in Down Town? It was a little like that, but it didn't get into my head through my bios. It was more personal. Unfiltered, raw. Like a memory or a thought. My father said it was only an approximation of the Bright Moment, but even so, it was . . . astonishing.'

Another silence. They were embarrassed again.

Riyya said, 'My father was fearless. He liked to argue with end-timers. With anyone.'

'About his work.'

'About the Bright Moment. It was all he wanted to talk about. It was all he had in his life.'

Salx Minnot Flores had been experimenting with entoptics, according to Riyya. Basic visual patterns hardwired into the human visual system. She picted a brief flutter of images. Cave paintings. Markings on a desert playa. Details of paintings. A sequence of geological features on planets and rocks that resembled human faces.

'He used a pulsed magnetic field to trigger them,' she said. 'He said that it wasn't anything like the way the Bright Moment had been

161

triggered, but the effects were very similar. That was what Dr Gagarian and the others were working on, weren't they?'

'On how it was transmitted,' Hari said.

'My father was interested in how it affected the brain's visual system – the entoptics built into the visual pathway. If they are triggered in the right sequence, they create a rough outline, and your mind puts it together. We see what we want to see, my father said. The trick was to push it in the right direction.'

Hari, remembering that Mr D.V. Mussa had said something similar, asked Riyya if she had ever met the tanky.

'I didn't meet any of my father's friends,' she said. 'I don't think he had very many.'

There was another short, uncomfortable silence. Hari thought of Dr Gagarian. It wasn't hard to imagine the tick-tock deciding to cut off all contact with people he didn't need any more. A purely practical decision, lacking any measure of human emotion or empathy.

'Those people down there,' Riyya said, pointing with her chin towards the bright little tents of the festival. 'They're celebrating their different versions of hidden truths. My father and yours, Dr Gagarian and the others, they were searching for a different kind of truth. The real truth, the truth at the bottom of everything. But what good did it do them?'

Hari said that his father thought that it was important because it would demystify the Bright Moment. 'He wanted to use philosophy to drive out superstition. He wanted to prove that Sri Hong-Owen, whatever she'd become, wherever she went, hadn't broken the fundamental laws of physics. He wanted to prove that the Bright Moment wasn't some kind of miracle, that she hadn't become some kind of god. It was like the seraphs, my father said. They had become something else, but they weren't gifted with superhuman powers. They were still only machines, constrained by the same laws that constrain everything else in the universe.'

Riyya said, 'One of the sects in Down Town believes that the seraphs are a kind of distraction. That the QIs didn't vasten after all, but went into hiding. That after causing the Long Twilight and the fall of the True Empire, they have continued to secretly manipulate human history.'

Hari said, 'If that's true, they can't be very smart. Based on the evidence.'

Riyya laughed. He discovered that he liked to make her laugh.

He told her about his adventures on Vesta and in Fei Shen, how he had met Rav. They talked about what the Ardenist might be planning, about what might be inside Dr Gagarian's head, and why Rav was really interested in it. They talked about growing up in the Climate Corps and aboard *Pabuji's Gift*, and discussed the small coincidences of their lives – that they were more or less the same age, that they both had two brothers, had both served apprenticeships in practical philosophies, and so on, and so forth.

In the company of this forthright young woman, in sunlight and fresh air, with the tremendous view spread to the horizon, Hari was possessed by a premonition that the world was trembling on the threshold of something new and wonderful, felt that he had reached a point where things could only get better, that he would soon discover the secrets hidden inside Dr Gagarian's head and find and destroy his enemies, begin his life again . . .

At last, late in the afternoon, Rav came scrambling up the rocky slope, carrying a brace of rabbits.

'We should eat before we set out,' he said.

Hari and Riyya shared rice cakes and savoury bean paste that she fetched from her scooter; Rav skinned and gutted and quartered the rabbits, and roasted the joints using a signal laser at its highest setting.

'I don't know why you baseliners are so squeamish,' he said. 'You're made of meat, so why not eat meat? Or are you worried about consuming the animals' souls, or some such groundless superstition?'

'Tell us about your plan,' Riyya said.

'Tell us everything,' Hari said.

Rav made a pass with his hands, held up a faceted vial containing a dark sliver. A replica of the trinket that he'd fabricated in a maker while Hari had been redeeming Dr Gagarian's head from the bonded store.

'All we have to do is substitute this for the original. The Masters of the Measureless Mind worship the idea it represents. As long as they don't know it's a copy, a copy will serve their needs as well as the original. But Gun Ako Akoi needs the original, because only the original can do what she wants it to do.'

'Is it really part of a seraph?' Riyya said.

'A fragment of one of the self-aware QIs that vastened into the seraphs,' Rav said. 'One that called itself the Lonesome Road of Exculpation. They were sprawling, complex things, those old QIs.

They accumulated self-awareness the way a genome accumulates complexity. By accidents of transcription, deletions, repurposing, borrowing from smaller intelligences, infections and infestations, and so on. Each one was different, and all of them were dead ends, leftovers of the dreams of an age long past. Created to show it was possible to create real self-aware machine intelligence, and then abandoned. Until they were vastened by a shared conceptual breakthrough, they were each about as intelligent as the average baseliner.

'Some say that they were vastened when the Trues attacked them, and infected them with djinns. Some say they became portals, neither wholly in this universe or in the pocket universe they opened up or created or became. The Saints and other equally deluded cults want to penetrate their information horizons because they think it will open the way to their individual versions of heaven. Others think the seraphs have become frozen accidents, consumed by self-engulfing iterations of an incomprehensible message from the far side. Who knows? Who cares? All that matters is that Gun Ako Akoi wants the original fragment of that old QI, wants to use it as the substrate for a new companion, or a memory engine, or some such tinker work. And we'll get what we want if she gets what she wants.'

Rav tossed the vial high into the air and it flashed like a star and he caught it and showed Hari and Riyya his open, empty hand.

'Hey presto!'

He finished his meal, and explained what he wanted Hari and Riyya to do. Tearing flesh from bones as he talked, cracking the bones between his teeth and sucking out the marrow, tossing the splintered bones over the edge of the sheer drop, licking grease from his fingers.

'Any questions?' he said. 'Good. Time's a-wasting. Let's go and play our parts.'

9

Light in the sunstrip was dying down towards the curved horizon of the lake as Hari followed the white road along the shore towards the festival. The kitbag was slung over his shoulders; the replica of the relic was in the breast pocket of his jacket; he was reviewing Rav's plan for the ninth or tenth time, the part he had to play.

Men and women were bathing on the broad beach of black sand at the water's edge. Standing waist-deep amongst islands of foam, scrubbing their torsos and arms, raising their arms towards the overhead and pressing their hands together and bringing them down and touching fingertips to their foreheads. Further out, children frog-kicked around a raft and clambered on to it and jumped off, locking their hands under knees tucked high and cannonballing into the water with loud screaming and laughter.

There was an iron smell on the cool breeze blowing off the water. Dark clouds were drifting in above the lake, dimming the last of the light.

Hari passed pilgrim encampments scattered across a broad meadow, joined a stream of people making their way towards the big tents pitched along the broad white road. Square tents with peaked roofs, long tents, pyramids, transparent domes. Most were reefed open, displaying carved idols standing amongst constellations of flickering flames, or complex light sculptures burning against black backdrops, or heads of humans or animals or chimeras staring out of glass tanks. A bulky white pressure suit with a gold-visored helmet stood in the centre of one tent: the armour of one of the heroes of the long ago, when humans had first ventured beyond the sky of Earth. In another, the brief vision of the Bright Moment played, the man on the bicycle smiling and turning away and vanishing into a flash of light, smiling and vanishing.

Several passers-by greeted Hari, pressing their hands together, touching fingertips to foreheads. Hari mirrored their gestures, feeling like a fraud. The small weight of the fake relic burned over his heart.

The crowd thickened. Here were several monks in scarlet robes walking with their hands clasped behind them, talking animatedly. Here was a skyclad sadhu arguing with an invisible opponent, jabbing at the air with clenched fingers. Indigents sat with begging bowls in their laps or at their feet. A naked Blue Man sat cross-legged in the shade of a flowering tree, eyes closed, hands resting on his knees, palms upturned and forefingers and thumbs pinched together.

Children ran everywhere. Many wore masks. Two men stripped to the waist were stirring a cauldron of soup with wooden paddles. A woman was selling shaved ice in paper cones. A child was selling garlands of white flowers. A man was selling tea, deftly pouring it into white porcelain cups from the long spout of the pot he balanced on a pad on top of his head. Two ascetics went past, clad in their parti-coloured robes, tapping a slow beat on small drums tucked under their arms. A woman sat cross-legged, playing an unfretted spike fiddle. Another woman sang an atonal praisesong. There were pairs and trios and quartets of musicians spaced along the grassy verge at the edge of the beach, and men and women stopped to listen and then moved on. Banners hung from tall poles, rattling in the breeze off the lake. The silvery teardrop of a balloon floated high above the tents, reflecting the last of the sunlight, and in the basket hung beneath it a holy man sang a wailing prayer.

As he mingled with the gaudy parade, passing intricately crafted altars and shrines, breathing the odours of sandalwood and incense, woodsmoke and cooking, hearing strange musics drifting on the warm wind, Hari felt an unbounded delight at the rich variety of human imagination. He supposed that his father would have been dismayed by the unabashed veneration of imaginary sky ghosts, the endless elaboration of superstition, the flaunting of pointless scholarship, but it seemed to him that although these people had gathered to honour and exalt their various prophets and gods, what they were really celebrating was themselves. One of the itinerant philosophers who had taken passage on *Pabuji's Gift* had once told Hari that small groups of like-minded people generated a gestalt, a group overmind or harmonic mindset that

166

enhanced problem-solving, enhanced empathy, and reduced conflict. A useful survival trait, according to the philosopher, when the ancestors of all human beings had been a few bands of man-apes on the veldts of old Earth. Hari's father had dismissed this and similar explanations of human behaviour as fairy tales, but it was easy to imagine a kind of benevolent overmind permeating the encampment, binding everyone to a common purpose.

A small parade was coming down the road. Eight men holding poles on which was balanced a huge red skull with elongated, toothy jaws, followed by men beating drums or tossing firecrackers to the left and right, and a man who swigged a clear greasy liquid from a bottle and touched a burning torch to his lips and breathed out fire. As the crowds parted to let them pass, Hari saw the tent of the Masters of the Measureless Mind on the other side of the road, square and butter-yellow, just as Rav had described it. A black pennant strung from the top of its central pole snapped in the wind.

One side of the tent was open to the road. Inside, a dozen men and women sat cross legged on rugs that covered the floor. They were swaying from side to side, arms raised, hands fluttering, chanting a slow and steady prayer. The altar reared above them, a starburst of silver and gold centred on a crystal lens that housed the relic, the real fragment of the QI. According to Rav, the Masters of the Measureless Mind believed that it emanated rays which, when the brains of the congregation were appropriately tuned by chants and devotional exercises, multiplied the complexity of their neuronal pathways.

Hari loitered on the other side of the road while the congregation inside the tent chanted and swayed. Dusk stained the air. Cloud sheeted the overhead. Dark layers, wispy streamers slowly turning. Something cold kissed Hari's cheek and he touched the spot with a fingertip and it came away wet. Another kiss, and another. People around him looked up, hurried on. He looked up too, and a drop of water struck his eye. He thought of the showers on the ship, how a cloud of droplets expanded from every direction. Here, droplets condensed inside clouds, and fell straight down. Here, the overhead wept . . .

It was part of Rav's plan. Riyya was using the climate machinery to wedge a cold front under the warm, moist air above the lake. There would be rain and strong winds, and in the confusion of the storm Rav would sneak into the tent and smash the altar and steal the relic. Hari would chase after Rav, chase him into the trees, and then he'd return, claiming he had confronted the thief and retrieved the relic, and present it – the fake relic – to the Masters of the Measureless Mind. And no one would know that the real relic, the fragment of the QI, had been stolen.

Hari heard a familiar music and saw the old ascetic he'd met at Down Town's train station, her patchwork coat billowing around her as she walked through the crowd of passers-by at the head of her little band of acolytes, their drums and guitars. She raised a hand when she saw Hari. Her acolytes halted and stopped playing, and she stepped towards him.

'It seems obvious to me now,' she said, 'but if you had told me in Down Town that the different paths we follow would cross here I would have called you a fabulist.'

Hari remembered the fragment that the book had displayed after the hermit had thrown it from his tree. ' "Streams rise in many places and flow by many paths, but all at last reach the sea." '

'You have been reading in your book.'

'I'm not sure how much I understand.'

'Some of those gathered here will claim that they can help you understand. A few might even be right, but amongst those of true faith there are many frauds and false prophets. We've already drawn out some, and we'll draw out more before the dogs bark and the caravan moves on,' the ascetic said. 'We have a lot of fun, teasing them, and sometimes we learn something from them, and sometimes they learn something from us. Of course, we don't have anything to lose. We're free to talk to fools, or to make fools of ourselves. But you should be more careful, I think. Be careful about who to trust.'

'I'm not going to give the book away to anyone who asks for it, if that's what you mean.'

'You asked me a question when we met before, and I gave you an answer. What you make of it is up to you.' A rainy gust blew over them. The ascetic drew her coat around her and said, 'We are camped in the meadow beyond these tents. If you need shelter and food, you are welcome to share what little we have. Perhaps you can teach me a song from your book, and we'll teach you one in return.'

'It's a kind thought, but I'm waiting for a friend.'

'The Ardenist? He's also welcome to share with us, but I rather think he prefers to walk alone.'

The ascetic bowed to Hari and walked on, and her acolytes struck up a new tune as they followed her. He felt a surprising pang as he watched them disappear into the crowds. As if a path he could have followed into another life had closed up.

But he wasn't following a path, hadn't set out on a spiritual quest or some kind of wandering, unfocused personal journey. He was on a mission. He was fixing a great wrong, repairing a hole or rupture in the world just as he would have repaired a broken machine, by working through a logical sequence of tasks, ticking them off one after the other.

Steal the relic, open the files in Dr Gagarian's head, discover what the hijackers wanted and use it against them.

The rain was falling harder now. Falling from clouds that seemed to squat about ten metres above his head, driven here and there in unfurling gusts. Hawkers were folding their blankets. Acolytes and priests and monks scurried about, gathering possessions, pounding loose stays into the ground, ducking inside tents. Tents were closing like flowers, like fists. Tents were altering their shapes. The tent of the Masters of the Measureless Mind extruded flaps and sealed itself up and hunkered down.

Hari joined several people in the scant shelter of a solitary pine tree. Waves slapped the beach, broke in lines of white foam. Rain billowed through the dark air. Tents flapped and strained. The silver balloon was hauled down, settling amongst the peaks and crowns of the tents like a clumsy bird. Rain walked and seethed in water running off the white road. One by one the people under the tree ran off in search of better shelter until only Hari was left.

He turned up the collar of his jacket, clutched it around himself. Water beaded its black brocade, dripped from its hem. His slippers were soaked through. He was wondering if something had gone wrong, was debating whether or not he should call Rav, when he saw something moving across the dark and restless lake. A tall whirling figure that cut a foaming white groove in the waves, drunkenly bending and tottering, wandering right and left, but steadily advancing, suddenly towering above the shoreline. Wind howled around Hari and a sudden smash of water drenched him, knocked him down. He staggered to his feet, spluttering and coughing. A swathe of tents had been flattened, including the butter-yellow tent of the Masters of the Measureless Mind.

Hari ran across the road. He had forgotten Rav's plan, was caught up in the moment, thinking that he could burrow under the ruin, find the altar, and replace the relic with its replica. People were beginning to struggle from the pancaked heap of sodden cloth. Hari circled left, and someone loomed out of the pelting rain. It was Rav, gripping his shoulder, bearing down, forcing him to his knees, leaning over him and saying, 'My game, my rules.'

An electric shock numbed Hari from head to toe; the Ardenist's hard fingers had pinched a nerve cluster. He couldn't speak, couldn't breathe.

Rav shouted into the rain and wind that he'd caught a thief, then reached into the pocket of Hari's jacket and pulled out the fake relic and held it up. 'Here it is. Here's what he stole,' he sang out, and when the men and women came crowding up he gave Hari a shove that sent him sprawling, and tossed the relic into the air.

Someone jumped high and caught it as it fell; others seized Hari, hauled him to his feet. He tried to speak, but his tongue was a blunt knot. Men gripped his arms, a woman shouted at him, her face thrust into his, and a clean cold spear pierced his head.

Light glowed on the blur of faces crowding in around him, sharp blue light that transmuted blowing raindrops into fugitive stars. The men let go of Hari's arms and stepped backwards. Several people knelt, knuckling their foreheads. Others stared gape-mouthed, sapphire sparks shining in their eyes.

A shadow stooped down. Hari flinched, saw blue highlights sliding over the fairing of a scooter, felt a wash of air as the machine settled in front of him. Rav leaned from the saddle and grabbed his arm and hauled him aboard.

The scooter rose into the wind and rain, cut a half-circle above the tents and shot out across the lake. Hari, hunched in the shelter of Rav's bulk, said, 'What were you trying to do?'

'I improvised. After Riyya conjured that waterspout and smashed down the tent, I dived under wreckage and snatched the relic. And then it occurred to me that there was no need to pretend I had stolen it.'

'So why did you pretend I had?'

'You had the replica. You couldn't just hand it over, could you?'

'Where is it?'

Rav held up his right hand, the relic's crystal vial pinched between thumb and forefinger.

'I meant the head,' Hari said. 'What have you done with Dr Gagarian's head?'

His own head felt as if it had been split with an axe. A sharp stink of char seared his nostrils.

Rav said, 'You're sitting on it. There's a locker under the saddle. I took it to keep it safe from the angry acolytes.'

'There was no need.'

'So I saw. That trick with the light was interesting. Did you mean to do it?'

'I don't know what happened,' Hari said.

'No doubt it was the djinn, stepping in to save you once again. I wonder if that's what the hijacker saw after she took down the skull feeders. A veil or shell of virtual light. Luckily, the Masters of the Measureless Mind aren't the kind of holy fools who give up their bioses so that they might see their god more clearly.'

'Yes, otherwise they might have lynched me.'

'I came back as quickly as I could. You're angry because you think I set you up. But it was part of the trick. Your surprise, when you discovered that you were the thief and I was the hero, played very nicely. And now we have Gun Ako Akoi's trinket, and the Masters of the Measureless Mind think that the replica is their holy relic. Everybody's happy. All's well that ends well.'

Hari was wondering about what might have happened if the djinn hadn't conjured the shell of virtual light. Wondering if Rav had been planning to run off with the head and the relic, and leave him to the mercy of the mob.

He said, 'Where's Riyya?'

'Directly behind us.'

Hari twisted around in his seat, searched the dark sky. After a few moments, his bios vectored in on a tiny shadow rising towards them.

Rav said, 'Shall we lose her?'

'She knows where we're going. And she deserves to know what Dr Gagarian knew.'

'Once again I am reminded that you baseliners think that sentiment is a virtue.'

10

The two scooters flew side by side through the tattered fringes of rain clouds, crossing the dark lake and flying above the forest beyond, turning to follow a road that cut through the trees. Hari's bios enhanced the crepuscular night glow of the sunstrip – everything seemed to be its own ghost, pale and insubstantial. Pale road, pale trees, a scattering of pale buildings in a clearing wheeling by, vanishing into the gloaming. The pale shadow of a bulkhead rose up, advanced with unnerving speed. Hari felt an airy rush in his blood as Rav angled their scooter into a steep dive. The bulkhead leaned above and they dropped with a plunging jolt and shot through a square port and began to rise again.

A narrow margin of forest gave way to threadbare grassland punctuated by stands of thorny trees and crests of bare rock like the thrusting prows of ships from the long ago, ships that had sailed the seas of Earth. The scooters flew on, travelling antispinward, a little faster than the rotation of the world city. Presently, light flared at the horizon and began to fill the skystrip.

Rav said that this sector had been one of the hunting grounds of the True optimates who had ruled Ophir at the height of their pomp. When Hari asked what they had hunted, the Ardenist pointed off to the left. Hari saw something move in the middle distance, zoomed in, saw large, bipedal animals standing knee-deep in a meadow of ferns. Muscular hind legs and shrunken forelimbs, paddle-tails fringed with dark feathers, feathers cresting along prominent ridges of their spines. Several stood watch, small eyes alert under bulging foreheads that were mostly bone, while the rest grazed. His bios couldn't identify them, but they looked a little like the animals carved into the roof beams of houses of the Nihongoni.

'I thought all the big dragons had been hunted to extinction,' he said.

'They're better than any dragon,' Riyya said. She was flying off to their right, matching the long curves Rav that put into their course. 'The ancestors of birds, conjured by gene wizards from fossil genes and guesswork. One of the wonders of Ophir. We have more of Earth's history than is left on Earth. I could show you the Taj Mahal. The pyramid of Cheops, and the Sphinx. Ankor Watt. The Library of Alexandria.'

'The whole dismal junkyard of history,' Rav said.

'It's your past too,' Riyya said.

'You baseliners are welcome to it. We own the future.'

As they flew on, Riyya told Hari about the treasures of Ophir. She picted images, said that the Climate Corps had a good relationship with the Curator Corps, she could get access to places most people never saw. They passed over random scatters of little round lakes – craters left by beam or kinetic weapons during the battle for control of Ophir, according to Riyya. And then something rolled above the close, curved horizon. A town-sized palace hung from the overhead, conical, mostly white. Hari saw sheer walls and broad terraces. He saw flying buttresses and viaducts, towers, a fringe of horizontal spars, slanting domes of green or blue glass, bridges spanning deep infolded crevices.

It was the home of the tick-tock matriarch, Gun Ako Akoi.

They rose towards it, floated in a long curve around its lower levels. Rows of narrow ports, a terraced garden, its lawns and clipped hedges sere and long-dead, a cluster of cubical buildings jutting from a vertical wall, a landing field scribed with arcane hieroglyphs. Hari and Rav's scooter leaned sideways, drifted towards a paved square. Riyya followed, and they touched down side by side.

White roses foamed down a broad fan of steps and threw tangles of thorny runners across the square. The cool, dry air was packed with their musky scent. At the top of the steps, a square of light glimmered in a facade of huge stone blocks.

Rav hinged up the saddle of his scooter and lifted out the kitbag and handed it to Hari, then turned to Riyya and told her that she couldn't enter the palace. Looming over her, smiling his barbarous smile, saying, 'Gun Ako Akoi stands at the head of a long lineage that includes Dr Gagarian. She is very old and very paranoid. By any normal measure quite insane. No one sees her without an invitation, and I confess that I forgot to tell her about you.'

'Tell her now,' Riyya said, fists on hips, glaring up at the Ardenist. 'Tell her that I'm coming in with you.'

'That isn't how it works,' Rav said. 'I made a bargain with her. The relic in exchange for access to the files in Dr Gagarian's head. An audience of two. The terms aren't flexible.'

Riyya looked at Hari. He felt embarrassment and pity, and said, 'I didn't have anything to do with this. I'm sorry.'

Something hardened in Riyya's gaze. 'That's how it is,' she said. 'You shook me down for information. Used my talent for weathermaking. And now you want to get rid of me because you don't need me any more.'

'Wait here if you like,' Rav said. 'But if I were you, I'd go back to the Corps. Go back to your mother. This was never really about you or your father anyway. He was, I regret to say, collateral damage.'

'I'll tell you everything that happens,' Hari told Riyya. 'Everything. You've earned it.'

'*Earned* it?'

Hari blushed. 'I mean you deserve to know. As much as I do.'

'Gun Ako Akoi is expecting us, and she doesn't like to be kept waiting.' Rav said.

'I'm sorry,' Hari said again, and shrugged the kitbag over his shoulder and followed the Ardenist up the ruined staircase, picking his way between stretches of broken stone and tangles of roses towards a square doorway framed by massive pillars carved with slaughterhouse scenes. Naked bodies writhing under the blows of armoured troopers. Hacked limbs, spilled viscera, a trooper in a horned helmet holding up a severed head. The crude, brutal realism of True art. This is this.

A long corridor stretched away inside, stone walls hung with red silk banners that shivered and shimmered as Hari and Rav walked past. Tiny lights hung at different heights in the air. Lights burned at the feet of statues that stood in recesses, painting highlights and shadows on folds of cloth and straps, on muscles and fluted armour.

'We wouldn't be here without Riyya's help,' Hari told Rav.

'She was conveniently to hand, but we could have managed without her.'

'Is that what we are to you? Tools to be used and discarded?'

Hari was thinking again of the trick that Rav had played on him. His little dominance games.

'You feel sorry for her because you share a trauma,' Rav said. 'In other words, you feel sorry for yourself.'

'You really don't know much about people, do you?'

'I know that your sympathy is temporary, that you will forget about it once you discover what Dr Gagarian stored inside his head. Don't worry about the feelings of the little weathermaker. She'll get over it. And don't worry about them, either,' Rav said, as small figures emerged from the edges of red silk banners and stepped out into the corridor.

They were child-sized manikins, dressed in antique uniforms. Scarlet jackets, blue jackets, ornamented with gold braid and tasselled shoulder pads and sashes and starburst badges. Belts hung with miniature swords and pistols and coiled whips, trousers with narrow stripes down the outseam, puffed breeches, polished knee-high boots with jangling spurs. One small figure was clad in a white pressure suit whose backpack emitted a jet of steam at every other step. Another, its face painted silver, wore a riveted corselet and a conical cap with a kind of chimney or spout.

'What are they?' Hari said.

'Aspects of Gun Ako Akoi,' Rav said. 'Her familiars and companions. They're mostly harmless, but don't make any sudden or threatening moves. Be polite.'

'We are her guests. Of course I'll be polite.'

Escorted by this miniature army, Hari and Rav entered a huge cylindrical shaft. Soft lights glowed beneath a floor of translucent plastic; a stair spiralled around the curve of the wall, rising into darkness high above. The little army of mismatched dragoons and paladins gathered at the foot of the stair, looking up expectantly, and a shadow detached from other shadows high above: a womanly figure descending turn after turn, accompanied by a loose halo of firefly lamps and small machines sustained by gauzy wings.

Gun Ako Akoi was taller than Rav, bone-thin, dressed in a crimson, ankle-length dress with a high collar. Her legs moving inside tight fabric as she came down the stair with delicate mincing steps. White gloves sleeved her arms to the shoulders. Her black hair was done up in a spire with little caves woven into it where insectile machines crouched and blinked coloured pinlights; her face was masked with an oval dish in which different faces came and went like spectators jostling at a window. At intervals it blanked with a blue as fathomless as the sky of Earth.

Pabuji's Gift had several times carried displaced autocrats or minor members of royalty as passengers. Watching the tick-tock matriarch progress towards him, Hari was reminded of one in particular, Princess-in-Exile Sihan-Djina of the Augusta Archipelago, a young woman about his age who had possessed the tranquil authority of someone accustomed to having their every wish expedited. Gun Ako Akoi shared the princess's absolute assurance, but there was something chill and predatory about her, too. Sihan-Djina's assumption of authority was charming and naive because it didn't extend beyond her immediate retinue and a few thousand monarchists scattered across the Belt; Gun Ako Akoi's authority, in this remote, ruined palace, was absolute. She could kill Hari on a whim, confiscate the head of her dead scion . . .

As she came down the last of the steps, and her little army parted to let her through, Rav did something that startled Hari: he went down on one knee and bowed his head and held out his arms on either side so that his wings stretched like a cloak. After a moment, Hari, feeling foolish and more than a little afraid, knelt too.

Gun Ako Akoi laughed, told them to stand. Her familiars clustered around her knees. She spread her left hand on the helmet of the one in the pressure suit. Its visor matched the parade of faces that came and went on her mask; its jets of white vapour swirled around her thighs.

'I've brought what you asked for,' Rav said, and held up the vial containing the relic.

'I never doubted that you would,' Gun Ako Akoi said.

Her voice was compounded of softly beaten gongs and tinkling bells.

A miniature general marched forward and took the vial from Rav and saluted and marched away across the soft lights of the floor.

'I see that there are three of you,' Gun Ako Akoi said.

For a moment, Hari thought that Riyya had crept in behind them; then he realised that the tick-tock woman must be referring to the head of Dr Gagarian. He started to explain how he had come by his burden, but she raised her right hand and he fell silent. Her fingers were very long, and appeared to have extra joints.

'I mean the djinn in your skull.'

'I was wondering about that myself,' Rav said.

Hari looked at him. 'The djinn is in Dr Gagarian's head.'

'It is in your head, funny little baseliner,' Gun Ako Akoi said. 'In your neural network.'

'Why don't you show him what you've found?' Rav said. 'You know how it is with baseliners. Seeing is believing.'

A pict appeared in the dusky air. A head two metres across, semi-transparent, slowly rotating, like the pict of Dr Gagarian's head in the head shop in Fei Shen. But there were no modules embedded in this head. Instead, a bright, tightly knitted tangle bridged the base of the hemispheres – a bios – and an intricate network of microscopic filaments ramified everywhere . . .

'It is very fine work,' Gun Ako Akoi said. 'Designed and seeded by the Memory Whole. Those filaments are just twenty nanometres across. You could fit a bundle of several hundred of them inside a single neuron, and each has a much larger carrying capacity than any axon. Do you remember its inception?'

Hari shook his head. His scalp felt as if it was trying to shrink into his skull. .

Rav said, 'Is it an independent entity?'

'Aside from the djinn? No. There are few points of contact with the baseliner's sensory centres, and none in his cerebellum. Most of the traffic appears to be modulated by his bios. I would guess that it is a high-capacity storage device.' Gun Ako Akoi stared down at Hari. The face in her mask was that of a young, beautiful girl. 'You really knew nothing about this.'

Hari dry-swallowed, nodded.

'You have no voluntary access.'

'No. None that I know of.'

'Then if you want to know what your neural network contains, you must consult its makers. I cannot open it for you.'

Rav said, 'Surely someone as skilled and puissant as you wouldn't be troubled by a mere djinn.'

The young girl's face dissolved, replaced by the face of an old man with blank white eyes and an agonised expression.

'I could dismiss the djinn easily enough, but the network is a very old design, based on obsolete principles,' Gun Ako Akoi said. 'They're older than me, those tankies down in the Memory Whole. Very conservative, very clever.'

'I have already paid you,' Rav said.

'You paid me to open Dr Gagarian's head. And this is no ordinary neural network. It has grown and elaborated itself from a seed rooted in the boy's brain. Before I could begin to unpick its encryption I would have to reverse-engineer and build the necessary tools, a task that would be neither quick nor easy. We would have to come to a new agreement, and in any case I doubt that you could afford my fee.'

Rav smiled. 'Are you telling me that you don't want to do it, or you can't do it?'

'I'm telling you that it would be easier to consult the makers of the net, or the person who commissioned it.'

'The person who commissioned it is dead,' Hari said.

He felt faintly insubstantial. If it was real, if there really was a neural network inside his head, woven through his brain, if it wasn't some kind of trick cooked up by Rav and the tick-tock matriarch, his father must have put it there. His father must have commissioned it. Who else had known? Nabhomani? Nabhoj? Had Agrata known about it? If she had, Worden Hanburanaman had probably known about it, too. *Worden will help you understand Dr Gagarian's work, and how to carry it forward.* And Worden Hanburanaman had been kidnapped and killed, and Nabhoj was a prisoner of the hijackers, so they probably knew about it too . . .

He said, 'I need to know. I need to know what's inside my head.'

The pict dwindled to a point of light, winked out.

'You will have to visit the Memory Whole, and find the tanky who designed and planted the seed,' Gun Ako Akoi said. 'Meanwhile, there is this other business – the head of my grandchild, Dr Gagarian.'

'Are you certain that you can open that?' Rav said.

Gun Ako Akoi ignored him and said to Hari, 'Dr Gagarian was murdered by the people who hijacked your ship.'

'Yes.'

'They wanted his head. You took it from them, and now you want to use it to ransom the ship and any hostages.'

'I want to find out why they want it. I came here because I was told that you could help me,' Hari said.

But he was wondering what he was carrying in his own head, next to his thoughts. He was wondering what his father had written into the neural network during those sessions when he had seemed to spend only an hour or two in the viron while days had passed outside, in the real world.

Gun Ako Akoi said, 'And if I claim the head of my murdered grandchild?'

Rav said, 'We have an agreement. I've done my part. Now it's your turn.'

'Remember that you are in my house.'

'Oh, is that how it is?'

'It is as it always has been.'

'Things have changed,' Rav said. 'I know that's hard for you to understand, living as you do in this tomb. But I owe you nothing, now. And you owe me.'

The Ardenist and the tick-tock matriarch stared at each other. Rav was smiling, showing all his teeth, and his wings were half-unfurled. The manikin familiars rustled around Gun Ako Akoi, hands finding swords and holsters.

Hari shrugged off the kitbag, held it out to Gun Ako Akoi. 'Take it,' he said. 'But if you love Dr Gagarian half as much as I love my family, you'll want revenge for his murder. We can help you get it, if you give us copies of his files.'

Gun Ako Akoi's laugh was like a hundred small bells cascading down a staircase. The face in her mask was the face of a sleepy young boy. 'I never met Dr Gagarian,' she said. 'Yet I know him, and I love him. I love all my children, and I love all their children, and their children's children. Ours is the truest form of human AI. We are woven from algorithms that learn to mimic particular elements in our global neural maps. And at the same time our neural maps learn to exploit the higher functions of the algorithms. It is a dynamic process that requires close supervision and takes many hundreds of days. Longer than the gestation of any mammal. I know all of my children intimately, and they know me. We share the same algorithms, similar patterns of thought, similar emotional riffs, similar inventories of qualia. And so it is between them and their children. We are all of us variations of a single intricate theme. The death of one diminishes the rest. The death of Dr Gagarian diminishes me.'

Gun Ako Akoi's mask darkened. The face looking out now was inhuman. Grey skin, huge black eyes, a small downturned mouth. The familiars lowered their heads and clasped their hands to their breasts.

'I want to know how he met his end,' she told Hari. 'We'll talk about that, you and I.'

They talked a long time. Gun Ako Akoi wanted to know every detail of Dr Gagarian's work, and Hari had to apologise over and again because he couldn't answer most of her questions. For the tenth or

179

twentieth time, he wished that he had paid more attention when he had set up the tick-tock philosopher's experimental apparatus, wished that he'd asked more questions, cursed the indolence of his younger self.

'He was a romantic,' Gun Ako Akoi said, at last. She spoke slowly and sonorously. She was composing an epitaph for her dead grandchild. 'He believed that the universe was comprehensible, that its complexity was an emergent property of a few fundamental rules. He believed that attempting to understand it was the finest occupation to which any kind of human being could aspire. The Bright Moment challenged his perception of the universe, and he tried to rise to that challenge. He saw giants where we see windmills. He tried to fly to the Sun. He searched for the Holy Grail. And like all such searches, his search ended in tragedy. Poor Gagarian. Poor parfait knight.'

There was a long silence in the shadowy chamber. The tick-tock matriarch was looking beyond Hari and Rav, looking at something in her past. The face in her mask was Dr Gagarian's, black leather and gristle twisted around a slot mouth and burning red eyes. Around her, the familiars stood still and silent, heads bowed, faces shuttered.

Hari said, 'I did not know him very well, but it seems to me that he wasn't given a chance to fail.'

'That's part of his tragedy,' Gun Ako Akoi said, her mask now showing the face of a young woman glowing with a warrior's fierce arrogant beauty. 'He was chasing a prize others wanted. He failed to see that. Or if he did see it, he failed to understand the consequences. And your father failed too, but because he was time-bound and unable to adapt to new circumstances that's not so surprising.'

Hari said, 'I think that Dr Gagarian and my father were murdered because they were right. Because they were close to success.'

Rav was giving him a hard stare, but he didn't care what the Ardenist thought. Didn't care in that moment whether or not Gun Ako Akoi would grant their wish. He wanted to defend his father and his family. And he wanted to justify his quest for revenge.

Bells tumbled and tinkled and clanged. The manikins around Gun Ako Akoi laughed too. Childish giggles, high ululations, a shrill whistle as the pressure-suited figure vented a tremendous blast of vapour.

Gun Ako Akoi said, 'None of my children are fools, and they do not choose fools to turn. But it's clear that Dr Gagarian was a clever man on a foolish quest. He sought knowledge for knowledge's sake, but he lived in a fallen age where knowledge is currency. Your family knew

that. They made their living rooting through ruins, looking for knowledge to sell. And because there's very little that's new, Dr Gagarian
made himself more valuable with every discovery he made. Until at last
someone attempted to snap him up.'

Hari said, 'If you think his research foolish, then I suppose I'm also a
fool. Because I want to understand what he discovered.'

'No. You want revenge. Which means that you're very much of your
time. As far as you're concerned, understanding Dr Gagarian's research
is a means to an end. Currency. Trade goods.'

'You see things very clearly,' Hari said. 'What do you see inside Dr
Gagarian's head?'

'Forgive the youngblood,' Rav said. 'He's yet to learn any patience.'

'He's hungry for the future,' Gun Ako Akoi said. 'As far as you and I
are concerned, the future is only more of the same. To children like
him, it's full of sweet and toothsome possibilities.'

'I'm not yet ready to retire to a mausoleum,' Rav said.

'Don't think you're any better than me, just because you are out and
about, walking up and down in the world,' Gun Ako Akoi said, and
looked down at Hari. 'Every one of my children and grandchildren is a
special snowflake, but they are all patterned on me. You know about
snowflakes, boy?'

'It's a kind of water ice,' Hari said.

'They do snow here, sometimes. The weathermakers. The cloud
wranglers, the climate cowboys, the friends of the little friend who
is waiting for you outside. It is a special kind of ice. Small crystals with
six-fold symmetry,' Gun Ako Akoi said, and opened a window.

White crystals slanted through darkness. Each with six facets around
its central axis, each different. Some ornamented hexagons, others with
six spiky arms, or six fractal branches, or six spikes bearing miniature
hexagonal platelets . . .

'The encryption of my changelings is based on snowflake forma-
tion,' Gun Ako Akoi said. 'Organised according to a certain symmetry,
every pattern different from moment to moment. But if you have the
base algorithm, you can unlock any of them. As I have unlocked Dr
Gagarian's.'

The view in the window changed. Dense columns of symbols scroll-
ing down unendingly.

'Unfortunately, there's a problem,' Gun Ako Akoi said.

The view changed again, racing above the columns of symbols as they deformed and branched and tangled into each other like a forest of crippled banyans.

Rav said, 'Is that Dr Gagarian's mindscape?'

'What's left of it,' Gun Ako Akoi said. 'I told you that I mourned my child. This is why. Something has eaten Dr Gagarian's memory.'

Hari said, 'Can't you fix it?'

'In some other universe shattered fragments may leap up and jigsaw themselves into a cup, complete, whole, unharmed. But not here. And this is not a ruin; it is more like a cancer. It has devoured Dr Gagarian's files and turned them into something else. Keep the head. You may still have some use for it, and I already have enough mementos.'

The tick-tock matriarch did not dismiss Rav and Hari. Instead, her manikins parted to form a line on either side, and she mounted the stairs backwards, ascending in silence, step by step by step, into the shadows high above.

11

Hari and Rav walked down the long corridor towards the entrance, past banners of red silk and illuminated statues. The manikins marched after them, stepping into doorways one by one.

'Now we know why the skull feeders were so interested in you,' Rav said, when the last of the manikins had departed.

'Assuming Gun Ako Akoi told us the truth,' Hari said. 'Assuming she didn't show us some kind of illusion.'

'Mmm. I suppose it must be hard, realising that you've been made over into a storage device.'

Hari did his best to ignore the taunt, saying, 'She could have copied Dr Gagarian's files, erased the originals, and faked that image of a neural network. Tried to persuade me that it didn't matter, because I had a copy in my head.'

'We think the files are important,' Rav said. 'She doesn't. She's a cantankerous old bitch, but she kept to our agreement.'

'For all the good it did,' Hari said.

'We've come this far, you and I, because we both wanted to know what's in Dr Gagarian's files. We've had a setback. Things didn't work out the way we hoped. But the hunt is still on. What we need to do now is find out what's stashed inside your head. We need to find a really good head doctor.'

'Or go to the Memory Whole.'

'I can't afford the Memory Whole's fees, and neither can you. So we'll have to make do. But don't worry,' Rav said, 'I'm very good at improvising. This is a setback, but nothing I can't fix.'

'I should be angry,' Hari said. 'My father used me, and he didn't tell me how, or why. I should be angry, but I'm not. Because he trusted me. He trusted me to keep his work safe—'

Rav had seized hold of Hari and pushed him against one of the walls and pressed a hand over his mouth. Hari tried to struggle, but the Ardenist held him firm, and smiled down into his face.

'Don't come out until I tell you that it is safe,' he said, and bounded down the corridor and ran straight through the square doorway.

Hari counted out a minute, and another, then crept forward. Light and shadow flickered beyond the doorway. There was the soft sound of falling rain. Hari called to Rav, took another step towards the doorway, and a tiny dark star floated in: a cluster of tiny needles, microbots. His bios locked on to them as they fanned out and whispered through the air towards him. He couldn't look away. Pain swelled behind his left eye and something reached past him towards the needles and they exploded in a stuttering sequence of supernovas. The corridor swung around him, the floor struck the length of his body, and someone was pinching his cheek, telling him to wake up.

It was Riyya. Her coppery hair was plastered to her scalp and water beaded her shift and trousers and dripped on Hari as she helped him to stand. His legs were unhinged, and the walls of the corridor and the doorway's carved columns seemed to reel around him as he and Riyya staggered into the rainy dark. Rav sat just outside, the cloak of his wings folded around him, droplets of rain running down his face and bare chest. Light beat at the bottom of the staircase. One of the scooters was burning from stem to stern, the bones of its frame white-hot inside a haze of hot blue flame and steam. The other scooter, Riyya's, was parked beyond it.

Rav turned his head and looked at Hari. His vertical pupils were huge ovals. 'Old,' he said, speaking with a deliberate effort. 'Getting old and slow.'

'He took your kitbag,' Riyya told Hari.

'Rav?'

'The thief. He drove me off with a smart bullet and set fire to your scooter. When your friend came running out, a swarm of little drones zapped him. The thief went inside, came back out with your kitbag, rode off.'

Hari tried to pull his thoughts together. His left eye pulsed hotly. His tongue felt swollen, scorched. He was trying to remember where he'd seen something like the dark little star before, and then he had it. Mr Mussa's avatar. Its nucleus of microbots.

'Where?' he said. 'Where did he go?'

'We'll find out,' Riyya said, and pulled Hari towards the steps.

Rav called out. Hari turned, saw that the Ardenist had managed to get to his feet.

'The thief is getting away,' Riyya said. 'Stay or come. It's all the same to me.'

Rav tottered forward, swaying like a man crossing a tilting deck. His wings flared as he tried and failed to keep his balance. He fell to his knees, reached towards Hari.

'Wait,' he said.

Hari said to Riyya, 'Can you catch him?'

'I think so.'

'Do your best.'

Hari swung into the saddle behind her, a transparent canopy closed over them, and the scooter rose, turned, tilted its nose down, and shot out into sheer air, curving past the tapering base of the palace, flying out of the shadow of the clouds into sunlight. The drumming of rain on the canopy stopped so suddenly that Hari thought for a moment he'd lost his hearing.

Riyya said that she was tracking the thief using the Climate Corps' panopticon. 'Strictly against regs. But so is conjuring a storm without permission.'

She'd been waiting outside the entrance, she said, using the panopticon to keep watch in case the Corps came looking for her, when she'd spotted a smart bullet coming in over the horizon.

'It was aimed right at me. I barely had time to fire up the scooter, and I flew like I'd never flown before, dodging and diving around the walls. And I managed to conjure a quick rainstorm, too. I thought it would confuse the damn bullet, but it was persistent. It was locked on to me. At last, I swung close around a giant statue and the bullet smacked into the statue's head. Blew it clean off. It screamed at me, just before it exploded,' Riyya said. 'I can still hear that scream. So then I headed back, arrived just in time to see the thief zap your friend and steal your kitbag. And then I found you, and here we are.'

Hari leaned against the length of Riyya's back, into the warm scent of her hair. 'Do you know where he's going?'

'There's nothing in this sector but scrub and swamp and saurians. If he doesn't double back, if he keeps heading antispinward, I reckon he's heading for the port.'

'All the way around the world to Down Town?'

'There's a second port, opposite Down Town,' Riyya said. 'They counterbalance each other.'

Hari remembered watching Ophir as Rav's ship had spiralled in. A silvery sphere shining in the sunlit dark, a thin thread extending from its waist, thickening into a spiky little blob at its far end: the beanstalk elevators running out to the docks in synchronous orbit. But as the world city had revolved another beanstalk had appeared, exactly opposite the first. As if Ophir had been pierced by a very long and slender needle.

'He's going to leave,' he said. 'He's going to meet a ship and leave Ophir.'

'If he gets there first,' Riyya said. 'He has a good head start, but his scooter is a civilian model. Mine is a little faster.'

'Fast enough?'

'Let's see.'

They were following a roadway now. A black line slashed straight through scrub and red rocks. Rugged cliffs rolled up from the horizon, with a transparent bulkhead looming above. Hari felt an airy rush in his stomach as the scooter swooped down and the cliffs smashed towards them. Towering masses of obdurate rock. He flinched with his whole body, and the scooter shot through a round hatchway, the smooth walls of a tunnel blurring past on either side, and came out into sunlight and rose above thick forest studded with grassy clearings in which white pyramids stood.

'There he is,' Riyya said, pointed to a small black pip high in the air.

Hari's bios gave him a close-up of the thief's scooter. He glimpsed its rider, a small slim person in black, pale-skinned like Riyya, and then it was gone, dropping sharply towards the trees.

Riyya said, 'He knows we're following him.'

'Can't you bring him down with some kind of weather?'

'He's travelling too fast. But if he's heading where I think he's heading, I may be able to work up a little surprise.'

The thief's scooter was flying just above the treetops now. They chased after it over long reaches of forest, past clusters of white pyramids. There was no sign that any were inhabited. The only animals

Hari saw were birds labouring in a ragged vee above the forest's green sea, scattering when the scooter overtook them.

Spires and stacks of rock came up over the curve of the horizon, standing at the foot of the sector's far bulkhead. The thief's scooter shot between two spires and disappeared. Riyya whooped and flew at the spires full tilt, passing so close to one of them that Hari could have reached out and touched its back flank. The scooter kicked, rising above a rocky turret. The branches of a thorn tree rooted on its flat top passed just a metre below. Riyya dropped down again, into the long groove of a gully, heading towards the foot of one of the biggest of the spires. Hari glimpsed the round mouth of another tunnel; then the scooter shot into it and they were suddenly in twilight with dabs of luminous stuff flickering past on either side.

Hari put his mouth close to Riyya's ear. 'How do you know he went this way?'

'It's the only way out of this sector for thirty klicks on either side,' Riyya said. 'The elevators to the port are beyond. Don't worry. We chase each other like this all the time, for fun.'

'This is fun?'

'If it isn't, I don't know what fun is.'

A small circle of brassy light appeared ahead, rushed towards them. A few moments later the scooter shot out into open air and immediately began to climb. Riyya's head turned this way and that as she searched the sky for her prey.

'There!'

Hari followed the line of her arm, saw a small bead against the sunstrip's glare.

Below, broken roads crossed sandy scrubland potholed with craters. Another ancient battleground. Ahead, a lip of green appeared at the horizon with a thread rising beyond it – the slim shaft of the elevator stack, rising straight up from the floor and punching through the overhead, the shell of the world city. Clouds hung close to its lower levels, growing thicker and darker, grey and purple-black, merging, revolving, like a giant version of one of Rav's smoke rings. Light blinked in the shadows they cast and a few moments later Hari heard a distant drum roll.

Riyya's weather.

'We can't catch him before he reaches the elevators,' Riyya said. 'But the storm might bring him down. Hang on. We're in for a bumpy ride.'

The churning cloud ring trailed skirts of rain. The thief's scooter was silhouetted against them as it fled across a series of tiered structures. Riyya and Hari followed. Flat platforms packed with soldierly rows of plants rose in helices around central columns, and the columns were linked by slender swooping ramps to roadways that ran between their footings towards the elevators.

Lightning lit the interior of the clouds, flashed rain into silvery sheets. The thief's scooter jinked and lunged as it dropped towards the collar of buildings at the base of the elevator stack.

'I'm having a problem,' Riyya said.

'What kind of problem?'

'They've found me. And they've commandeered my scooter.'

She was hunched forward in her seat, twitching the steering yoke as the scooter slowed and began to plane through the air in a long, curving fall.

Hari said, 'Is this the thief's friends?'

Riyya gave the yoke a final twist and sat back and pushed her hands through her coppery hair. 'The Corps. They've been looking for me ever since that unscripted rainstorm at the festival. And now they've locked me out. Of the scooter, of everything. I'm sorry, Hari. I malfed our mission.'

'It isn't over yet,' Hari said.

But he felt a cold dismay as the scooter fell between tiers of elevated fields. The ring of clouds around the elevators was thinning. Breaking up into ragged fragments. There was no sign of the thief. And the scooter was skimming towards a flat, vivid green meadow, slowing, thumping down, slewing to a halt in a fantail of mud and water.

'That's that,' Riyya said, and popped the canopy.

Hari asked if the port had a train station.

'Of course it does. But we won't be able to catch the thief now. And the Corps police will be coming for us.'

'I think I know who the thief is working for, so I'm not about to give up the chase yet. How about you?'

Riyya turned in her seat and studied him. Her expression was grim, pinched with frustration, but after a moment a small smile plucked at the corners of her mouth and she said, 'Why not? I can hardly get into more trouble than I'm already in.'

As they splashed through ankle-deep water blanketed with ferny fragments – azolla, according to Hari's bios – towards the edge of the field, Hari told Riyya about Mr D.V. Mussa. His interest in Dr Gagarian's head, his avatar and its nucleus of microbots.

'He paid someone to follow me,' Hari said. 'To take Dr Gagarian's head after the tick-tock matriarch had unlocked it. He's a free trader. He has a ship. That's where the thief must be headed.'

'You think he's planning to leave Ophir,' Riyya said.

'Rav has a ship too. It's docked at Down Town's port.'

'He might not forgive you for leaving him behind.'

'He needs me. And it seems that I still need him.'

'But can you trust—'

A window scrolled open in the air directly in front of them. A woman looked out, looked at Riyya.

'There you are, sweetheart,' she said. 'What a time we've had, looking for you.'

'I'm not coming back,' Riyya said. 'I won't come back.'

She stepped sideways, but the window drifted in front of her.

'I don't believe I've met your little friend. Did he put you up to this?'

The woman was smiling, but there was no warmth in it. Her skin was pale and her hair was wheat-coloured and cropped short, but Hari could see the resemblance to Riyya in the bones of her face, the shape of her eyes. There were two gold bars pinned to the collar of her white shift.

'It was entirely my idea,' Riyya said, and began to walk forward.

Hari walked beside her, sloshing through ferny water. The window drifted ahead of them.

'You will have to stand in front of a disciplinary board, but I'll be there with you,' Riyya's mother said. 'I'll speak for you. I'll help you in every way I can.'

'If you want to help, stop and arrest the thief we're chasing,' Riyya said. 'He stole something that's connected to the murder of my father, and the hijack of my friend's ship. We need to catch him, and the person who hired him. We need to ask them some serious questions. You can help us, or you can get out of our way.'

'I'm afraid that's outside the Corps' jurisdiction. As are the troubles of your friend Gajananvihari Pilot. Yes,' Riyya's mother said, looking at Hari, 'I know who you are.'

'Then you'll also know why your daughter and I are helping each other,' Hari said.

'And why you should help us,' Riyya said.

'I'll help you get through this,' her mother said. 'You have my word.'

'But you won't help me catch the people who killed my father,' Riyya said.

'You already know the answer to that. We have talked about it a dozen times.'

'And you won't do anything that will violate protocol. That doesn't have a *precedent*,' Riyya said, and bent and scooped up a handful of fern and mud and flung it at the window.

Her mother didn't even blink as the clot spun through her image. 'You're still grieving for your father,' she said. 'I'll make sure that the board takes that into account. You'll be demoted. That's inevitable. But I promise that any sentence they pass will be suspended. We put this behind us and start over . . . What are you doing, sweetheart? Is that in any way sensible?'

Hari and Riyya had reached the low rail at the edge of the field. Riyya climbed over it; after a moment's hesitation Hari followed her. They balanced on a narrow fringe twenty metres above a steady traffic of trucks moving along a roadway. The window hung in the air in front of them.

'I really think you should wait for the police,' Riyya's mother said.

Riyya took Hari's hand. 'Ready?'

Hari looked down at the drop. The railing was pressed against the back of his thighs. 'I don't know much about falling. Is this survivable?'

'I know what I'm doing,' Riyya said.

'Don't let her do this,' her mother said.

'On the count of three,' Riyya said. Her grip on Hari's hand was hot and tight. She was watching a truck approach. Its big hopper was heaped with red sticks.

'Wait,' her mother said. 'Wait, youngbloods.'

Her voice was slurred and something strange was happening to her image. It was stretching, breaking apart in fountains of coloured dots that spun and coalesced.

'Wait,' Rav said. 'I'm coming straight for you.'

Hari looked all around, saw something small and white streaking through the air above the tiers of fields, a small boat or gig in the shape of a white, long-necked bird. Rav sat in the hollow between its furled wings, behind one of Gun Ako Akoi's manikins, the one with the silvery face and riveted corselet and conical cap.

The white bird shot past the edge of the field, curved back, and came to a halt directly in front of Hari and Riyya. It was coated in what looked like real feathers, ruffling in the warm breeze. Its small head had a black mask, an orange beak. It extended a short pont towards them and Rav stood up and smiled at Hari.

'You shouldn't try to fly before you're fully fledged. Hop aboard, youngblood. The little weathermaker's friends are on their way.'

'Riyya is coming with us,' Hari said.

'I don't think so.'

'Then she's coming with me.'

'And you'll both go directly to jail,' Rav said, and pointed towards the elevator stack.

Four scooters were rising from the collar at the base of the stack, spreading out as they accelerated through the tattered remnants of Riyya's storm.

'She helped us,' Hari said. 'Now we must help her.'

He and Rav stared at each other; then Rav shrugged. 'Sentiment will be your downfall, youngblood. Climb aboard, both of you. We'll give these bravos from the Climate Corps a run for their credit, and when we've shaken them off we'll head directly to the docks.'

'No,' Hari said. 'We'll head to Down Town. I need to have a few words with my uncle before we leave.'

12

'Are you sure you want to do this on your own?' Rav said.

'It's family business,' Hari said.

'Just you and him and his killing machine.'

'He won't use it against me.'

'Your people are very different from mine,' Rav said.

They were sitting amongst dry weeds on top of a half-ruined tower, looking out across clumps of palms and stretches of zebra grass towards the Pilot family compound. It was early in the morning in Down Town's sector. Riyya had ridden the elevator to the docks and Rav's ship, where she would be safe from the Climate Corps police, and her mother.

Hari said, 'Of course, if there should be any trouble . . .'

Rav said, 'I'll be right there.'

'I want you to call the police.'

'You think I can't deal with a single myrmidon?'

'I'm not worried about the myrmidon,' Hari said. 'I'm worried that my uncle may have taken other precautions.'

As he walked along the wide empty road towards the family compound, dawn light brightening in the sunstrip high above, his shadow wheeling hugely behind him, Hari thought that it would be much easier to go up and head out after the thief than do this. Easier, yes, but then he'd never know if his uncle had betrayed him. He'd never know what his uncle knew about his father and his family.

It was like one of Professor Ari Aluthgamage's hinge points. Diverging paths leading to very different histories.

The gate recognised him. He walked past the dry bowl of the fountain in the weed-grown courtyard, down the short corridor with statues of his ancestors on either side, through the big double door into his uncle's chamber.

Tamonash Pilot was eating breakfast at the far end of the long, blue-tinted room. Looking up as Hari walked towards him, greeting him warmly, telling him to sit down, asking if he would like a little something.

'I came here to talk,' Hari said. He shrugged his kitbag from his shoulders and sat on the other side of the little table.

The myrmidon behind Tamonash was shuttered and still, but Hari felt its attention sweep over him. He had to assume that the machine hadn't noticed the packet he'd sent before entering the room, or the response he'd received.

'I've been very worried,' Tamonash said, although he did not sound or look worried, perched on his chair in black pyjamas, white hair falling around his face as he bent over his bowl of porridge. 'You did not come back from your appointment with that tick-tock woman, I could not contact you, and then the Climate Corps contacted *me*, and asked me to verify your identity. What kind of trouble did you get into, Gajananvihari?'

'Nothing I could not handle, Uncle.'

'The Ardenist led you on, no doubt. You would do better to listen to the advice of your uncle rather than that of your so-called friends.'

'Talking of friends, where is your friend Mr Mussa? His ship has just left Ophir. Did you have a falling-out?'

'Mr Mussa's business is his business, not mine.'

They were staring at each other across the breakfast clutter. After a moment, Tamonash smiled and said, 'You have been on an adventure. Perhaps you'd like to tell your uncle about it. Did the tick-tock woman help you find what you are looking for?'

'Actually, I lost something,' Hari said, and opened the kitbag and showed Tamonash that it was empty.

Behind the old man, the myrmidon shifted very slightly.

Tamonash looked at the kitbag and then looked at Hari, his spoon halfway to his mouth. A pearl of porridge splashed on the hammered-brass tabletop. He said, 'What have you done with the tick-tock's head?'

'It was stolen by Mr Mussa.'

'Don't be ridiculous. He is an honest trader.'

'I was knocked out by a little cluster of microbots exactly like the microbots of Mr Mussa's avatar. You remember, I'm sure, that I told you a djinn is protecting me. It reached out to the microbots, and they exploded. A series of very bright flashes that knocked me out. I chased the thief to the port on the opposite side of the world. The port from which Mr Mussa's ship departed soon after the thief escaped.'

Rav had tagged the cryoflask when he and Hari had arrived at Ophir – 'Of course I did, youngblood. Don't expect me to apologise for what turned out to be absolutely necessary' – and his son had tracked it from Gun Ako Akoi's palace to the elevator stack, tracked it as it had risen to the docks, and to Mr Mussa's ship.

'It is a very interesting story,' Tamonash said, 'but the evidence is entirely circumstantial.'

'The thief knew the djinn would trigger the microbots. Who told him about it, I wonder?'

'You lost the head of Dr Gagarian, and you come here making wild accusations—'

'Swear,' Hari said. 'Swear on the honour of our family that you didn't.'

The myrmidon jacked to its full height, turret head prickling with the muzzles of various anti-personnel armaments, targeting systems throwing a pattern of red and green cross-hairs and dots across Hari's torso.

'I would be careful, if I were you,' Tamonash said. 'Making wild and unfounded accusations can be very dangerous.'

'We should both be careful,' Hari said, and sent a command to the repurposed battlebot that stood amongst the line of old machines that faced the view of Earth's icy sea.

The myrmidon took a step forward, flanking Tamonash, as the battlebot marched to the centre of the room. Its clanking tread shivered the floor. It raised its two pairs of flexible arms, the multitools at their ends spun, and the teardrop of its body blistered and dimpled with internal adjustments. Many of its sensors were offline or permanently disconnected, but Hari believed that the basic array would be more than enough to deal with the myrmidon, believed that the myrmidon's tactical weapons, designed to put down human assassins, would be no match for the bot's mass and armour and hardened nervous system.

'Now I did not know that was still functional,' Tamonash said thoughtfully.

'There's only a fractional charge in its fission batteries,' Hari said. 'But it should be more than enough.'

For a moment, there was dead silence in the cold, blue room. Then

Tamonash smiled and gave a verbal command to the myrmidon, telling it to stand down. Saying to Hari, 'We are family. We should be able to talk to each other without making silly threats.'

Beside him, the myrmidon retracted various muzzles and discharge spikes.

Hari sent a command to the battlebot. Sharp spurts of compressed air hissed as it lowered its arms.

'Why did you do it?' he said.

'It is a long story, nephew. Long and painful. It began many years before I met Mr Mussa.'

'Then you admit that you and he—'

'Allow me to tell it my way. From the beginning. But first, please, have some tea,' Tamonash said, and poured a measure into a white porcelain cup and set it in front of Hari.

Hari drank the bitter black tea and smashed the cup down 'Now tell me everything. From the beginning.'

'Do you know what a coin is?'

'A kind of portable credit.'

Nabhomani had once brought several coins back to the ship. Handing them out as presents, laughing, saying, 'Look! Look how far we've fallen!'

Tamonash said, 'When it comes to family, love and hate are two sides of the same coin. I'm sure you were sometimes angry with your brothers, Gajananvihari. But you always loved them, no matter what. It was like that with me and your father. I loved Aakash when I was about as young as you were now, and he was two years older. And then things changed, and the coin flipped from love to hate. All because of your mother. All because of Mullai. Who was once my lover. Did Aakash ever tell you about that? I thought not.'

Tamonash leaned back in his chair and crooked one leg over the other and clasped his hands across his belly. The nails of his bare feet were painted bright red. He wore a silver ring on one big toe.

'It began when Aakash had the idea to turn our family's fortune around by buying a wreck of a ship, renovating it, and using it as a base for trade and the research into old technologies in which we were both interested. We were young, we were ambitious, it seemed that there was nothing we couldn't do. And I was in love with Mullai, and she was in love with me.

'We had first met, Mullai and I, when we bid against each other for various salvaged machines. This was on Ceres, where she had been born and raised. I won the bid, we fell to talking about the defunct ship that Aakash and I were refurbishing, and when I returned to Ophir she came with me and joined our crew.

'I named it. Did you know that? I named the ship *Pabuji's Gift*. An homage to our family's long history. The fashion amongst baseliner families and clans to undo the homogenisation of the True Empire by reviving old traditions and customs is beginning to fade now, but it was still strong then. Like many others, our family had traced their ancestors, given their children names of their storied dead. So why not name our ship for the local god of the region where our family lived before it was scattered across Earth and other worlds? Aakash said at first that it was a silly superstition, but I prevailed. And I wonder now if it was part of the reason for his betrayal. That he betrayed me to assert his strength, his will over mine.

'I failed to see that Mullai was falling in love with your father, even while she was still in love with me, and I with her. I was so in love, in fact, that when one of my friends tried to warn me I had him banished from the crew. We baseliners pride ourselves that we are a kinder, more rational people than the True. But in truth, like them, we have not lost all of our ape heritage. We are drawn to powerful people. And Aakash was one such. I was – I am – clever enough. I am admired by those who share my special interests. But Aakash had that particular quality that transmutes base admiration to the gold of love. He was one of those men for whom people will give up their lives. They will leave everything behind to follow him. They will die for him. That was how I lost Mullai.'

Tamonash was looking past Hari. Looking past everything in the room, the compound, the world city.

'The ship was not finished when Aakash took her on her shakedown voyage. I spent every waking hour fixing systems that had revealed flaws when they became fully operational, attempting to complete work that should have been finished before we set out. I was very busy, but I was also a fool. A blind fool. I did not see what was happening. I did not know anything about it until we returned to the docks at Ophir, and Mullai told me. Told me that she had been Aakash's lover for some time before we had set out, and that during that voyage she had realised that she must choose between him and me. And she had chosen him. So that was the end of that, and that was the end of my relationship with

Aakash. I allowed him to buy out my share in the ship. I stayed here, in the family home. Where I have been ever since.

'Your father is a selfish man, Gajananvihari, as many powerful men are. Ambitious, single-minded, and utterly selfish. Unable to see that other people may have other ambitions, other dreams. That is why he made your two brothers in his likeness. That is why he chose to pass over into a kind of life after death, rather than give himself back to the Wheel. Yes, I know that your brothers are his clones, and I know how Mullai died, and Rakesh. I kept track. I even tried to contact Aakash, once or twice. After Mullai died, after he passed over. He never replied. I told myself it did not matter. I made a life for myself here. I partnered with a kind and loving woman, may she rest in peace. I have a strong, capable daughter, and she has given me two grandchildren and we are building a business together.

'And then Aakash's ship was hijacked, and you arrived here. Perhaps you do not know it, but you look so much like your mother. And you were – you are – caught up in your father's obsession. It broke my heart to see it. When Mr Mussa came to me with his plan, his proposition, I thought that if the damned head was gone you would be free. You would be able to take up your own life. Perhaps you would come to work for me, perhaps not. But you would be free of your father's influence. And yes, I admit it, I would have been free of it too,' Tamonash said, looking at Hari with a steady gaze. 'Well, who knows why we do the things we do? But I did not think, I really did not, that it would end as it has.'

Hari didn't know how much of the story to believe. He knew only that he couldn't forgive his uncle. Couldn't accept his confession, or his guilt. He was gripped by a cold, angry purpose.

He said, 'Tell me about Mr Mussa's proposition. Tell me everything.'

Tamonash said, 'You share half my brother's genome, and you have something of his single-mindedness, and something of his ability to attract and influence other people. You don't realise that yet, I think. I doubt that you were given much of a chance to use it, on the ship. It is a gift, a very useful gift, but be careful. Like a coin, it has two sides.'

'Humour my single-mindedness, Uncle.'

'Mr Mussa told me that he had a client who wanted to know what Dr Gagarian had discovered. He promised me that no harm would come to you or the Ardenist. And in that, at least, he has kept his word.'

'Who is this client?'

Tamonash studied Hari for a moment, hands steepled under his chin. Then he said, 'When we made our arrangement, Mr Mussa told me that he would be able to sell the knowledge to a rival of Dr Gagarian's. He did not give his client's name, but dropped enough hints to allow me to guess it. To let me think I had discovered a secret he wanted hidden. The person he pointed me towards was Ioni Robles Nguini, a philosopher who lives in Greater Brazil, on Earth. I see you recognise the name.'

'He was working with Dr Gagarian and my father,' Hari said. 'Is he still alive? Have you talked to him?'

'I talked to a representative of his family, who claimed to know nothing about Mr Mussa. I suppose that he was attempting to conceal the identity of his real client by pointing me in the wrong direction.'

'But you agreed to this proposition of his anyway.'

'I wanted to free you of your burden, nephew,' Tamonash said blandly.

It was impossible to make out if he was telling the truth.

'You told Mr Mussa where I was going,' Hari said. 'And he made arrangements to steal the head.'

Tamonash didn't deny this.

'Who ambushed us?' Hari said 'Who stole the head? Was he working for you and Mr Mussa, or for this client? Is he still here, on Ophir?'

'It was Mr Mussa's daughter. He created her during his last days in corporeal form. She's a kind of clone. Her genome contains two copies of his X chromosomes, and she has been tweaked, and she is a lot older than she looks. Be careful, if you ever meet her. Hope that you don't.'

'Mr Mussa's ship is heading towards Tannhauser Gate,' Hari said. 'Rav's son tracked it when it left Ophir, and is tracking it as we speak.'

'You are going to chase after him. You and the Ardenist.'

'Of course.'

'I suppose that it would be pointless to attempt to persuade you that it would be dangerous and foolish.'

'It would.'

'My offer still stands, nephew. You are welcome to come and work for me. You could spend some time on Earth. You could visit Ioni Robles Nguini. Talk to him. If Dr Gagarian found anything of any significance, if you and Ioni Robles Nguini can work out what it was, I will do my best to help you understand it. I have many contacts. Make use of them. Make use of me. We are, after all, family.'

There it was.

'I have lost my family,' Hari said. He pushed to his feet and turned his back on his uncle and walked away. Tamonash calling after him, pleading with him to stay, saying that the people who wanted the head would come after both of them, as he walked through the cold blue light of Earth, walked out of his family's old home.

The battlebot followed him. As protection, and because he had one more use for it.

'I would have killed him,' Rav said.

'Our peoples are very different,' Hari said.

'You are very different. Your blood runs much colder than mine. You realise that your uncle will be targeted by the Saints. They will want to know what you told him, and they won't want to leave any loose ends . . .'

They were riding the elevator up to the docks, and *Brighter Than Creation's Dark*.

'I've taken care of that,' Hari said. He opened a window showing the viewpoint of the battlebot as it stamped along the road towards Down Town, and told Rav its destination.

Rav laughed. 'You're almost as crazy as me. Those particular Saints are strictly local. Low-grade recruiters. They didn't have anything to do with the hijack. Or with the murder of Salx Minnot Flores, either.'

'But if their superiors did, if those superiors sent that message to me, well, now I have sent them a reply. Also, the police will trace the battlebot back to my uncle. Maybe they will arrest him, maybe not. But if he has any sense he will tell them the whole wretched story, and ask for protection.'

'Mmm. That's actually almost smart.'

'Thank you.'

'How long will it take that thing to reach Down Town?'

'About forty minutes. And it will take ten or twenty minutes more to find the school and start its work.'

'And by then we'll be on our way to Tannhauser Gate. Which is just as well, because Ophir's police really won't be happy about the trouble you're about to cause.'

'I have no plans to return,' Hari said.

PART FOUR
PIRATES OF
THE ASTEROIDS

PART FOUR

1

At age sixteen, Hari jumped ship.

It was in the Commonwealth of Sugar Mountain, shortly before Dr
Gagarian came aboard. Hari had gone shoreside with Nabhomani, his
first time off *Pabuji's Gift*, to observe how trade negotiations were
handled.

'It will be dull and tedious work, entirely lacking in excitement,'
Nabhomani told Hari. 'Which is no doubt why Aakash allowed you to
come along. The lives of these people are bound by rules and regulations they've been accumulating and refining and discussing for over
a thousand years. It's their religion, their great work, but as far as
outsiders are concerned it's about as thrilling as cataloguing every grain
of sand on Mars. They even managed to bore the Trues into allowing
them to become a neutral enclave, way back when. But boring work,
tedious work, that's no bad thing, Hari. You'll witness contract negotiations without the usual distractions – drinking, drugging, bribery and
corruption, all the other good things that make life worthwhile. Pay
attention, little brother, work up a detailed and accurate report for our
father who art in his own little heaven, and I'll make sure we get some
of the good stuff next time.'

The Commonwealth was a free-fall reef, seven gardens between one
and five kilometres in diameter set at irregular intervals along a central
spine spun from comet CHON. The whole looking, as *Pabuji's Gift*
approached it, like a string of soap bubbles pierced by a needle, each
bubble brilliantly lit by banks of sun-mirrors.

Hari and Nabhomani rode for some sixty kilometres down the spine
in a rail car with fittings of real wood and metal, and padded walls clad
in hand-sewn tapestries showing heroic scenes from the construction of

the reef. Once luxurious, the rail car's appointments were now worn and shabby. Like everywhere else, Sugar Mountain was pinched by the long, belt-wide recession.

The rail car traversed three bubble habitats – gulfs of sunlight and air and cloud forests, stacks of tethered or floating platforms – before arriving at the trading centre, which was set just outside the interchange station of the fourth and largest habitat. A cylindrical installation of about twenty storeys, offices and meeting rooms, and chilly guest suites where Hari and Nabhomani were the only occupants.

The negotiations concerned the renewal of the Commonwealth's collision-protection system, using components that *Pabuji's Gift* had salvaged from a dead garden. Terms of payment for the components and for the supply of rare earths and metals required for fabrication of spare parts, contractual guarantees, penalties for overrun costs . . . Arid and interminably prolonged discussions that anatomised every clause and footnote in interminable detail. The Commonwealth's officials were tall and mostly pale-skinned, dressed in trousers and collarless tunics of various shades of grey. Austere, earnest, unsmiling. Hari and Nabhomani were restricted to the trading centre, shuttling between their guest suite, presentations by various officials and endless discussions of minor changes to sub-sub-clauses in contracts, and formal meals where edible morsels were extracted with special instruments from stringy pods or spiny clusters of leaves, and dipped in simmering pots of melted cheese or bubbling oil using another set of special instruments, with appropriate gestures of politeness and in strict rotation amongst the diners.

Despite the tedium, Hari was constantly on edge, worried that he'd violate some important protocol or custom, or fall asleep at the dining table while one of their hosts was explaining the superiority of the Commonwealth's culture and biomes, its arts (very long atonal operas, nanosculpture, dabbing pigments on stretched canvas to represent mindscapes produced by exotic mathematics, flower-breeding) and, most of all, its political system, in which every citizen voted ten or twenty times a day on the distribution of various resources between habitats, minor changes in civil and judicial codes, and so on and so forth, boredom and fear and resentment knotting inside Hari's chest until he felt that he could scarcely breathe.

The third meeting of the second day was enlivened by the attendance of several technicians who gave short presentations about potential problems uncovered during inspection of the control system. One of the technicians immediately caught Hari's attention: she looked a little like Sora Exodus Adel. Sora, whom he still loved with a kind of hopeless Platonic idealism because she represented the possibility of a life other than the life he had. It wasn't so much the physical resemblance as the way the technician held her head and tilted her chin, the way she sometimes smiled when one of her co-workers made a point, a brief faint twitch at the corners of her mouth, sly and private. After she and the other technicians had finished their presentations and left, Hari felt a dull echo of the hopeless yearning sadness that had swamped him after Sora had disembarked at Trantor, and Jyotirmoy had run away from his parents.

Nabhomani told Hari that introducing the technicians into the negotiations was an attempt to drive down the price of the components. 'They insist that the flaws they have uncovered are worse than they actually are; we must pretend that we are not insulted by the implication that we are trying to sell them damaged goods, and prove that the flaws are minor and easy to fix. What you have to remember, brother, is that the good citizens of the Commonwealth love this kind of thing. They live for it. When they aren't negotiating with traders and other governments, the Commonwealth's habitats are negotiating amongst themselves, or arguing over refinements of their political system. It's a massive sink of time and human energy, and generates nothing of any value. That's why the Commonwealth has such a huge internal economy, but so little trading credit. All it has to offer in exchange for essential imports is the use of its ship-repair facility – which admittedly is much better than most – and the products of its guest workers. Who because they get their hands dirty doing actual work are never allowed to become citizens.'

The next day, Hari rebelled. After the last meeting ended, he and Nabhomani had two hours of so-called free time before the beginning of the long evening meal. Nabhomani retired to his room for a nap; Hari broke out of the trading centre. Or rather, he simply swam out: the Commonwealth believed that its guests, like its citizens, would unquestioningly obey every rule and regulation, and did not see the need to enforce any of them. Hari reached the station without encountering any guards, locked doors or paranoid security bots, caught the next rail car out and alighted at the second stop, one of the guest-worker towns.

He had a simple plan: he wanted to look for the young technician, whose name was Sharma Song. He didn't much care whether or not she lived in this town (there were dozens of guest-worker towns, and he couldn't use his bios to search for her in the Commonwealth's registry). It was the quest rather than the prize that was important. Escaping the prison of protocol. Exploring this strange new world. Embarking on an adventure.

The town was a crowded labyrinth of narrow corridors and tunnels and common spaces threaded around, through, and between irregular stacks of buildings. Domed gardens and roofed yards were set in the perimeter walls, and shafts let in filtered sunlight in some places, but otherwise it was lit by luminous panels and chains of floating lamps. There were workshops and fabbing mills, cafés with tiny counters and perches for just two or three customers, augmentation parlours specialising in tattoos or cosmetic surgery or implants, little stores selling everything from handmade food to vat-grown pets. There were churches and chapels and temples, many featuring iconography venerating the Bright Moment: portraits and effigies of the cyclist in a hundred styles, replicas of his bicycle, looped picts of the flare of light reaching out, engulfing him. Hari found it odd and disturbing to see these familiar images in this strange place.

Most of the town's inhabitants were smaller than him. Dwarfed descendants of Outers, enclaves of refugees from Earth, a few clades and races that Hari recognised, many he'd never seen before, an unending stream of strangers hurrying past on mysterious errands and missions, glimpses of incomprehensible lives. Strange buildings, strange signs, strange customs, snatches of strange music, strange odours from strange food . . .

One sector specialised in manufacturing pressure suits. There were workshops dedicated to making different components – liners, helmets, gloves and boots, lifepacks, avatars. There were parlours that measured and fitted customers. There were studios where artists worked on customised and elaborate paint jobs for chestplates and helmets, in the ancient tradition of Outers. Familiar work on familiar, utilitarian equipment.

When Nabhomani found him, Hari was talking to one of the suit painters, an old woman dressed in an ankle-length smock with many pockets. They were sitting outside the spare little cubbyhole of her workshop, drinking tea and nibbling salted curds, olives, and raw vegetables that were much tastier than anything Hari had eaten in the trading centre. A chestplate stood on a rack, marked out with the lineaments of a design – a standard, idealised representation of Sri Hong-Owen, her hands cupped around the star Fomalhaut and the halo of its dust ring – that the old woman was creating for a devout follower of the Church of the Human Uplift.

When Nabhomani swam out of a corridor mouth and drifted past the lighted alcove of a café towards him, Hari wasn't especially shocked or dismayed. He'd been expecting it. He'd known that he wouldn't be able to escape for long.

Nabhomani spoke to the old woman in a language that Hari's bios didn't recognise, full of clicks and aspirants (he later learned that it was a bastard dialect of Xhosa and Pinglish). The old woman replied in the same language, and told Hari in Portuga that it had been a pleasure talking with him, and should he ever need his suit decorated he should come to her. If she could not satisfy his requirements she knew everyone else in the trade here; she would make sure that he got what he wanted for the best price.

'Let me give you something for your hospitality, mother,' Nabhomani said, but the old woman said there was no obligation, it was a pleasure to meet his younger brother.

'No obligation is the worst kind of obligation,' Nabhomani told Hari a little later, after he'd found them seats at a tiny bar that sold pineapple juice and spicy bean-sprout pancakes.

'We were just talking in a general way,' Hari said. 'I didn't tell her anything about our trade.'

'I'm not worried about that. You don't know anything about anything worth knowing. But I am worried that you fell into that old she-devil's clutches,' Nabhomani said. 'I bet you don't even know who she is.'

'I suppose you're going to tell me she doesn't really paint p-suits.'

'She also runs this ward, which means she runs about a quarter of the town. And she does most of her business through a system of favours . . . Did she offer to introduce you to that technician you were mooning over? Or tell you where she lived?' Nabhomani smiled. As always, he was impeccably groomed, hair lustrous with scented oil, his shirt luminously white and fastened by silver pins, little finger cocked as he fed himself a morsel of pancake. 'You're going to tell me I'm a hypocrite. That you only wanted to have a little adventure, like the adventures I'm always talking about. The thing is, Hari, there's a time and a place. It isn't just that the old woman would have expected you do to her a favour in return for her help. If you'd found that technician, if you'd slept with her, it would have been an act of industrial sabotage. It would have blown the deal. You would have been arrested, I would have been arrested, and I don't like to think what would have happened to the technician.'

'I didn't do anything.'

'And no harm's been done. I patched over your absence at dinner. And tomorrow, after we've endured the contract-signing ceremony, we're finished here.'

'Assuming I come back with you.'

Hari felt guilty, was angry because he felt guilty. He hadn't told the old woman about Sharma Song, but he had been thinking about telling her. He knew he'd done wrong, knew his so-called rebellion was dull and obvious, but resented Nabhomani's patronising homilies.

Nabhomani sucked on his bulb of pineapple juice, pretending to think about that. He said, 'It isn't difficult to become a guest worker, but it is almost impossible to leave if you do. And even more difficult to become a citizen of the Commonwealth.'

'Who says I want to become a citizen?'

'I know I wouldn't. The endless debates, endlessly considering and voting on infinitesimally trivial matters . . . It must be like being stuck in a trade meeting for the rest of your life. No, it would be much better to claim refugee status. After two or three years of trying to live on welfare you'd be allowed to become a guest worker. And then you'd have to learn a trade, and stick at it for your entire life, never doing anything that other people haven't already done. Because that's how it is here. Custom and convention stifles enterprise and innovation. Maybe you'd even meet someone you liked enough to partner, although your choices would be pretty limited because there isn't much exogamy here. The clades and clans and enclave nations like to stick to their own. And, of course, you'd spend your whole life in a little town like this one,' Nabhomani said, 'because guest workers aren't allowed to leave Sugar Mountain, ever.'

'You're good at this,' Hari said. 'At selling a place.'

'If I'm selling anything, I'm selling you what you already have, because it's a better deal than anything you'll find here.'

'Yet the people here seem happy.'

'Because they don't know any better. And because they are too polite to express their real feelings. Politeness is a survival trait in crowded, confined places. If the denizens of this town weren't so incredibly polite, they'd all have killed each other long ago. But you know more than they do, Hari. You know what's out there. All kinds of people, all kinds of places, all kinds of ways of living. Cities and settlements, worlds and worlds and worlds. You want to jump ship for the first place you've seen? Fine. But if you want my opinion, you should see a few other places first. Live a little, little brother. I know I have,' Nabhomani said, and commenced to tell several improbable stories that at last wore through Hari's shell of sulky resentment and won a couple of smiles from him.

They swam through the town's mazy corridors to the station and rode the next rail car back to the trade centre, and caught a few hours' sleep before the last round of negotiations, and the interminable contract-signing ceremony. And that was the end of Hari's first and last act of rebellion against his family and his birthright.

2

Hari told Riyya about his adventure in the Commonwealth of Sugar Mountain because he wanted to show her that he knew a little about running away – running away from a family that had mapped out every detail of your future. He wanted her to know that he understood how she felt, that they had something in common, but Riyya pointed out that he was trying to find his way back to his family, hoping to save any still alive and win back *Pabuji's Gift*, while she had left everything of her old life behind and had no intention of returning. And besides, leaving the Climate Corps had not been a spur-of-the-moment decision. She had been thinking about it for several years, ever since she'd started to visit her father. Wondering what direction her life might take if, like him, she quit the Corps. Daydreaming about seeing something of the other cities and settlements of the Belt. She'd even ridden up to the docks not so long ago, and found a place where ship crews hung out – although she hadn't dared say anything to anyone, and had bolted when a woman her age had offered to buy her a drink.

And then she'd met Hari and Rav, and after their little adventure it had become impossible to stay in the Corps, in Ophir.

'My father showed me that there was more to the world,' she said. 'Another reason for my mother to hate him. She was always complaining that the disgrace of his desertion had held her back, that her rivals used it to rob her of opportunities and promotions that were rightfully hers. That was why she put in a claim to his house and the rest of his stuff. He wanted to leave everything to me. He had the crazy idea that I would carry on his work. As soon as my mother heard about it, she put in a counterclaim. She said that even though she had annulled their partnership when he left the Corps, she had a right to be compensated for the way he had hurt her and damaged her reputation. It's possible, I guess, that she was trying to prevent me from making what she believed would be a bad decision. But the way she went about it only made things worse.'

Riyya made a kind of peace with Rav. She listened with uncritical attention to his tales of unlikely adventures in the cities and settlements of the Belt; Rav questioned her about the Climate Corps and its work, and told Hari that the algorithms that controlled Ophir's weather systems were trivial, but not without interest. Another day, he asked Hari if he and Riyya were having sex yet.

'I'd have sex with her, if I was inclined that way and if I happened to be baseline,' Rav said. 'She's what passes for intelligent amongst your people, and as far as I can tell she isn't deformed. You'll go your separate ways after this little adventure, so you won't be inconvenienced by any lasting emotional attachment. And you'd be better for it. It would relieve some of your tension. It would be harmless fun.'

'Once again, you demonstrate your ignorance of us simple-minded baseliners.'

'Oho. I've embarrassed you. One thing I do know about baseliners: you make basic human interactions needlessly complicated. A consequence of your primitive wiring, I suppose.'

'It's true that I don't know why you spend so much time with her.'

Rav smiled. 'Perhaps I'm trying to make you jealous.'

He had touched a nerve. Seeing Rav and Riyya together, talking easily, laughing, studying windows and picts hung in the air between them, made Hari feel suspicious and, yes, envious. Made him feel that he was watching the kind of life he wouldn't ever be able to enjoy, reminded him of the way he'd felt about Sora and Jyotirmoy and all the other passengers he'd briefly befriended, reminded him of the ease and comfort of his family.

The dull ache of grief and loss. Always there, even when he didn't notice it.

Brighter Than Creation's Dark maintained a constant distance behind Mr Mussa's ship. Hari and Rav had no intention of catching up with it. They planned to follow it to Tannhauser Gate, to give Mr Mussa a chance to make contact with the people who wanted to buy Dr Gagarian's head. The people, Hari was certain, who'd been behind the hijack of *Pabuji's Gift*. Who'd be ready to make a deal with him, when they discovered that the files in the tick-tock philosopher's head had been turned into a spew of random noise.

Early in the voyage, as they cut a chord across the inner edge of the main belt, Hari borrowed time on the ship's comms and fired off a brief message to Earth, to Ioni Robles Nguini, explaining who he was and why he was interested in the young mathematician's collaboration with Dr Gagarian. Two days later he received a brief reply from a representative of the Nguini family: a solicitous young woman who offered her condolences for his loss, said that Ioni Robles Nguini was not prepared to discuss his work with Dr Gagarian, asked him to refrain from sending further messages. Hari sent them anyway. They were not answered.

'His family know what happened to my father, and to Dr Gagarian and your family, and the others,' Riyya said. 'They're protecting him.'

'His family is powerful and wealthy,' Hari said. 'It survived several revolutions, and the rise and fall of the True Empire. One of his ancestors was President of Greater Brazil. An aunt and his eldest brother are senators in the government. His mother is the head of the country's judiciary. Other relatives are senior officers in the army. And they're frightened of me?'

'Or the hijackers, the assassins . . .'

'It's possible.'

'Is that a polite way of saying that you don't think it's likely?'

'Perhaps he has secrets that his family doesn't want us to know. Something he discovered, or something Dr Gagarian told him,' Hari said. 'Tamonash said that Mr Mussa tried to distract him by pretending that Ioni Robles Nguini wanted to buy Dr Gagarian's head. I'm beginning to wonder if it wasn't some kind of double-bluff.'

'We'll find out about the tanky's client soon enough,' Rav said.

They were talking in the big spherical compartment that Rav shared with his son. Sitting on what was presently the floor, in the fractional pull of the ship's acceleration. Padded walls curving around them, randomly studded with light panels. Rav's son was busy with some menial task in a recess, doing his best to be invisible. When Hari had explained the relationship between Rav and his son to Riyya, she'd said that she thought it horribly sad that they were trapped in a tradition that no longer had any meaning. 'The son can't find out who he is until Rav dies, and Rav can't ever really know his son,' she'd said, and hadn't been consoled when Hari had told her that Rav wasn't interested in anyone but himself.

Now, Riyya studied a pict that Hari had discovered in the public archives of the institute where Ioni Robles Nguini worked, and said, 'He's so young. Younger than me.'

'He's a mathematician,' Hari said. 'And most mathematicians do their best work when they're young.'

'A universal fault of baseliners,' Rav said. 'You're cute, as children. Bright-eyed, fearlessly curious, with an insatiable appetite for novelty. And then, all too soon, your brains calcify.'

'Unlike you, the everlasting child,' Hari said.

'Everlastingly creative and ingenious, always open to new ideas,' Rav said.

'Easily bored. Never entirely serious.'

'It's true,' Rav said. 'I *am* easily bored. I'm bored with speculating about whether this boy-genius could be some kind of criminal mastermind. The Saints hijacked your family's ship, youngblood, and hired the assassins who killed Riyya's father and the others. They want the files inside Dr Gagarian's head, and I have absolutely no doubt that the rogue tanky will try to sell it to them when he reaches Tannhauser Gate.'

'An ancestor of Ioni Robles Nguini once used cloned assassins,' Hari said. 'Grown in ectogenetic incubators, any number of them, tailored and trained for infiltration and murder. Just like Deel Fertita and her sisters.'

'More than fifteen hundred years ago, during the so-called Quiet War,' Rav said. 'Why the look of surprise? Did you think you had at last discovered something I didn't already know?'

'Clearly, I discovered something you didn't want to tell me about,' Hari said.

'Something I didn't bother to tell you about, because it's meaningless,' Rav said. 'I admit that I fleetingly entertained the idea that either the boy wonder or someone else in his family commissioned the assassins, but tailored clones have been used with varying degrees of success in hundreds of wars and disputes. Human history is finite, and seems to be full of recurring patterns. But coincidences all too often are no more than coincidences, given spurious significance by observer bias.'

'Yet the assassins killed every one of Dr Gagarian's associates except Ioni Robles Nguini,' Hari said.

'The Saints believe they will become as gods,' Rav said. 'But they are not gods yet. They cannot throw lightning bolts to Earth. Everything will become clear when we reach Tannhauser Gate. And then, I promise you, there'll be a reckoning.'

3

Anyone could sell anything to anyone else in Tannhauser Gate's free zone, but all goods were tagged on entry, every transaction had to be certified and taxed by its bourse, and its owners, the League of Christ Militant, severely punished anyone caught trying to evade paying their dues by smuggling contraband, japing tags, or bribing officials and brokers. Hari used Rav's account to access the bourse's register, looking for someone who specialised in tracing dubious deals and tracking down stolen property. He found something else. He found Rember Wole's sister. And when he reached out to her, he discovered that she had been looking for him.

Her name was Khinda. Khinda Wole. Like her brother, she was a broker. A friend in Tannhauser Gate's police had told her that the commissars of Fei Shen had tried to contact her brother; that they'd been seeking information about the son of one of his clients, who claimed to have escaped from dacoits. She had sent a message to Hari, but he had already fled the city. And she had also traced Tamonash Pilot, who had promised that he would pass on any news about his nephew or any other members of his family.

'But I heard nothing, and thought it was a dead end,' she said. 'Imagine my surprise to hear from you now.'

'My uncle is somewhat unreliable,' Hari said.

It was difficult to hold any kind of conversation because of the signal lag between *Brighter Than Creation's Dark* and Tannhauser Gate. They sent short statements back and forth. Speaking, waiting for a reply, responding.

Hari told Khinda about the hijack of *Pabuji's Gift* and his adventures on Themba and in Fei Shen and Ophir, told her about Mr Mussa's theft of Dr Gagarian's head. She told him that Rember and Worden had disappeared after setting out for a meeting with the crew of a salvage ship.

'It seems that they were lured into a trap,' Khinda said. 'No one in the salvage crew talked to them – the police questioned them and checked their comms records, and there is no evidence that Rember and Worden went anywhere near their ship. Their bodies were found in the free zone two days later. Their bioses and the files and caches in their workshop had been purged. And there were signs that they had been tortured. The police believe that it was a transaction that had gone badly wrong. One of the hazards of trying to make illegal trades in the free zone, they said. I tried to tell them that Rember and Worden had never dealt with dacoits or reivers, that they'd always worked through the bourse, but the police wouldn't listen. I don't have any traction with them, or with the synod, because I'm not a member of the League, and neither were my brother or Worden. So that was that, file closed. My friends and I have been trying to find out what we can, but we haven't turned up anything useful. And now you tell me that it is something to do with the hijack of your ship. Okay. What I want to know is, how can you be so sure?'

Hari told Khinda about Deel Fertita and Angley Li and the other assassins, told her that Angley Li had travelled to Ophir from Tannhauser Gate, asked her to find out what she could about the woman, her friends and associates, whether they had any connection with the Saints. He sent the pict of Angley Li he'd found in Ophir's commons, told Khinda that one or more of her sisters might be living in Tannhauser Gate.

A long wait, then Khinda asked if he thought that one of Deel Fertita's sisters had killed her brother and his partner.

'It is possible,' Hari said. 'But there is more to this than these women. They work for the hijackers. Who may be the Saints, or may be someone else. That is why we need to find out who Mr Mussa contacts, when he arrives at Tannhauser Gate. Who he meets. Every detail of any transaction he makes on the bourse. My friend thinks we should hire an impartial broker. I think he's wrong. What do you say?'

'That was a good touch,' Rav said, afterwards, 'making her think I don't think she can do the job. A nice bit of reverse psychology.'

Hari said, 'It's the truth, isn't it?'

'It's true that I don't trust people I haven't met. Are you sure she won't go to the police?'

'Even if she did, the police wouldn't care. And even if the police did take an interest, they wouldn't stop Mr Mussa from trying to sell the head. He's just another trader in stolen goods. As long as the League gets its cut, he can sell whatever he likes to whoever he likes.'

'Sometimes – not often, but once in a while – I think I've underestimated you.'

'We were lucky to find her,' Hari said. 'And we need all the luck we can get.'

'Luck is something you make, not something you're given,' Rav said. 'Has it occurred to you that she might be using us, just as we're using her?'

'I hope that we are all helping each other, because we all want the same thing.'

Rav smiled. 'Yes, why not?'

This was some two hundred hours before Mr D.V. Mussa's ship was due to dock at Tannhauser Gate. *Brighter Than Creation's Dark* was twenty-six hours behind it.

Hari discussed tactics with the eidolon of his p-suit, which possessed a cache of old war-gaming files. He practised negotiations with her. He worked up various strategies he could fall back on in case the negotiations failed. The eidolon advised him that they were all too dangerous, said that he did not know enough about his enemies, and lacked the capability to confront them safely.

'When I neutralised the hijackers' drone on Themba,' she said, 'I accessed combat files I did not know that I possessed. Unfortunately, I am unable to access them now. Perhaps I require a trigger to do so.'

'Perhaps,' Hari said.

He hadn't told her about the neural net in his skull, and the djinn that crouched inside it. He hadn't told Riyya, either; neither had Rav.

'She's a minor player in a game much bigger than she can imagine,' the Ardenist said. 'The less she knows the better.'

They all had their secrets.

Sometimes Hari sat quiet and still in his little sleeping compartment, eyes closed, mumbling his little mantra, *all things shall be well and all manner of things shall be well*, trying and failing to feel his way into the neural net that was wrapped around the inside of his skull, trying and failing to evoke the djinn. Sometimes he'd open a mirror window and study his reflection: gaze into his own eyes. He knew it was foolish, pure superstition, but he looked anyway, trying and failing to catch a glimpse of a spark or a shadow, daring the djinn to show itself.

He read in his book. It was presenting him with more stories now, as if responding to the way he flicked – tap tap tap, on/off – past everything else.

Two in particular stayed with him. In the first, a young woman on Saturn's giant moon Titan discovered one of the fabled gardens created by the great gene wizard Avernus, hidden inside a bubble habitat buried at the bottom of a deep rift. When she cycled through its airlock the young woman found that it was still lovely and perfect centuries after the gene wizard's death: groves of slender birch trees standing amongst black rocks and lawns of thick black moss, lit by bright chandeliers. But as she walked through it, it began to die. Chandelier light dimmed to an eldritch glow. Her p-suit boots left white prints in the moss that began to grow like puddles of spilt milk. The fresh green leaves of the birches around her darkened, turned red, and began to fall, a red snow fluttering down across the dying piebald lawns. And the paper-white bark of the trees began to darken too, turning black as soot. The young woman realised that she had triggered the garden's death, that she had become Avernus's collaborator in a work of art. That she was the sole witness to its transient beauty. The spills of white widening across the floor. The red leaves fluttering down. The skeletons of the leafless trees blackening as if consumed by an invisible fire. She sat in the middle of the garden, aching with sorrow and wonder and awe.

The second story began in a holy city threatened with invasion by a True battle fleet. The city's two priest-kings burned the sole copy of the sacred book at the heart of their religion, so that it would not fall into the hands of the infidels, and divided their people into two groups and fled into the Kuiper belt. The priest-kings had memorised every word in the book; each established a refuge where the children and children's children of their followers learned the sacred text by heart. But as generation succeeded generation errors crept into the memorised text, subtly changing it, subtly changing the creed and customs of the religion. A million years passed. At last, the long, slow orbits of the icy kobolds of the refuges brought them close. After first contact the two groups immediately declared war, each convinced that the other was a nest of heretics, and the bitter battles left no survivors.

Hari discussed these stories with Riyya, and she told him stories about her work with the Climate Corps. Tending the superconducting nets that balanced temperatures across the world city, the air-conditioning plants with their vast grids of catalytic polymers that absorbed excess carbon dioxide and generated oxygen. Generating weather by altering the strength and direction of air currents, heating or cooling them, seeding them with moisture. Precipitating falls of rain or snow by lifting and cooling moist air currents, or by spraying aerosols of microscopic particles that nucleated raindrops or snowflakes. Creating radiation fog, advection fog, evaporation fog, supercooled freezing fog . . . Weather-work was an art, and Riyya had been learning how to be good at it: how to make rain fall in an area as small as a field or a town block for a precise duration; how to ramp up a storm or a blizzard; how to prevent chaotic runaway events in which small errors could, if not checked, quickly become magnified into catastrophes.

She grew animated as she told Hari about the tricks of her trade, about treks across the snowy wilderness of the water-ice reservoirs at Ophir's south pole, about supervising caches of ancient machinery in the world city's outer skin, about duels in desert sectors involving dust devils and small lightning storms. She said that she'd miss weather wrangling, but wouldn't miss the Corps. It was, she said, a little like the Common-wealth of Sugar Mountain. A bureaucracy that clung to obscure and pointless traditions, fixed by rules and procedures administered by inflexible hierarchy.

'They teach you to love the Corps, but sooner or later you learn that it doesn't love you back,' she said.

Hari and Riyya spent much of their time in the passenger module of *Brighter Than Creation's Dark*, a hemispherical array of small compartments set around a central commons. Riyya discovered and activated a nest of cleaning bots, programmed the maker in the commons to produce a variety of novel and tasty meals, generally kept busy and always appeared cheerful, but Hari twice heard small soft sounds of grief behind the stiff curtain drawn across the hatchway of her compartment, and felt a helpless embarrassment. Agrata would have known how to comfort her, would have known the right thing to say;

Nabhomani would have kept her amused and distracted. But Hari felt as clumsy and awkward as Nabhoj, and besides, he didn't want to get too close. He'd done the right thing when he'd helped her to escape the Climate Corps and Ophir, but anything else would complicate things. It would be an unwelcome and dangerous distraction. His duty to his family came first.

Sometimes he went outside, floating out on a tether until the ship could be eclipsed by the palm of his gloved hand, thinking about what he needed to do, calling up a view of Saturn's ringed globe and trying and failing to pick up a signal from *Pabuji's Gift*. He always went out on his own. Riyya, who had otherwise adapted to shipboard life, refused to go outside; Rav said that he didn't see the point. Tannhauser Gate lay directly ahead, the brightest point in the dusty arch of gardens and rocks that swept across the black sky and the shoals and scatters of the fixed stars.

Six hours after Mr Mussa's ship had arrived at Tannhauser Gate, Hari was outside, watching Tannhauser Gate and waiting for news from Khinda Wole, when Rav pinged his comms and told him that another message from the hijackers had arrived. A plain compressed file, free of any detectable djinns, apparently sent from Tannhauser Gate.

'I haven't opened it,' Rav said, after Hari came inside. 'Frankly, I don't think there's any need. We know what it means. Mr Mussa sold Dr Gagarian's head to the Saints. Or tried to.'

'And they found out that its files had been corrupted,' Hari said. 'And sent me some kind of threat or ultimatum.'

'I wonder if Mr Mussa survived his clients' disappointment.'

'I wouldn't be surprised. He's slippery enough.'

'We'll have to see.'

'Yes, we will.'

Hari knew that Rav was right. He knew that he shouldn't look at the message. He looked anyway.

It was worse than he had expected. He told himself that it was not really Nabhoj. That it was a construct, an eidolon in a virtuality. It made no difference.

Afterwards, he pulled on his p-suit, numbly working through safety checks, switching off its eidolon when she came on line, going back outside and floating away from the ship, staring at the bright star dead ahead. Trying to contemplate the infinite. Trying to lose himself in thoughts about insignificance, mortality, the smallness of human affairs and the grandeur of the universe. Trying not to think of the thumb-sized maggot-things eating Nabhoj's face while he screamed and screamed, and a woman's voice explained what would happen if Hari didn't agree to surrender when he reached Tannhauser Gate.

4

Built by one of Earth's nation states several centuries before the rise of the True Empire, Tannhauser Gate was a long, blunt cylinder that had once sleeved a habitat rotating around its long axis to provide a centrifugal pull of around 0.1g. In its pomp, it had been one of the hubs for exchange of goods and services with the ten thousand gardens that orbited at the outer edge of the main belt. Later, it had become one of the True Empire's most important military bases, and towards the end of the empire's reign infiltrators had sabotaged the cylinder's axial bearings and the sudden deceleration had destroyed everything and killed everyone on its inner surface. Its present owners lived on the exterior; the ruined interior housed the infamous semi-autonomous free zone, where dacoits, pirates, reivers, free traders, and political refugees met and mingled, stolen or looted goods were traded, and hostages were ransomed.

Mr Mussa's ship was parked at one end of a rake of pylon docks. *Brighter Than Creation's Dark* drifted in towards a neighbouring rake, in the shadow of a much larger ship, *The White Brigades,* an ancient design with a delta profile for atmospheric entry. According to Rav, it had fought against the True Empire but was now a so-called free-nation ship. Dacoits in all but name, like many visitors to Tannhauser Gate these days.

'Pirates,' Riyya said. 'Pirates of the asteroids.'

'Pirates, dacoits, reivers, marauders and common cut-purse criminals,' Rav said. 'You'll find them all in the Gate, but don't expect too much excitement. Successful pirates look like crew leaders and traders because that's what they are, and only successful pirates can afford to trade here. I met the admiral-president of *The White Brigades*, once. She looked like a functionary in the government of a conservative and not especially wealthy settlement, but she commanded enough firepower to blow my ship to fundamental particles. And she'd have done it, too, if she thought it was necessary.'

'You admire them,' Riyya said.

'They're fellow predators. And they maintain an extensive network of informers and spies. If anyone has any news about the hijackers who took down *Pabuji's Gift*, the admiral-president of *The White Brigades* will know about it. And she'll share the information with you, for the right price. Something to think about,' Rav told Hari, 'if your game with your dead friend's little sister doesn't work out.'

But Hari wasn't yet ready to put his trust in information purchased from dacoits. He had at last reached the place Agrata had aimed him at, in those last desperate moments aboard *Pabuji's Gift*. Rember Wole and Worden Hanburanaman were dead, but he had found Rember's sister and she was willing to do all she could to help. His mission was back on track at last.

Khinda Wole was a small, middle-aged woman, dressed in a pink jumpsuit with many pockets and loops. A cap of beaded braids splayed out from her shapely skull like so many exclamation points. Most of her family were traders from Ceres, and most of them were still there, she said, selling biologics to each other.

'My mother brought back dogs. Do you remember dogs?'

'One of our passengers owned one,' Hari said. 'A small animal he carried everywhere in a sling scarf.'

'You could remove dogs from every biome they inhabit,' Khinda Wole said, 'and it wouldn't change a thing. They are ornaments. Companion animals. But they made my mother rich.'

They were sitting at a small table with Rav and Riyya, sharing bulbs of water and tea, little bowls of gels and pastes, flatbreads tinted green or pink with tinctures of exotic herbs. It reminded Hari of the family conferences aboard *Pabuji's Gift*. Sharing food, sharing the familiar squabbles and jibes, the familiar jokes, with Nabhomani and Nabhoj, Agrata, and a manikin ridden by his father. As he talked with his co-conspirators, he felt an echo of that old happiness, that harmonic mindset of blood on blood. For a little while, he could believe that he might not yet fail.

This was in the cluttered living space tacked onto a string of storage compartments that jutted out from the docks, with its own jetty. Like everywhere else in Tannhauser Gate, it was in microgravity. While Hari picked politely amongst the dishes and Rav ate with careless gusto, Riyya sat pale and still, suffering from a touch of free-fall sickness. She had managed to swim along the cordways of the docks without disgracing herself, but said that it felt like falling for ever through a place where basic directions like up and down kept switching around or vanishing entirely.

Khinda said that she didn't have any fresh information about Mr Mussa. She had been updating Hari ever since the free trader's ship had docked at Tannhauser Gate. So far, neither his avatar nor his daughter had left the ship, and no one had visited it, either.

'That you know about,' Rav said.

'We're keeping a close watch,' Khinda said.

'Visitors aside, he could be talking to any number of people right now,' Rav said.

'He could,' Khinda admitted. 'But he hasn't contacted the bourse. He has an account, but it has not been activated. He hasn't attempted to sell the item in question on the open market. And none of my friends and contacts have heard anything about a clandestine sale involving a tick-tock's head.'

'Which doesn't mean he hasn't tried to sell it,' Rav said.

'If he has, no one has come to collect the goods,' Khinda said.

'That you know of,' Rav said again. He was bored, or was presenting a very good imitation of being bored. We'll meet this broker, he'd told Hari while *Brighter Than Creation's Dark* had been making its final approach. We'll find out what she knows, which won't take long, and then we'll go into the free zone and talk to my friends and acquaintances, find out everything we need to know about the people who want what's inside your neural net, and work out our next move. When Hari had said that it didn't sound like much of a plan, Rav had said that the only alternative was to wait until the hijackers contacted Hari again and gave him instructions to surrender.

'And I'm not about to let you do that. I've grown fond of you, youngblood. I'd hate to see you give up your life in some kind of noble but pointless sacrifice. Besides, we don't yet know what's in your neural net.'

'I'm prepared to do anything that will get me close to the hijackers.'

'The foolish hunter flies straight at the flock and scatters it across the sky. The wise hunter hangs back, shadows the flock, studies its behaviour and marks the weakest members before he screams and stoops. We'll find out what this broker knows. Then we'll find out what my friends know. And then we'll be ready to stalk our prey, or set a trap. Trust me,' Rav had said. 'I was born to hunt. Postulates or people, it's all the same. It's my life.'

Now Hari told Khinda Wole, 'I think Mr Mussa tried to sell Dr Gagarian's head. Because why else would he come here? He tried to sell it, but the buyers discovered that it was damaged. That's why they sent me that message. They know I'm coming here, and they want me to know that they know.'

Khinda said, 'But have they sent any instructions or demands? Have they told you how to contact them?'

'Not yet. But now that I'm here, I think they will,' Hari said.

Rav yawned. 'The free trader has been squatting inside his ship, he hasn't seen anyone, he hasn't talked to anyone that you know of. In fact, you don't have any idea about what he may or may not have been doing. Is that it? Are we done here?'

'I do have some information about the assassins,' Khinda said. 'One of my friends has a contact in the transit police. It seems that Deel Fertita and Angley Li arrived at Tannhauser Gate on the same ship. An itinerant freighter, *The Heavenly Chrysanthemum*. They boarded at Ritsurin-kōen.'

'I know it,' Rav said. 'One of the gardens along the outer edge of the main belt. A big place, but a backwater. The assassins may have boarded *The Heavenly Chrysanthemum* there, but they started out from somewhere else.'

'They arrived there sixteen days earlier,' Khinda said, 'on a ship that came from the Saturn system.'

'Oho,' Rav said. 'I have to admit that's slightly interesting.'

An electric thrill plucked at Hari's heart. The wheel habitat of the leader of the Saints, Levi, orbited Saturn. And that was where *Pabuji's Gift* had been aimed, after its gravity-assist manoeuvre around Jupiter . . .

'Specifically, from Paris, Dione,' Khinda said. 'I can see that it means something to you.'

'It emits a definite odour of sanctity,' Rav said. He was staring across the table at Hari. His silver-capped smile. His frank green gaze. His careless confidence.

'There's something else,' Khinda said. 'A third passenger boarded *The Heavenly Chrysanthemum* at Ritsurin-kōen. A woman named Ang Ap Zhang. Deel Fertita and Angley Li lodged together in a hostel for transients after they reached Tannhauser Gate, but Ang Ap Zhang vanished after she disembarked. And as far as I can tell, she is still here.'

Hari said, 'Do you have an image of her?'

'Alas, no.'

'But we know what she looks like,' Rav said. 'Because she looks like her sisters. Angley Li. Deel Fertita. Ang Ap Zhang. Ang-*ley* Li. De-*el* Fertita. Ang *Ap* Zhang. It's like found poetry, isn't it?'

Riyya said, 'They didn't bother to change their appearance. They had similar names. They didn't care if people knew that they were related. They're either careless, or very confident.'

'Or it didn't occur to them that it mattered if people knew,' Rav said, 'because they were raised in a place where the identity of the individual is subsumed to the will of the whole. One of the eusocial clades, or a soldier clone-line. They needed names to travel under, outside their nest. War names. And because names don't mean anything to them, they used a simple-minded algorithm to generate them.'

'Then they aren't Saints,' Riyya said.

'They may not be Saints,' Rav said. 'But they work for the Saints.'

Khinda said that it was likely that Ang Ap Zhang was hiding somewhere in the free zone; there was no trace of her in any of the topside hostels or caravanserais.

'The Saints could be sheltering her,' Rav said. 'They have a big school here.'

'We have been keeping watch on it,' Khinda said. 'And we have also been looking for her in the free zone. So far we haven't had any luck, but it's an easy place to disappear into.'

'Now you'll be able to see how a real hunter works,' Rav said. 'We'll head for the free zone and flush out this so-called assassin, and we'll ask her some hard questions about who she works for, and how we can talk to them. How you can talk to them, Hari. How you can negotiate the release of your family and their ship.'

'First,' Hari said, 'we should deal with our good friend Mr D.V. Mussa.'

'If he came here to sell the head to Ang Ap Zhang, she probably killed him when she discovered that its files were corrupted,' Rav said. 'Him and his daughter. Forget them. They're dead meat.'

'I would know if anyone entered or left his ship,' Khinda said.

'Give me ten minutes, and I'll prove you wrong,' Rav said.

'Mr Mussa stole something from me,' Hari said. 'I want it back.'

'It's worthless,' Rav said. 'We hoped it would flush out the Saints, but it didn't work. And now we have other quarry.'

'Dr Gagarian was a passenger on my family's ship,' Hari said. 'I owe him a duty of care. Before we do anything else, I want to talk to Mr Mussa. I want to work out a deal for the return of the head. My family has credit here. I'll pay Mr Mussa for the head, if he still has it, and for the name of the person who wanted to buy it.'

And he wanted to have a serious conversation with the tanky about his uncle.

'We know who wanted to buy it,' Rav said. 'The Saints. And Mr Mussa won't be able to talk to you because he's dead. Killed by their hired assassin after he tried to sell her a head full of futzed files. Forget about him. We need to find Ang Ap Zhang.'

'We don't know that he's dead,' Hari said. 'And it won't take long to find out.'

Riyya said to Khinda Wole, 'This is usually where they get their dicks out, and start comparing length and heft.'

'Not for the first time, you mistake me for someone who hasn't evolved much beyond his ape heritage,' Rav said.

Riyya said, 'I may be second cousin to an ape, but I've thought of something you missed.'

Rav said, 'I doubt it.'

Riyya said, 'If this assassin, Ang Ap Zhang, did somehow get on board Mr Mussa's ship, if she killed him and his daughter – well, don't you think that she might be hiding there?'

Afterwards, after Hari had called Mr Mussa's ship, after he had talked to the tanky, or to someone using the tanky's avatar, after a long discussion about tactics, after everyone was finally talked out, Khinda Wole drew him aside.

'I found out something else about Deel Fertita. Something I think I should tell you privately. You asked me how Rember found her, when he hired specialists to help your family at Jackson's Reef.'

'And you told me that his work files had been purged,' Hari said.

'His assistant kept a duplicate set,' Khinda said. 'According to her, Nabhomani chose Deel Fertita and the other specialists.'

Hari said, 'Nabhomani hired them?'

Khinda said, 'He asked Rember to hire them. Rember drew up their contracts and arranged for the bottle rocket that took them to your family's ship, but your brother asked for them by name.'

Hari asked Khinda if she could be certain that the assistant was telling the truth.

'She is completely reliable.' Khinda paused, then added, 'I dug into the backgrounds of the specialists. At least one of them, Odd Samuelson, was a reiver. He traded in biologics, but he also hired out as freelance security. He was part of the crew that took over Thor Five thirty years ago.'

Hari thought about that. He said, 'It doesn't mean anything. Nabhomani could have met Deel Fertita long before we took Dr Gagarian aboard. He met many people. He knew many people. And it's no secret that my brother liked women. They met, she seduced him, and asked him to remember her the next time he was recruiting specialists.'

Khinda said, 'I'm sorry if it's bad news.'

Hari thanked her for her discretion. 'One thing is clear. My enemies have been planning this for a long time.'

5

'I'm at the front door,' Rav said. 'Ready to do my best to kick it down. How about you? Are you ready? Are you able? Are you willing?'

'Absolutely,' Hari said.

He was floating in the shadow of a service module close to the hull of Mr Mussa's small, sagittiform ship. The eidolon of his p-suit glimmered beside him. Beyond, the combs of the docks dwindled towards a curved, prickly landscape crowded with domes and tents, blockhouses and bunkers, towers and turrets and steeples and spires. Most of the spires were wrapped in gold foil and topped with golden crosses or giant picts of bleeding hearts or crowns of thorns. The League of Christ Militant believed only the fittest could attain Heaven, and that fitness was measured by accumulation of wealth – most especially the accumulation of gold, which they believed to be as incorruptible as the justice of their prophet.

'Of course, it's not too late to switch our roles,' Rav said. 'I admire your pluck, youngblood, but I've done this kind of thing before and you haven't. I'd take it badly if you got yourself killed.'

'Neither Mr Mussa nor the assassin want to kill me,' Hari said. 'They both want what's inside my head. Let's do this before I lose my nerve.'

Khinda Wole cut in, told Hari and Rav that her friends were ready to intercede if the police were called; a few moments later Riyya said that she had established contact with Mr Mussa's ship.

'An eidolon is screening calls,' she said. 'Do you still want me to go ahead?'

'If someone is on board, they'll be listening in,' Hari said.

Rav said, 'You know what would really distract them? Blowing a big hole in their airlock and storming aboard.'

'Start knocking,' Hari said. 'I'm going in.'

As Riyya began to explain that she had discovered a vacuum organism capable of extracting and concentrating vanadium from very low levels, Hari sculled across the short gap to Mr Mussa's ship and attached the emergency airlock package that Khinda Wole had located in her stores of miscellaneous salvage.

Riyya said, 'It's a fast-growing variation of the old RUR-three-eighty strain.'

'I'm not interested in purchasing vacuum-organism strains at the moment,' Mr Mussa's eidolon said.

The package unfolded into a disc that clamped to the hull with billions of microscopic hooks and sticky pads. A puff of gas, enough to create a pressure of less than a hundredth of a millibar, inflated its dome and triggered a charge that flowed through two hoops of memory wire and configured its airlock.

'I also have a robust ten-sixty-eight-dash-em strain,' Riyya said. 'It grows true.'

'I have no interest in it.'

Hari unsealed the flap of the outer hatch, scrambled inside, and resealed the outer hatch before pushing through the inner hatch into the little dome of the tent. So far, so good. It was a standard method for entering a pressurised vessel or habitat whose locks were in some way compromised, employed routinely during salvage work. Nabhoj had taught Hari the technique, but Hari had never before tried to solo it, and he was using it to gain entry to hostile territory.

Riyya said, 'Do you have anything to trade in exchange? I have a client who is looking for a specialised sunflower strain. I heard you might have a culture line that doesn't have the usual cis-em-dash senescence error.'

'Your information is not accurate,' Mr Mussa's eidolon said.

'How about a germanium accumulator?'

'I do not have any accumulator lines in stock at this time.'

Hari unwrapped the rope of polarised explosive from his waist and began to lay it in a circle.

Riyya said, 'You do trade in vacuum organisms.'

'Of course.'

'But not only in vacuum organisms.'

Hari flinched. Riyya had gone off-script.

'I am fully occupied with other business at the moment,' Mr Mussa's eidolon said.

'There's talk that you have a tick-tock person's head,' Riyya said. 'I know a collector who'd pay good credit for it.'

Silence, while Hari glued a strap of flexible fullerene across the point where the two ends of the rope overlapped. He felt a jittery static in his body. Then another voice said, 'I assume you're working with the Ardenist.'

Riyya said, 'I'm a sole trader.'

'An Ardenist is attempting to force the hatch of the jetty to which my ship is moored. Tell him to desist.'

Hari triggered the explosive rope. There was a faint tremor as the polarised explosive sliced through a circular section of the hull, and then the circle hinged up, pushed by air rushing out of the ship to fill the tent's blister. Hari triggered the cylinder of incapacitating agent and sent it spinning through the narrow hole, then threw a flashbang grenade. There was a percussive blast and brief stutter of fierce light, and he swarmed head first through the hole, trying to look everywhere at once.

As planned, making use of a model created by a single pass of the deep radar of Rav's ship, he'd entered some kind of hold or storage area. A cramped cylindrical space, walls dappled with the flittering shadows of debris shaken loose by the detonation of the grenade and tumbling and bumping around a coffin-sized tank cradled in a web of pipes and hoses and pumps.

Hari realised that it must be the tank where what was left of Mr D.V. Mussa's corporeal body was maintained. He started when the p-suit's eidolon appeared beside him.

'Tell me what you see,' he said.

'I cannot detect any movement. But waste heat from the tank is interfering with my infrared imaging, and the noise of the pumps is affecting my motion detectors.'

'Switch everything off,' Hari said, and someone swam up from the far side of the tank. A small figure in a black p-suit, aiming a pistol with a flared muzzle. The eidolon shot past it, vanished into a bulkhead.

Lights snapped off; the churn of the pumps slowed, stopped. Dull red emergency lighting kindled.

'You're early.'

It was a young girl's voice, soft and calm. Mr Mussa's daughter.

Hari said, 'Why don't you put away that pistol? Then I'll restore your ship's systems, and we'll be able to have a sensible conversation about our common interests.'

Rav had patched the system-killing routine into the eidolon. He claimed that he'd tricked a dacoit into giving it to him years back, said that he'd always wanted to try it out. Hari hadn't been certain that it would work, and wasn't sure that he could undo the damage, but it was the only bargaining counter he had. So far, there was no sign that the djinn was going to come to his aid. He hoped it was a good sign, hoped that it meant he wasn't in any real danger.

'I can fix anything on this ship myself,' Mr Mussa's daughter said.

'Then you had better get to work. The tank that keeps your father alive has been knocked out.'

'He's already dead.'

Hari was reflected in the mirror of her helmet visor. The muzzle of her pistol seemed to be about the size of a cargo lock.

'I'm sorry about your loss,' he said.

'No, you're not,' the girl said.

The eidolon appeared behind her. 'Her suit is hardened,' she said.

Hari told the girl, 'I admit that you appear to have the upper hand at the moment, but your ship is crippled, and I have friends outside.'

'The Ardenist, and the girl pretending to be a trader? Or the crew of amateur sleuths who have been keeping watch on me ever since I docked?'

'We can help you find the person who killed your father.'

'Take off your helmet,' the girl said.

There was a hard, unforgiving tone in her voice. It reminded Hari that she was much older than she appeared to be. He wondered why the djinn hadn't taken an interest in her. Because he was negotiating with her, perhaps. Or because she was a little girl . . .

He said, 'I don't think so.'

'But I do,' the girl said.

The eidolon merged briefly with the girl's p-suit, backed out, spread her hands in a gesture of helplessness.

A sudden glow was reflected in the visor of the girl's helmet. Hari turned, saw Mr Mussa's avatar floating in front of him. Its luminous sphere broke apart into a cloud of little needles, microbots, that swarmed over him. The row of indices and virtual switches under his chin blinked out; the p-suit's musculature hardened around his arms and legs; the latches in his neck ring clicked back and the helmet rose away from his head. There was a strong, sweet odour – the incapacitating agent – and the red glow of the emergency lighting deepened to darkness.

6

Hari jolted awake with a chemical taste burning in his mouth and pain pulsing behind his eyes. He was held fast by bands across his chest, hips, knees and ankles, lashed to a fragment of wall that stuck up from a field of rubble like a grave marker. He had been stripped to his suit liner, something was clamped over his scalp, and his bios was blocked. He could not tell where he was or how long he had been unconscious, could not reach out to anyone. It was like being back on Themba. It was like being deaf and half-blind, like being unable to read or to recall the proper names of things.

He sucked spit into the foul cavern of his mouth and softly called to the p-suit's eidolon. Nothing.

A smashed ruin of rubble curved up on either side and stretched away into a dim vastness. Little sparks glimmered far off in the unresolved distance. One or two were moving, but most were set in scattered clusters, thickening towards a hazy and irregular disc like a primordial galaxy. Hari began to understand where he was. Inside Tannhauser Gate's cylinder. In the free zone, where anything could be bought or sold, where there were no laws except the tithe law.

He called to the eidolon again, softly, urgently, and something moved at the edge of his vision.

The little girl, Mr Mussa's daughter, floating down through the air.

She still wore her black p-suit, but she had taken off its helmet and hung it on her hip. She looked about eight years old. She planted one hand on the fragment of wall and leaned in close.

'Your suit is presently heading sunwards,' she said. 'I did some serious damage to its comms back on the ship, and launched it from the escape-capsule tube. Don't expect your neural net's security to help you, by the way. It works through your bios, and I've been neutralising that ever since you boarded my ship. What do you find so funny?'

'Everyone but me seems to know what's inside my head.'

'I spotted it the first time we met. When you met my avatar. A simple neutron backscatter scan revealed it. I wasn't interested in it at the time, and neither were my clients. But things have changed. Very soon, I'm going to tell their representative where you are. And I'm going to tell your friends, too.'

'They're the Saints, aren't they? Your father's clients.'

The girl's smile, a quick, cold flicker, reminded Hari that she wasn't what she appeared to be.

'You'll find out soon enough,' she said.

'And the head. Dr Gagarian's head. Did you and your father sell that to them, too? Is that why he was killed?'

'I didn't try to sell the head to anyone,' the girl said 'Did you really think I wouldn't check the integrity of its files? I paid one of Gun Ako Akoi's granddaughters to take a look as soon as I arrived here. When she told me that the files were irrevocably corrupted, I realised that I was bait for your trap. It was clever, by the way, to let me think I'd got away with the theft, so that I would draw out the people who wanted the head.'

'I thought so,' Hari said.

'But not quite clever enough. I knew you were chasing me. I knew you would come here, to find out who wanted to buy the head from me. When I told my clients that Dr Gagarian's files were corrupted, I offered them your neural net. After that, all I had to do was wait. And here you are. I won't stick around to watch the fun, when the representative of my clients meets your friends, but you'll have a grand-stand view. And there's a good chance it will kick off something amongst the local inhabitants. When there's trouble in the free zone, people come running. And not to help.'

'If this is because you think I'm responsible for your father's death—'

'You made many mistakes, but that's your biggest. Believing that someone killed him because of that head.'

'Then who did?'

The girl flashed her quick, cold smile again.

'You,' Hari said.

'Care to guess when? I'll give you a clue. It wasn't here.'

'Not on Ophir either, I suppose.'

'The problem with being a tanky is that you are stuck in a tank,' the girl said. 'You have to rely on avatars, and the kindness of strangers. Like many tankies, the old man fettled up someone to act as his eyes and ears in the real world. She did all his dirty work, and guarded him against those who wanted to harm him. But then he tried to cheat some bad people, and they found out, and they killed his little helper. She was blameless, but she was on the spot and he was a long way away, safe in his tank. So then he had to make a new little helper. Who was just as skilled, and just as loyal. At least, to begin with. Because the old man didn't learn from his mistake.

'That's another thing about tankies, you know? They are semi-detached from the world. After a while, it all seems like a saga to them. They forget that actions have consequences, that you can't reboot and start over when things go wrong. So the old man tried to swindle someone else, his new little girl barely escaped with her life when it all went wrong, and she began to wonder if he'd made the same kind of mistake before. She wanted to help him because that was how she'd been made, and the best way to do that, she thought, was to learn how to save him from himself. She broke into the old man's files, and found out about her predecessor. Saw the pict that the bad people had made after they'd caught her, saw what they'd done to her. And she began to realise that the old man considered her to be disposable.

'So, when he started to plan another dubious deal, his little helper tried to persuade him out of it. She was trying to save him from himself, and save herself, too. But he didn't see it that way. He thought that she was rebelling against him, thought she was being disloyal. And he punished her. Hurt her badly. After she recovered, she decided that things couldn't go on like this. She didn't kill him. Not immediately. First, she locked him down in his tank. She took control of his avatar and his business. She let him know what he was doing, and told him why, and tried to reason with him. But he managed to open a back channel to a former associate, and the associate tried to kill me. So what could I do? I killed the associate and I killed the old man, and because I had no other way of earning a living, I continued to run his business.

'I moved to Ophir, set up the old man's tank as if he was still alive inside it, and went into business with your uncle, supplying exotic biota which he sold on to his contacts on Earth. I dealt with Tamonash through the avatar. He had no idea it was me and not the old man. And it was good, for a while. A nice, simple little business, with the promise of some real profit down the line. And then I heard about Dr Gagarian's research, that people thought he'd discovered something significant about the Bright Moment. Something valuable. My clients mislaid you and that head, but their carelessness gave me the opportunity to sell it to them again. And here we are.'

'You told them. The hijackers. You're the one who told them about Dr Gagarian. I thought it might have been my uncle, but it was you.'

'Let's put it this way: this is the second time I've sold you to them. That's why we aren't doing the handover directly. For some reason, they blame me for your escape the first time around. And I think they think I had something to do with those corrupted files in the tick-tock's head. The credit is already deposited with the bourse. It will be released when their representative takes custody of you. Your friends will create a distraction when they try and fail to rescue you, and I'll be on my way to somewhere else. Somewhere far, far away. And since you cut a hole in my ship's hull and futzed its systems, I believe I'll take the Ardenist's ship,'

'I don't think so,' a voice said close by, and a small drone dropped out of the dark air and aimed a brilliant light at Hari and his captor.

7

The little girl kicked away from Hari, somersaulted in midair, and drew her pistol and shot the drone, all in one fluid movement. Its light went out and Hari tried to blink away swarming after-images, glimpsed the girl skimming away above fields of rubble, saw someone swoop down and smash into her.

It was Rav. As the girl tumbled away, he beat backwards, steadied himself in the air, and pointed at her. A thread of intense blue light flicked out from his fist and she burst into flames, kicking, writhing, dwindling cometwise into the dim volume of the cylinder. There was a brief shower of sparks when she struck a finger of stone, and then she was gone.

Rav swept in towards Hari with three swift strong beats of his wings, neatly reversed, and caught hold of the edge of the wall.

'She liked to talk, didn't she?' he said. 'I thought she'd never get to the point.'

'You shouldn't have killed her.'

'Why not? She tried to kill me. And caused me a good deal of inconvenience, too.'

'Even so. It wasn't right.'

'We're in the free zone. There's no right or wrong here. And I don't believe in little weaknesses like mercy or forgiveness.'

The Ardenist flourished a knife and began to saw at the strip that pinned Hari's ankles. 'I don't know about you,' he said, 'but I'm having a serious case of *déjà vu*.'

Hari saw a dark wet gleam on Rav's bare shoulder. 'You're hurt.'

'It's only a scratch. My boy won't be growing hair on his balls just yet.

It was a nice trick, firing off your p-suit. Good enough to fool the trader and her friends, anyway.'

'But not you.'

'But not me. When you broke into the ship, I suited up and went outside as fast as I could. I saw her sneak out of an access hatch in the stern, towing a storage pod. She was fast. Almost got away from me. Almost, but not quite. You know the rest,' Rav said. He cut the last of Hari's bonds and caught him by one arm and smiled into his face. 'You also caused me a good deal of inconvenience, youngblood, but all's well that ends well. I won't let you out of my sight again, I promise.'

Hari pulled off the cap that Mr Mussa's daughter had clamped over his scalp. His bios rebooted; the volume of the cylinder immediately gained scale and clusters of names and other signifiers.

'Mr Mussa's daughter told me that the representative of her clients will be here soon,' he said.

'You would like to work up some kind of ambush. Ordinarily, I'd like nothing better, but we're exposed here, and almost certainly outgunned,' Rav said, and clasped Hari to his chest and kicked away from the stub of wall.

As they arrowed through dim air towards the little galaxy of lights at the far end of the cylinder, Rav told Hari that it was time to regroup.

'I'm not ready to leave until we've found Ang Ap Zhang,' Hari said.

'I'm not ready to leave, either. But we've been compromised, thanks to your little adventure with the tanky's spawn,' Rav said. 'The assassin has had more than two hundred days to establish herself here. We're right in the middle of her territory. She knows about us; we haven't had time to find out about her. It won't be easy, getting you out alive, but I'm going to do my best. We'll get back to my ship, and work out what to do next.'

'What about Riyya? Where is she?'

'Oh, I made sure she's safe, although I don't expect she'll thank me for it.'

'I confess that I'm not very happy either,' Hari said.

'Your pride is hurt. Look at it this way. You weren't the first to be fooled by that little girl, but you were definitely the last.' Rav looked at Hari. His sharp smile and green gaze very fierce, very close. 'You really *are* upset because I killed her. You shouldn't be in the revenge game, youngblood. You're too sentimental.'

'I know what she was, and what she wanted to do,' Hari said. 'And I also know that you didn't have to kill her. If only because she could have told us who her clients were. Whether they were the Saints, or someone else.'

'Forget about that for now,' Rav said. 'Let's concentrate on getting out of here alive. I'm going to do my best to save you, but you'll have to work with me. Do what I say when I say it. Can you do that?'

'I can try.'

They were skimming over hills and valleys of broken flowstone, bright shards of plastic, twisted rebar. Here and there rubble-pile islands floated like baby asteroids, lashed together by nets and tethered by cables. Hari tried to imagine what it must have been like when the habitat had stopped spinning and centrifugal forces had torn everything loose. Buildings ripped apart, smashing into other buildings. A whirling hurricane of debris plastering itself against the cylindrical wall . . . Amazing that the habitat's sleeve had survived. Amazing that anything recognisable had survived.

Rav pointed out latticework spheres scattered across a bowl of pale green grass. Most were ten or twenty metres in diameter, but one was easily as big as *Pabuji's Gift*.

'Combat cages,' he said, 'where the good citizens of the free zone thrash out their differences. I've taken down a few braggarts there, over the years. Maybe we could set you up with the mastermind behind the hijack.'

Lights thickened ahead. Archipelagos of rafts, erratic piles of cubes, towers that leaned out of the rubble at improbable angles, girdled with platforms or scabbed with the bubbles of small tents. Free-fall settlements of scavengers and dacoits, outlaws and pirates. Places where a person could buy any kind of mod or tweak, satisfy every kind of sexual desire, every appetite.

Hari and Rav flew through a passage that twisted and turned between anarchic free-fall architecture, lit by dabs of luminescence, signs and images hung in garishly coloured blocks of light, the glow of gardens enclosed in transparent spherical tents like small, erratic moons. People moved in every direction, swimming along cableways, riding scooters and varicopters and jetbikes, towed by hand-held fanmotors, navigating the air with judicious squirts of propellant from a variety of pistols and jets. Children riding airboards burst from a narrow space between two square towers like a flock of birds, shouting taunts as they split around Hari and Rav. The air seemed thicker and warmer, tainted with the sweet stink of garbage.

'We're almost there,' Rav said, and a moment later changed course with a single strong beat of his wings.

Hari looked around. A scooter was turning back towards them, ridden by a woman with long black hair and a familiar face. It was Deel Fertita. It was Angley Li. It was Ang Ap Zhang.

Cold shock jolted through Hari. His bios popped warnings as his heart rate and blood pressure increased; a sliver of icy pain pierced his left eye. The djinn was waking up. Blue light exploded as he and Rav swept through a huge sign hung in the air; Rav told him to curl up as tight as he could, and gave him a hard shove.

Hari flew through an open window, skimmed across a room where two women were tending rows of plants bristling from hydroponic tubing, shot through a window on the far side. A slab wall loomed dead ahead, and then Rav caught him and they stalled with a clap of wings and rose towards the underside of a platform. Rav caught at its edge and swung around. Everything flipped, and then Hari was clinging to one of the tethers stretched across a garden patched with dozens of different crop plants. His pulse was pounding in his skull and there was a dagger twisting behind his eyes and a feeling that something stood at his back.

'That was intense,' Rav said, and laughed.

He was aiming a pistol here and there with sharp precise flicks, looking for and failing to find a target.

'Khinda was right,' Hari said. 'The assassin was in the free zone all along.'

'The representative, so-called, of your late little friend's clients,' Rav said. 'She wants to snatch you, youngblood. She wants your head. Let's try to make sure that doesn't happen.'

He pulled a knife from a loop on his harness, handed it to Hari, asked him if he knew how to use it.

Hari squeezed the grip. The thin blade blurred with a vibration he felt all the way up his arm.

'Could you cut or kill someone if you had to?' Rav said.

'I suppose I'm going to find out,' Hari said.

'If she doesn't come after us again, she'll be waiting at the gate,' Rav said, and pointed towards the living wall of a giant banyan patch beyond the far end of the platform. 'Think you can follow me?'

Hari slid the knife into the cinchband of his suit liner. 'I grew up in microgravity. Let's go.'

They both kicked away from the garden platform and plunged into the labyrinth of branches and leaves, zigzagging past platforms, past rooms like giant insect cocoons woven from living leaves or fibrous ropes. Hari felt a primal exhilaration. It was like the games of tig he'd played as a child – but now everything was at stake. He was thinking with his muscles, following a heartbeat behind Rav, flying through air, through screens of big green leaves, swinging around branches. Rav smashed through a bower of flowers and Hari followed, bursting through an expanding storm of petals and shooting out across a spherical volume of open air. A man stared out at him from the window of a hut lodged amongst sprays of leaves. Hari laughed and saluted him, saw Rav grab a branch at the far end and kick sideways, grabbed the same branch, pivoted, followed.

He caught up with the Ardenist when they reached a wide cordway on the far side of the banyan patch. They swam along it, using their fingertips to skim over the warp of the fat orange threads. Workshops along one side, a wall of leaves and branches on the other. They overtook people, passed people travelling in the opposite direction. After a couple of minutes, Hari realised that half a dozen young women in leather corselets and knee-length trousers were keeping pace with them, some twenty or thirty metres behind.

Rav said that they were locals, not Saints. 'It's probably just a territorial thing. Ape posturing. But if they come at us, we'll have to deal with them. Strike first, and strike hard.'

'Right.'

'Use the knife, but don't try anything fancy. If you try to stab something vital, you'll probably miss. Slash. Quick, tight strokes. It doesn't matter where you hit your opponent. Even shallow cuts hurt, and they bleed a lot, too.'

'Right.'

Hari's mouth was parched. The djinn had retreated, leaving behind a bright pulse in his left eye.

'We're almost there,' Rav said. 'No turning back now.'

Curtains of leaves fell away, revealing a huge shaft or corridor with bubbles and platforms and buildings cantilevered out into it and a swarm of people moving through the air, swimming along cableways and cordways, riding all kinds of machines, shouting, blowing whistles.

Fanjet tractors towed strings of cargo sleds up and down the periphery of the shaft, sounding mournful horns. Strings of red and blue lights sketched traffic lanes that everyone seemed to ignore.

All this stretching away for more than two kilometres, terminating in a black wall or shield pierced by tunnel entrances set in a hexagon, each ringed with red or green lights. The end cap of the cylinder. The gates to the exterior.

Rav gripped the cord he'd been following, stopping so quickly that he swung through one hundred and eighty degrees. Hari stopped too, both of them hanging there, looking down at the gates. Their followers clustered some ten metres away, beside a pod with a dim red-lit interior and a banner sign printed with Pinglish ideograms rippling inside an underwater fantasia of bright fish and waving waterweed: *Lete's Eats*.

Rav flung his arms wide, so that his wings spread from shoulders to ankles. Calling out, saying, 'Like what you see?'

'I see fresh meat,' one said.

'And I see children who don't know what they're getting into,' Rav said. 'Run along. Play somewhere else.'

'This is our playground, fresh meat. We go where we please.'

'The only thing we have in common,' Rav said, and kicked away from the branch.

Hari followed. They kept inside the banyans as they moved towards the gates, making their way through curtains and fans of leaves, skimming around clusters of pods. Near the end of the long tangle, Rav snatched at a branch and waited for Hari to catch up with him.

'If I was trying to snare us, I'd set an ambush at the only way in or out of this place,' he said. 'We'll have to go under cover. We'll have to sneak out.'

'How are we going to do that?'

Rav pointed to a short train of cargo sleds puttering past. 'By hitching a ride. Ready?'

Before Hari could answer, Rav kicked off and flew straight at the train. Hari kicked off too, shooting out into open air, smacking into a transparent bladder swollen with water, snatching at the straps that lashed it to a sled as he rebounded. Rav grinned at him, pointed. The gang of women arrowing out of the banyans, landing one after the other at the far end of the train's string of sleds, moving towards them.

Rav drew his pistol. Hari pulled out his knife, tingling with nervous anticipation.

The leader of the gang laughed and said, 'Is that all you've got?'

She hung from the flank of the neighbouring sled by a hand and a foot. Her toes were as long as fingers, terminating in flat pads. Her hair was swept back in stiff wings on either side of her lean and eager face. Her eyes were white stones with tiny black dots at their centres. She raised her free arm and flung it forward and something snaked towards Hari – a whip divided into a hundred threads at its end, each tip armed with a vicious hook. Hari flattened himself against the taut bladder, felt the whip snap above his head, slashed at it with his knife, and lost his balance and tumbled into empty air. As he turned, he saw two women coming towards him from different angles. Then Rav struck him and held him, and they flew away from the train, banyans and gates and a ladder of buildings turning over and around.

Rav's wings beat around Hari. Their tumbling trajectory stabilised. The women were diving towards them, using little squirt bottles to steer themselves. Rav told Hari to catch hold of his harness, and pulled out his pistol and took aim. There was a blink of blue light and one of the women flared into a shrieking fireball that slewed sideways and struck a stack of platforms.

The others sheered away in every direction. Hari clung to Rav's waist as the Ardenist beat towards the gates. All around, people and vehicles were swerving around burning debris that sprayed across the shaft. Two trains crossed and collided, spilling wobbling blobs of water and expanding clouds of plastic pellets. Hari and Rav dropped through the debris. A hard rain of pellets stung Hari's face and hands. As they came out of the far side, a scooter sliced past, Ang Ap Zhang leaning out, slashing at Rav with a long knife, gone. Rav gasped and jerked, and his wings folded as he and Hari arrowed towards a building jutting into the gulf of air and crashed through a wall, paper stretched across wooden framing, into a small room where a single sleeping cocoon was strung on a tether.

Rav was bleeding badly, blood pumping from his thigh, tumbling away in scarlet droplets. 'The knife,' he said. His voice was tight with pain.

Hari handed it over at once. Rav squeezed the handle and the blade vibrated and began to whine and shone a dull red that brightened to yellow, white. The Ardenist set his teeth in a jagged grin and plunged the knife into the wound.

Hari gagged on the stink of seared meat.

When Rav pulled the blade free the bleeding was much reduced. Hari took the knife from him and cut of a strip of material from the ankle of his suit liner, twisted it into a rope and wrapped it around Rav's thigh, and caught a floating splinter of wood and used it to tighten the improvised tourniquet until blood stopped flowing.

'We can't stay here,' Rav said. 'If the assassin doesn't find us, that little gang of bad girls will.'

'Can you move?'

'I can still fly. The assassin is fast, but I'll take her if it comes to it. You understand that the only way out is through the gates.'

'We'll do it together.'

Layers of smoke obscured the gulf of the shaft. People were fighting a small fire in the banyan wall on the far side, whacking at flames with blankets, spraying foam. The building that had been struck by the body of the burning woman was a charred shell wrapped in a pearl of smoke. There was no sign of the rest of the gang, and the shaft was mostly clear of traffic.

Rav went first, pushing away with his good leg, spinning out and down towards the gates. Hari followed, a fast exhilarating swoop. They fell past windows and platforms, past some kind of manufactory where elephantine machines shuddered and pulsed. They punched through a string of glowing signs, and that was when the gang of women ambushed them.

They shot out from a tier of platforms, impossible to avoid. A whip snapped around Hari's leg as one of the women flew past; as they spun about a common axis Hari grabbed the whip and hauled close and slashed at the woman and felt the knife catch on something. He kicked free, flying towards the wall of the shaft as the woman he'd wounded tumbled outwards. A knot of women was writhing around Rav. Hari caught a branch and swung and got his feet under him, saw one of the women lock her arm around the Ardenist's throat, saw two more hammering at his chest with the spiked handles of their whips. Saw a scooter sidle in, saw the women push away from Rav as Ang Ap Zhang stood up in her saddle and delivered the killing stroke.

Rav's body tumbled in a mist of blood. The women were swarming after his severed head. And Ang Ap Zhang was heading towards Hari, standing astride her scooter, flourishing a whip. Her unbound black hair flew behind her like a banner; her long knife was sheathed at the waist of her white shirt.

Hari barely had time to draw his knife before she was on him. Leaping from the scooter as it went past, knocking him backwards through a tangle of branches. He struck out in panic, and the assassin hit his wrist with two stiff fingers and he dropped the knife. She spun him, pushed him away, lashed out with her whip. It spiralled around him, binding his arms to his sides, gripping with hundreds of tiny teeth.

Ang Ap Zhang pulled him close. There was nothing human behind her gaze. A spray of blood glistened on her pale face. Rav's blood.

'I should kill you now, for what you did to my sisters,' she said. 'But you are wanted alive, and I am merely the arm and the hand.'

She towed him to the edge of the maze of leaves and branches, where her scooter was waiting. The pressure was back inside Hari's head. Light pulsed in his left eye, obscuring pop-up warnings from his bios. He felt as huge and heavy as a water bladder.

Ang Ap Zhang paused at the edge of the banyans. Down the shaft, something inflated around the string of glowing signs. A giant figure jigsawed from shards of light, from compressed signage and images, its misshapen head turning, jagged eyes fixing on the assassin, an arm stretching out towards her, stretching a hundred metres. She flinched as talons tipped with flame whipped past, and the giant somehow grabbed hold of a fixed spot in the air and hauled itself towards her.

Hari drifted sideways as the burning giant yawned and breathed out a ball of flame that engulfed the assassin. She tumbled free, and a black ball thumped against her white shirt and writhed and burst, spurting thousands of threads that tangled around her arms and legs, swiftly wove a cocoon that held her in a close embrace.

The giant began to shrink and fade. Two broomstick scooters dropped through its dimming image. Khinda Wole steered one, Riyya behind her, clinging to her waist; two men rode the second.

Khinda Wole halted neatly beside Ang Ap Zhang's cocooned figure. She pulled the threads from the assassin's face and met her fierce stare without flinching, then looked at Hari. 'This is the woman who killed Rember?'

'I think so. Yes. She killed Rav. Her and those women. They must have been working for her . . .'

'I saw it,' Khinda said. 'I wish I could say that I was sorry.'

'He knocked us out,' Riyya said. 'He came out of the jetty and knocked us all out.'

Hari was about to ask her exactly what Rav had done when Ang Ap Zhang started to shake and quiver inside the rigid weave of the cocoon.

'Don't struggle,' Khinda told her. 'The threads will keep tightening. All the way down to the bone if you keep it up.'

'Something's wrong,' one of the men said.

There was white foam on Ang Ap Zhang's lips. Her eyes had rolled up. The two men hauled her close to their broomstick and started to work on her, but she was already dead.

8

They left the free zone and returned to the docks without incident. Khinda Wole was in a grim mood. Ang Ap Zhang's suicide had cheated her of her revenge, and she was still angry about being tricked by Rav.

Riyya told Hari that Rav had emerged from the main lock of Mr Mussa's ship. 'He flew out of the jetty with a pistol in his hand. Shot us with tranquilliser darts. Me and Khinda and her friends. I didn't know what had happened until I woke up, he moved so quickly. Khinda's friends in the free zone spotted both of you. When we caught up I tried to use the weather against him, but the machinery was too different.'

'You saved me, anyway,' Hari said.

They were swimming down a broad corridor, heading towards Khinda Wole's workshop. Hari, Riyya and Khinda Wole, Khinda's friends. Skimming along cordways greasy with the touch of thousands of hands, past walls livid with half-life signs and slogans deposited by rival crews and cults and engaged in a slow and patient Darwinian war for *lebensraum* that reminded Hari of the vacuum-organism pavements on Themba. And he had the feeling he'd always had under the empty black sky of the asteroid: the tingling sense of being watched, of being stalked by some invisible, implacable and all-knowing enemy. It had never entirely left him, but it was stronger than ever now. He was preternaturally alert, starting every time someone came into view. But they all seemed harmless, the few passers-by, men and women dressed in work clothes and suit liners.

Pirates of the asteroids.

He was exhausted, badly bruised, lacerated by the teeth of the assassin's whip, but he wanted to keep things moving forward. Khinda Wole said that she would attempt to arrange what she called a parlay with the Saints, but Hari wanted to talk to Rav's son first. He wanted to tell him that his father was dead. He wanted to ask him what Rav had been planning to do. He wanted to try to retrieve Dr Gagarian's head from Mr D.V. Mussa's ship, too. But first he needed to rest and regroup, organise his thoughts, work out the extent of this disaster.

They had turned off the main drag and were swimming down the branch that led to the workshop when it happened. Three figures dressed in white, white masks covering their faces, appeared ahead of them; three more crowded in behind. One of Khinda's friends reached for the slug pistol on his hip, there was the howl of an energy weapon, its beam hot and bright in the confines of the corridor, and the man spun backwards, trailing globs of blood through the air.

Riyya, Khinda and the second man held out their empty hands, drifting in mid-air, and Hari felt the hot pulse of the djinn, saw livid tangles of repurposed graffiti whip out at the ambushers, and the air was suddenly full of a blizzard of what looked like scraps of white paper. He thought of Ma Sakitei's butterflies; he thought of Gun Ako Akoi's snow. And then he was blinded as a fluttering storm of white scraps whirled around him, fastening to his face and scalp, flowing together, tightening. His body locked in a powerful cramp; his bios blanked; all sense of the djinn vanished.

Someone gripped his shoulder, turned him. A woman spoke in his ear.

'The Saints bid you welcome, Gajananvihari Pilot.'

PART FIVE

THE COLD
EQUATIONS

PART FIVE

1

Afterwards, after each session of the long, slow exorcism, the Saints allowed him to wander out into their garden. Gradually, he would remember who he was, where he was. Why he was there. He would say his name. He would say the names of his dead. Speaking slowly, shaping the syllables as if they had never before been uttered. He would sit on the blood-red lawn outside the tented cluster of rooms and stroke the half-life grass. Tough haulms hissing under his palms.

'This is real,' he'd say. 'This is really happening.'

He walked paths with no particular destination in mind, stopping now and then to stare at the trail of footprints he had made in the black sand, an echo of a half-remembered story. The nearest and newest were white and sharply printed; those further back were losing definition, dissolving into the default black of the smart grains. He climbed the endless slope of the garden, wandering among trees and meadows until he found the place he recalled from times before, and climbed the steep stair to his favourite vantage point.

It was a broad ledge rebated under the top of a cliff assembled from chunky blocks of flowstone. Rivulets of seep-water pulsed amongst mosses and ferns that grew in the erratic joints of the clifftop, feeding a braided stream that tinkled into a pool of clear water. He liked to study the intricate miniature jungles of liverworts and mosses and ferns. Droplets beading actual leaves and stems. Laddered arches of leaves. Transparent hairs bristling from ridged stems. He studied the falling water, the ripples in the pool. He studied the tiny transparent shrimp that flicked over black sand like erratic ghosts, like his thoughts. Water lipped the edge of the pool and fell past the cliff, angling away, torn to mist before it reached the treetops.

On either side of his perch the rising curve of the gardened floor bent towards the vanishing points where floor and roof intersected, and the inner surface of the wheel habitat flexed above, the bright stars of chandelier lights hung beneath a pale blue overhead interrupted at regular intervals by window-strips. One hung directly above the ledge, a long, narrow quilt of diamond panes. It glowed with weak, reflected sunlight during the day, and at night, when the chandelier lights dimmed, gave Hari a view of spars dwindling towards the white cylinder of the central hub, and the arch of the opposite side of the wheel, more than two kilometres away.

Mostly, he liked to sit on a saddle of stone and look out across the treetops. Wind walked and whispered in the leaves. Birds sang, bright interrogative threads of music rising near and far. There was always a drone hanging close by, watching him, sometimes asking him questions, sometimes darting off and returning with morsels of food or a thimble of red tea or gritty black java.

Sooner or later Jyotirmoy would find him, stepping lightly up the stair of artfully set stones to the ledge, sitting beside him, telling him that he'd done well.

Hari had only hazy memories of the exorcisms. Perhaps it was a kindness of the remembrancers and philosophers, or perhaps it was a side effect of their drugs and the clamp on his bios. In any case, he was grateful that he couldn't remember much, because what he could remember was bad enough. What was done to him, to wake the djinn. Its inchoate rage and pain.

It was powerful and stubborn, but the exorcists were making progress, according to Jyotirmoy.

'The djinn is subtle and malicious,' he told Hari. 'We can't begin to recover the files until every trace of it has been eliminated, and eliminating it has been harder than we first thought it would be because it has deep roots in your brain and in your nervous system. But the worst is over, now. Your father used you cruelly. He turned you into a slave, and burdened you with his secrets and lies. But with our help you will be able to unlock his shackles and remove that burden. With our help, you'll soon be truly free, free to find out who you really are.'

'You pretend that this is for my own good. You pretend to be kind,' Hari said, with a feeble flicker of defiance. 'It would be kinder to kill me.'

Jyotirmoy sat quietly, looking off in the distance, while Hari wept. He was a slim, handsome, elegantly composed person, glossy black hair swept back from his high forehead and gathered at the back of his neck in a short pigtail. Like Hari, he wore a white spidersilk jacket fastened by two rows of plastic toggles, white spidersilk trousers. Perched on the rock, his back straight and his legs crossed at the ankles and his hands resting on his thighs, he gave the impression that he had paused in the middle of a dance. He made Hari feel like a clumsy child.

Hari's old friend had joined the Saints soon after he had jumped ship and run away from his parents. The work he'd found in the docks of Trantor, driving dumb, strong machines, had left him too tired to practise properly, or to work on his choreography. Sometimes he would perform solos from old classics in one or another of the city's parks, but few people were interested in him or in the stories his dances evoked.

Every day, he'd see the Saints process through the streets of the city. They were enthusiastic, but lacked skill and discipline. They shuffled along with lumpen solemnity; when they struck poses while their leader declaimed a short piece against the seraphs or about the triumph to come, their transitions were stiff and awkward and their expressions were little better than frozen grimaces. Masks they did not properly inhabit.

He mentioned this to one of the Saints who asked him for a donation to support their cause, and a few days later a young woman approached him after he'd finished one of his routines in the park, asking questions about his dancing, why he did it, the meaning of his performance, and so on, and so forth. She was waiting for him in the park the next day; they talked again. She asked him why he had run away from his parents, asked him what he wanted from life, and explained how she had come to realise that the Saints spoke the truth, how she had decided that she must help them take their message to every part of the Belt. They talked a long time, sitting in the park, rambling through streets. They ate at a stall. At last, Jyotirmoy took the woman to the cubicle he rented in a stack near the docks. Early the next morning he woke to find that she was already dressed, sitting on the edge of the sleeping niche, watching him. 'You should meet some friends of mine,' she said. 'I think you can help them.'

And so Jyotirmoy began to visit the school of the Saints. He led classes in movement and dance. He listened to the sermons of the adepts, took part in group discussions. Soon, he gave up his rented cubicle and his job, moved into the school, and began to lead their processions through the city. He did not sleep with the woman again, but after he had been baptised he sometimes accompanied her when she went out into the city to recruit new members.

Forty days ago, almost three years to the day after he had joined the Saints, he had been summoned to a meeting with a high adept, who told him that dacoits had hijacked a ship whose crew and only passenger, a tick-tock philosopher, had been working on the problem of the Bright Moment. Jyotirmoy knew the ship, the adept said. *Pabuji's Gift*. She told him that one of the crew, a young man named Gajananvihari Pilot, had escaped the hijack and taken important files with him, and now he had fallen into the hands of the blessed.

'You were his friend,' the adept said. 'You will help us bring him into the true light.'

And then Jyotirmoy knew with a great glad surge that his entire life had been shaped towards a single purpose.

'You are part of a noble and holy work,' Jyotirmoy said, after Hari's slow seep of tears had ceased. 'With your help we will do things that will echo down the halls of human history.'

'I'm trying my best.'

Hari was embarrassed by his stupidity and weakness. He knew that it was a side effect of the drugs that helped his brain and body endure the exorcisms, but he hated himself for it. Hated the way his emotions spilled like water from his cupped hands.

'We know it is hard,' Jyotirmoy said, 'but the end is in sight. Soon, we will be able to access the files cached in your neural net. Soon, we will know what the tick-tock philosopher discovered, and we will use that knowledge to reshape history. We will make the crooked way straight. We will walk the true path, in light and in love.'

His face shone with a pure, simple joy. He took Hari's hands in his.

'We're so fortunate to live in such times!'

2

Sometimes, Hari would see Levi walking in the garden. A tall, slender man dressed like any ordinary Saint in a plain white jerkin and white trousers, ankling along at the head of a small congregation of adepts and sacristans, the five mind sailors in their golden suits, and the drones that recorded his every moment. Intricate patterns unfurled from his footsteps, racing out across the path in a steady and unbroken wave of white on black. Pictures from his life. The faces of martyrs. Over and again, a single moment from the Bright Moment. The young man on his bicycle, turning to look out at the viewer before he was engulfed in a flare of light.

Levi and his crew trod on holy ground.

Three of the adepts were Ardenists, broad-shouldered giants whose faces and arms and chests were scarred by old disputes, the folds of their wings falling from shoulders to wrists and hips like leathery cloaks, golden hair bushed out from white ribbons knotted at their brows. They talked gravely with Levi as they walked, conjuring windows and picts.

Hari had felt a cold, sharp pang the first time he saw them. The memory of his friend, his friend's betrayal and fall, pierced him like sunlight falling through glass. His feelings about Levi were more complicated.

He had not yet met the prophet. The leader of the Saints. He watched the procession from a distance but didn't dare approach it. Here was his enemy. Here was the man who had changed the course of his life, passing by in his pomp.

Jyotirmoy and other adepts had told him that the Saints were not responsible for hijacking his family's ship and the murders of Dr Gagarian and his associates. They said that the assassins were nothing to do with them, that they had not sent the messages, that they were not holding Nabhoj or any other members of his family prisoner. Hari didn't believe them. He was stupefied by drugs and bone-deep exhaustion, but whenever he saw Levi walking in the garden he felt the beast stir in its basement lair. Had fantasies of flying at him, attacking him with a stone, a broken branch, fists, teeth.

He never acted on these fantasies. Never took one step towards Levi when he passed by at the head of the little procession. He forced himself to watch, to stand calmly with no particular expression on his face. It was a discipline, this small show of defiance: like all prisoners, Hari had discovered the importance of self-control. But although he told himself that attacking Levi would be futile, that he would be shot or peppered with paralysing darts, zapped by drones or brought down and beaten by acolytes, that it was better to watch the man and sharpen his hatred and wait for the moment when he could act quickly and decisively, when he could scream and stoop, he knew that the moment would never come, knew that it was a fantasy as futile as the fantasies of revenge he'd conjured in the long and lonely days of exile on Themba, and felt a filthy mixture of fascination and anger and helpless self-loathing wash through him like a sickness.

The worst thing of all was that neither Levi nor any of his followers spared him a glance. No one noticed Hari's tremendous simulation of calm. He was invisible, of no consequence. He didn't matter. The pain inflicted on him didn't matter. Only what he carried in his head mattered. Only that. The remembrancers and sacristans told him that the ceremonies of exorcism were done with all of their love, but it was a lie. It had to be a lie, because how could anyone love someone they did not care about?

Hari always tried to remember that. Tried to remember that he meant nothing to the Saints. That he should never hope for mercy or kindness. It was another form of discipline.

During the days of Hari's long exorcism, Jyotirmoy told him stories about Levi's life and the rise of the Saints. Dancing for Hari as he had once danced on *Pabuji's Gift*, now as then teaching him how to make the appropriate genuflections and expressions, how to flow from position to position, moment to moment. Telling the story of Levi's rebellion after the Bright Moment, and his revelation during his exile. Telling the story of Levi's overthrow of the elders of his church and the establishment of the company of Saints, of how Levi had led the first Saints out of their garden into cities and settlements of the Belt, where they discovered that dozens of sects had sprung up in the aftermath of the Bright Moment, each claiming to possess exclusive knowledge about its true meaning. But only Levi and the Saints knew the truth, Jyotirmoy said. That was why so many had recognised him as a true prophet. That was why, just three years after his rebellion against the elders of his church, he had been at the head of an army of tens of thousands, and had begun to plan his assault on the false gods of the seraphs.

The story of Levi's invitation to the Republic of Arden and his long discussions with the old philosophers was Jyotirmoy's masterpiece: a virtuoso performance that evoked the aerial displays and fights of the Ardenists, and the slow forging of a plan to use the information horizons of the seraphs as portals to a universe whose physics would allow merely human intelligence to vasten, as Sri Hong-Owen's intelligence had been vastened.

It was not a new idea. Several cults had already tried and failed to destroy, invade, or co-opt the seraphs. Others trailed after the seraphs as they orbited Saturn, transmitting prayers and petitions and entreaties. But Levi and the Ardenists believed that they alone would triumph because only they could forge an alloy of faith and philosophy into a blade that could cut through the seraphs' defences. Jyotirmoy told Hari how Levi and the old ones from the Republic of Arden had supervised the voyage of the wheel habitat to Saturn. How, after a great ceremony of prayer and blessing and purification, a capsule containing the first of the mind sailors had been shot into the folds of frozen light around one of the seraphs. How the capsule had vanished in a flare of false photons and hard radiation, and a djinn, or something as relentlessly aggressive and unforgiving as a djinn, had violated the ship from which the mind sailor had been launched, driving its crew insane and firing up its motor and committing it to a trajectory that had intersected with Saturn's atmosphere.

Two more attempts had likewise failed, and then someone had tried to assassinate Levi while he was preaching in one of the floating cities of Ceres. It was a low point for the Saints. Their dream of vastening a human agent had been thwarted; their leader had been infected with a virulent half-life virus, and spent three years in coldsleep while his physicians devised a cure.

But now, according to Jyotirmoy, Hari would help the Saints to achieve their holy mission.

'You did not know it, but you were travelling along a predestined path,' Jyotirmoy told Hari. 'And at last it brought you here. Just as my own path brought me to *Pabuji's Gift*, four years ago. We did not meet by chance, Hari. We are here because we are meant to be here.'

Hari did not question any of the stories, and Jyotirmoy never asked him if he believed any of Levi's teachings. The Saints were not interested in testing his faith. They were entirely focused on purging the djinn that stood at the entrance to his neural net.

The djinn defended Hari by subverting and twisting the functions and capabilities of other machine intelligences. It had used the eidolon of Hari's p-suit, the algorithms in the skulls of the skull feeders, the signage in the free zone of Tannhauser Gate, and much else. And the Saints were using that ability to destroy it. At each stage of the exorcism, Hari's neural net was stimulated to trigger the djinn, and its manifestation was captured in a sandbox where simulations of various machines churned in futile cycles. While sacristans prayed over Hari, remembrancers located areas in his brain and neural net where activity was correlated with the djinn's ferocious attempts to escape the trap, and zapped them with tightly collimated beams of neutrons that created microscopic cascades of lethal radiation where they crossed.

The remembrancers assured Hari that his brain would find routes around the damaged areas, and because his bios had been deactivated, and because he inhabited his damage and could not see it from the outside, he had no way of knowing how much he'd been changed. But after each session he was aware that his thoughts had become a little foggier, could feel that some small part of him had been cut away. A word he could not quite remember, a pict half-glimpsed in the moment of its dissolution.

And so it went, a brutal cycle of ceremonial torture and recovery, and each time Hari was weaker and more tractable than the last. Until, one day, he woke at the end of a session to find Levi studying him.

As usual Hari was seated in a padded chair with a flock of small drones hung around him, measuring his metabolic activity and the activity of his brain and major organs. The remembrancers and sacristans stood to one side, heads bowed. And Levi stood in front of Hari, with the Ardenists and the adepts and the mind sailors at his back.

His blond hair was done up in tight cornrows; his face was ashen, as white as the skulls and long bones that Hari and his family had once discovered stacked in neat patterns along the walls of an ossuary in an airless settlement. As if something paler and colder than blood ran in his veins. His hands joined prayerwise just below his chin, fingertip to fingertip, he studied Hari with a tranquil unblinking gaze while one of the adepts sang a kind of sura and the others chanted *Praise God* at the end of each verse. *Praise God. Praise God.* When at last they fell silent, Levi stepped forward and cradled Hari's face in his cool hands, and kissed him on the forehead and drew back and made a small gesture.

Sacristans and remembrancers, the Ardenists and the adepts and the five mind sailors in their gold one-piece suits, plugs and implants bristling from their bare scalps, left the room in a bustle of respectful obedience. The drones rose up and followed, and the little lights scattered across the ceiling of the room dimmed until only Levi's face was illuminated.

Hari did his best to meet the prophet's gaze. It took all his concentration, all his strength. He began to sweat, felt as if he was being forced backwards, crowded into a smaller and smaller space. A pressure grew behind his eyes. He wondered if the djinn would step out, but it did not. The pressure swelled, squeezing out his thoughts until only Levi's implacable gaze was left. Hari felt that he was falling into it, a dust mote spiralling down a beam of light.

Then Levi laughed, and closed his eyes. His lids were each painted gold, with a red dot in the centre. The pressure in Hari's skull vanished, but the blind unblinking stare of the painted eyes held him fast.

Levi said, 'Do you believe in karma?'

His voice was soft, with the faintest trace of a lisp.

It took Hari a moment to gather his thoughts. 'My father taught me that we are responsible for our actions, and we are judged by them in this life, not in any other.'

'Yet both of us are shaped by previous lives. Your father turned you into a vessel for his heresies; I am the reborn prophet of an ancient cult. We are emergent patterns that repeat over and again in the warp of history. Hero and nemesis. Prophet and sacred book. You are part of my story, and I am part of yours. It was inevitable that you would be delivered to me.'

Hari remembered Professor Aluthgamage, and thought of the steps that had brought him here. Any one of which, by some small deviation, could have led him elsewhere.

He said, 'Prove that it was inevitable.'

'Here you are. What other proof do you need?'

Levi opened his eyes. The shock of his ocean-blue gaze was like a physical blow.

'I was gifted with a vision,' he said. 'I saw how history has diverged from the holy ideal. I saw the Bright Moment could help us make that crooked way straight. And I also saw how history has been manipulated and is still being manipulated by the seraphs. Just as they once locked Earth into the long winter from which it is still recovering, they want to lock history to its present path.

'The missions of my mind sailors were sabotaged by agents of the seraphs. I was almost murdered by one of them. And your family's ship was hijacked by their agents, and they murdered Dr Gagarian and your family. They attempted to suppress me, and attempted to suppress your family. Yet I survived, and you escaped, and your search for those who stole your ship has brought us together, and delivered to me the means of creating a new crusade that will at last storm the citadels of the seraphs. You still do not believe in karma, Gajananvihari Pilot?'

Hari said, 'I believe that it wasn't chance that brought me here. You have been searching for me ever since your followers hijacked my family's ship and I escaped. I escaped you over and again, but then my luck ran out.'

'We did not hijack your ship. Your enemies are our enemies.'

'Prove it. If you didn't hijack the ship, show me who did.'

'All in good time. The remembrancers tell me that the djinn or demon that once rode you has been entirely excised. Let's test that, shall we?'

A small bright ball of white light snapped on, hanging in the air between Hari and Levi. It seethed and spun and crackled, and radiated heat like a tiny sun.

'If the remembrancers are wrong, your djinn will defend you,' Levi said. 'It will push away this little star before it can harm you. It will use it to attack me.'

The bright hot light drifted towards Hari. Its heat began to scorch his face.

'Push it away, if you can,' Levi said. 'Take hold of it and throw it at me. I am quite undefended. You could kill me. I know you want to. Do it!'

The hot glare blotted out Levi's face. Hari tried to flinch away from it, but a strap across his forehead held him fast. The scorching air stank of electricity. He screwed his eyes shut; the light burned blood-red on his eyelids and grew brighter and hotter. His skin was withering, shrinking against the bones of his face, his eyes were boiling in their sockets . . .

Then the light vanished. There was a point of intense pain at the centre of his forehead, but otherwise he seemed unharmed. He opened his eyes. Somewhere beyond the afterimages swarming in the dark, Levi said, 'Now we can begin our real work. My people will extract the secrets locked in your head, and they will explain why we are not your enemies, and how we can work together.'

After the remembrancers and the sacristans returned, after they worked on him for several hours, Hari was set free and allowed to wander out into the gardens. It was night. The half-life lawn glowed with soft red light. Fireflies pulsed in trees and bushes. He made his way to the pool on the ledge above the treetops, splashed water on the puffy burn in the centre of his forehead, stretched out on a flat rock. Saturn's ringed ball, tiny as a toy, hung in the black sky beyond the dim architecture of the roof.

This is real, he told himself. I am really here.

He tried to process what had happened, what Levi had told him, but he was so very tired, and his head felt like a hollow gourd stuffed with black sand. He slept, and if he dreamed he did not remember his dreams, and woke to sunlight and bird song. Jyotirmoy sat nearby, watching Hari, smiling like a small child on the dawn of its birthday. Every trace of the djinn had been exorcised and the files were at last accessible, he said. The remembrancers had extracted them and the adepts were even now studying them.

'We believe that we have all of Dr Gagarian's work, and the work of his associates,' he said. 'We have everything we need. Your long trial is over, Hari! You have borne it well and bravely, and it is almost over! Almost, but not quite. But there is still some work to do. Your neural net still contains a set of files protected by deep layers of encryption. The remembrancers believe that they were created when the seed of the net was planted in your skull by the tankies of the Memory Whole.

They also believe, from their size and structure, that they are a copy of a human personality. A copy of your father, perhaps.'

Hari laughed. 'Who else would it be?'

'You knew, and you did not tell us?'

'I didn't know, but I should have known,' Hari said. 'I should have guessed.'

Like all those who passed over, his father had cached a copy of himself in a safe place. And because he didn't trust strangers, he'd kept it close. On the ship, inside the family. Updating it and checking it when Hari had visited his viron. All those times when only an hour or so had seemed to pass inside the viron, but days had gone by in the real world . . .

Jyotirmoy said that Levi had hired a specialist skilled in the old techniques used by the Memory Whole. She was on her way, riding a swift ship from Tannhauser Gate. She would crack open the last of his files, and then there would be no more secrets.

'It must be a shock,' he said, 'to discover how badly your father used you.'

'It's a shock to discover how badly I failed him.'

Hari was certain now that Agrata hadn't aimed him at Tannhauser Gate so that he could open the files cached in Dr Gagarian's head, and enter into negotiations with the hijackers. No, Worden Hanburanaman would have translated the copy of his father into a new viron. And even though Aakash and Agrata hadn't trusted him, had manipulated him, used him, lied to him, Hari would have been proud to have helped to resurrect his father, would have been proud and happy to carry out his every wish, obey his every order.

'I suppose you will want to quicken him,' he said. 'So that you can force him to tell you everything he knows.'

He thought of his father waking and realising where he was and somehow taking control, but knew it was a hopeless fantasy. If the Saints ever quickened his father, they'd do it inside a sandbox, and vivisect him.

'The expert will access the files, and determine what needs to be done,' Jyotirmoy said. 'And when we have done what needs to be done, we will know everything. And you will know everything, too. Everything your father did not want you to know. But please, don't worry about that now. The worst part is over. The exorcism is finished; the files have been extracted. It is a great thing. A great day. The first of many.'

But it wasn't really over, of course. The remembrancers subjected Hari to batteries of tests and probes while the sacristans prayed and sang. There were long interviews with the Ardenists, who showed him the files they'd extracted: raw data and logs from experiments; algorithms and models based on extrapolations and conjectures; notes and picts exchanged between the tick-tock philosopher and his associates. Hari found most of this stuff as incomprehensible as his father's monologues, but he quickly realised that something was missing. Although Dr Gagarian had preserved every message sent by his colleagues, there were no records of his conversations with Aakash. Hari wondered if these were cached inside the encrypted set of files still lodged in his neural net; wondered what else was hidden there, wondered if he would ever know – after the specialist opened him up, the Saints might kill him. Dispose of him, or throw him into some deep hole for the rest of his life.

But then the Ardenists showed him something else and, for the first time since they'd captured him, Hari allowed himself to feel a little hope.

3

Several days later, after one of the interminable sessions with the remembrancers and sacristans and Ardenists, Hari was walking in the gardens when Jyotirmoy hailed him. The young dancer emerged from the spreading shade of a cedar tree at the far end of a long lawn and advanced with small, quick, bouncing steps that terminated in a spin through three-hundred-and sixty degrees. He landed with arms outspread and one knee bent in a graceful half-bow, and smiled up at Hari. 'I've brought a friend.'

Behind him, someone started across the lawn, walking with the tottering steps of an invalid, dressed all in white. After a few moments of confusion, after wondering if the specialist had finally arrived, Hari realised that it was Riyya Lo Minnot.

They wandered along paths of black sand, across lawns, through shadow-dappled woods, past stands of bamboo and long banks of flowering bushes. The garden always rising up ahead of them, green and lovely in the warm chandelier light, as if they were treading a new world into existence.

Riyya had not been awake long. 'They stored me in a hibernaculum until they needed me, revived me a few days ago. Six days, seven. This is the first time I've been allowed outside.'

'I'm sorry they brought you here,' Hari said. 'Sorry you are caught up in this. But I'm pleased to see you, too. It's selfish, I know. But still. It's good, I think, that they have allowed us to be together. A good sign. *Another* good sign.'

He wanted to reach out to her. He wanted to embrace her, comfort her, wanted to tell her that everything was going to be all right, but she was defensive, hunched into herself. She'd fallen several times as they ambled along, and each time she'd refused Hari's help, saying that if she had to learn how to walk all over again she'd do it herself. So they walked and he let her talk, hoping they could get past her anger and bitterness and discuss his great good news, and how they could move forward.

'I'm your reward,' she said. 'For cooperating. For giving them what they wanted.'

'I didn't have much choice, Riyya.'

'I know. They showed me what they did to you.'

Hari felt a blush of shame. 'That was cruel and unnecessary.'

'They were proud,' Riyya said. 'They were proud of their work. They believed they were doing a great good thing, and wanted to share it with me. I thought they were killing you.'

'They didn't quite manage it, as you can see.'

Riyya gave him a look that turned his heart. Her coppery hair had been cropped short, and her face was thinner than he remembered, pale skin taut on her cheekbones, dark scoops beneath her eyes.

'No,' she said. 'Not quite. But they destroyed your djinn.'

'And found Dr Gagarian's files in my head, and pulled them out. But there's something else in here,' Hari said, tapping his forehead. 'Something big and deeply encrypted. I think it's a copy of my father. Or, at least, a copy of what he became after he passed over. A copy of a copy. I'll find out soon enough. The Saints have hired a specialist to open it.'

'So it isn't over,' Riyya said.

'The worst of it is over.'

He almost told her then, but she had turned away to watch a flock of scarlet parakeets burst from a stand of trees, chase each other above a lawn, and disappear into the green shade of the trees on the other side.

Quietly, dispassionately, as if reporting something that had happened to someone else, far away and long ago, she said, 'I told them everything. They showed me instruments, after they revived me. They explained what would happen to me if I did not answer their questions. They gave me a demonstration, with what they called an excruciation needle. Just the lightest touch. It felt as if I'd been burned to the bone. So I told them everything. I told them about my father and his work. I told them about you. Everything. Because I was scared of what they would do it if I didn't.'

'Don't feel bad,' Hari said. 'Everything you told them, it's probably in the files they pulled out of my neural net.'

Riyya turned to him, said with a sudden flash of bitterness, 'I betrayed my father – his trust in me. I should feel better because it was pointless?'

'I meant you did the right thing.'

She didn't seem to hear him. She said, 'It *was* pointless. After we left Tannhauser Gate, their friends on Ophir gained access to my father's possessions. They bribed one of the police, just like we did. And now they are building a duplicate of his apparatus. They showed it to me. And I don't know if this is funny or scary, but they expect me to approve of what they are doing. To be pleased that they are carrying on with my father's work.'

They walked a little way in silence.

Hari said, 'This copy of your father's apparatus – does it work?'

'They are close to finishing it,' Riyya said. 'They told me that they want to use it to inject some kind of thought bomb into the information horizon of one of the seraphs. They think it will allow them to get a mind sailor past its defences.'

'And the mind sailor will vasten, or fuse with the seraph,' Hari said. 'And then they will be able to use the vastened mind sailor to reach out to everyone on every world and worldlet, and begin a new age of peace and harmony.'

'Do you think any of it is possible? Could they actually invade and exploit one of the seraphs? Or use my father's discovery to manipulate people? Control them, inject ideas into their minds . . .'

'I think they've confused magical thinking with actual philosophy.'

'I hope you're right. But they seem so certain. So sure that they are on the threshold of a great change.'

'They've been selling that story for twenty years,' Hari said. 'They're very good at it. But it doesn't mean it's true.'

Riyya appeared to think about that. Then she said, 'They told me something else. They told me that they didn't have anything to do with the hijack of your family's ship, or my father's murder. His assassination. They said that he had been killed by agents of the seraphs. They showed me the confessions of agents they had uncovered. Agents of the seraphs pretending to be Saints . . .'

'I saw those confessions, too,' Hari said.

'You said that they were very good at selling their ideas,' Riyya said.

'But those so-called confessions were obviously fakes. Performances by mimesists, or real confessions made by poor, crazy people who believe that the seraphs talk directly to them.'

'I wondered about that, too. But then they showed me something else.' Hari was smiling. He couldn't hold back any longer. 'They showed me where my family's ship is. They showed me that they didn't have anything to do with the hijack.'

It was orbiting close to the outer edge of Saturn's rings, amongst the pack of ships and bubble habitats and platforms that trailed after the seraphs. The Ardenists had told Hari that it was listed in the registry of the city of Paris, Dione as the *Jindray Khinchi*, had shown him several picts obtained from a follower who worked there. Picts of its captain supervising repairs in Dione's orbital docks.

Nabhoj. Nabhoj or Nabhomani, it was hard to tell. He was dressed in a black blouse and black trews, Nabhoj's habitual costume, but his hair was long and caught up in a net, and he had a neatly trimmed beard. Alive a little over a hundred days ago, long after the hijack, accompanied by a woman whom Hari recognised at once.

His first thought had been that his brother was a prisoner. He'd wanted to believe it. Wanted to believe that his brother had been coerced into cooperating with the hijackers. But then he'd remembered what Khinda Wole had told him. That Nabhomani had known Deel Fertita; that he had told Rember Wole to hire her. And there he was, there was Nabhomani, or maybe it was Nabhoj, with one of Deel Fertita's sisters . . .

Hari wasn't ready to tell Riyya about that. Not yet. Perhaps not ever. It was family business.

She said, 'If the Saints know where your ship is, why haven't they tried to capture it? It has Dr Gagarian's equipment on board. It may have copies of his files, too.'

'Perhaps they don't care to get too close to the seraphs and their supplicants. Or perhaps they tried to hijack it from the hijackers, and failed,' Hari said. 'They didn't tell me everything.'

'That's the one thing we can be certain about,' Riyya said.

Hari took her to his favourite place in the garden. They sat at the edge of the little pool and looked out across the treetops, the sea of leaves heaving in the restless wind. Coriolis wind, according to Riyya. The wheel habitat was spinning to deepen its gravity: objects near its floor moved slightly faster than objects near its overhead because the path around the centre of spin was slightly longer. That was why water fell at a slant. And as with water, so with air. Different layers of air moved at different speeds, and friction between the layers created eddies. Climate-control machinery and landscaped windbreaks broke up these eddies before they grew too big, but couldn't eliminate all turbulence.

'I suspect a parable,' Hari said, trying to keep things light.

'It is what it is. A simple philosophical statement. This is an old world,' Riyya said. 'An old design from the age of expansion. At least a thousand years old, maybe more. A lovely place, but fragile.'

They sat side by side on a saddle of black rock in the sunlight that fell through the window-strip in the overhead, sipping from beakers of hot chocolate delivered by a pair of hummingbird-sized drones. Their bare feet planted on a thin gutter of damp moss, the drop to the treetops directly below. Rainbows glimmered in the feathering braid of water that fell from the pool's lip.

'All gardens are fragile,' Hari said. 'Too big, too open, stuck in their orbits, unable to manoeuvre . . .'

'This one's more fragile than most,' Riyya said. She drank off the last of her hot chocolate and tossed the beaker out into the empty air. It was blue, the beaker. Blue plastic with a frieze of white interlocked squares at its lip. As it tumbled past the black blockwork of the cliff, a drone flashed through the air and caught it and carried it off. A gust blew across the treetops and leaves heaved and tossed and showed their silvery undersides, a furrow of silver racing after the drone, racing away around the wheel of the world.

Hari said, 'The Saints made me an offer. They want me to help them capture *Pabuji's Gift*. They'll get any files and equipment left on board; I'll get the ship, and the hijackers.'

'It was cruel of them to show you your ship, Hari. Cruel of them to give you hope.'

'We'll find who killed our people, Riyya. And we'll get our revenge. I swear it.'

Riyya gave him a strange, tender look. 'That's all you care about, isn't it? Revenge. That's all you have left.'

'They owe us for what they did,' Hari said. 'And I intend to make them pay.'

4

Hari and Riyya explored the gardens, walking around and around the little world. They kept away from the Saints, and the Saints kept away from them. They found a cluster of woven sleeping pods hung from the lower branches of a grandfather live oak. Humps in the half-life lawn beneath the tree's canopy formed seats and tables. There were pools of warm water amongst the black rocks beyond, and a patch of smart sand that absorbed bodily wastes. Drones brought food, the simple fare of the Saints – discs of unleavened bread, harrisa, chickpeas in salted vinegar, ripe figs, apples, pomegranates.

Every day, Hari felt a little stronger. Every day, his mind was a little clearer. He and Riyya told each other stories about their childhoods and their very different lives. There was little left to say about their plight, no point yet in making plans for the future.

One night, Hari woke to find Riyya leaning over him in the faint luminescence of the pod's weave. He started to speak, fell silent when she pressed a finger against his lips. His mouth was dry and he had an airy feeling of falling. He'd been forbidden to sleep with any of the passengers, but he'd sometimes fantasised that Sora or one of the other young women travelling on the ship would come to find him. Now, as in his fantasies, the pleasure was heightened by the excitement of transgression, the electric immediacy of Riyya's presence. She reached down, moved her hips against his until he slid into her heat. The pod rocking as they rocked against each other. Hari came almost at once, and Riyya held him inside herself and ground against him until she gasped and trembled.

They curled together, afterwards, on the yielding floor of the pod, in

271

the dim hush of the garden. When Hari woke, daylight shone through the pod's translucent weave, and he was alone.

Riyya didn't want to talk about it. 'I don't want to talk about it,' she said, when Hari tried to talk about it. And: 'It wasn't anything. Back in cadet school, we played around with each other all the time. It didn't mean anything then, and it doesn't mean anything now.' And: 'Why do people need reasons for what they do?'

So they didn't talk about it. She deflected his fumbling attempts at intimacy; he began to resent the way she had used him. For relief, to escape the terror and uncertainty of captivity, to assert herself. Instead, they had a kind of argument about their adventures, about whose story it really was. Hari tried to tell Riyya that everything would come right, but she wouldn't listen to him.

'Do you think that what the Saints did was necessary?' she said. 'Do you think that they tortured you because it served a higher cause? And what about you, Hari? Do you want to punish the people who killed your family because it will satisfy some kind of cosmic balance? Or is it because you are angry and hurt? Do you think you'll be any less angry, any less hurt, afterwards?'

At last she walked away and left him alone with his guilt and doubt. He had come to believe that his suffering was necessary. That it was part of a transaction. The Saints wanted to know everything about Dr Gagarian's research; he needed their help to reach *Pabuji's Gift*. But he could think of no good reason for what the Saints had done to Riyya. She had been humiliated and hurt. Her wounds were still raw. They might never heal. And he was responsible. He had walked into her life. He had drawn the Saints' attention to the hijack, to Dr Gagarian's work and the work of her father.

She came back to him after two days, and they didn't talk about it again. But Hari's guilt lingered. Guilt and doubt.

And so the days passed, each much like the rest. One day, they were sitting up on the ledge, looking out across the treetops in companionable silence, when a raw white flash took the world away. A moment of no time, no thought. And then the world came back, as if it had been rebooted. Hari and Riyya looked at each other, and knew that the Saints had tested her father's apparatus.

Later that day, two adepts came for Hari, and escorted him down one of the spars to the hub of the wheel habitat, the dock at the spin axis. Levi was waiting for him in a gig, a small gold-tinted sphere that darted out from the wheel habitat, followed by half a dozen identical gigs, bubbles of air rising through the sunlit black until Hari could blot out the tiny, turning world with his thumbnail. A ship hung out there, a fat argosy from the last days of the True Empire. As the gig slowly circled it, Levi told Hari about the progress of the Saints' great work.

'They have already downloaded a mind sailor,' Hari said to Riyya, after he returned to the wheel habitat. 'They took her brain apart, neuron by neuron, and copied her connectome into a viron. They are trying to do what the Ghosts tried to do, out at Fomalhaut. They were going to create mind sailors too, the Ghosts. Somehow fuse them with the alien intelligence that inhabits the core of the gas-giant planet, Cthuga.'

'My father says they failed because there was no alien mind,' Riyya said. 'There were epiphenomena, created by the planet's magnetic field, that mimicked aspects of intelligent behaviour. Sprites, apparitions. But there was no world-mind until Sri Hong-Owen downloaded or re-distributed herself into the sprites.'

'Well, Levi plans to vasten his mind sailors in a similar way,' Hari said. 'He talked for a straight hour about how it's supposed to work. Half of it philosophy, half theology. I asked him why the seraphs hadn't tried to stop him. If he could vasten a human mind and interfere with their control of history, why hadn't they destroyed the habitat, and the ship? He said that the human agents who had tried to kill him before couldn't reach him out here, and the seraphs themselves responded only to immediate threats. He said, "A man will brush a fly from his face, but he won't go to war against flies." Do you have flies, in Ophir?'

'They're a useful part of the biosphere,' Riyya said.

'I had to ask about them. I told Levi that perhaps the seraphs hadn't reached out to him because they didn't consider him a threat. He said they were arrogant, and that would be their downfall.'

'You were trying to annoy him.'

'I discovered that it isn't possible. His fantasy is entirely airtight.'

In the little bubble of the gig, Levi had told Hari that he was looking forward to talking with his father because they had so much in common, had laughed when Hari said that they held completely opposing views.

'We have taken different paths, your father and I, but we both started from the same place, and we both want to reach the same destination.'

'You want to prove that Sri Hong-Owen is a kind of god,' Hari said. 'My father and Dr Gagarian wanted to prove that she is not.'

'She is beyond our understanding,' Levi said. 'Beyond the reach of ordinary human comprehension; beyond the reach of philosophy and the experiments of Dr Gagarian.'

He launched into another monologue, telling Hari that philosophy could not give a complete account of the universe because of limitations in its reductive methodology. Philosophy reduced the universe of things to its components, catalogued them, tried to fit their properties and interactions into mathematical models. Large-scale properties that could not be anatomised – beauty, grandeur, the splendour and sublimity of scale – were considered to be trivial by-products, emergent accidents that triggered spurious human responses. Philosophy stripped away metaphor, Levi said. And that was where faith was strongest: bridging the reality of the universe and the reality of human experience.

'Philosophy also fails to give a complete explanation of the universe on its own terms,' Levi said. 'Many properties are chaotic: initial conditions are underdetermined, and cannot be used to predict accurately the final state. Measurement of the behaviour of every atom in a small volume of gas will not provide any useful information about the way those same atoms behave in a solid or liquid state on a larger scale, because the phase change from gas to liquid is an emergent property. There is no reconciliation between the very small and the very large, no smooth transition. So we do not need to invoke a god of the gaps, hiding in places philosophy cannot reach, or a god who intervenes with miracles that circumvent the usual natural order or exploit causal lacunae. Divine agency is an emergent property of the universe. If the activity of our neurons affects our consciousness from the bottom up, then divinity affects it from the top down.'

Levi floated above his couch, pale-skinned, dressed all in white, ghostly against the black vacuum. Every now and then a faint tremor passed through his body. He had never completely recovered from the assassination attempt. There had been irreversible nerve damage; he was in pain all the time. But the pain was useful, according to him. A useful discipline, a reminder that he was mortal, and fallible.

'Philosophy may claim that it does not need our faith and beliefs,' he told Hari. 'But we do not renounce philosophy. It provides our basic needs. And if you grant the utility of a maker or an air scrubber, it would be illogical to spurn the rest. The work of Dr Gagarian will be of great use to us; so will the device of the father of your friend. I am told that it is based on a weapon developed by the Trues. And while it is a very poor imitation of the Bright Moment, and its power diminishes with distance, it will play a crucial role in the vastening of my mind sailor.

'And so all things have followed different paths, yet come together at the same point. As if foreordained. As if through the workings of a subtle plan beyond the comprehension of merely human minds. The work of Dr Gagarian and his colleagues complements our work. Your father complements me. He will challenge my ideas and my faith, and make them stronger. Yes, I very much look forward to talking with him, and I will not have to wait much longer. And you will help me too, of course, as I will help you. You see how it all fits together?'

Riyya said, 'He's crazy, but he thinks that he needs you. That's a weakness. Something you can exploit.'

'Unfortunately, I need him,' Hari said.

They were walking through a grove of birch trees and ferns. Sunlight slanted between the white trunks of the trees and a bird was singing somewhere in the distance – it reminded Hari of the forest biome where he'd been interviewed by Ma Sakitei. He wondered if the gardens of the wheel habitat had been designed by the Free People.

'You need him to take back your ship,' Riyya said. 'But after that?'

Hari knew that she wanted to know if he had a plan to defeat and escape the Saints, but he couldn't talk about that, and not only because the Saints were almost certainly eavesdropping.

'Levi told me that the specialist will arrive very soon,' he said. 'Once the last file left in my neural net is unlocked, he said, I can head out to *Pabuji's Gift*. I don't trust him, Riyya. But if I'm given the chance, I'll go. Even if there are secrets hidden aboard the ship that will help the Saints get closer to their fantasy, even if there's no chance that I'll be able to escape, I'll go. Because that's what this is all about. To find out who hijacked the ship, and employed those assassins.'

'Agents of the seraphs, according to Levi.'

'We'll see.'

Riyya said, 'If this was one of the old stories, we'd somehow escape just before Levi launched his mind sailor. There would be a desperate fight for control of a crucial machine, and at the last moment one of us would key in a sequence that would shut it down. The seraph would no longer be distracted, the mind sailor would be destroyed and the Saints would be thwarted, the universe would be saved.'

'It's a nice thought.'

'It's a story. What we're caught up in isn't anything like that. For one thing, we're talking about the kind of story we're caught up in,' Riyya said. 'And in those old stories they didn't ever stop to think if they were doing the right thing in the right way. They just did it.'

'We look backwards for inspiration and guidance because everything's old. Because everything's been done before,' Hari said.

A sudden sharp breeze blew through the birches and their leaves danced and flickered.

Riyya said, 'You know what scares me most? That if we are trapped inside a story, it isn't yours or mine. It's Levi's fantasy of becoming a god.'

'This thing we're in, whatever it is, we're in it together,' Hari said.

But it didn't reassure her.

5

Several days later, Hari and Riyya were eating breakfast in the shade of the grandfather live oak when Jyotirmoy appeared, traversing the half-life lawn with his usual languid elegance. Hari knew why he had come, knew what he was going to say. Felt it like a stone in his stomach. He scarcely noticed when Riyya reached out and gripped his hand.

Jyotirmoy took Hari to the little cluster of rooms where he had been exorcised, and the crew of remembrancers and sacristans prepared him in the ordinary way. Stripping off his clothes. Strapping him to the chair. Fitting a mask that delivered a chilly draught of dry, oxygen-rich air. Treating him with drugs that paralysed him and distanced him from the world.

The remembrancers and a small woman in a grey smock and black leggings were studying windows that showed different views of Hari's brain and the neural net wrapped around it, quietly conferring with their backs to him. At last the senior remembrancer leaned over Hari, asked him if he was ready. Hari tried to smile. He wanted to let the man know that he wanted to get this done, but could do little more than move his eyes.

The remembrancer turned and looked at someone and said, 'He's yours.'

The woman in the grey smock stepped towards him. Child-sized, her bare scalp tattooed with spidery symbols. Hari had met her before, in a city halfway around the Belt. The head doctor, Eli Yong.

She studied him with a cold and clinical gaze, said something to the chief remembrancer. And then there was a blank space, and then she was inside his head.

*

Black water lapped islands of white moss. The yellow eyes of torches pulsed in the twilight. Skulls hung from poles like clusters of bony fruit. A sprawl of bodies – the small congregation of skull feeders, the dead woman. The assassin killed by Hari's djinn. His father's djinn. She lay on her back, bloody stars glistening on her black bodysuit.

'Trite and melodramatic, I know,' Eli Yong said. 'But it's easy to model and its cues trigger useful subsets in your dynamic core. Do you remember when we last met?'

She was a solid presence, fully realised, but Hari was little more than a floating viewpoint. He couldn't move, but discovered that he could speak.

'I remember that you said that you couldn't help me. Either you lied to me then, or you're lying to the Saints now.'

'I told you the truth then, and I'll tell the truth now. I didn't come here to help the Saints. I came to help you.'

'You had better tell me why.'

'You walked into my shop with an exquisite neural net inside your head, and a djinn fiercer than any I'd ever had to deal with. I wanted to know more, but before I could get in touch with you again, you and Rav had fled Fei Shen after some trouble with a group of skull feeders. I knew Rav by reputation, and reached out to him. He told me that he had other plans for you, involving a tick-tock matriarch in Ophir, but I made myself useful to him. I studied the image of the neural net I'd captured, and researched the techniques of the Memory Whole. I talked to one of the skull feeders. I reported the conversation to Rav and sent him the commissars' file on this woman,' Eli Yong said, gesturing towards the dead assassin. 'She arrived on Fei Shen shortly after you. A trader, according to her bios, but the settlement where she claimed to live had no records of her. She was progeric, and had been tweaked in several interesting and rather antique ways. They used to make warriors like her in the long ago.'

'I know. I've met some of her sisters,' Hari said.

'I constructed this simulation from a file Rav sent me. Isn't the level of detail wonderful? He has eidetic recall – if only I'd been able to look inside his head,' Eli Yong said. 'As I anticipated, Rav had no luck in Ophir. Tick-tocks are skilful, in their own way, but rather specialised. I knew the matriarch wouldn't be able to get past your djinn, although I expect she faked disinterest to disguise her failure.'

'We went to her to open Dr Gagarian's files,' Hari said. 'But they had been destroyed.'

'That's why *you* went. Rav wanted to look inside the tick-tock philosopher's head, yes, but he also wanted to know what you were carrying inside that neural net of yours. When it didn't work out, he called me. As I knew he would. I was supposed to meet him at Tannhauser Gate, but by the time I arrived he was dead and you had vanished. So I made a new arrangement.

'The Saints were once a power, but they are much reduced now. The near-assassination of their leader, schisms during his long recovery, the failures of their so-called mind sailors . . . It was easy to intercept the message to their school in Tannhauser Gate, easy to fool them into thinking I was an agent of the Memory Whole. I gave them advice about dealing with the djinn, then told them I would have to unlock the last of your files in person. And here I am,' Eli Yong said. 'And I will unlock those files. But not now, and not here. A ship is ready to take us away: *Brighter Than Creation's Dark*. I believe you know it.'

'Rav's son. You were working for Rav, and now you're working for his son.'

'*With* him, not for him. Luckily for you, he isn't anything like his father. He has interests of his own. He'll tell you all about them when we get back to the ship.'

'It's a pretty story. Why should I believe you?'

'This little shared experience is taking place in only a few seconds as measured in the world outside, and our time is almost up. But to prove that we want to help you, I'll tell you the name of the original of this assassin and her sisters. The name of her mother. The commissars couldn't find a match for her genotype, but they were looking in the wrong place. Looking for people still alive. Rav found her elsewhere. In the deep past.' The head doctor, Eli Yong, smiled at Hari. 'It turns out that the assassins are tweaked clones of Sri Hong-Owen.'

'She went to Fomalhaut,' Hari said. 'She and her children left the Solar System for Fomalhaut fifteen hundred years ago.'

'Not all of them, it seems. I know where they live. If you want to find out, come with me,' Eli Yong said. 'And now it's time to wake up.'

'Tell me what you and Rav hoped to find. Why you wanted to open my neural—'

Hari woke to the roar of wind and water blowing somewhere outside the dim room. A light flickering in one eye, then the other.

'You'll do,' Eli Yong said, and helped him sit up.

He was naked. A fat white patch was stuck on his right arm. Eli Yong crossed the room, stepping around the bodies of adepts and remembrancers and sacristans, came back with his clothes.

'Can you dress yourself? Of course you can. Quickly now. We don't have much time.'

Hari wanted to get out, wanted to follow the woman – it was a physical desire, a force lifting him out of himself – but a stubbornness at his core resisted the impulse. 'Wait,' he said, and ripped the patch from his arm.

'That was feeding you antidotes to the remembrancers' drugs,' Eli Yong said.

'And what else? Something to make me obedient, compliant?'

'Well, it doesn't matter. It's probably done its work by now. Get dressed. Hurry.'

'I need to understand something.'

'I'm here to rescue you from these fanatics,' Eli Yong said. 'That's all you need to know for now. Get dressed, I'll explain everything else on the ship.'

Hari remembered the question he had tried to ask in the dream. 'Why did you and Rav want to open my neural net?'

'To find out what was inside, of course.'

'I had a lot of time to think about what Rav wanted,' Hari said. 'Why he was happy to take me to Tannhauser Gate. Why he turned on my friends there. Why he wanted to hide me on his ship. He wanted you to pull the files from my neural net, yes, but not because he wanted to help me. It was because he wanted to sell them.'

'We really don't have time for this,' Eli Yong said.

'Who was he going to sell the files to?'

'I was able to knock out most of the Saints because their bioses are cross-linked via the commons of this garden. A foolish and easily exploitable design flaw. But I couldn't incapacitate everyone – I couldn't touch the Ardenists. They are rebooting the system right now. And the others won't remain unconscious for long. Get dressed. We need to leave right now.'

'I won't leave until you tell me who Rav's clients were,' Hari said.

'It doesn't matter any more. Rav is dead. Things have changed.'

'Prove that I can trust you. Answer the question.'

They were staring at each other. Eli Yong looked away, looked back.

'It was the Saints,' she said. 'The Saints, to begin with.'

'He hated the Saints. He wanted to destroy them.'

'Is that what he told you? He told me that he had talked to Levi. He wanted to sell them Dr Gagarian's head, at first. And when that didn't work out, he was going to sell you,' Eli Yong said. 'That's why he didn't simply steal the tick-tock's head. He knew about your neural net even before I told him, guessed that your father had stashed a copy of the files inside it.'

'X-ray spex,' Hari said.

'I told him I could get inside your neural net and copy whatever it contained. I also told him that he needed to keep you alive. That your neural net wasn't anything like the tick-tock's storage modules: the files it contained might be compromised if he killed you and cut off your head. I saved your life then, and now I'm saving it again, if you'll let me,' Eli Yong said.

'Gun Ako Akoi tried and failed to open my neural net. That's when Rav accepted your offer.'

'He told me to travel to Tannhauser Gate. If I could extract the files from your net, he was going to sell copies through its free zone to whoever wanted them. The Saints, the assassins . . . And if I couldn't extract the files, he was going to sell you. But none of that matters now,' Eli Yong said.

'You and Rav. And now you and Rav's son,' Hari said, and pulled on his trousers.

'Rav's son doesn't want to sell you or your cache of files to anyone. He wants to know what Dr Gagarian knew. He wants to carry it forward. You can talk about it, the two of you, on the ship. Are you ready? Come on, then.'

They hurried through the chain of rooms, out into the lashing roar and sulphur light of a storm. Wind and rain smashed into Hari, drenching him from head to foot; Eli Yong grabbed his elbow, pulled him across the drowned lawn. They splashed through ankle-deep water, ploughed through squalls that lashed rain sideways.

'Your friend is helping us out,' the head doctor shouted. Her tattooed scalp gleamed. Her grey smock was plastered to her slender body. 'In exchange for a ride.'

Hari followed Eli Yong up a steep slope of trees and black rocks. Trees heaved and writhed as if trying to tear themselves out of the ground. Splintered branches and windrows of green leaves lay everywhere and whirled on the wind and smashed against Hari's body, his face. He clawed them off, slogged on up the muddy slope, possessed by a fierce wild elation that Riyya's storm had woken in his blood, in the marrow-heart of his bones.

Eli Yong climbed ahead of him, small and hunched and tenacious. He yelled to her, asked if they were heading towards an airlock. The docks were at the hub in the centre of the turning ring of the habitat, but there might be emergency airlocks along the rim . . .

'There's another way!' Eli Yong shouted back. Her sodden leggings and smock were spattered with mud and there was mud streaked on her face. She looked like a proxy got up for war.

A path threw narrow switchbacks as it climbed towards the overhead. Water cascaded from level to level. The wind was growing stronger, a relentless howling force, but when Hari and Eli Yong reached the top of the path the rain suddenly stopped, the last of it torn into scatter-shot fusillades that blew away down a long pavement of bare black rock.

Riyya stepped from the shelter of one of the folds in the low cliff on the other side of the pavement. She was soaked from head to toe. Her cropped hair was plastered to her skull. Her fierce smile reminded Hari of Rav.

She said, 'You took your time. I almost ran out of rain.'

Hari said, 'How do we get to the ship?'

Riyya pointed at the overhead. One of the habitat's window-strips was directly above them, and something hung beyond its diamond panes. A froth of spherical pods, a long spine tapering away . . .

'Rav's ship!'

Hari tried to imagine how Rav's son had managed to match the spin of the inner surface of the wheel. Crabbing his ship down one of the spokes with cables and grapples, perhaps, or gradually increasing its velocity as it spiralled out from the hub . . .

Eli Yong said, 'I've just lost my connection to the system. We must keep moving.'

They climbed a helical stairway to a service walkway beneath the overhead. Wind lashed them; the stairway hummed like a plucked wire. Far below, clumps of debris pelted through the air and trees heaved and surged, mostly stripped of leaves now. Riyya clutched Hari's arm, pointed. Small black shapes, scooters, were coming towards them, riding close to the overhead.

'We need ninety seconds,' Eli Yong said.

She was clinging to the rail of the walkway with both hands and looking up at the ship. A rectangle of dim red light had opened in the curve of the largest of its pods, above the far end of the window-strip.

Hari understood, and said, 'Where's our emergency lock?'

'We don't have one,' the head doctor said.

A sudden raw blast struck Hari and drove him against the rail. His wet clothes flattened against his skin. The scooters were very close now. Levi rode in the lead, standing in his saddle, aiming a short black staff at Hari. The Ardenists were right behind him. Then a howl of wind struck them and they checked and slid backwards, bucking and spinning. One of the Ardenists leaped from his machine, wings outspread, was caught in a gust that tumbled him head over heels, and dropped straight down and smashed into the restless trees. Levi brought his scooter around and looked straight at Hari, and wind struck him broadside and swept him away.

'Twenty seconds!' Eli Yong said.

Something moved in the warm red light, a figure emerging, casting something on to the panes of the window-strip, retreating. Hari grabbed Riyya by the waist, clung tight to the rail. There was a sharp crack, a vast howling scream: a ragged hole had been blown into the triple layers of the window-strip and a torrent of air was blasting through it into vacuum.

Half a dozen thick black cables dropped down, their blunt ends studded with little red lights, questing this way and that. A cable whipped around Eli Yong, lifted her, dragged her through the hole. Two more snaked towards Hari and Riyya. He told Riyya to close her eyes, felt a cable loop around them and tighten, and pushed away from the rail as hard as he could.

The rush of escaping air spun them as they were hauled up. Hari yelled in exhilaration and terror. His ears popped and he and Riyya jerked to a halt, spinning clockwise, counterclockwise. There was a rushing roar and his ears popped again. He opened his eyes, saw that he and Riyya were hanging inside the padded cubical space of a cargo pod, saw someone in a p-suit standing beside the rim of a big hatch, reaching up, unlatching his helmet, smiling at Hari.

'Welcome back,' Rav's son said.

6

The wheel habitat of the Saints traced an orbit some twenty five million kilometres from Saturn, a sixth of the distance between the sun and Earth. Recklessly squandering reaction mass, *Brighter Than Creation's Dark* drove inwards, outpacing the cutter that had belatedly given chase, crossing the retrograde orbits of shoals of irregular outer moons. The Saints bombarded its comms with pleas and threats. If Hari returned, all would be forgiven; if he failed to honour the agreement he'd made, he and his friends would suffer Levi's wrath. Once, one of the drones launched by the cutter managed to evade the collision-protection system, clamp itself to the hull, and extrude threads that infiltrated the outskirts of the ship's mind. A few moments later, Jyotirmoy's eidolon floated in front of Hari, asking him to make direct contact, promising him every kind of help with his quest if only he would return.

'You have what you wanted,' Hari told him. 'Now I'm going to take back what's mine.'

'You need our help,' Jyotirmoy said.

'I have all the help I need.'

'No, you don't. There are many people who want to know what you know. Who would kill you and your friends to get it. We can protect you from them, and help you take back your ship.'

'How's the storm, by the way? Has it blown out yet?'

Riyya had found it easy to infiltrate the wheel habitat's old, open-source climate-control machinery. When Eli Yong had locked out the Saints and given her complete command, she'd turned all the ventilators in the same direction and set them pulsing on maximum thrust, ramping up a storm that had grown towards hurricane force as it chased its tail around the world.

Jyotirmoy said, 'Your childish trick badly injured three of our people, but I would like to think that we are still friends. That we can forgive each other and patch up this misunderstanding.'

Hari said, 'You were an interesting passenger. I admired you. I admired your skill and enthusiasm. I even admired the way you jumped ship. But I don't want to follow your path.'

'You can't take back your ship without our help, Gajananvihari.'

'Watch me,' Hari said, and told Eli Yong, who had by now traced the parasitic feed, to cut the connection.

Rav's son told Hari that they were bound by ties of blood. 'The people who hijacked your family's ship also killed my father. We have common cause against them. And I feel an obligation towards you. My father pretended to be your friend, but he was planning to extract the files in your neural network and sell them.'

'To the Saints,' Hari said. 'Blaming them for the hijack of my family's ship, claiming we had common cause against them, it was all a fantasy. An attempt to hide his real plans. And it worked. I really thought he wanted revenge for being expelled from the Republic of Arden. I really thought they were his sworn enemies.'

'He had many enemies, but they were all of his own making,' Rav's son said. 'And he was exiled from the Republic some years before it went over to the Saints. He quarrelled with one of the old ones about an obscure mathematical point, lost the duel, and refused to apologise or admit that he was wrong. Ever since then, he'd been living by his wits. You're not the first he preyed on. You're a very long way from being the first. I am ashamed of my part in it. In all of it. I had to obey him – it was my duty, it is how we are – but I swore that I would not follow his path. And after he died, after he was killed, I swore to help you in any way I could. A small attempt to make good all the crimes in which I have been complicit. And here I am.'

'You'll help me take back my family's ship?'

'I'll do what I can.'

'And then we'll find these assassins.'

'Yes.'

'Are they really Sri Hong-Owen's daughters?'

'My father matched DNA from skin cells taken from the assassin in the skull feeders' chamber with records held in Ophir's commons. He also discovered where they lived,' Rav's son said.

286

'It's somewhere in the Saturn system, isn't it? Somewhere ahead of us.'

'On Enceladus,' Rav's son said, and opened a window that displayed various views of domes and spires crowding a broad setback in the shadow of a vast pleated ice-cliff. 'They were satraps of the True Empire. They supplied cloned, tweaked soldiers, and cadres of elite guards. They created the janissaries who served two suzerains. Of course, they've greatly dwindled since then. But they still live on Enceladus.'

Hari said, 'Rav found all this out in Ophir.'

'So it would seem.'

'And he didn't tell me.'

'I'm sorry.'

'Did Rav contact them? Did he try to negotiate with them?'

'I know he talked to the Saints, To Levi. He told me about his negotiations when we arrived at Tannhauser Gate. Told me what he was going to do. If he also talked to Sri Hong-Owen's daughters, or if he decided that dealing with them was too dangerous, he left no record of it. He did not tell me everything,' Rav's son said.

He had changed since Hari had last seen him. He was straight-backed now, looked Hari in the eye while they talked, and spoke as he pleased. He had been a cypher, a shadow; now he had presence, the heft of character. He had come into his own. He had taken charge of his destiny.

They talked about whether Eli Yong could unpick the files still locked inside Hari's neural net. Rav's son said that she was surprisingly resourceful, but not entirely trustworthy. Hari agreed, and said that he wouldn't need to rely on her expertise if his father could be retrieved or recovered from the memory cores on *Pabuji's Gift*.

He still hadn't told Riyya about the picts he'd been shown: Nabhoj with two of the assassins. Nabhoj, or Nabhomani. He didn't tell Rav's son either. He secretly wished that the assassins had killed his brother after he'd helped them repair *Pabuji's Gift*, and was ashamed and disgusted because he knew that he was hoping he wouldn't have to confront his brother and deal with his treachery.

He gave an account of how Rav had died; Rav's son said that he was surprised that it hadn't happened sooner.

'The old man put himself in danger so often that he should have died a thousand times. He took unnecessary risks. He liked to take his time, stalking his prey. He liked to have what he called fun.'

Hari said, 'Is that what he was doing with me? Having fun?'

'His idea of fun. He was easily bored, but you caught his interest.'

'I suppose I should try to be flattered.'

Hari's feelings about Rav were complicated. He did not feel that he had been betrayed. Duped, fooled, used, yes, but not betrayed. It was clear that Rav had intended to steal and sell Dr Gagarian's files from the outset. As soon as he'd heard Hari's story. As soon as he'd seen what was inside Hari's head. Yet he'd twice saved Hari's life, and without his help Hari would not now be heading towards *Pabuji's Gift*. And although he'd been a thief and a trickster, he hadn't been as ruthless as he'd often claimed to be. He might have been planning to sell Hari to the highest bidder, but he hadn't cut off Hari's head, or dumped him in a hibernaculum. So Hari's anger was tempered by gratitude and, yes, sorrow. Rav had been a thief. Deceitful, dishonest, unscrupulous. But he'd also been a friend.

He tried to explain this to Rav's son, who was much less forgiving.

'Everything he did was part of a plan to enrich himself at your expense. Any good that came from it was accidental.'

'Well, if I was a fool to trust him, I was a lucky fool,' Hari said.

'You were naive. An innocent targeted by a skilled and experienced predator. And now he is gone, caught up in and killed by his deceptions, and I am free to make a name for myself. I have sworn that it will grow longer and more intricate than his, and that when I get a son I will be a kinder father than my father ever was. Rescuing you was the second step in honouring that promise.'

'And the first?'

'Before I left Tannhauser Gate, I retrieved your p-suit. Would you like to speak with it?'

'Very much,' Hari said, surprised and delighted.

Although the p-suit's comms had been comprehensively trashed, the eidolon appeared as soon as Hari invoked her. A shadowy sketch in the red light of the stowage locker, her eyes faint and flickering sparks. 'Something happened,' she said. 'I'm not what I was.'

'I know, and I'm sorry for it,' Hari said. 'I'll try my best to fix you, but I'm not sure if I can get you back to what you once were.'

He had stretched the p-suit in a repair frame. The eidolon gestured towards it, said, 'I'm not in there any more.'

She guided him to his cubicle in the passenger module, to the book that had once belonged to the ascetic hermit, Kinson Ib Kana. Hari had left it behind when he'd crossed to Tannhauser Gate. When he picked it up, a single sentence shimmered in its black face:

Whether I shall turn out to be the hero of my own life, or whether that station will be held by anyone else, these pages must show.

He said to the eidolon, 'Is that you, or the book?'

'The book has a mind of its own.'

'It tries too hard to show how clever it is. How did you manage to insert a copy of yourself in its memory?'

The eidolon hummed and shrugged. 'I'm not what I was.'

'Perhaps I can port you back into the suit, when I've fixed it.'

'I don't think that would be a good idea, Gajananvihari.'

'Why not?'

The eidolon bent close, whispered. 'There's someone else in here with me.'

7

While Hari and Rav's son revised and re-revised their plans to storm *Pabuji's Gift*, Eli Yong and Riyya separately studied the copy of Dr Gagarian's files that the head doctor had ported into *Brighter Than Creation's Dark*'s mind. Riyya was looking for anything associated with her father's research, and soon found something that distressed and disturbed her. A sheaf of messages from her father elaborating details about a conspiracy to suppress his work, orchestrated by agents working for the seraphs.

'He thought that these agents were controlled by entoptics derived from the Bright Moment. He was treating himself with his own entoptics, trying to make himself immune. I never knew,' Riyya said, with pained bafflement. 'We talked about his work, but he never told me about this.'

'It doesn't mean he was crazy,' Hari said. 'There was a conspiracy, after all. Maybe the seraphs weren't involved, but it killed him, it killed my family. And we're still caught up in it.'

Riyya said, 'It goes much deeper than that. Deeper and weirder. My father believed that entoptics coded in the baseline human visual system are evidence that something had altered the structure of the brains of our distant ancestors. Some kind of backward-acting influence from their deep future – our present. He thought that the seraphs had reached back in time and bootstrapped our ancestors to intelligence, so that their descendants would create the QIs which were the seeds of the seraphs . . .'

'I'm familiar with the idea,' Hari said. 'But it wasn't the seraphs who did it, in the version I was told. It was Sri Hong-Owen. She somehow became distributed through the entirety of human consciousness. Not just contemporary human consciousness, but the mind of every person who ever lived.'

Aakash had talked about this hypothesis more than once. It was possible, Hari supposed, that he'd been influenced by Riyya's father. Spooky to think that they had been discussing bizarre ideas and making plans based on them, all unknown to their children. Who were now beginning to understand that they'd been entangled in those plans for far longer than they'd suspected.

Riyya said, 'I always knew that Salx was unusual. Obsessed, driven, But this isn't any kind of philosophy. It's a maze he lost himself in. It's magical thinking.'

She was disturbed and angry. She said that her father seemed to have worked up an elaborate and grandiose conspiracy theory to justify resigning from the Climate Corps and abandoning his family.

'He tried to turn it into a story,' she said. 'He thought he was a hero battling dark and mysterious forces. He thought he was saving human civilisation.'

'He built his apparatus,' Hari said. 'That's real. A real accomplishment. You should be proud of him, Riyya.'

But she wouldn't be comforted. 'This thing my father and your father and the others shared, it poisoned their lives. And it poisoned mine, and it poisoned yours. Not because their work was wrong, or blasphemous. Not because they were trying to discover things that mere mortal humans aren't supposed to know. But because they turned it into a conspiracy. They tried to keep it secret.'

'They worked long and hard to uncover the secrets of the Bright Moment. That's why it is so valuable.'

'My father once told me the difference between magic and philosophy,' Riyya said. 'He was trying to explain the importance of his work. He said that magicians refuse to share their secret knowledge because it is hard-won and personal. Every magician practises a different form of magic. Every act of magic is affected by the operator's skill and state of mind. But philosophers deduce universal laws by deducing the simplest possible explanations for observable phenomena, and testing those explanations with experiments designed to falsify them. There are no secret philosophical laws because all laws are derived from the universe. The observable universe; the universe of things. Anyone can discover those laws. Anyone can use them. Anyone can repeat anyone else's experiment and obtain the same results. My father's work cost him everything he had. And for what? For something anyone could find, if they looked hard enough.'

'But they didn't,' Hari said. 'Your father, my father, Dr Gagarian, they were ahead of everyone else. They had the prize everyone else wanted.'

'They shared a secret,' Riyya said. 'But they couldn't keep it secret for ever. Because it was derived from common experience. From something that happened to everyone who was alive when the Bright Moment passed through the Solar System. It wasn't magic; it wasn't a secret. But he forgot that, my father. After Dr Gagarian stopped communicating with him, he began to think like a magician. He was afraid someone would steal his work, or use it against him . . .'

'And someone did try to steal it,' Hari said. 'And we're going to make them pay for what they did. You'll see. We're almost there, Riyya. We're almost at the end of it. We have fought off assassins and fanatics. We have tracked down my family's ship. We'll find the answers to all our questions there.'

Brighter Than Creation's Dark crossed the orbit of Iapetus and entered the realm of Saturn's inner moons and their storied cities and settlements. Some of the first colonists of the Solar System had settled there, and won their independence from Earth's power blocs. Descendants of those colonists had fought against the True Empire, bitter battles that had ended in the destruction of many of their cities, and the second conquest of the Saturn system. But although the True Empire had fallen after the seraphs had imposed the Long Twilight on Earth, its defeat had not revived the fortunes of the cities of Saturn's moons. Ten million people had once lived there; now, less than thirty thousand eked out an existence in half-ruined cities and settlements.

Unchallenged by any traffic system, detecting no other vessels but the cutter that was still doggedly pursuing it, *Brighter Than Creation's Dark* crossed the orbit of Hyperion. It crossed the orbit of Titan, and Rav's son shut down the motors and began to adjust the ship's configuration. The pods crawled over each other, lining up along the spine of the ship, and the outermost layer of the largest pod jacked up and spread out to form a hemispherical heat shield.

The motor flamed on again, and they were accelerating inwards. Past the orbits of Rhea and Helen. Past Dione. Past Calypso and Telesto, past Tethys, Enceladus and Mimas. Flying on across the plane of the ring system.

The rings were not what they once had been. Centuries of human activity and interference had altered them. The Cassini Division, between the two major segments, the A and B Rings, was much wider, and there were new gaps in the spiralling lanes of the rings. As the ship sailed inwards, Hari glimpsed black flecks orbiting within the bright ring segments: manufactories the size of shepherd moons which had once swept up icy chunks of ring material and digested them and used their water and primordial soot to construct bubble gardens. A pharaonic project begun long before the rise of the True Empire. And there were hundreds of gardens orbiting inside the rings, too. Most, like the gardens in the Belt, were dead. Yet some still lived, and the stars of their chandelier lamps glittered in little constellations along the edges of ring segments and within gaps swept clean by the manufactories. Hari wondered if anyone lived there; wondered if anyone marked the passing of *Brighter Than Creation's Dark*.

And then the inner edge of the rings slipped past and they were falling towards the blurred butterscotch pastels that banded Saturn's vast globe. The feathery swirls of an equatorial storm lay dead ahead. The motors cut off again and for a few minutes they were in free fall, and scrambled for the acceleration couches that extruded from the floor of the big pod. Gravity returned, grew steeper and steeper as the aerobraking manoeuvre converted the kinetic energy of the ship's excess velocity to heat. Windows showed a shell of ionised gases flaring from rose to white, incandescent flecks of fullerene foam tumbling away from the heat shield, as *Brighter than Creation's Dark* scratched a thin bright chord across the outer edge of the planet's deep ocean of hydrogen and helium. Slowing, slowing, slowing . . . and at last its motors fired up to drive it above the atmosphere and out across the rings towards apogee, a hundred and seventy thousand kilometres distant, out beyond the orbit of Titan.

Hari and Riyya shared a meal and searched for the Saints' cutter. It hadn't been able to copy the aerobraking manoeuvre, had instead shot past Saturn, decelerating hard. Riyya spotted its bright star far beyond the little constellation of the seraphs, which floated above the apex of the ring-arch.

Brighter Than Creation's Dark swung around the night side of the gas giant. The pale, shrunken sun dawned beyond the sweep of the rings and the seraphs lay ahead. Blossoms of filmy veils hundreds of kilometres long, insubstantial and beautiful, funnelling out from the dark stars of their information horizons, where minds vastened beyond all human measure were rooted in boundless arrays of knotted and linked optical vortices. Standing waves twisted and non-linearly modulated around fundamental solitons that, according to some philosophers and the beliefs of many cults and sects, tunnelled into other universes where exotic physics supported supernal forms of intelligence.

Five hundred years ago, at the height of its pomp, the True Empire had declared war on the seraphs. They were the final enemy, the last redoubt of unconquered and uncurbed posthuman intelligence. They had to be eradicated. A battle fleet matched orbit with them, bombarded them with hordes of djinns, blitzed them with fusion pinch bombs, raked them with exotic particle beams. One seraph was destroyed; the rest retaliated. Djinns emerged in the nervous systems of every ship and drone in the fleet, fired up their motors, and sent them hurtling out of orbit on random trajectories. Many plunged into Saturn, or shot across the plane of the rings and were torn apart by impacts with icy bolides. The rest drove outwards until the reaction mass in their tanks was exhausted, flying beyond the orbit of Neptune, beyond the Kuiper belt, beyond the bow shock of the sun's heliosphere, dead ships crewed by the dead, dwindling into the outer dark of interstellar space.

A little over seventy minutes after the battle fleet was scattered, Earth's day side dimmed. A warp or twist in the fabric of space-time had appeared beyond the orbit of the Moon, absorbing fifty per cent of the sunlight that passed through it. Earth lay in the cone of its shadow. The Long Twilight had begun. After two years, most of Earth's cities had been destroyed by food riots and insurrection, and suzerains and scions were fighting each other for control of Mars and the Belt and the moons of the outer planets. After ten years, as ice marched out from Earth's poles, the True Empire fell; weakened by civil war and massive and futile efforts to re-engineer Earth's global climate, it was unable to resist a ragged alliance of posthumans, reivers, and rebel baseliners. After fifty years, with much of Earth mantled in snow and ice and ninety per cent of its population dead, the sunshade warp vanished.

Earth was still locked in a new ice age. The seraphs appeared to be unchanged. They occasionally swatted a drone or ship that approached too close, but otherwise seemed indifferent to human affairs, and to the prayers and petitions of their flock of followers.

As *Brighter Than Creation's Dark* swept past them, maintaining a respectable distance, Hari opened a window, centred it, zoomed in. He wasn't interested in the seraphs, but in their followers. Little stars brightened, resolved into the cylinders and cones and discs of ships and orbital platforms, fled beyond the margins of the window. At last, only one was left. A tiny twisted ring: *Pabuji's Gift.*

8

Brighter Than Creation's Dark sidled through the scattered cone of supplicants amidst a flurry of chatter and crosstalk. Rav's son answered direct enquiries with a bland statement about a resupply mission, fended off several attempts to probe his ship, matched *Pabuji's Gift*'s orbital velocity and her slow rotation. The two ships turning like partners in a dance, just a kilometre apart. The ring ship's hatches were shut. Its running lights were dead and its beacon gave out only its false identity; it did not respond to pings or to family code.

After Rav's son had tried and failed to detect any movement inside it, Hari explained that its paint job reflected radar, microwaves and neutron backscattering.

'My father made her combat-ready because we worked in remote and lonely places,' he said.

And it hadn't made any difference, in the end, because they'd been betrayed from within.

'Sketch the internal layout,' Rav's son said. 'I can't resolve any detail.'

Hari pulled down a window and captured an image of the ship and quickly limned the main corridors, the cargo spaces, the levels and partitions in the crew and passenger quarters. Rav's son examined the diagram, asked questions, agreed that the service airlock next to the cargo hatches would be the best entry point.

'I'll wait here,' Eli Yong said. 'I have no experience of free fall. I've never even worn a pressure suit.'

Rav's son studied her for a few moments, then said, 'Work on Dr Gagarian's files. The ship's systems are locked, and I'll know if you try to open them.'

'I wouldn't know where to begin,' Eli Yong said.

'I hope not,' Rav's son said, and flared his wings and smiled a sharp-toothed smile.

Eli Yong almost managed not to flinch. She drew on her dignity and said, 'Suppose the worst happens? Suppose you don't come back?'

'You think I care about what happens after I die?'

They crossed to *Pabuji's Gift* on two broomstick scooters. Riyya rode with Rav's son; Hari rode solo, carrying his book inside his p-suit. He hadn't told anyone what it contained, or how he planned to use it. He still hadn't told anyone that one of his brothers had collaborated with the assassins, either.

Family secrets. Family business.

He studied the ring ship's familiar contours and landmarks as they grew closer. Spars and tethers anchoring the motor pod in the centre of the ring ship's Möbius strip. Cubical modules and domes of various sizes scattered over the surface. The two big rectangular hatches of the starboard garages. The cluster of dish antennae where he'd done his first work on the ship's skin, helping Nabhoj swap out a frozen servo. The workshop blister where he'd assembled much of Dr Gagarian's experimental apparatus. The hatch for the garage that housed his utility pod, 09 *Chaju*, a tough little unit with pairs of articulated arms either side of the diamond blister of its canopy. The hours he'd spent in the couch that took up most of the pod's cramped cabin, ferrying and assembling components, welding . . .

Everything looked the same. Everything had changed.

No one challenged them as he led Rav's son and Riyya towards the inner surface of the ship, opposite the control and command tower. He brought his broomstick to a halt with a little flourish and shot anchoring tethers fore and aft and without waiting for word from the others kicked away from it, caught a grab rail next to a small square hatchway, popped the cover of the manual controls, and threw the power switches. He felt a brief vibration through his gloves. Silently, smoothly, the airlock's outer hatch slid back and lights flicked on inside.

The three of them made a tight fit. The outer hatch closed; the lock pressurised with a hiss that grew in volume and cut off with a sharp crack; the inner hatch opened on a spherical staging area. As soon as he was inside, Hari attempted to access the ship's control systems and the family commons, and wasn't surprised to discover that the codes had been changed. The passenger commons was down, too, but he was able to force a connection between his p-suit's comms and the little mind of the airlock.

He told Rav's son he was shut out of the ship's systems, said that he would need to reach the access point to perform a manual reset.

'Where is this access point?'

'In the command and control tower.'

'Where any hijackers are most likely to be.'

Rav's son's stare was sharp and vivid behind the visor of his helmet. Hari wondered for the fifth or tenth time if the Ardenist suspected that he was withholding information.

'If there are any hijackers on board, I expect they will be coming to greet us,' Hari said. 'We should find them before they find us.'

'Wait here,' Rav's son said, and kicked off across the staging area, falling neatly through the hatch on the far side.

Hari called up the eidolon, told her it was time to get to work. 'Try to keep the djinn quiet until I ask you for help.'

The eidolon said that she would do her best. 'It is good to be home, Gajananvihari.'

She had claimed that she did not know when or how a limited copy of herself had been ported into the book, had become flustered and sulky whenever Hari pressed her about it. She didn't know how a copy of the djinn, also much reduced, had been ported into the book either. Hari suspected that the original in his neural net had been responsible, and was using the eidolon as an interface, as it had used other machine intelligences to defend him elsewhere. He also suspected that the djinn had made the copy long before he'd escaped from Themba. It had mostly remained dormant, escaping detection by the commissars in Fei Shen and the tick-tock matriarch, but Hari believed that it had manifested itself at least once: after he'd left the book with the ascetic hermit in Ophir, it had frightened the man into throwing the book away, so Hari would retrieve it.

The eidolon hadn't been able to tell him if the copy of the djinn influenced the book's mind, whether it had chosen the stories he'd read, but she had assured him that it would help him take back the ship. He had broken the procedure down into a series of steps and constructed a simple virtual model, and he and the eidolon had rehearsed what needed to be done a score of times. The eidolon had always been dutiful and compliant, but despite her assurances Hari did not trust the djinn. It was his father's agent, after all. Some of its objectives coincided with his; some, he suspected, did not.

Now he said, 'This isn't like the time on Themba, with the drone. Or the time I was being held prisoner by the skull feeders. I'm in no immediate danger. And I may be able to take back control of the ship manually. The best way of protecting me is to stay in the background until I ask you for help. And then – and only then – to do everything I told you to do, in the order we agreed.'

'We both understand,' the eidolon said.

'I can't access the commons, so I'll have to port you into the airlock's mind. After that, you'll have to do a point-to-point migration. Leave a link in the airlock's comms node. Listen out on the common band.'

'As we rehearsed.'

'Yes. Exactly as we rehearsed,' Hari said, and opened the channel.

'We will not fail you,' the eidolon said, and then she was gone.

Riyya asked if he was all right; he told her that he had been trying to find a way into the ship's systems. She hadn't been privy to his conversation with the eidolon, and he hoped that Rav's son hadn't been able to eavesdrop either.

She said, 'You really aren't going to tell me what you're going to do, are you?'

Hari was watching the data flow through his comms as the copies of the eidolon and the djinn migrated from the book to the airlock's mind. 'I don't know what I'm going to do until I find out what I need to do,' he said.

'And I was hoping for some kind of plan.'

Hari liked the way she said it. Trying to keep it light, trying to pretend that taking back the ship was a harmless game. He felt a pang, a little pinch of guilt and sorrow, hoped that she'd forgive him.

Rav's son returned and said that he had released a swarm of drones but so far hadn't found any trace of activity. 'It may not mean anything. The internal walls and bulkheads are as opaque as the hull. We'll have to hunt down any hijackers in the old way.'

The idea seemed to please him. He was his father's son, all right.

They kept their suits sealed as they sculled along the curve of the corridor. Familiar scuffed, off-white wall quilting. Familiar insets glowing with soft light. But here was a long scorch mark; there was a rachet spanner slowly turning in mid-air . . .

Riyya snatched the spanner from the air as she passed. It was as long as her forearm, and the shift in her centre of mass spun her against the wall. She let go of the spanner as she tried to steady herself, and Rav's son caught it and flicked it away down the corridor.

'What I am supposed to do when we meet the hijackers?' Riyya said. 'Charm them into submission?'

'You will stay behind me while Hari and I deal with the situation,' Rav's son said.

They were only lightly armed. Rav had preferred to use his wits to get himself out of trouble, and his teeth and claws if talk and charm failed. *Brighter Than Creation's Dark*'s maker lacked templates for hand weapons; its armoury consisted of an ancient pistol that Rav's son wore on his hip. Hari carried a cutting wand he'd found in a maintenance kit, and the shuriken he'd programmed the maker to manufacture on the voyage between Ophir and Tannhauser Gate, using the template he'd worked up back on Themba.

He asked Rav's son what his drones were telling him.

'That the way ahead is clear.'

'That's convenient.'

'Isn't it?'

As they neared the intersection with the main throughway that ran around the ship, a manikin, naked in its grey plastic skin, drifted out to meet them. It wore the face of Deel Fertita. She smiled at them and the manikin opened its right hand and scattered a drift of little black pips in the air. The infiltration drones.

Hari sent the family's distress code through the common band and Rav's son fired his pistol, snap snap, and the manikin was knocked backwards and its chest burst open, spraying shards of debris cased in little flames that flickered blue and yellow and snuffed out. Riyya drifted past, kicking and flailing as she tried to reach the wall, and Hari sensed a movement at his back. A displacement of air. A shift in the shadowless light. Rav's son must have sensed it, too. He turned with Hari, both of them somersaulting and planting gloved hands on the wall quilting to steady themselves.

Manikins crowded the corridor. As Hari reached for his cutting wand they surged forward, moving so fast that Rav's son managed to shoot no more than three before the rest swarmed over them.

9

Stripped to their suit liners, manikins gripping their arms, manikins crowding ahead and behind, Hari and Riyya and Rav's son were swept through corridors and companionways to the omphalos, the heart of the section of the ship once given over to passengers. Sailing through the central shaft to a platform that jutted from the wall of architectural weave, where a woman in an acid-yellow bodysuit was studying a clutch of windows. Eli Yong and a burly, black-bearded man slouched in sling chairs nearby.

Hari recognised the man at once. Nabhoj. His brother, Nabhoj.

Riyya was escorted to a sling chair; a manikin snapped tethers around the wrists and ankles of Rav's son, tethering him to the platform. The Ardenist had been sedated, was curled up inside the caul of his wings.

The woman gestured; the manikins dragged Hari towards her. She had the same pale skin and sharp, angular face as her sisters, her sister assassins. Her shock of black hair was brushed back and stiffly lacquered into a hundred points.

'Welcome home,' she said.

Hari looked past her, looked at Nabhoj. He tried to speak, wet his lips, tried again. 'Hello, brother. I wish I could say that it's good to be home.'

'I'm sorry,' Nabhoj said. 'This is necessary.'

Hari saw a flash of movement in the corner of his eye. A boxy drone darting in, clamping a thin band around the top of his head. Something gross and irresistible shouldered through his thoughts. His bios cut out; a window scrolled down in front of his face. It was black and infinitely deep, and a star twinkled in its centre, jittering around a fixed point with an engaging eccentricity. He couldn't look away, the star commanded his entire attention, and it was suddenly exploding towards him, a wavefront of searingly bright rapacious light . . .

When he came back to himself, the assassin was closing up windows one by one. He felt the functions of his bios begin to return, suppressed the urge to call out to the eidolon.

'People keep doing this to me,' he told the assassin. 'It never ends well for them.'

'Oh, I don't know,' the assassin said. 'We have Dr Gagarian's files and we have you, and the files locked in your neural net. We have your friends and their ship, too, and your brother will be of no help to you. You caused us a little trouble in the past, but now everything you are and everything you have belongs to us.'

'They came through the hull,' Eli Yong said, leaning forward in her sling chair, her voice sharpened by distress. 'There was an explosion and a howling gale and I couldn't breathe, and a dozen manikins came crowding in. They shoved me in a box and told me they would expose me to vacuum if I didn't give up the files. I won't apologise. They already had my cache, I was helpless, I didn't have any choice. So I gave them the key and told them about the copy in the ship's mind. I won't apologise. They would have killed me if I didn't.'

'Be grateful I didn't kill all of you,' the assassin said.

'No more killing,' Nabhoj said. 'That was the agreement.'

Hari said to the assassin, 'Where are your sisters?'

'I need no help, as you can see.'

'One of them, Deel Fertita, died here, on this ship. Two died on Themba, another died in Fei Shen. Two more killed themselves rather than surrender. Angley Li in Ophir; Ang Ap Zhang in Tannhauser Gate. Are you the only one left?'

'We are many,' the assassin said, and turned to Nabhoj. 'Your father's backup is still in the boy's neural net. We will unpack him and put him to the question.'

Nabhoj said, 'If you hadn't trashed his viron, we could have restored him here.'

'And if we did that, he would immediately attempt to take back the ship,' the assassin said. 'Given your unsatisfactory actions when we took control, there is a strong probability that he would succeed.'

They stared at each other. Nabhoj was the first to look away. He said, 'I will talk to my brother before you take him away.'

'Talk, then,' the assassin said, as if it meant nothing to her.

Nabhoj said, 'I will talk with him alone.'

'You'll talk now or not at all,' the assassin said.

'This is a family matter,' Nabhoj said, with a flash of his old authority.

He was dressed as usual in tan coveralls cinched by a utility belt. Sitting straight-backed in the embrace of his chair, elbows on knees, hands joined beneath his beard, hooded eyes gleaming under tangled eyebrows.

Hari said, 'I no longer have any family.'

'Like you, I wish that things had taken a different course,' Nabhoj said.

'Wishes won't bring back your dead,' Hari said.

Nabhoj tried to stare him down. When Hari didn't look away, Nabhoj said, 'We did not know that it would lead here, Nabhomani and I. But we are where we are, and we cannot go back. We must move forward. And we can do that together, Gajananvihari.'

'You and Nabhomani have already done enough,' Hari said.

'We did what we had to do. Aakash was ruining our family, and he would not listen to reason.'

'So you decided to kill him,' Hari said.

'No. No, no, that was never our intention,' Nabhoj said. 'We wanted only to depose him before he did more damage to our business. He was stuck, Gajananvihari. He was obsessed with Dr Gagarian's work. It had consumed him. It had driven him mad. You didn't see it because you were too close to him. You lacked perspective and experience. And Agrata, well, Agrata was always unquestioningly loyal. But we saw it, Nabhomani and I, and it was . . . so sad. So sad, so painful. Aakash thought he could revive the golden age of the Great Expansion. That's what he told you. That's what he told us. That's what he told himself. But he was wrong. The golden age is long gone. Nothing can bring it back. Our father was chasing a dream of past glory, driving us in the wrong direction. We did what we had to do to save the family, and our business, and our ship.'

'Aakash is gone. Agrata is dead. I almost died,' Hari said. 'And Nabhomani isn't here, so I guess that he's dead, too. And you tell me that you were trying to save the family?'

Hanging above the platform, outstretched arms clamped in the iron grip of the two manikins, he was neither angry nor afraid, felt only a cold forensic pity. His brother was a prisoner too, stripped of his competence and command, his potency. He had failed and he was trying to justify his failure, redefine it as an inescapable tragedy.

'Nabhomani and I, we served the old man for almost fifty years,' Nabhoj said. 'We were loyal. We were faithful. We did everything asked of us. We agreed to allow Dr Gagarian aboard. We agreed to help him with his research. But it was a bad decision. You know that. You know what happened. It was a bad decision. Two years passed. Our reserves of credit were almost gone. We were losing the reputation we had cultivated over many years. And we had nothing to show for it. Nothing. Nabhomani and I endured the fiasco for longer than we should have done, out of misplaced loyalty and respect for our father. We tried to persuade him to give up his obsession, but he would not listen to us. And when at last we realised that we could not persuade him to do the right thing, we knew we had to act.'

'You were too cowardly to do it yourself. You hired Deel Fertita and the reivers.'

'They contacted us. When we put in at Porto Jeffre to pick up consumables and components for Dr Gagarian's experiments, for those probes of his, Nabhomani was approached by a free trader who told him that someone was interested in Dr Gagarian's research.'

'This free trader, she was a tanky, wasn't she?' Hari said. 'She called herself Mr D.V. Mussa.'

'I never met him. Or her. We started a conversation with the interested party, Nabhomani and I, and we came to an arrangement. We would give them Dr Gagarian and his partners; they would give us control of the ship. We didn't have the operating codes for the ship's security, its reaction cannon and all the rest, and we didn't have the expertise to neutralise any of it. So we agreed to a plan that would allow experts to come aboard. People who could help us.'

'You betrayed your family by making an agreement with these reivers, and then they betrayed you. It was their idea to head out to Jackson's Reef, wasn't it?' Hari said.

He'd been thinking about it ever since Khinda Wole had told him that Nabhomani had hired Deel Fertita and others. He was certain that he knew what had happened, but he wanted to hear Nabhoj admit it.

'We needed an excuse to bring specialists aboard,' Nabhoj said. 'Jackson's Reef seemed as good a destination as any. It was a simple plan, but things went wrong. I admit that things went badly wrong. The tick-tock fought back. Agrata and the old man fought back. We had cut the manikins and the drones and bots out of his control loop, but he found a way back inside that we didn't know about. Nabhomani was killed before I could trace it. And then I tried to find you, but you had escaped from the cargo hold. I had sent you there and locked it to keep you safe, and you were gone, and so was Agrata.'

'She rescued me. She saved my life, and she died trying to save the ship.'

'I tried to keep both of you out of harm's way while we dealt with the machines and the security systems,' Nabhoj said. 'But it did not work out.'

'You didn't try to keep Agrata "out of harm's way". You killed her.'

'Not me.'

'If not you, then your friend here, or one of her sisters. Don't try to tell me that makes a difference. Because it doesn't.'

'She wouldn't surrender. She killed Deel Fertita and two of the reivers, and she refused to surrender.'

'Did she know? Did she know what you and Nabhomani did, before she died? Before she was murdered?'

Nabhoj opened his hands, palms up. A kind of shrug, one of Aakash's gestures.

Hari said, 'It must have broken her heart when she realised that you had betrayed our father.'

Nabhoj looked away, looked back. He said, 'Our hearts were already broken. Mine and Nabhomani's . . .'

Hari was no longer listening. The eidolon had pushed into his bios, breathless and happy. Suddenly, he was in the commons and he was in other parts of the ship.

Riyya was saying to Nabhoj, 'Do you know what you did to Dr Gagarian's colleagues? To their families?'

'You will stay out of this,' Nabhoj told her.

'I am already in it,' Riyya said. 'My father was murdered by one of this woman's sisters. You're responsible for that, too.'

'You should have come alone, Gajananvihari,' Nabhoj said. 'You shouldn't have involved other people in this.'

Hari made himself pay attention to his brother. He said, 'They were already involved, thanks to you and Nabhomani.'

'I have explained why that was necessary.'

'And now strangers control our ship. And you're their prisoner. Bait to lure me back. Was it your idea to send those messages, or theirs?'

'The ship is mine.'

There was a familiar congestion in Nabhoj's face, a force pushing through his impassive calm.

'Prove it,' Hari said. 'If you're in charge of the ship, order these manikins to free me.'

'You'll be freed once the files have been extracted from your neural net.'

'Is that what they told you? You're a fool if you believe them. They killed everyone else who had anything to do with Dr Gagarian's research. They'll kill us, too.'

'We have an agreement,' Nabhoj said.

'Of course we do,' the assassin said. 'Have you and your brother finished?'

'Absolutely,' Hari said.

The floating lights around the platform snapped off. In the sudden darkness, panels of emergency lighting kindled, dim red glows pulsing like hearth fires in the wiry thickets of the architectural weave, amongst the shadows of rooms and platforms, pulsing faster and faster, strobing, spraying sparks into the dim air of the central shaft. Firefly constellations whirled and thickened, coalesced into spidery figures with hinged jaws and blazing eyes that flung themselves at Nabhoj and the assassin.

Nabhoj shouted out and cringed as the figures lunged and snapped at him. The assassin did not move. She said, 'I am not affected by silly tricks. And I still have control of the ship.'

'Maybe you do,' Hari said. 'But I have control of everything else.'

The two manikins let go of his arms and there was a sudden commotion at the entrance to the omphalos as a crowd of manikins and service and maintenance bots rushed in, clambering along the architectural weave or swimming through the air, swarming towards the platform.

Nabhoj shouted again, and launched himself at Hari. Hari had barely enough time to bring his knees up to his chest. He kicked out, pushing against Nabhoj's chest, the moment of contact shocking: a hard, shocking jar in his feet and spine. They flew apart. Action/reaction. Hari shot backwards across the shaft, grabbed a strand of the architectural weave and hung there, breathless. Nabhoj was intercepted by Riyya, who crashed into him and crooked her forearm under his beard and braced and hauled back, choking him into silence as they spun in the air.

The assassin watched this, calm and still between the pair of bristling maintenance bots that had settled on either side of her. 'You still don't have the ship,' she told Hari.

'Perhaps I can help,' Eli Yong said.

'I don't need any help to take back my ship,' Hari said. 'But there is something you can do for me.'

10

After Hari had performed the reset that gave him control of the drive and navigation systems of *Pabuji's Gift*, after he had confirmed that his father's viron had been comprehensively trashed, Eli Yong helped him download a copy of Dr Gagarian's files into the ship's mind. He told her that she could keep the original.

'It's more than you deserve. But then again, it's worth less than you think.'

Eli Yong met his gaze, attempting to project her version of sincerity. 'The arrangement I made with Rav, that was strictly business. I had nothing against you personally.'

'Tell me something. Were you planning to cheat Rav after you extracted the files?'

Eli Yong's gaze didn't waver. 'What do you think?'

'I think that neither you nor Rav were interested in what the research meant, or how it could be used. You were only interested in what it was worth. How much you could sell it for. And because it's only worth something to people like you while it remains a secret, I intend to seriously devalue it.'

Hari watched Eli Yong think about that. Her posture and the mask of her face didn't change – she was very good at hiding her emotions – but something in her gaze hardened. Small shifts in the muscles around her eyes, a slight narrowing of her pupils.

She said, 'If you're going to do what I think you're going to do, you are making a foolish mistake.'

'I have no doubt that you hid a copy of the files somewhere. Either on *Brighter Than Creation's Dark* or inside your head. The Saints may have made copies you didn't have time to find. It's possible that the tick-tock matriarch lied, and made a copy. The skull feeders probably made a copy, too,' Hari said, remembering Rav moving from pole to pole on the moss island, methodically crushing the bouquets of skulls. Not out of malice, as Hari had thought at the time, but in case the skull feeders had unlocked Dr Gagarian's files and downloaded them into the mindscape of their dead.

He said, 'Riyya was right. Once an idea is out in the world, it's impossible to suppress it or keep it secret. Only a fool would try.'

'She is an idealist,' Eli Yong said. 'The worst kind of fool.'

'She's too honest, perhaps. Too trusting. But she sees the world more clearly than you or I. She sees it straight.'

'She's a fool,' Eli Yong said. 'And so are you.'

'Cheer up,' Hari said. 'If you're as clever as you want everyone to think you are, you have a good chance of winning the race to find something useful in the files. And if you aren't, well, at least you have a head start.'

Hari knew that Riyya would be angry when he told her about his plan. He tried to harden his heart. He told himself that it was strictly business, family business. He told himself that he was protecting her, that he was saving her life. But it still wasn't easy.

'I made no secret about what I wanted to do,' he said. 'The assassin and her sisters have to pay for what they did. And I have to go to them because they will not come to me.'

He'd tried and failed to contact the assassin's sisters – the assassin had refused to help him, saying that she was their arm and their hand, not their voice.

'This isn't just about what you want to do,' Riyya said. 'It's also about how you're going about it. We got here, you, me, and Rav's son, because we helped each other. And we helped each other because we have all lost people. But you think that your loss counts more than anyone else's. You think it gives you the right to abandon us and do whatever it is you want to do. Well, it isn't right, Hari. It's entirely selfish. And without our help you'll probably get yourself killed.'

'I don't ask for or expect forgiveness, but I have to do this alone,' Hari said. 'I can't explain why, but you'll understand soon enough.'

Riyya looked away. Hari waited out her silence. He knew what she was going to say, knew she was going to condemn him, hoped that things would go more easily once she had decided that he was a monster.

But when she looked back, her gaze was softer, sadder. 'You've changed,' she said.

'Long before I met you, while I was still marooned on Themba, I vowed that I would find out who destroyed my family and my future. That I would have my revenge. That was me then. This is me now.'

'You want to balance out greed and foolishness and murder with more of the same,' Riyya said. 'How does that work? It won't bring back your dead. It won't bring back mine. You have your ship. You have your brother. You know what he did, and why. Isn't that enough?'

'The ship was hijacked and my father and Agrata were killed far beyond the jurisdiction of any city or settlement. And there's no common police force in the Saturn system. There isn't even any traffic control out here. I can't invoke a higher authority. So if I'm going to make this right, I have to do it myself.'

'You don't have to do it by yourself. Let us help you.'

'I don't need any help.'

'It must have been a terrible shock, finding out what your brother did, how he betrayed you. You're angry,' Riyya said, 'and you want to hurt the people who hurt you. I understand. I do. But if you run straight at them, they'll kill you. Let me help. Let Rav's son help too. We've all been hurt by these assassins. We all want to make them pay. Talk it through with us. We can work up a plan—'

'I already knew,' Hari said. 'I already knew what Nabhoj had done before he confessed – when the Ardenists told me where my ship was, they also showed me picts of him and the assassin in Dione's orbital docks. I didn't tell you because it was family business. And that's why I didn't tell you what I was planning to do. That's why I don't need or want your help. You left your family, Riyya. You ran away. I don't think you are in any position to tell me what I should or shouldn't do now that I've come home.'

It was easier, after that. After he had said a few unforgivable things, after Riyya had told him that he deserved to die alone, he called up half a dozen manikins, hustled her into the only gig left in the garages, and sent her across to *Brighter Than Creation's Dark* with Eli Yong and Rav's son. The Ardenist was still unconscious, sedated by the ship's doctor thing. Hari reckoned that he wouldn't recover consciousness for at least a day. More than enough time to do what needed to be done.

After the gig returned, Hari fired up the motors of his ship. *Brighter Than Creation's Dark* and the seraphs and their supplicants dwindled into the darkness astern. He was on his way.

11

The Saints' cutter was driving towards Titan, presumably planning to shed its excess delta vee and swing back and resume the chase, and Hari had a lot to do before he reached Enceladus. But before he started work he had a last conversation with his brother, the last of his farewells. Nabhoj hung between two manikins in one of the staging areas for the ship's lifepods. Lifting his head when Hari floated into the bright spherical space, saying, 'It has done you good to get off this ship, Gajananvihari. You've changed. You've grown up. You've had an education. You've learnt that there's more to life than salvage work and serving the old man. Think about those lessons, brother. Think hard. Think about what you want to do with the rest of your life.'

'You've had two hours to work up that speech,' Hari said. 'Is that the best you can do?'

He felt very cool, very calm. Watching everything as if it was a scene in a saga, as if he and his brother were mimesists playing out pre-ordained parts.

Nabhoj had difficulty meeting Hari's gaze, but he retained some of his dignity and authority.

'I am not pleading for my life,' he said. 'I know that you want to kill me, and I understand why. All I ask is that you do what you want to do, not what you think you should do. Forget me, forget our father, forget the family. Save yourself.'

'I'm doing exactly what I want to do,' Hari said.

'Nabhomani and I thought we were going to escape the old man's influence,' Nabhoj said. 'We thought that we were going to make a new life for ourselves. Instead, we were following a course he'd already taken. We planned to steal his ship, the same ship he'd stolen when he broke the agreement he'd made with our uncle, Tamonash. Do you know that story?'

'I met Tamonash. I know that our father stole more than the ship.'

'Nabhomani met Tamonash's daughter some years ago, and got the story from her. Perhaps it began then,' Nabhoj said, as if he'd thought of it for the first time. 'Perhaps that was the seed of our decision to take charge of the ship.'

'You could have left the ship and our family, and started a new life elsewhere. Or you could have killed our father and taken command of the ship by yourself. Instead, you and Nabhomani relied on outsiders. That's what I can't forgive.'

'Perhaps we were cowards,' Nabhoj said. 'Yes, I admit that's possible. Or perhaps our father inserted subtle checks and balances into our minds that made it difficult for us to rebel. We knew that our father's obsession with the Bright Moment would destroy the family. We knew we had to do something. We could think about it. We could make plans. But when it came to acting on those thoughts, those plans . . . Well, we needed help. We needed a push. And if the old man did that to us, he did it to you, too. He made us all in his image.'

'We weren't ever a family. It's clear to me now. We were a cult. Controlled by the old man, doing whatever he wanted to do without question. He had passed over. He was dead. And he refused to let go. He would not give up the world, and he would not allow us to live our own lives. I always hoped you'd rise above that, Gajananvihari. That you'd be the first of us to escape, to make a life for yourself. And you can still do it. You can still put an end to this poisonous thing of his. My life is over. I know that. But whatever it is you're planning to do, walk away from it. Erase the old man's backup. Give him true death. Leave all this behind and find your own path.'

'You betrayed our family to outsiders,' Hari said. 'You are responsible for the erasure of our father, and the deaths of Agrata and Nabhomani and Dr Gagarian. But you are still my brother, Nabhoj, and I still love you. I'm not going to kill you, but I can't let you stay here. So I'm going to send you away.'

'If you had any kind of spine you'd kill me,' Nabhoj said.

'If you had any kind of spine you wouldn't ask for the easy way out. I'm going to send you to a remote little rock. 207061 Themba. It isn't much of a place, but I know from first-hand experience that with a little work it's possible to survive there. Perhaps you'll even contrive to escape, as I did. If you do, don't bother coming to look for me. I'm going to confront the people who helped you destroy my family. There's only a small chance that I'll survive it.'

Nabhoj began to speak, but Hari didn't listen. He signalled to the drone controlled by the doctor thing and it moved forward and injected his brother with a soporific. After that, the mechanics of the operation were easy. The manikins dressed Nabhoj in a pressure suit and stowed him in a lifepod, and Hari launched the pod on the long, long course that would take it out of Saturn's gravity well and across the vast gulf to a remote and unremarkable rock at the outer edge of the Belt.

Then Hari was outside, riding in good old utility pod 09 *Chaju*, supervising a gang of manikins as they made alterations to *Pabuji's Gift*'s motors and laid the explosive charges he'd spun in the ship's maker. For a few hours, he lost himself in the details of the work. It was almost like the old days. Enthroned behind the little pod's diamond blister, choreographing the stately dance of its arms and tools. The lower left-hand arm still had that stiffness in its rotator cuff he'd never been able to fix . . .

Two hours passed. Three. Working as quickly and accurately as he knew how while the hard bright point of the sun dropped past the lower edge of the inner rings and set in a glorious arc of amber light that extended through the outermost layer of Saturn's atmosphere towards the north and south poles, and *Pabuji's Gift* swung into the giant planet's shadow. Four hours, five. Trying to ignore the tick of time passing, everything outside the overlapping pools of light dropped by the pod's lamps. And at last he was finished, and he drove the utility pod back to its bay and powered it down, and swam along the curve of the maintenance shaft to the docking garage.

Manikins had already dressed the assassin in her antique p-suit and loaded her into the little prospecting gig, *Jnana-chaksu*. She lay in a crash couch, lashed down by six hoops, deep in induced sleep. As soon as Hari had settled into the neighbouring couch, *Jnana-chaksu*'s cradle everted, and it drifted away from *Pabuji's Gift* on a light puff from its manoeuvring jets.

Hari called up the eidolon, and they rehearsed what she needed to do. He told her that he was sorry he couldn't take her with him.

'I would rather not return to the book,' she said. 'It was very cramped, very limiting. And I am pleased to serve, as always. I will do my best, if the Saints try to take the ship.'

'I know you will protect the ship as you once protected me,' Hari said, certain that the djinn was listening.

There was a pause, then the eidolon said, 'We have had some fine adventures together.'

'Yes, we have,' Hari said, startled and touched.

And then she was gone and *Pabuji's Gift*'s motor fired up, a diamond scratch dwindling across the black shadow of the ring plane, spiralling into a lower orbit as it accelerated away.

The gig swung on around Saturn's nightside. At last the edge of the vast dark globe was defined by a widening crescent of dawn light. Beyond, the arch of the rings soared away into sunlight, packed lanes narrowing towards its apex, where a tiny half-disc hung against the outer dark.

Enceladus.

12

The little moon was a bright, cold ice-world. Smooth, snow-white plains crazed with ice-blue cracks and shallow troughs, bordered with belts of icy grooves and ridges; spatterings of snow-white craters. But although its surface was one of the coldest places in the Solar System because it reflected most of the sunlight that fell on it, there was a small ocean of liquid water beneath its south pole, warmed by tidal kneading as it swung around Saturn. And that was why its surface was so bright, so cold. Vents in the floors of deep chasms exposed the surface of the ocean to vacuum. Water seethed and boiled and fed geysers that lofted ice dust hundreds of kilometres above the surface. Some of the dust spiralled inwards to Saturn; some went into orbit and eventually collided with other moons inside or just outside Enceladus's orbit, coating their leading surfaces with sprays of frost. But most of it fell across Enceladus's surface. A faint, constant snowfall that over centuries, millennia, millions of years, had built deep drifts that had smoothed out most of the small moon's contours, buried ridges and small craters, filled the slumped bowls of the oldest craters to the brim.

As the gig approached it, Hari thought that Enceladus looked like a fragile ornament spun from frost and fine glass.

A swarm of tiny throwaway probes flew ahead of *Jnana-chaksu*, spying a handful of small settlements scattered around the equator, a wrecked city inside a circular crater, its angular tent shattered and the terrain around blackened and pitted, and a vertical city clinging to the side of a deep rift in the tiger-stripe terrain of the south pole, exactly where Rav's son had said it would be.

Now the gig decelerated, achieving an elliptical parking orbit that approached to within fifty kilometres of Enceladus's surface. It wasn't stable, thanks to the insistent tug of Saturn's gravity, but Hari did not plan to stay in orbit for long.

Pabuji's Gift was halfway around Saturn's dayside, travelling just above the division between the outer and inner rings, and the Saints' cutter was accelerating towards it. Hari had anticipated this – the eidolon was primed to deal with any attempts to board the ship – but he still felt a tremor of unease.

A second tranche of probes spiralled towards the south pole, blurting packages of multispectrum and radar images before they crashed into the surface. Hari studied 3-D renderings stitched from the data, then woke his cargo.

The assassin showed no emotion when Hari told her where they were and where they were going.

'I will meet your sisters to discuss reparations for the harm they did to my family,' he said. 'But I am not surrendering. We will meet as equals, or not at all.'

'And yet you are delivering yourself to them,' the assassin said.

'Tell me how,' Hari said.

Enceladus's icy shield curved away on every side, details resolving out of its bright surface as the gig descended. At the horizon, the faint plume of a geyser scratched the black sky.

Hari piloted the gig towards a spot to the west of the geyser. Ridges and valleys drifted past. Boulders scattered along the tops of narrow, winding ridges. Steep slopes plunging into chthonic darkness. *Jnana-chaksu* killed the last of its momentum and hovered at the edge of a long rift, balanced on a whisper of manoeuvring jets.

The city was directly below, a step-like series of narrow terraces cut into the wall of the rift. Everything frozen and dusted with ice glitter, everything at ambient temperature, cold as liquid nitrogen, except for a faint infrared glow radiating from a building perched at the edge of the lowest terrace.

Hari picted the image to the assassin. 'There?'

'There. If your craft attempts to descend past the city, defence systems will target it.'

Rows of buildings dropped past, one after the other, as Hari guided the gig towards a landing pad at one end of the last and lowest terrace. Fine ice crystals blew away in a circle as *Jnana-chaksu* touched down, washing against windowless, unornamented walls of low bunkers, everything settling back into immemorial silence and stillness.

Hari warned the assassin that if she tried to harm him the musculature of her p-suit would freeze and he would leave her to die, and then he freed her.

She sat up on her couch, smiled at him behind the visor of her helmet. 'I am delivering you to my sisters. Why should I harm you?'

'I'm making the generous assumption that you may possess a vestige of human irrationality.'

'I am the arm and the hand.'

'Lead on, then.'

They skated along frozen walkways to the building that was leaking a trace of heat. It was a severe cube three decks tall, partly cantilevered out from the edge of the terrace. A door irised onto a tall lighted space where transparent capsules nestled side by side against a long platform. Cables strung on horizontal stays dwindled away into absolute shadow.

Hari and the assassin descended in one of the capsules, passing through several intermediary stations. Reflections of the capsule's riding lights glimmering from vertical slabs of ice, from massive folds and pleats, from setbacks where drifts of ice crystals had collected. At first, the far wall of the rift was lost in darkness, but it slanted closer as they plunged down, until they were sliding between two walls no more than a hundred metres apart. Dim lights resolved below, illuminating an angular tent that stood on a ledge above a chaos of tumbled ice blocks pinched between soaring cliffs.

The capsule slowed and eased through an aperture in the roof of the tent, passing through a long chimney of flexible black leaves, halting at a small platform. Hari followed the assassin along a spiral walkway that descended past dark clumps of banyans. No lights, no movement. The tent, once pressurised, had long ago lost its air. Everything in it was dead and frozen, glitter-dusted with frost.

The walkway ended at a kind of plaza littered with fallen leaves that shattered under the featherlight tread of Hari's boots, the whip of his waist tethers. A row of airlocks gaped like corpse-mouths. Outside, a wide walkway or road rimmed with little lights swooped out across the ice-block sea. Hari and the assassin followed it between ragged embankments, past rough facets and tilted slabs, the walkway turning now, descending to a long and ragged slash that might once have been the mouth of a geyser but was now capped with a rough slather of diamond-fullerene composite.

A small dome squatted at the base of this cap; two figures in antique p-suits stood outside its airlock.

Hari stopped when he saw them. Turned, and saw two more figures behind them. He knew he had reached his destination, and sent a brief squawk to his ship.

'He is here, my sisters,' the assassin said. 'I have brought you the last of the family of heretics.'

13

Escorted by the assassin and her sisters, Hari passed through an airlock into a short tunnel lined with stained white ceramic, where hidden machines blitzed him with microwaves, neutrino beams, and X-rays. He was forced to surrender his book, felt a small surge of relief when it was returned to him after it had been interrogated inside a virtual space as ancient as the tunnel's security protocols. It was the only thing he'd brought with him. He'd left everything of his old life behind, but he hadn't been able to abandon or give away the book, and not just because it was a memento of the dead man who had saved his life, or because it had smuggled the copies of the eidolon and the djinn aboard *Pabuji's Gift*. He had carried it through adventures and hardships; its stories had amused and amazed and informed him; he was bonded to it by something stronger than sentiment or gratitude. And he hoped that some trace of the djinn might still be hidden inside it; it was a faint and foolish hope, but he needed all the help he could get.

With two of the assassins in front of him and two behind, he descended a ramp that spiralled down a vertical shaft. A small zoo of machines squatted in alcoves and niches cut into the raw, rough ice of the shaft's wall. Most were dead, mantled with frost, but a few reached out with brief whispers of microwaves and a man-shaped bot stepped forward to watch the little procession go past, its eyes burning red in the chilly shadows of its crypt.

A string of lamps hung down the centre of the shaft, and presently Hari saw that their little lights were reflected on a black circle below.

Water. The still surface of the buried sea.

Three streamlined scooters were moored at the bottom of the ramp. Hari climbed aboard one behind one of the assassins, as he'd once ridden behind Riyya, and the scooters drove down a long tunnel and at last emerged into a limitless dark sea. An icy overhead stretched away in every direction, lit by chains of floating lamps. Swales and humps like inverted hills, fins, long gashes fringed with stalactites dozens of metres long. Grids of illuminated rafts hung all around, dangling streamers of dark red or brown or black weed. In the far distance, a chain of fat spheres dwindled into the deep dark.

Hari felt a flutter of relief. As he'd guessed, as he'd hoped, Sri Hong-Owen's daughters hadn't entirely thrown off their human instincts. They lived close to the overhead of their pocket sea. They were vulnerable. And, because they hadn't shut down his p-suit's deep radar, he could see the floor more than two kilometres below, could glimpse immense bulkheads, walls, curving away, delimiting a chamber that was less than five kilometres across. He supposed that it had been sealed off from the rest of the subsurface ocean so that it could be warmed and oxygenated. A small, vulnerable bubble habitat.

His escorts drove him to a pod hung from a smooth bulge of ice where small schools of fish flickered amongst a fuzzy turf of red weed and clusters of fleshy flowers pulsing on bony stalks. They pushed him through the entrance, a moon pool at the base where external hydrostatic pressure was balanced by internal atmospheric pressure, and sealed him in. It was spherical, the pod, chilly and damp, divided into three levels by mesh platforms. In the lowest level, a teardrop-shaped cleaning bot that had clearly gone insane was slowly working its way around the rim of moon pool, following a shallow, circular groove it had carved into the floor. It might have been working there for centuries.

There was no link that Hari could latch on to, either through his bios or the suit comms. He couldn't open any windows in the pale walls.

He wondered if the Saints had managed to intercept *Pabuji's Gift*. The manikins controlled by the eidolon and the copy of the djinn should be enough to hold them off, but even if they gained control of the ship it didn't matter. By now, its course had been set and its motor had been shut down. If the Saints tried to take control, if they tried to restart the motor, they'd trigger his little surprise; if they didn't, it would activate itself in a little under seven hours. Meanwhile, there was nothing Hari could do until Sri Hong-Owen's daughters decided to talk to him.

He had a long wait. He couldn't detect any toxins or contaminants in the pod's atmosphere – a standard nitrox mix – but he kept his p-suit sealed. He watched the clock he'd set up in his visor's display tick down, tried not to think about the potential flaws in his plan. Such as it was. He mostly sat still, trying to seem calmer than he felt.

The insane cleaning bot completed a painfully slow circuit, began another. At last, with three hours remaining on the countdown, a patch in the opaque wall cleared. He ankled towards it, felt a flutter of relief when he looked out and saw a little cluster of faint shapes rising through the black water. Sri Hong-Owen's daughters were coming for him.

There were five of them, five weird sisters fluttering up from gelid depths like the phantoms of drowned sea-sailors. Their legs were vestigial, fused into short flat tails. Their arms were long and bone-thin, and filmy veils stretched from arms to hips, beating in slow synchrony as they ascended.

Hari found a shelf facing the window, an ancient design that sucked air through mesh to tether him in the vestigial gravity, and composed himself as best he could. Running through the flow of his pitch. Trying to channel Nabhomani, his easy charm, his sincerity and sympathy. *You have to understand the client better than he understands himself,* Nabhomani used to say. And: *you have to believe in what you are selling. You have to convince yourself of its worth before you can convince the client.*

Hari told himself that he was doing what his father would have wanted. He told himself that it was possible to win both revenge and redemption.

The five weird sisters sculled up to the window in the pod's wall and stared in at him. Their faces were identical, with prominent cheekbones and large, black eyes. Racks of red-rimmed gills slashed their flanks. Organs could be dimly seen through their translucent skin, snugly cased inside chests and abdomens. Beating hearts, trees of blood vessels.

Hari opened the visor of his helmet, breathed in cold damp air, the prickling odour of ammonia. The ghost of his smile floated in the dark window amongst the frank stares of Sri Hong-Owen's daughters.

At last, a whisper rustled in his bios: 'You are the son who inherited the sins of his father.'

'As you inherited the sins of your mother,' Hari said.

'We serve our mother, now and always.'

'And I came here as the last representative of my family.'

'You are here because we brought you here.'

'I chose to come here,' Hari said, trying to project a confidence he didn't feel. 'I came here because I want you to tell me why you tried to destroy my family. And because I want to make you an offer.'

All five shrugged, a human gesture that made them seem all the more inhuman.

'The path you followed does not matter, because every path you could have chosen had the same destination,' they said.

'I came here to make you an offer,' Hari said again. 'But before we can talk about that, you must allow me to communicate with my ship.'

'There is no point in talking to it because you no longer control it,' the weird sisters said.

An inset opened in the window, tracking across fields of stars towards a small bright fleck that hung beyond the rippled, ruffled ringlet at the edge of the ring system. Centring on the fleck, zooming in to reveal the kinked circle of *Pabuji's Gift* with a splinter jutting from one side: the Saints' cutter.

Hari imagined the Saints closing on *Pabuji's Gift*, pinging and signalling and probing, obtaining no response. Sending a scouting team across, trying and apparently succeeding to hack into the control and command systems. Everything quiet and dead inside the ring ship. Everything abandoned in place. The cutter nosing into the docking garage, its crew disembarking, scattering through *Pabuji's Gift*, searching for secret files of forbidden knowledge, and ambushed one by one by manikins, by the djinn . . .

The inset closed. The weird sisters said, 'That was the situation exactly one hour ago. We have no doubt that the Saints will soon gain complete control of your ship, and take it where they will.'

'We'll see,' Hari said.

He had expected that the Saints would attempt to board *Pabuji's Gift*. He had planned for it. And now that it had happened there was no going back. Meanwhile he must remain calm, refuse to be cowed or coerced, project confidence and control.

'You hijacked my ship,' Hari said. 'You erased my father, killed the woman who raised me, and killed the tick-tock philosopher Dr Gagarian. I escaped, and vowed to hunt you down and destroy you. But I know now that my brothers were equally guilty. You agreed to help them take control of our ship if they helped you to kill Dr Gagarian and pointed you towards his associates. Have I got it right?'

'We could have done what needed to be done without them. But their help made it easier.'

'Dr Gagarian was close to finding out something important about the Bright Moment. Something you wanted to remain hidden.'

'What people call the Bright Moment was not a gift. It was a message. A message aimed at us, and only us. The method of delivery meant that everyone saw it, but only we understood it.'

'And you are frightened that other people will prove you wrong. By studying it, by discovering what it really means. Is that it? Is that why you killed Dr Gagarian and his colleagues, and stole their discoveries?'

A silence stretched. Sri Hong-Owen's daughters hung outside the window, filmy veils fluttering, gill slits pulsing, faces shuttered. Hari began to believe that he'd blown it, that he'd gone in too hard. But then their collective voice whispered in his comms.

'Most care only for the message itself. They imbue it with significance it does not possess. They build religions around it. They see in it, as in a mirror, a reflection of their desires and fears. Our mother would be amused. It would confirm everything she believed was wrong with the human species.

'But a few people were not interested in the message, but in the way it was sent. In how it propagated. In how it acted on each and every human. They were a danger. They were the children whose fingers curl around the trigger of a weapon whose power they cannot comprehend.'

Hari said, 'You took it on yourselves to kill the people you believed to be dangerous. You assassinated them. Executed them without any warning.'

'If we told them that what they were doing was dangerous, would it have stopped them?'

'You had no right,' Hari said.

'Sri Hong-Owen was our mother. Whatever she became, before her vastening and afterwards, she is our mother still. And we are her arm and hand.'

Hari studied their blank faces and felt sorry for them. The blind worship of the past that had flooded most of what passed for civilisation these days ran deeper here than anywhere else. How could he have thought to overcome the immense foolishness of human history? But he had to try. He had to try to give some shape and meaning to his loss.

The weird sisters were talking, telling him that his family's struggle was over. That they would keep what was left of it alive. He realised that they meant him.

'It is good that you came to us. We will keep you here,' they said. 'We can learn from you.'

'It isn't over,' he said. 'One of Dr Gagarian's colleagues still lives. At least one.'

'The boy on Earth? The mathematician? We will reach out to him, by and by. He is not important.'

'And then there's everyone else,' Hari said, and explained what he had done.

Hari had escaped the hijack of *Pabuji's Gift* with Dr Gagarian's files, but by the time he had returned to his family's ship the so-called secrets hidden inside the files were longer secret. Too many people had been able to examine them, copy them. And then there was the question of revenge.

'I won't deny that I wanted to hurt you,' he told Sri Hong-Owen's daughters. 'I wanted to avenge what had been done to my family. I wanted to put an end to the intrigue and the killing. And I realised that the best way to do it would be to make it impossible for you to keep your secrets secret. So, after I gained control of *Pabuji's Gift*, I broadcast copies of the files across the Solar System.'

With the help of Eli Yong, he had compressed Dr Gagarian's files and tagged the package with a brief explanation and used *Pabuji's Gift*'s comms to send it to as many people as possible. To Ma Sakitei, in Fei Shen. To his uncle, in Ophir. To Khinda Wole, in Tannhauser Gate. To every contact and business associate of his family – scores of government entities, several hundred individuals. To the cities of Saturn's moons. And to the seraphs, aiming the big dish of *Pabuji's Gift*'s comms at each of them in turn. He knew that it was probably as futile as the prayers and petitions of their supplicants, but it had seemed necessary to let them know that merely human minds had attempted to approach the mystery of Sri Hong-Owen's Becoming. It was a fitting memorial for his father and Dr Gagarian and the others: a kind of closure.

'I don't know what the seraphs and everyone else will do with the information,' Hari told the weird sisters. 'Most will probably decide the files are fake, or pseudo-philosophical gibberish, or some kind of trick. And even if no one finds them interesting, if no one is inspired to set out on the same path as Dr Gagarian and his colleagues, it will have been worth it, because the knowledge you wanted to bury beneath the ice of Enceladus is scattered far and wide across all the worlds beyond. You can't undo it. You can't unshatter a broken cup. But there is something you can do. Something we can do together.'

He paused, waiting to see if they'd take the hook. He felt as if he'd run a long race in deep gravity. Breathless, heart pumping.

The weird sisters hung beyond the window in the wall, veils beating against some slow cold current. Their large unblinking eyes suggested deep reserves of patience and composure. After all, what was time, down here, where nothing changed and nothing wanted to change?

Their small mouths did not move, but their collective voice whispered in his comms.

'You underestimate us.'

'I hope I do. I hope you're better than I think you are. I hope that you'll work with me, help me make amends for all the people who have died because of this.'

Another pause. Then:

'How?'

'I was brought up in a family of junk peddlers. We dug through the ruins of history, extracted information and artefacts, and tried to get the best price for our finds. Then my father became involved in the research of Dr Gagarian and his colleagues. He gambled that their work could be used to develop new technologies, to build a business empire. Instead of mining old ideas, we would forge new ones, revitalise philosophical investigation, and sweep away the cults and sects that sprang up in the wake of the Bright Moment. They promise their followers entry into utopias based on claims of exceptionalism. We would provide the foundation for a utopia based on hard facts and philosophical principles, and open to all.

'My father failed,' Hari said. 'I freely admit it. He failed because he made the same mistake as you. He thought he could police ideas. That he could collect them and make a profit from by selling them, just as we sold old machines. But ideas aren't artefacts. They don't exist in any one place – they can be found by anyone who goes looking. And in any case, there's no intrinsic value in ideas. It's what you do with them that counts. You say that you serve Sri Hong-Owen. That you are her arm and hand. Let me help you. You know things other people don't know. Let me connect you with them.'

He told the weird sisters about his family's contacts. He explained that there were still many philosophers in the Belt. Their influence was greatly diminished, he said, and they were scattered amongst the cities and settlements, but they exchanged ideas and argued and collaborated, as Dr Gagarian and his colleagues had collaborated. Hari's family had been part of that network. Carrying philosophers from rock to rock, garden to garden. Giving them a place to work, a place where they could discuss their work. He told the weird sisters that they could join this network. And because they were the daughters of Sri Hong-Owen, one of the greatest philosophers in the history of the human species, they would be an important voice. With his help, they could promote their mother's ideas and discoveries.

'You know things other people don't know. We can use that knowledge to make things right. To move forward from the mistakes of the past. You don't have to give me an answer now. I want you to think about it. I want you to discuss it. But even if you decide against helping me,' Hari said, 'you'll have to let me go.'

'We have others plans,' the weird sisters said.

'I didn't come here to surrender. I came to tell you what I did, and to make you an offer. And because we can't yet trust each other, I took precautions. Keep watching my ship. You'll soon see what I mean.'

'The ship is not yours to command. The Saints have control of it now.'

'Think it through,' Hari said. 'I knew that the Saints were chasing me. I knew that they would try to take my ship, after I left it. Do you really think I'd let them? If they try to start the motor, it will uncouple from the ship. If they don't, it will uncouple anyway. And when it does, it will fire up and aim itself at the weakest spot in the roof of your little sea. And only I will be able to stop it.'

Hari sweated out a short silence. He'd made his pitch; Nabhomani couldn't have done better. What happened next was up to the clients.

'When we return, we will wake your father,' the weird sisters said at last. 'He will live again, and we will force him to help us. You, unfortunately, will not survive the process. We will have to strip your brain neuron by neuron, your neural net link by link. But be comforted that your death will help us find a way of undoing the harm you have done.'

'You can't unshatter a cup. You can't unring a bell.'

'You underestimate us. As Aakash Pilot will discover, when he wakes.'

'I'm your prisoner, but you are prisoners too. Sri Hong-Owen quit the Solar System more than fifteen hundred years ago. She reached Fomalhaut, and then she went somewhere else. And you're still here. Trapped in this little pocket sea under the surface of this small moon. Trapped in a fantasy that you can police or suppress investigations of the Bright Moment. I've shown you that you can't. Everything you've done since the hijack of my family's ship shows that you can't. Think about that, but don't take too long. If the Saints don't trigger it first, the motor will fire itself up in a little over an hour.'

'We will return,' the weird sisters said, and the window blanked.

'Sooner than you think,' Hari said.

14

The wait was much worse, the second time Hari told himself that everything had gone as expected. That this was just a stage in the process. The weird sisters wanted to see if he had been telling the truth; they'd come back as soon as they saw the motor fire up. And if they didn't, well, he would die a good death. He'd have the revenge he'd dreamed about, back on Themba. At least he'd have that.

He talked to the insane cleaning bot, tried to persuade it that its work was done, that it could rest. It wouldn't listen.

He tried to read in his book, a long story about a young man trying to escape a vast, ancient, populous city, but the words and sentences wouldn't stay put. He'd look away for a moment, distracted by some stray thought, and discover that he'd lost his place. He'd find himself reading the same paragraph or line for the second or third time.

Thirty minutes passed. An hour. The clock counted down to zero, began to count up.

Hari supposed that condemned men knew how this felt. How it felt to watch the approach of the preordained moment of your death.

At last, without warning, a window opened and Sri Hong-Owen's daughters were there, leaning in the black water.

An inset opened too, showing a chunky cylinder throwing out a long violet spear of fusion light. *Pabuji's Gift*'s motor, flying free. Hari felt a clean shock of relief. His plan had worked. Either because the Saints had tried to start the motor, or because the clock he'd set up in the motor's mind had been triggered. In any case, the explosive charges had severed the motor's cables and spars, and the motor had fired up and aimed itself at a particular spot in Enceladus's south pole.

'You will stop it,' the weird sisters said.

Hari stowed the book in his p-suit's pouch, saying, 'I can change its course, if you let me speak to it.'

'Speak, then.'

Channels opened in Hari's bios.

He said, 'I'll order it to miss Enceladus on this pass, but it will swing around Saturn and come back. And it won't change course a second time. If you let me go, I'll send a command as soon as I return to my gig. The motor will destroy itself. Flare its reaction mass and blow itself into harmless fragments. There may be some damage to surface structures, but the roof of your little world will protect you. But if you don't let me go . . .'

'You will die too.'

'I'm prepared to die. Otherwise I wouldn't have come here. But I wanted to meet you. To talk, face to face. To tell you about what I did, yes, but also to make my offer. And if you let me go, I hope you'll think about that offer. I hope you'll think about it seriously, and I hope that we will be able to discuss it seriously. I want to honour my father's memory by continuing his work. As I think you want to honour your mother's memory.'

'We will talk about this when you have done what needs to be done.'

'Of course,' Hari said, and opened a link to the motor.

For a moment, he inhabited its control system. He saw that it was burning harder than it should be and that it was much closer to Enceladus than he'd anticipated. Very much closer: alarmingly close. He called up the eidolon, but something else leaned towards him and smiled in his face. His father's sly, shrewd smile, worn by the djinn.

'As always, I do your father's will when you will not,' it said.

The connection snapped shut. Hari tried and failed to reopen it.

'It still comes,' the weird sisters said.

'Wait,' Hari said. His thoughts fluttering like a panic of wings as he tried to understand what had just happened. The eidolon was supposed to be riding the motor, driving it towards Enceladus, towards the weak spot that Hari had mapped in the icy floor of the rift; the djinn was supposed to be aboard *Pabuji's Gift*, harrying and distracting the Saints . . .

'You lied,' the weird sisters said, and turned as one and swiftly swam away.

The moon pool burst open and two assassins shot through, masked, dressed in supple skintight black. At once, a churning ghost light filled the pod, alive with snapping jaws and burning eyes. The cleaning bot sprang at one of the assassins and she knocked it aside and it smashed into the pool and sank. The ghost light snapped off and both assassins dived at Hari.

He barely had time to close up the visor of his helmet before he was dragged through the pool into open water beyond. The assassins spun him, crammed him into a net, scrambled onto a scooter and took off, dragging him behind them.

Down, down.

All around, rafts were sinking through the water, seeking refuge in the depths. A school of pods scattered away into darkness. There was a flash of light far above, a concussion like the door to another universe slamming shut. Hari saw bright lines whipping through black water. Shock waves. Then they hit.

The scooter was wrenched sideways and went tumbling end over end. Hari slammed into it, was jerked away, slammed into it again. His p-suit's tethers whipped out and fastened to the scooter's flank and he clung there, still wrapped in the net. The two assassins were gone, ripped away. He tumbled in a wild welter of bubbles and clashing currents.

Then the last of the shock waves passed. Debris sank all around him, silhouetted against a wedge of weak light.

The scooter, obeying some kind of survival tropism, was rising. A collapsed chain of rafts, crumpled as if squeezed by a giant hand, frames stripped of weed, drifted past. Debris spun in cross-currents. The p-suit's collision warning flashed and Hari looked all around, expecting to see a raft or pod bearing down on him, saw by deep radar a complex shear surface rising through black water – the reflections of the shock waves from the floor of the pocket sea.

A strong and pitiless force caught him and spun him, and he was suddenly rushing upwards. Smashing through a seething shudder of water boiling at less than zero degrees Celsius. Hari's p-suit stiffened to protect him as the scooter bucked and slammed, rising between ice walls on a seething wave that broke and dropped it with a precipitous lurch. The scooter skidded and slewed in a receding wash. Hari saw something looming out of a freezing fog and closed his eyes. The scooter slammed into it. And stopped.

All around, a furious froth of water was draining from a broad setback littered with fragments of ice large and small. It bubbled and boiled, exploded into storms of ice crystals, feeding a fog that thickened in veils and blew sideways to reveal glimpses of smashed and broken ice.

A fresh wave broke, caught Hari and the scooter, dragged them towards a seething churn that slopped at the edge of a long gash in the ice.

The net was wrapped tightly around him, binding his arms and legs. He extruded cutting edges from the fingers of his gloves, sawed at the mesh as best he could. Water washed over him, pulled him closer to the gash, coated his p-suit in a glaze of ice that crackled and broke as he wriggled and sawed. At last, he freed one hand, quickly cut himself out of the net and pushed to his feet.

He had washed up on a tilted slab of ice jammed amongst a shattering of shards and blocks. Everything was obscured by restless billows and sheets of icy fog. Radar showed the footings of the great cliff of the rift's wall rearing up three hundred metres away, but there was no sign of the tented settlement or the cableway, and chunks were falling from the cliff in swooning slow motion and bursting on impact. The slab shuddered and bucked; there was a general grinding vibration. The fog blew aside for a moment and Hari glimpsed a vast rushing column leaning into black space, rooted at the close horizon of the little moon, the point of impact of the motor of *Pabuji's Gift*.

Anyone watching Enceladus would have seen a new geyser rising from the south pole.

The p-suit's radar pinged. Shapes were sliding towards him through the streaming rush of fog. Two, three of them, platforms perched on squat reaction motors, ridden by people in antique p-suits. Assassins.

As they manoeuvred close, calling to Hari, telling him to surrender, something fell out of the sky. At first Hari thought that it was some great shard of the cliff; then he realised that it was a ship.

His p-suit's radar showed a figure detaching from its bulk, flying with astonishing speed and accuracy at the assassins. They peeled away, and the figure bounded after them, leaping from point to point in the shattered, restless chaos, launching in a long and graceful arc, colliding with one of the platforms and embracing its rider in a quick vicious struggle, leaping away as the platform spun towards the cliff.

A quick blink of fire lit the fog. Rav's son howled in triumph and chased after the two remaining assassins.

Now something else detached from the ship: a figure riding a broomstick scooter that swooped past Hari, halted with a flourish of reaction jets, sidled back.

Riyya leaned towards him. 'Climb on,' she said.

Far off in the fog, two tiny stars bloomed and died. Rav's son howled again.

'Wait,' Hari said.

A copy or fragment of the djinn had tried to use the cleaning bot against the assassins. And he knew where it was lodged.

He stepped towards the edge of the long lead of boiling water. A wave washed to his knees, a seethe of froth and fog. When he pulled the book from the pouch of his p-suit, the fog lit up and his father stood there. Dressed as usual in a white dhoti, bare-chested, lips moving in his white beard.

'Don't be foolish, Gajananvihari. I'm here to help you.'

'It was never about me,' Hari said. 'It was always about you.'

Faces crowded in, long-jawed, red-eyed, raving. Warnings popped across the display in Hari's visor: something was forcing its way through his comms. Within moments, it would be trying to get inside his head. Hari raised the book, skimmed it towards the water. Burning faces screamed at him, and then it smacked into the churning flood and whirled and tilted and sank, and the faces guttered out.

Hari turned away, and walked back to where Riyya was waiting for him.

PART SIX
DOWNWARD TO
THE EARTH

1

Three years after Hari's confrontation with Sri Hong-Owen's daughters on Enceladus, the Saints mounted a second crusade against the seraphs. By then, Hari was working with a tanky free trader who called himself Rubber Duck, on the shifting triangle run between the Flora Wolds, the Koronis Emirates, and Ceres. They'd just left Ceres when Riyya, presenting as an eidolon in the cramped lifesystem of Rubber Duck's dropship, contacted Hari and gave him an account of the crusade. She was working with Rav's son, helping to refurbish an old garden that orbited in the Cassini Division in Saturn's rings, and had more details of the debacle than any of the news services.

She showed Hari several views of Levi's argosy, accompanied by a small constellation of gigs, lumbering towards the seraph's vast, gauzy blossom, told him that the gigs had aimed transmissions packed with so-called holy algorithms into the seraph's information horizon. Based on her father's work, the algorithms had been meant to paralyse the seraph with topological hallucinations so that mind sailors could infiltrate and vasten themselves.

The plan had failed, spectacularly. Hari watched three tiny capsules, each containing the stripped personality of a mind sailor, fly out from the argosy. They fell free on diverging trajectories, spiralling down the funnel-flower of pastel veils towards the dark star at its root. But long before they reached the seraph's information horizon, the capsules began to slow, ploughing up shock waves that thickened around them in layers of nacreous luminescence. Corona discharges flickered around the capsules and they grew hot and bright, miniature novas that burned through their pearlescent shrouds before flaring and fading. Beyond the seraph, the argosy and its retinue of gigs were flung abruptly sideways towards the ring plane, as if struck by a hurricane blast. One view tracked the argosy as it ploughed through mountainous clouds of material at the outer edge of the B ring. The fat ship jolting and spinning as a hail of icy pellets hammered into it, sections of its hull peeling away, debris spewing from ruptured compartments, until at last it collided with a bolide twenty metres across and disintegrated in a flash of superheated gases.

Riyya's eidolon said that Levi and his Ardenist advisers had been aboard the argosy. 'Also Eli Yong. She'd been working with the Saints for the past two years.'

'She had a knack for choosing the wrong side,' Hari said.

The eidolon said that the Saints had not given up their holy mission. 'They claim that Levi was instantly reincarnated. They are preparing a mission to find the vessel of that reincarnation and install him in their wheel habitat.'

'I feel sorry for them,' Hari said. 'They won't ever give up because they really do believe that history is on their side. That something elsewhere or elsewhen, some impossible ideal, is shaping their destiny.'

'None of us can escape who we are,' Riyya's eidolon said, reminding Hari of their quarrels before they had agreed to part company.

After the Saints had abandoned it, Hari had sold salvage rights to the wreck of *Pabuji's Gift* to the government of Paris, Dione. He had briefly returned to the ringship, but had found no trace of either the eidolon or the djinn. The ship's mind and control systems had been ransacked and destroyed by the Saints, and they had futzed the power systems, too, and left the lifesystem open to hard vacuum. And because the Saturn system had a surplus of wrecked and obsolete ships, the sale hadn't yielded as much credit as Hari had hoped. It had been barely enough to purchase citizenship on Ceres for himself and Riyya; he'd used most of what was left to purchase Dr Gagarian's head from the synod of Tannhauser Gate, which had confiscated Mr Mussa's ship and its contents in lieu of docking fees. He'd sent a message to Gun Ako Akoi, asking if she wanted to take custody of the mortal remains of her grandchild, and when it became clear that she wasn't going to reply he'd had the head and its scrambled files incinerated, and one bright day he and Riyya had hired a skiff and scattered the ashes on the frigid waters of Ceres's Piazzi Sea.

Riyya had taken up a position with the biosystem management of one of the dwarf planet's floating cities, but Hari had found it hard to settle down. He'd been convinced that either the Saints or Sri Hong-Owen's daughters would try to kidnap or assassinate him, had spent too much time chasing down rumours about them. He'd tried his hand at various menial jobs, tramped all the way around the equator on what the locals called a wanderjahr, and at last had taken up with Rubber Duck. Shortly afterwards, Riyya had returned to the Saturn system. She had never really forgiven Hari for betraying her and trying to deal with Sri Hong-Owen's daughters on his own, and after their adventure had ended there had been little to keep them together.

Now Hari asked her eidolon if she had ever heard anything from the weird sisters, asked if they had shown any interest in the Saints, or in the work of Rav's son and his friends. Riyya's eidolon told him that if any were still alive they were keeping a low profile. Perhaps they had all been killed, or perhaps they had retreated to the depths of their pocket sea to contemplate their next move. No one knew, and neither Riyya nor Rav's son had tried to contact them.

'We are thinking about our future,' Riyya's eidolon said, 'not our past.'

She and Hari talked about their diverging lives. Riyya's eidolon told him that she was busy with work that was good and satisfying, and as far as she was concerned that would do for now. Rav's son, who now called himself Ji, the first syllable of what he hoped would grow into a long and storied name, had gathered a crew of like-minded refugees from the Republic of Arden, and they had colonised an abandoned garden and were delving deep into the intricate puzzles that Dr Gagarian had not had time to solve. It would take years, according to Ji. Decades. Meanwhile, Riyya was tweaking the garden's climate control, and helping the Ardenists to design and populate its biome. Ji already had a son, and was talking about quickening a second. He, at least, was content.

'And you?' Riyya's eidolon asked Hari. 'Are you happy?'

'I hope I'm getting there,' Hari said.

He was busy, anyway. Even though Rubber Duck said that there had never been a worse time for trade, they were always on the move, plying their regular three-cornered route and making the odd side trip to chase down unique machines and other artefacts Hari found through his contacts.

Rubber Duck claimed to be more than a thousand years old, claimed that he'd been piloting his ship before the rise of the True Empire.

Tankies were given to boasting that they had witnessed or played crucial roles in turning points in history, or that they were actual historical personages who'd passed over to cheat death, or had been resurrected by faithful followers, and so on and so forth, attempts to make them seem important to a future that didn't really care. But whether or not Rubber Duck was older than the True Empire, his ship was definitely very old, the oldest that Hari had ever seen: an old dropship powered by three pulsed fusion motors, with a stubby utility spine that sported a pair of comb racks for self-guided pods that, in the halcyon days of centuries long past, had been dropped off or picked up in transit during long, looping runs through the Belt. Half a dozen pods of various sizes were permanently welded to the racks now. One contained Rubber Duck's extensive collection of trinkets and memorabilia; two more were tricked out to accommodate passengers; the rest stored cargo and trade goods.

Rubber Duck was inextricably wedded to his ancient ship, stripped back to his nervous system and plaited though her spine, augmented by traits he'd been using for so long he couldn't remember what was original and what wasn't. When she goes dark, he liked to say, so will I. 'That's why we have the same handle. She's my muscle; I'm her brains.'

The tanky was represented in what he called the happening world by a semi-autonomous avatar and a trio of maintenance robots that took care of parts of the dropship's structure and systems that were no longer (or never had been) self-repairing. But mostly he presented as a face in a window. The face was, according to him, the face of his lost meat self: a cheerful old man with unruly white hair bushed up by a scarf neatly folded to display his logo, a bright yellow cartoon duck with a red bill and large blue human eyes.

Rubber Duck claimed that the scarf and his persona were part of a rebranding he'd undergone a century before the rise of the True Empire. At one point, he said, there had been a small franchise of Rubber Ducks weaving through the Belt, but he was the only one left. 'I'm pretty sure I'm the original. Not that it matters. We shared everything, back then.'

Hari revived the old contacts that Nabhomani had used when *Pabuji's Gift* had still been in the salvage business, and worked up several more. After three years, Rubber Duck made him an equal partner in their enterprise, and began to talk about reviving the old franchise. But there really wasn't that much trade, any more. Travel to the outer belt was increasingly risky; and dacoits were beginning to harass or hijack ships along the outer edge of the main belt.

Rubber Duck claimed to have known some of the first dacoits, tanky pilots who'd gone rogue, preying on other ships for consumables and reaction mass. He talked about black fleets that had set up a network of stealthed bases on comets and kobolds, run by slaves recruited from the crews and passengers of ships they'd infiltrated or chased down. He talked about the time that several cities had united and gone to war against the dacoits, breaking up the black fleets and rescuing the surviving slaves.

'*Those* were dacoits,' he said. 'These newbies, they're just chancers who sometimes trade and sometimes raid. Part-time pirates who don't have any respect for tradition.'

'I heard some of the old-time dacoits are still out there,' Hari said.

As a child, he'd been fascinated by his father's tales of the wars against the black fleets. Colourful, grand, and simplistic dramas of good versus evil. Stories that might have shaped him, he thought now; that had perhaps influenced him when he had decided to set out on his path of revenge.

Rubber Duck said that there were all kinds of stories about the remnants of the old black fleets.

'Some say that the survivors are heading out to settled stellar systems, aiming to kick up trouble there. Others that they are aiming for systems that aren't yet settled, planning to set up their own brand of civilisation. Or that they have been lurking in the outer dark all this time, sleeping it out, waiting for an opportunity to take control of the Belt. Which might be soon, the way things are going. Posthumans are disappearing up their own assholes, and don't need or want to trade. And base-liner worldlets and gardens are growing poorer, trading less and less. How many ships were docked at Tannhauser Gate, when we were last there? I'll tell you. Twenty-two. Back in the day, there would have been ten times that number. And nine of those twenty-two were semi-permanently docked, no place to go, unable to pay off debts accruing each day. That's how it is everywhere. Not enough work to go around, and if you don't find work you end up stuck, trying and failing to work off your debts. Becoming indentured labour for whatever worldlet you end up on.'

They didn't talk about the hijack of *Pabuji's Gift*, Hari's abduction by Saints, his confrontation with Sri Hong-Owen's daughters. Hari was trying to put that behind him. He'd broadcast the contents of Dr Gagarian's files to every part of the Solar System: it was up to others to make of it what they would. He tried to keep current on the various nets used by philosophers, but there was little talk of the Bright Moment. Only a few people had ever been interested in the philosophy of its propagation, and Dr Gagarian's research had barely caused a ripple of interest.

Maybe Rav's son, Ji, and his crew of young Ardenists would make a breakthrough. Maybe someone else would, in ten or a hundred years. Hari tried to let it go, tried to move on.

He ploughed the triangle run over and again with Rubber Duck, making a few deals on the side, hoping to save enough to purchase or rent his own ship and get back into the salvage trade, perhaps start his own family. And one day, a little over six years after the debacle of the Saints' second crusade, he received a message from Ophir. His Uncle Tamonash had died, and Hari had inherited a portion of the old family estate.

Hari was surprised. He'd never tried to contact Tamonash after he'd left Ophir, and Tamonash hadn't tried to contact him, either. He talked with Tamonash's daughter, Aamaal, who was still living and working on Earth, and quickly reached an agreement about selling the estate. Hari's inheritance was by no means enough to purchase a ship, but he worked out that he could at last pay to have a question answered, and for the first time in their partnership he and Rubber Duck quit the Belt and headed sunwards, towards Earth, and the Memory Whole.

2

The dropship looped around Earth's Moon and closed on a small, stony asteroid, one of several orbiting the L5 point. A Greater Brazilian corporado had deflected it from its Earth-crossing orbit fifteen hundred years ago, and mined its regolith for platinum-group metals, rare-earth elements, and hydrogen and oxygen. Now it housed the Memory Whole.

Hari appraised it as the dropship spiralled into a close orbit. An irregular, heavily cratered spheroid with a major axis of a little less than a kilometre, gouged by strip mines, riddled with test bores and extraction shafts. Plantations of vacuum organisms that resembled black, bushy rocket ships packed the floors of craters and marched in phalanxes across inter-crater plains. A rack of railgun catapults. The remains of an ancient refinery. An interesting labyrinth of interconnected pods buried under a mound of shaly spall. You could always find something useful in old installations. Construction steel, cables and ancient electronics that could be rendered down for copper and germanium and gallium, personal artefacts abandoned by former occupants . . .

But these ruins were inhabited. The discorporate tankies who had founded the Memory Whole had used intersecting beams of protons and antiprotons to bore a shaft through the asteroid's rotational axis, and the fused rock wall of the shaft was coated with a network whose complexity was several orders of magnitude larger than that of the human brain. Parts of it were based on a variety of hardwired platforms, but the majority was rooted in probability fields generated by billions of loops of metal-rich ZNA within clades of slow-growing alife bacteria.

This was the information sea where the founders of the Memory

Whole now lived. They had been discorporate for more than fifteen hundred years, early pioneers whose brains had been scanned by a variety of primitive techniques and replicated in digital simulations. Although they claimed to be the first true posthumans, the first to have transcended baseline human consciousness and escaped what they called meatspace, their minds were crude, unaugmented replicas of their original selves. This was partly due to technical limitations, but was also the expression of a shared ideology. The discorporate of the Memory Whole wanted to live for ever, but they did not want to change. They wanted to preserve themselves as they had been in their so-called prime, and that they had largely succeeded was both their glory and their failure. They had won the amortality they craved, but did not realise that they had built a prison and willingly entered it. They were the last remnant of the old Western cults which had venerated the primacy of the individual. The ghosts of libertarians trying to keep their little candle-flames of ego-self alight for as long as possible, refusing to understand that flames are never the same but are always dancing, always changing.

After the first swaggering flush of creation, when they had constructed solipsistic kingdoms and squabbled and gone to war with each other, re-enacting universe-spanning crusades out of the fantasies of the long ago, they had settled into a long, staid era of mutual cooperation. They had become conservators of their own legend. They had taken in other simulations, given homes to failed attempts at true artificial intelligence. They had, like many of their kind, dabbled in projects to reach out to alien civilisations, and had created simulations of universes inhabited by all kinds of intelligent species. In one of those, Rubber Duck told Hari, a group of the discorporate claimed to have created a genuine self-aware civilisation and had contacted it and watched it recoil and self-destruct. There was another group who after centuries of research claimed to have solid evidence that the observable universe was also a simulation: that humans had been created by aliens like unto gods. And so on, and so forth.

'They do like their secrets and their conspiracies. They like to make themselves out to be more than they are. They want to believe that they are the last keepers of the true flame. That they haven't been left behind. That they are still *relevant*,' Rubber Duck said, with uncharacteristic scorn. 'When all they do, like the posthumans they clearly aren't, is burrow deeper and deeper into fantasy.'

The discorporate were, he said, the mirror image of posthumans. Posthumans tended to vanish into their own heads while they searched for the ultimate truths that underpinned the observable reality of the universe. The discorporate had vanished inside fantasies in which they were the microcosmic gods of their own creations. And meanwhile, human history flowed on around them both.

The Memory Whole's only connection with the rest of humanity was through the services they offered. Their techniques were old but entirely reliable, and had been modified to take advantage of new technologies. They traded in various forms of life after death, could implant all kinds of augmentations, provide backup systems and exo-memories, and install secure neural networks. Hari's father had gone to the Memory Whole when he had decided that his time had come. He had been discorporated and loaded into a corner of *Pabuji's Gift*'s shipmind. Later, he had returned and paid to have a neural network installed in his newly decanted son, with a copy of himself woven into its root.

That copy was still there. It had never shown any sign of wakening, but it was impossible to forget its presence. It was like a mortal illness, a shadow always at Hari's back. He knew that his life could never truly be his own until he had freed himself of his burden.

Rubber Duck did not dock the dropship because there was nowhere to dock. Instead, he matched delta vee with the Memory Whole's unprepossessing rock, standing off at twenty kilometres as requested.

Earth and the Moon floated far off, small, lonely islands in the black sky.

Presently, a drone flashed out from the battered asteroid, trailing a superconducting monocrystalline tether. After some to and fro regarding compatibility and handshaking protocols, it coupled with one of Rubber Duck's external interfaces and established a gateway to his fatline. That was how things were done, at the Memory Whole. That was why Hari had to travel to there in person. Connections to the outside were made through clunky old-fashioned hard links controlled by avatars of the Memory Whole crew. There was no point asking to use a qubit loop, a proxy, or even a randomly-modulated, highly-directional laser. The discorporate had survived the vastening of the seraphs, the True Empire, the humbling of Earth during the Long Twilight, and much else. They were paranoid about being hacked, invaded, turned;

the boundary of their utopia bristled with security protocols and lethal traps.

Hari linked the fatline to his bios and settled in a hammock and composed himself for a long series of tests and checks. At last he was given the all-clear, and in an eyeblink found himself in an avatar that mirrored his own body and was dressed in antique clothing: bib coveralls of stiff scratchy blue cloth, and some kind of wide-brimmed hat that was, he discovered when he took it off, woven from straw. All alone on a log raft riding a red river of molten sulphur.

It was a viron that replicated a section of Jupiter's moon Io with scrupulous fidelity. The lava river, fed by tributaries that pulsed down the slopes of a volcanic cone at the eastern horizon, was more than a kilometre wide, channelled between pillowy dykes. The rugged landscape beyond was patchworked in shades of red and yellow, orange and brown. Fallout deposits, fumarolic materials, remnants of local flows. The sky was hazed with a smog of frozen sulphur dioxide. Jupiter's huge crescent tilted in the west, and the fat star of one of the other Galilean moons hung beyond its bright limb.

The air shimmered at the other end of the raft, coalesced into a roughly man-shaped robot clad in silvery skin that reflected the molten river and the raft and Hari's avatar. The tiller of a steering paddle was tucked under one of its accordion arms. Its head was a glass turret in which a man's face floated. Pale skin, sleepy eyes, a neat black beard parting in a smile.

'Welcome to my favourite moon. Always changing, always the same.'

'It seems very real,' Hari said politely.

'A trivial exercise from my youth, but it makes a handy sandbox. You never know what people may bring with them from the outside. If you try to run some sneaky app or demon you'll find out what I mean.'

The robot gestured with its free arm, a curious looping snakelike motion. A plume of smoky gases spurted from the volcanic cone. A moment later, fat ripples coursed down the river's sluggish flow. The raft bucked and slewed; Hari danced on the spot, waving his arms to keep his balance. All around, a faint sulphur dioxide snow began to fall, flurries of gritty white flakes blurring the landscape, flashing into vapour as they kissed the molten currents of the river.

'I am as a god here,' the robot said. 'And you wouldn't like me when I'm angry.'

The face's lips didn't move when the robot spoke. It gazed out at Hari with a kind of abstracted serenity.

Hari said, 'I am happy to abide by your rules. My father had an agreement with you. I know you are an honourable people—'

'You want to invoke the guarantee. Before we get into that, I'd like to know how the client in question failed.'

'It was not caused by any fault in your work. My family's ship was attacked. Its systems were compromised. My father and his viron were destroyed. I am carrying his backup in my neural net.'

'I designed that backup, you know. Also its security, which I notice is missing.'

'It became . . . troublesome,' Hari said.

'You're undergoing one of your active periods out there, aren't you? The so-called Bright Moment has stirred things up. It spawned all kinds of prophets, each believing themselves to possess the only true key to its enigma. And there was a faction of Belters who were trying to unriddle it using what used to be called the scientific method – your father was involved in that, and so were you. See, we aren't as out of touch as you think we are. We keep an eye on developments. Mostly, it's a steady decline into barbarism, but every now and then there's a blip, a vexatious agitation, and we have to take measures to make sure we aren't affected. So there's a little more to your visit than honouring a contract. It could involve us in something we don't want to be involved in,' the robot said. 'That's why the service isn't free. That's why I require something in return.'

'But you will honour the guarantee,' Hari said.

'First, you're going to tell me exactly how the original was destroyed. Take your time. This river is fresh and hot. It runs on for several hundred klicks before it finally cools and hardens. And anyway, time as you understand it isn't a consideration. Every second that passes in your universe is a second lost for ever, and they pass at a steady rate. Here, in my universe, I control the rate at which time passes. You can spend an hour on your story, and when you are done we will still be in the same place. So speak out, kid. Tell me everything you know.'

What harm could it do to tell his story one more time? Hari started from the beginning, when he'd discovered that he'd been locked in the storage bay, moving from one incident to the next as if crossing a river on stepping stones. The escape from *Pabuji's Gift* with Dr Gagarian's head. Waking to find himself marooned on the rock. His escape from the two cloned assassins, his shipwreck on Vesta, and so on, and so on.

The face in the robot's glass turret watched him as he spoke, its expression carefully neutral. The particoloured landscape slid by on either side of the lava river. Ever-changing. Ever the same.

When Hari was finished, the robot said, 'It reminds me of an old joke. What do you get when you play a country-and-western song backwards?'

'I don't understand.'

'You came here to fix the story of your life. Trouble is, it wasn't much of a story to begin with.'

'It is the only one I have.'

'Did your father crack the meaning of the Bright Moment? Him and this Dr Gagarian?'

'I don't think so. But they might have made a good beginning.'

'Maybe it doesn't matter. Aside from the people who wanted to kidnap or kill you, no one else seems to have any interest in it. It isn't your fault, kid. Not many people want to do any heavy lifting any more. This is an age of superstition and wishful thinking. The sky is full of evening's empires, and every one of them is founded on sand.'

'I can't help what other people think,' Hari said. 'You've heard my story. It's as truthful as I could make it. Perhaps it isn't as exciting as you hoped, and has little in the way of revelation or resolution, but it's all I have.'

'Your wife comes back, your dog's alive again, and your pickup truck hasn't broken down,' the robot said. 'That's what happens when you play a country-and-western song backwards. You hope that the backup copy of your father might know something. Something that might unriddle the Bright Moment, maybe. Or something that will give shape and meaning to what happened to you. That will restore order. Fix your broken life. I hate to disappoint you, but life usually isn't that simple.'

'When Dr Gagarian came aboard, my father made me his assistant,' Hari said. 'Dr Gagarian designed experiments, my father sourced the hardware he needed, I helped to construct the probes and bits and pieces of experimental apparatus. Dr Gagarian didn't tell me what he was doing, or what he found, or what it meant, and I didn't ask. He discussed his work with my father, and my father tried to explain it to me, but I wasn't a diligent pupil. Oh, I truly believed that the work would change everything, but only because I believed everything my father told me. I never questioned it. I never asked what he really wanted from me. Perhaps the copy of my father that's cached inside my neural net can help me understand what I was caught up in. Perhaps not. Perhaps I won't ever be free of him, his influence. But I can't even try to begin to escape my past while he's still inside my head, and that's why I'm here. I want to get him out of my head. And I want to talk to him, one last time.'

'The past is always with us,' the robot said. 'It's where we came from. It's what we make, day by day. We leave it behind, but we can't escape it. All we can do is come to terms with it.'

It made the curious looping gesture with its arm again, indicating the lava river and the dykes of congealed sulphur along its edge, the riven landscape beyond, Jupiter's swollen, candy-striped crescent above.

'You might think that this sandbox is like a dream. A harmless hallucination from which you can wake at any time, and take up your life as if nothing had happened. The question is, can dreams change dreamers?'

'I don't know,' Hari said. 'Perhaps – if it is the right dream, at the right time.'

'You told me the story of how you got here. Let me tell you a story in return, about a dream I had when I was about your age. I dreamed that I had entered a great white city, and I knew, in the dream, that I had also travelled into the future, although I cannot tell you how I knew. Perhaps because such cities were often represented in popular fiction about the future, although the one into which I walked, in my dream, was far more detailed than any of those make-believe cities. There were many tall buildings, all built of white stone and fretted with rows of windows. Some cylindrical and buttressed with fins, like the dreams of the first spaceships before the first spaceships were built. Some narrow rectangles. Some square in profile. Some tapering to points. All shining white and clean in the bland sunlight. They stood in clusters, and at their feet were smaller buildings. All again built of white stone. Elevated roadways and monorail lines ran past the buildings or looped around them at different levels. There were open spaces, but they contained only gardens of raked gravel and stone fountains, and statues of people in heroic and noble poses. No trees, no growing things of any kind, no decoration or signs. In the time when I lived, cities were full of signs advertising all kinds of goods and services. Here, the buildings were blank canvases, and the everyday life of the city was unreadable.

'In many dreams, you are a bodiless viewpoint. People in the dream talk with you as if you were one of them, but you have no sense of your body. You are an observer. That was not the case in this dream. I was aware of every footstep, and the people who inhabited the city looked at me as I passed. Perhaps because I was dressed as I would have been dressed in waking life, which to them must have seemed as strange as a man in a suit of armour walking up Broadway.

'The people of the city all seemed to be members of the same family. They had light brown skin and black hair cut in various styles, and wore long shirts over loose trousers in combinations of pastel colours. In my day, birds nested on ledges of buildings, as if on cliffs, and people kept certain species of animals as pets. There were no animals that I could see. And no children. Only men and women of varying ages. There were a great number of them, but the walkways and monorail cars were not crowded because the city was so large.

'I wandered a long time, but did not dare to enter any building. At last, with shadows engulfing the feet of the tall buildings and reddened sunlight burning on their western sides, at the foot of a huge statue of a bare-breasted woman holding up a strand of DNA to the blank dish of her face (none of the statues had features), a man came up to me, and asked me if I was a traveller. I told him that I was dreaming. Often we do not know in dreams that we are dreaming, but I knew. I also told him that I believed that I was dreaming about the future. He looked at me quizzically, and said that this was his present, but not necessarily my future. He said that I might reach it, one day in the waking world, but there were other paths I might take instead.'

The robot paused, then said, 'Some philosophers claim that we are composites of multiple personalities, of agents. They share a common substrate of memory and traits, these agents, but are discrete entities, each knowing certain things that are forever hidden from all the others. If that's the case, then the people we meet only in dreams are part of us, yet not part of us. We do not find it difficult to believe that such a stranger would know things we do not. So it is in dreams, where we sometimes meet people who reveal to us new truths, or reveal to us that things we have always believed to be true are in fact false.

'The man who greeted me in that white city of the future was one such. He was tall, in his middle years, and strongly built. And he was confident, easily carrying the power he had been lent by his fellow citizens. The power he represented. His black hair was cut level with his eyes and shaved high around his ears and at the back of his neck, so that it resembled a cap tilted forward. His gaze I remember still. It was friendly, but it looked right through me. He told me that he was one of the citizens who had been chosen by lottery to protect the city. I asked him what he protected it from, and he looked at me gravely and said that he protected it from people like me. People who thought differently. Visitors from the outside. And then he laughed, and said that his job was easy because people like me were solitons, while the citizens all shared their thoughts, united and indivisible.'

Hari said, 'Did they possess a common bios?'

'I did not ask how they shared their thoughts. When monsters appear in dreams, you are as terrified as you would be in what is commonly called real life, but you don't ask why they have appeared or where they come from, or what they eat when they aren't chasing dreamers.'

'Because you know it is a dream. And you knew this story you're telling me was a dream.'

'Just so. I accepted that they shared their thoughts, but I did not ask how it was done. Later, I realised that it was a city of communists. That its citizens were in fact the ultimate expression of communism. All were equal. All shared all. Were they happy? I suppose they were, but only because they did not know any better. Their protectors kept them safe from thoughts that would contaminate their unthinking purity. I also realised that they had no ambitions, no drive to better themselves. Theirs was a way of life that was changeless, because change would destroy it. It was a city of the eternal present. A city of the eternal now, where every day was day zero.'

Hari said, 'There are clades of posthumans who share their thoughts and memories. But I do not think they are anything like the people in your dream city.'

The robot said, 'But they may be the first step on an evolutionary path that will lead to such cities, such citizens. Despite all we have done to try to avoid that future, it may yet come about.'

'You take this dream very seriously.'

'It was eighteen hundred years ago, and I have not dreamed a dream like it since. But I still remember every detail because it changed my life. I have not yet told you how it ended. Sometimes, when you meet strong and unique people in a dream, you wake up. As if they are gatekeepers who have the power to prevent you from travelling deeper into the dream. You may have met such people in your own dreams.'

'I suppose they are rationalisations for waking up. A last attempt to keep the dream coherent as it falls apart.'

'If that's true, where did you summon those people from?' the robot said. 'In any case, that isn't how it happened in my dream. It did not end when I met the protector of the city. We walked together through the streets and plazas that ran amongst the footings of the skyscrapers, some lined with humbler buildings, some not. The protector explained the functions of the larger buildings, pointed out various monuments and told me about the moments in history long past that they com-memorated. They were the only signs that things had once been different from the way they were now, in the city's eternal day zero. A remembrance of how the city had come into being, and why it must be as it was. I realised then that I was in the very far future. Not hundreds of years from my own time, or even thousands, but millions upon millions. And for most of its long, long history, the city had been changeless. Parts of it had worn out, and buildings or entire blocks had been destroyed in fires or floods, but everything worn away or destroyed had been replaced with an exact replica. And in the same way, the people of the city maintained and preserved their gene line. The city was changeless, and so were they.'

Hari said that it sounded unlikely.

'Certain species of eusocial insect, like ants and bees and termites, have changed little over more than a hundred million years. Why shouldn't a species of eusocial human that is able to police its gene pool remain unchanged for even longer? Especially if they remove all competition, all drivers of natural selection. That is what I learnt from my guide as we walked the empty streets. At last we ascended to a monorail station where a single car waited like a bullet in a chamber of a revolver. It sped us through the rest of the city, out across the green farmlands that ringed it, and at last reached a small and lonely platform at the edge of a desert that stretched away in the bloody light of a sun swollen to ten times its usual size and flecked with long chains of black spots.

'My guide explained that most of Earth was desert. The oceans had shrunk; the polar ice-caps had evaporated millions of years ago. A little life persisted in the deserts and what was left of the oceans, but most of what was left was preserved in cities like his. That was why it was important, he said, to exclude anything that threatened their stability. Then the door of the rail car opened, and I stepped out as if I had been commanded to do so. The rail car sped away, dwindling towards the white towers of the city. A squall of dust blew up and whirled around me, and that was when I woke,' the robot said.

'But the dream did not fade on waking, as most dreams do. I remembered every detail. Much more than I have told you. Some dreams are so powerful that they change us. This was the dream that changed me. The calm horror of it. The sense that it was inevitable. That it was waiting out there in the far future. That the seeds of what the world would become had already been planted in the present.

'At the time of my dream, I was living in a powerful country that had defeated both fascism and a perverted form of communism. This was before the effects of climate change had begun to alter the world and the lives of its people. My country was still the most powerful in the world. It was founded on principles that allowed every citizen to express his or her potential as best they could. It celebrated instances of individual enterprise, imagination, and heroism. It mythologised them. Of course, many people, then as now, were lazy. Or they were like sheep, content to graze their little patch of grass. But I had talent and ambition. I was one of the gifted. And my dream of the bleak changeless future in which everyone was like everyone else, reduced to the lowest common denominator, fed my ambition. I wanted to do all I could to make sure such a future did not come about.

'We had already passed from a mechanical age powered by burning fossil fuels to an electronic age where the sources of power were many. New technologies were creating new varieties of small, smart, efficient machines. Exchange of information was outgrowing exchange of goods. And we were beginning to learn how to tweak plants and animals, and ourselves. To improve existing species, and create new ones. But I knew that would not be enough. The resources of a single planet are not infinitely exploitable. There were already shortages of fresh water, farmland, phosphates, essential rare elements, and much else.

'So I went into the space business. I founded one of the first private space-transport companies, and helped to develop a city on the Moon. The city to which I, and others who had grown rich through talent and ambition, escaped when Earth's climate and weather systems finally collapsed. We moved outward from there. I was one of the founders of Rainbow Bridge, on Callisto.' The robot paused, then said, 'You told me that you met Sri Hong-Owen's daughters. I met their mother, once, in Rainbow Bridge.'

'What was she like?'

'Intense. Solitary. Single-minded. With a brisk and undisguised contempt for everyone she believed to be her inferior, which was just about everyone she met.'

'Her daughters were about the same.'

'It was just before the beginning of the Quiet War, when I met her. Or rather, it had already begun, but we Outers had not yet realised it. Sri Hong-Owen played a role in beginning it, and helped to end it, too. Earth's three major power blocs briefly occupied and controlled the cities of the outer system, but their rule was overturned, and a long golden age began. By that time I was more than two hundred years old. One of the oldest people to have ever lived. And at last I became what I am now. I translated. First into the mind of a ship, and now here. Where we still strive to keep the flame of individual achievement alight. Where lions and tigers and bears still live.

'Perhaps you think my dream has nothing to do with you. That it's the rambling justification of someone who has outlived his time and purpose. But I decided to tell you about it because it's possible that you might be a lion, too. One of those who know how to use knowledge to change the world. Who is not afraid of change.'

'It seems to me that lions can cause all kinds of damage, too,' Hari said. 'The leader of the Saints, for instance. Levi. He must have been a lion.'

'Lions kill because it's the nature of lions to kill. But without lions the common herd would grow weak and debased. Lions are a challenge, a test that all must pass if they are to survive. And since the weak fail that test more often than the strong, the fitness of the herd is increased. Lions drive change, and change is good. Change strengthens us all. You hoped to change the course of human history when you broadcast the research of the tick-tock philosopher and his friends. It didn't work out the way you hoped it would. Perhaps that's why you really came here. Not because you want to restore your father,' the robot said. 'Or not only that. But because you hope his backup contains information that the tick-tock philosopher's files lacked. Because you still hope to change things.'

'I was hoping to find out how he had changed me,' Hari said. 'Can you help me or not?'

'Of course. But if you want to talk to him, you'll have to do it here.'

'I don't believe that's part of the guarantee.'

'Don't presume to tell me what I can or cannot do,' the robot said. 'You are in my realm now.'

'My avatar is represented here. I am elsewhere.'

'Then go back,' the robot said, 'if it's that easy.'

That was when Hari realised that the link to the ship and his bios had vanished.

He said, 'I need to talk with my father. If you truly want to help me, you'll grant me that.'

A big wave passed down the molten river. It lifted the raft and dropped it and Hari fell down and clung to the raft's rough planks as it tipped and tilted. Geysers opened all around in the raw red lava – no, they were human mouths, each screaming at a different pitch, all spitting vapours that fed an acrid yellow fog. The ground on either side of the river broke apart and bright fountains of molten sulphur erupted. The robot grew, doubling in height, doubling again. The mild face in the glass turret of its head darkened, sprouting horns and a beard of writhing snakes; its eyes burned like red stars.

For a moment, Hari couldn't breathe. His mouth and nose filled with a parching reek. His coveralls were smouldering and his skin was burning, withering, as the heat of the lava river beat over him. Then heat and stench blew away on a cool breeze, and the robot dwindled, and its human face laughed.

'I control the physics here,' it said. 'I decide whether you can stay or leave.'

Hari stood up cautiously, saying, 'It's family business. It isn't of any interest to anyone else.'

He was trying his best to seem calm, to show that he had not been intimidated by the petty display of power. Telling himself that sooner or later Rubber Duck would realise what was going on and break the link. But what would happen then? Would he wake, back in his body, back on the ship? Would he be damaged by the equivalent of a hard reset? Or would his mind remain here while the uninhabited shell of his body aged and died? Perhaps his mind had been copied during the uplink. He would wake on the ship, but this version of himself would be trapped here for ever . . .

'I'll decide what's interesting to me and what isn't,' the robot said. 'If you don't want me listening to your conversation, you can leave.'

'If I agree to your terms, if I let you listen in to whatever I have to say to my father, and whatever he has to say to me, maybe you can tell me something first.'

A slow raster line passed across the image of the face in the robot's head.

'That depends on what you ask,' it said.

'On whether you can answer it?'

'On whether I want to.'

'It's simple enough. When my father passed over, did you encourage him in any way? In any particular direction?'

'When people come to us, they generally know what they want. They have a good idea of the shape their lives will take when they pass over. Of where they want to go and what they want to do.'

'Do you know what my father wanted to do?'

'He did not want to leave his family.'

'That's what he told you.'

'That's what he implied.'

'Perhaps he meant that he didn't want to lose control.'

'You must ask him that.'

'You helped him to pass over. And then he came back here some years later. After his son Rakesh had died. After I had been quickened, but just before I was decanted. He paid you to install a neural net in my head. Did he tell you why?'

'He wanted a place where he could hide a backup of his personality.'

'And did you do anything else?'

'What do you mean?'

'Did you talk with him about the Bright Moment?'

'You think we set him on that path?'

'It occurred to me.'

'Many believe that we turn people who come to us for help into our agents,' the robot said. 'That we sit at the centre of a web of intrigue and influence, plucking one thread, pulling another, reaching out to change things beyond our small world. It's understandable. We are old, and we possess certain powers and a great store of knowledge that's been lost or forgotten elsewhere. And this is an irrational age, where rumour is interchangeable with hard fact. But we have no such agents. We have no inclination to meddle in the affairs of the worlds outside our world, and we learn all we need to know about them from news feeds, such as they are.

356

'Your father was already set on his path before he came back to us. His first true son had been killed. He quickened you as a replacement. And he wanted some kind of revenge. He wanted to prove that the cults and sects were fools and charlatans. That's all I can tell you because that's all I know.'

'That's about all I know, too,' Hari said. 'That's why I need to talk to him.'

'I should warn you that the backup you carry was never intended to provide a full restoration. It isn't big enough. It lacks detail and nuance.'

'Will he be able to tell me what I need to know?'

'You'll have to ask him.'

'All right,' Hari said, and then he was somewhere else.

3

It was his father's old viron. A parched landscape saddling away to a shimmering horizon; scoured cliffs rising above fans of rubble; the hot blue sky and the unblinking glare of the platinum sun. Hari climbed the familiar path to the cave mouth. It seemed as real as the discorporate's sandbox. It seemed unchanged. And if it was unchanged, then his father must be unchanged, too . . .

His father wasn't there and then he was. Standing in front of the cave mouth, saying, as Hari came towards him, 'You took your time.'

'You have been keeping watch on me, then. I wondered.'

'I have a clock that tells me how much time has passed outside this world. I don't know what you have been doing out there, Gajananvihari, but I do know that I must have died the true death. Otherwise you wouldn't be here.'

'And now you live again.'

'I am greatly diminished. That is the first thing you should know.'

But he looked like Aakash. Bare-chested and barefoot in a white dhoti. Bead necklaces looped on his chest. White hair brushed back in a wave, his untamed white beard. He sat on a flat rock, and after a moment's hesitation Hari sat beside him.

'What happened?' Aakash said. 'What happened, out there? What happened to me?'

Hari told him about the hijack at Jackson's Reef.

Aakash said, 'You escaped.'

'Agrata got me out.'

'You escaped,' Aakash said again, and paused. 'Did you escape with Dr Gagarian?'

'Not exactly. He was killed, in the hijack. I took his head with me.'

'Was he alive?'

'No. He had been killed. Agrata gave me his head.'

'He was dead.'

'Yes.'

Hari had been planning to tell his father that Agrata was dead, that Nabhoj and Nabhomani were dead and *Pabuji's Gift* was lost, but he knew now that it would be cruel and pointless.

Aakash said, 'You took Dr Gagarian's head because it contained a copy of his files.'

'That's why Agrata gave it to me.'

'When you were given the head, did you know that you were already carrying a copy of those files?'

'I found out about the neural network later.' Hari paused, then said, 'Agrata didn't know about it, did she?'

Aakash didn't reply. He was staring out at the shimmering desert, stroking his beard with thumb and forefinger. Hari was reminded of an automaton they had once recovered from an old settlement long abandoned on a lonely rock. It had been woman-shaped, transparent, hollow. Its nervous system and musculature laminated into its thin tough skin. It had been dead for centuries and centuries, but Agrata had spent some time working on it, and at last it had woken. It was able to perform graceful acrobatics: it might once have been a dancer, or a mimesist. It could sing, too. It had a clear high voice. The songs were in no language they knew. It followed Agrata around; it had imprinted on her. It was eager to please. It was able to hold limited conversations. If it didn't understand something, it smiled and cocked its head and spread its hands, a gesture of helpless apology, and said, 'I don't understand.'

After a few days, that was almost all it said. *I don't understand. I don't understand.* Smiling, spreading its hands. *I don't understand.* It stopped singing, and developed a weakness in its left leg. And it became obsessed with a certain dance move: raising its arms above its head, palms pressed together, and bowing forward and extending the bow into a somersault. It kept losing its balance, spinning sideways in a thresh of arms and legs, and it would recover and try to repeat the move with dogged, futile persistence.

Agrata tried to fix it, but there was too much cosmic-ray damage to its distributed intelligence. At last, she shut it down and it went into one of the storage modules and Hari didn't know whether it had been sold or traded by Nabhomani or whether it had still been in storage when *Pabuji's Gift* had been broken up.

This copy of Aakash had some of the same traits. Hesitancy and repetition. Gestures used to hide a gap in comprehension. A blankness. A lack of affect.

It broke Hari's heart.

He said, 'You had something to tell me.'

His father didn't look at him. Saying slowly, as if to the air in front of his face, 'You were the one we chose, Gajananvihari. We did not entirely trust your brothers. We hope we were not mistaken, but there it is. That is one reason. The other is that you are our true son. And although it may be wrong of us, we love you above everything else.'

'And I love you,' Hari said.

But his father did not appear to hear him.

'I gave you the gift of the neural network, and did not tell anyone else about it,' he said. 'I did not tell your brothers. I did not tell Agrata. She might have suspected it was why we visited the Memory Whole the second time, but she never said anything. I planned to tell you, Gajananvihari, when you were older. When you came into your own. Did that ever happen?'

'I only came into my own after I left the ship,' Hari said.

'The neural network. I didn't tell you about it?'

'No, you didn't. I discovered it after I escaped.'

His father was silent for a little while, as if thinking about that. As they sat together on the low flat rock, in the hot bright sunlight, Hari noticed a glitch in the shimmering landscape: an editing flaw that revealed where the end of a short loop had been stitched to its beginning. He wondered how far he would get, if he walked out into the desert. Not very far, probably.

At last, his father said, 'I gave you the gift of the neural network. And during our conversations I inserted copies of the results of Dr Gagarian's research, and the research of his colleagues. Did you find those files?'

'I don't understand much of what they contain, but I hope I have made good use of them.'

'There is one more file. It is bound with this representation,' his father said. 'Would you like to see it?'

'Very much.'

A window opened in the air. It showed Aakash and Dr Gagarian sitting on canvas chairs inside the cave. A shaft of sunlight angled behind them, falling steeply from a cleft in the overhead and splashing on ferns and moss that grew on and around a spill of boulders.

Dr Gagarian was talking about his work, about refining measurements he had made several times before. 'I remain confident that the perturbation of the Higgs field was created by asymmetrical generation of virtual particles,' he said, 'but the question of how the virtual particles were generated is still unanswered. As is the nature of the asymmetry – the imbalance between annihilation and creator operators.'

'I thought time reversal accounted for it,' Aakash said.

'It accounts for the disappearance of the antiphotons, which travel backwards along the light curve to their inception point. But the creation of baryonic virtual pairs is another matter.'

'So that is the next problem. A hard one, I suppose.'

'I have some ideas about attacking it. Exploring Ioni Robles Nguini's hypothesis about wave propagation of Heaviside functions, for instance.'

The two men talked about experiments and experimental apparatus. They leaned forward to study windows.

'More time,' Aakash said at last. 'More time, and more credit. Nabhoj and Nabhomani will not be pleased.'

'They complain that they have no work,' Dr Gagarian said. 'But this is work. Real work on a real problem.'

'A hard problem in a series of hard problems. How close are we? How close are we to understanding this?'

Dr Gagarian sat back and looked up at the stony overhead of the cave. The leathery mask of his face was as inscrutable as ever. After a little while, he said, 'Long ago, there was a program that beamed information to extrasolar colonies. And that was based on even older programs, from the time when human beings had barely reached orbit around the Earth, when they had just begun to search for signals from other civilisations. Non-human civilisations. Aliens. They did not find any. And those who've looked since haven't found any, either. Either because intelligence is rare, or because in the future we'll make the universe more hospitable to humans and less hospitable to anything else. And since any alien species would do the same, it follows that because we exist, there can be no other alien species.

'But suppose that one existed, and we detected a message it aimed at us. It would not matter at first what the message meant. That we had received it would be enough. Perhaps the Bright Moment is like that. We don't know what happened to Sri Hong-Owen, where she went or what she became. We don't know how it was done. All we know is that she transformed into something beyond our comprehension. And in the moment of her transformation she manipulated space-time and sent a signal that did not attenuate as it travelled across twenty-five light years, and created an identical image in the minds of all those it touched.'

Aakash said, 'We know that she altered the local Higgs field. And we will soon know how she did that. We'll prove that it is no miracle, and confound the fools who believe otherwise. And we'll start a new philosophical revolution, and make back all the credit we've invested in this, and much more. That's what you promised, when we set out. And that's what we'll do. It's too late to have doubts.'

'There is a theory that when symmetry broke in the first few femtoseconds after the Big Bang, it determined not only the parameters of the four fundamental forces but also the limits of our intelligence,' Dr Gagarian said. 'One thing that we do know about Sri Hong-Owen, thanks to the observations of the colonists of the Fomalhaut system, is that she disappeared when she vastened. Her discorporate personality inhabited vortices and knots in the electromagnetic field of the gas giant Cthuga, and they moved away in a direction orthogonal to every known dimension. No one knows where she went, but the least worst guess is that she created a new universe that could support a higher level of intelligence, just as other universes in the calculable range of possible universes support different values for the fundamental forces, and other universal constants. The seraphs are rumoured to have done something similar. And if she did, it follows that we can never understand where she went, or what she became. Because we are constrained by the limits of this universe, and she slipped free of those constraints.'

After a short silence, Aakash said, 'We have not yet reached the limits of things we can understand, so there is no need to invoke other universes and higher planes of consciousness. Which sounds to me perilously close to the kind of nonsense touted by the end-time sects.'

Dr Gagarian said, 'Yet time and again we have seen how posthuman clades falter and fail, or become trapped in abstract and increasingly recursive speculation. Time and again they have demonstrated that boosting human intelligence may be of little or no benefit.'

Aakash said, 'The True comforted themselves with that notion. It didn't do them much good, in the end.'

'The Trues were wrong about many things. It does not mean that they were wrong about everything.'

'Are you are trying to tell me that you don't think you can do what you said you could do?'

'I am confident that it will be possible to understand how the message was sent, and how it was received. I am not confident about understanding anything else. Why it was sent. What Sri Hong-Owen was becoming, when she sent it. What she became, and where she went, afterwards.'

'Well, as long as we can find out how to manipulate the Higgs field, the rest does not matter.'

'It matters to me,' Dr Gagarian said.

'You want every question answered, everything squared away. It's in your nature. But if you started asking why people do the things they do, you'd never get to the end of it. And even if you could answer those questions, what use would those answers be?'

'I do not share your utilitarian outlook.'

'Perhaps not, but we do have an agreement that most would call utilitarian. I help you with your research, and we divide the profits.'

'I have not forgotten it. I do not forget anything.'

'Then you remember what we agreed about your colleagues.'

'I do. But it is not yet time. I still need their help.'

'You'll have to manage without it,' Aakash said. 'We're close to cracking this problem. If your colleagues know everything we know, it will be hard to make any kind of profit from it. They'll undercut our price, or give away the information. We still need Worden's help. And besides, he's my friend, and the partner of my broker. But *your* friends – Ioni Robles Nguini, Salx Minnot Flores, Ivanova Galchan – we're cutting them loose. You knew the time would come when I invoked that part of our agreement. Here it is.'

'And if I refuse to cooperate?'

'We're planning to make a run to Porto Jeffre for resupply as soon as you finish this present run of measurements. If we can no longer work together, I think we should head there at once. And when we arrive, you can disembark and begin to look for another sponsor. I'll keep all the equipment, of course. The probes and the rest. I paid for them; my son built them. Maybe Worden and I can find some use for them. Maybe we'll find another philosopher who can complete your work. I'd rather not do it. I hope I don't have to. But there it is.'

Dr Gagarian stared unblinkingly at Aakash. At last, he said, 'You know that I cannot leave. Not now. Not yet.'

'Good. We both have a lot invested in this thing of ours. I would hate to see you throw it away on a point of principle.'

'My colleagues have invested much time and credit, too.'

'You can finish your work without them.'

'I think so. Yes.'

'But they can't finish it without you.'

'Of course not.'

'There it is. I hope you see why it's the right thing to do.'

'I see why you are doing it.'

'We will go on together. We will put an end to all the nonsense that surrounds the Bright Moment, and get filthy rich.'

Dr Gagarian smiled his small, stiff smile. 'Yes, why not?'

The window closed and Hari saw that the robot was standing behind his father. Its silvery flanks and the glass turret of its head gleamed in the hot sunlight.

'I had hoped your father would be a lion,' it said. 'It seems that he was no more than a weak soul who tried and failed to match the reach of his ambition. He wanted to change the world, but only because he hoped to make a profit from it.'

Hari said, 'Have you or anyone else here taken up Dr Gagarian's research?'

'We have no interest in going where Sri Hong-Owen went. If she went anywhere.'

'My father wanted things to change, but you're stuck. You reached your limits long ago.'

'You aren't really angry with me,' the robot said. 'You're angry with your father.'

Aakash was watching them with a mild and somewhat quizzical expression, like a child trying to follow the conversation of adults.

'No, not with him,' Hari said.

It was true. He wasn't angry with his father: he was angry with himself for holding on to a last, foolish hope that it had been Dr Gagarian, not his father, who had started the long chain of causation that had led, step by step, with grave and terrible logic, to Mr Mussa's daughter approaching Nabhomani in Porto Jeffre, the deal with Sri Hong-Owen's daughters, the hijack . . .

His father had not changed after he passed over because the dead did not change. Aakash had so often talked about using the hard logic of philosophy to undercut the crazy beliefs of the end-time cults, about using technology derived from the Bright Moment to bring about a second age of expansion, and so on and so forth, but his idealism had been no more than a peg for a sales pitch. At bottom, he had only been interested in how he could profit from Dr Gagarian's research. He had been, as he had always been, a shrewd, unsentimental trader.

The robot said, 'I think we are finished here.'

Hari said to Aakash, 'Do you have anything else to tell me?'

'You know about the neural network and about the files it contains.'

'Yes, I do.'

'And you saw and understood the record of the last meeting.'

'It has given me much to think about.'

'I always wanted to do what was best for my family,' Aakash said.

'I know you tried, in your fashion.'

The robot said, 'We can take care of him. This viron does not take up much space, and he will be able to interact with other incomplete personalities. He might even be able to develop, if you could supply additional memories of his original.'

'No,' Hari said. 'He has done what he was supposed to do. It is time to let him go.'

'You would have me erase him?'

'He's already gone. What's left is no more than an eidolon.'

'And you will go on with this work?'

'I hope that someone will,' Hari said, and woke up in the hammock aboard the ship.

'That didn't take long,' Rubber Duck said. 'Did you get what you wanted?'

4

At one point on the short voyage to Earth, Hari asked Rubber Duck if he'd ever been tempted to head into the outer dark.

'When I can't get any more business, or if I acquire a debt I can't pay off, then maybe I'll decide it's time to go on the drift,' the tanky said. 'Hitch a ride on a long-period comet and go to sleep, wake up every century or so to see what's going on back in the system. Or maybe I'll go look for the Grey Harbours.'

'The place where old ships go to die?'

'The place where old tanky pilots like me go to merge with a heaven box that runs a parallel universe. Our own version of the Memory Whole, where a hundred thousand worldlets teem with every kind of civilisation, the free-trading spirit flourishes, and the running is free and easy. But not yet, not yet. I'm still interested in people. I want to find out what happens next. This thing you're caught up in, maybe it will shake things up.'

'Maybe,' Hari said.

The white pearl of Earth swelled in the window, an equatorial belt of ocean and land clamped between the fretted margins of two huge caps of ice and snow. And then Hari was down, amongst its cities and people and the weary weight of its gravity and history.

At first, he lived with his cousin, Aamaal, and her family. It took several months for his body to adapt to Earth's gravity and overcome assaults by viruses and allergies. He spent the time learning about the family business and absorbing the various protocols for dealing with representatives of the governments and co-ops of the nations and city-states of Earth. Aamaal was much older than him, a strong intelligent woman in her sixties, with two husbands and three children and five grandchildren. It had been her idea, not her father's, to set up the import/export business. She suggested to Hari that he could take charge of the Belt end of things. It was a kind offer, but Hari knew that her crew of factors were experienced and trustworthy and dependable, and he would be an unnecessary addition. And so he declined, saying that he wanted to see something of Earth before he could begin to think about returning to the Belt.

'You're worried that those weird sisters will catch up with you,' Aamaal said. 'Or that the Saints will.'

'If they were planning to come after me, they would have done so already. But perhaps I should move on, just in case. I've caused so much trouble to so many people . . .'

Hari was thinking of his dead, as he often did. His father and Agrata and Nabhomani. Dr Gagarian and his colleagues. Eli Yong and Levi, Sri Hong-Owen's daughters. And then there was Nabhoj, exiled on his lonely little rock . . .

He said, 'It doesn't seem right that I should have survived.'

'We're all glad that you did.'

'You don't know me. I wanted revenge, and the price was paid by others.'

'Hush,' Aamaal said. As if speaking to her youngest, soothing him after a nightmare. 'You're here now, and I wouldn't have it any other way.'

In the spring, Hari went out into the world and travelled through the ruins of the True Empire's hubris, through landscapes damaged by the Long Twilight. He attempted to drum up business, and delighted in the new places he saw, the new people he met. He tried to contact Ioni Robles Nguini, but the mathematician's family said that he had given up his research and did not want to be disturbed, and Hari did not press the matter. He found work for Rubber Duck, hauling cargoes between Earth and the Belt, and intermittently exchanged gossip with the old tanky, but he never went back up.

Ten years passed. Twenty. Twenty-two.

5

One night, Hari started awake with a fresh image printed in his mind: a pure white space resonant with arcane significance. People were shouting, somewhere outside his guest-house room. Angry, panicky voices. He rose and stepped to the window and looked out across the dark, low-rise city. Bamako, the capital of the Azawalk Fealties. It was a clear, cloudless night. Stars leaned over the city and the black ribbon of the Niger river. Lights were flickering on everywhere. Bells ringing out above a growing and restless murmur. A woman's voice below Hari's window asking the same question over and over. What happened? What just happened?

Hari knew what had happened. He knew what had passed through this world, and all the others.

Soon, the news was everywhere. It had been a second Bright Moment. As before, its wavefront had expanded across the Solar System at the speed of light, and everyone awake or asleep had been affected by it. But this time its origin had not been outside the Solar System, but within it. At Saturn, where the seraphs had vanished.

In the days that followed there were riots, several instances of mass suicide, flare-ups of old enmities, and other disturbances, but the trouble was localised and ended quickly. Humanity had survived the first Bright Moment; the second was disquieting, but lacked the shock of the unknown. People weren't asking what it was, but what it meant.

Hari's bios filtered messages from people who wanted to contact him, wanted to discuss the research that his father and Dr Gagarian and the others had done so long ago. One message immediately caught his attention. It was from Ioni Robles Nguini.

Fifteen days later, Hari arrived at Portlandia, an arcology on the western coast of what had once been the northernmost extent of Greater Brazil. He hired a scooter and travelled into the wilderness, following a broad valley that cut through a mountain range. The scooter was a blunt, powerful machine with a teardrop canopy that sheltered him from the freezing headwind. He flew above a river mostly covered in ice. Channels of open water smoked in the cold. Tall fir trees crowded the steep banks on either side. Green trees and white ice and black rock under a clear blue sky. Flying through this cold, clean landscape reminded him of riding with Riyya, in Ophir. The wild chase after Mr Mussa's daughter.

There was a series of falls bearded with enormous icicles. Hari jockeyed the scooter above them, flew across a broad gravel pan cut by braided, ice-choked channels. Presently, following the instructions he'd been given, he landed at the edge of the pan and walked up a steep path through stands of Douglas fir. Smaller trees grew in breaks in the thick cover. Yellow pine, sugar pine. Hemlock, incense cedar, maul oak. Hari began to sweat inside his heavy sweater and blue jerkin. It was very quiet under the trees. An intimidating silence broken only by soft slides of sloughed snow. No wind. His breathing and pulse loud in his ears.

The path twisted and turned. Sometimes it was hardly there. Dirty laceworks of old snow over slippery drifts of needles. The dry sticks of last year's weeds.

At some point he became aware that a drone was pacing him, slipping silently through the treetops high above.

He reached the edge of the trees, climbed through a nursery plantation where dense rows of seedlings grew in plastic tubes. Several bipedal, man-sized machines were working on the raw terraces of a distant slope. The path topped out on a broad bench that ran under the brow of a cliff, with a view across the valley towards a range of snow-clad mountains and a glacier spilling from the vast ice plain that covered what had once been high desert.

A small dwelling crouched under a bulge of stone deeply scored by ice-flow. A tan ferrocrete dome with skylight strips, a couple of out-buildings, a vegetable patch that was all tilled earth and dead stubs in this early season. A man stood where the vegetable patch gave way to rough grass. A large liver-coloured dog squatted at his side, rising as Hari approached.

'I came alone,' Hari said, spreading his empty hands at the level of his shoulders.

'I know you did,' Ioni Robles Nguini said.

'Maybe you could tell your dog I'm not a threat. I've been living on this world for more than twenty years, but I'm still not used to animals.'

'You don't have to worry about him if you don't give him anything to worry about. Come and sit down.'

They sat on a paved terrace that looked south-east, towards the iceblink of the glacier. The air was cold, but the terrace cupped the warmth of the sun. Ioni Robles Nguini poured spiced tea into translucent porcelain cups, set out a plate of honey biscuits.

Hari said, 'I suppose you know that I was looking for you, once upon a time.'

'That wasn't why I came out here to live. I haven't been hiding from you.'

'Did your family pass on my messages?'

'They told me that you were looking for me,' Ioni Robles Nguini said. 'That's all. And to be frank, I didn't ask. I wanted to put it all behind me.'

'I was angry, at the time,' Hari said. 'I felt cheated. I felt that the story I had been caught up in hadn't ended. I suppose I was still hoping for some kind of justice for what happened to me. To my family.'

'What do you feel now?'

'That the past I thought I'd left behind has caught up with me.'

'The past doesn't change, does it?'

'It's still there, same as it ever was. But we see it differently as we get older.'

'Yes. We do, don't we?' Ioni Robles Nguini said.

He was a slim, thoughtful man. Curly black hair clipped short and receding from a high forehead, three-day stubble. He was dressed in a woollen shirt and a sheepskin jacket, red jeans and sturdy boots. His dog lay near his feet, watching Hari.

Hari said, 'Are you still working on the Bright Moment?'

'I've begun to think about it again.'

'And this new Bright Moment, does it change anything?'

'It appears to possess the same properties as the first. There was a perturbation of the Higgs field, as before. The same characteristic propagation. The same universal effect on observers.'

'Sri Hong-Owen used the perturbation to send a message. The seraphs didn't.'

Ioni Robles Nguini smiled. 'Didn't they?'

'There wasn't any information.'

'There was a field of uniform information that our minds translated as a blankness.'

'An empty screen. Untrodden snow.'

'Similes are inaccurate. But yes, something like that.'

Hari was reminded of his conversations with his father. He said, 'They didn't have anything to say to us. That was their message. No last words, no farewell. They just did it.'

'I was never interested in why Sri Hong-Owen vastened herself, what she became, where she went,' Ioni Robles Nguini said. 'It's like asking what happened before the Big Bang. As with her, so with the seraphs. All we can do is speculate.'

'Dr Gagarian once said something like that.'

'He was a wise man.'

'Are you still working on the Higgs field? How to manipulate it, and how to fold information into it . . .'

'In my profession, you do your best work when you are young. And I'm no longer young.' Ioni Robles Nguini paused, then added, 'For many years I have been blocked. I have been unable to see any way forward. But now I am touched by the same enthusiasm I felt when I first began to think about the problem. I see new possibilities, new angles of attack.'

'What would your family say, about you telling me this? About us meeting?'

'Now we're getting to it, aren't we?'

'The sooner we get to it, the sooner we can get past it,' Hari said.

There was a short silence. They drank tea. They looked off at the view.

'When did you find out?' Ioni Robles Nguini said.

'Generally when a group of people die and you want to know who was responsible, you look for the last person standing.'

'I am not the last.'

'I suppose not. But someone told Sri Hong-Owen's daughters about Dr Gagarian's work. I'm pretty sure it wasn't anyone in my family, and I know it wasn't me.'

'It wasn't my idea,' Ioni Robles Nguini said.

'I rather thought it wasn't. Was it your family, then? Or the government of Greater Brazil?'

'Did you know that I am related to Sri Hong-Owen? She had two children. I don't mean the clade she created, her daughters, but the two sons born here, on Earth. One died without issue. The other, Alder Hong-Owen, was part of the revolution in Greater Brazil, at the end of the Quiet War. He helped to bring down the old regime, and to revive the idea of government for the people by the people.'

'How did that work out?'

'It lasted until the True Empire. A long time. My family took a strong interest in the Bright Moment when it became clear that Sri Hong-Owen was responsible. They felt that in some way it belonged to them. At first, they were happy that I was collaborating with Dr Gagarian and the others. They thought I would learn something useful. Something they could profit from. But then I was cut off. Dr Gagarian would no longer communicate with me, or with the others who were working with him. My family was afraid that he had solved the problem and wanted to keep the solution to himself. They were eager to find out what he had discovered, and also wanted to make sure that no one else knew about it, but they had no influence or presence in the Belt. You have lived on Earth for more than twenty years. You know how things are here.'

'I think I know a little.'

'A hundred years ago, all this was under ice. The ice was retreating then, and it is still retreating, but the thaw is slow. The damage was enormous. To Earth, to its peoples. We can scarcely reach low Earth orbit. We don't even have a presence on the Moon. But my family was trading with the Belt. It had certain contacts there. Including your uncle.'

'Tamonash.'

'I see this is new to you.'

'Yes. But not unexpected.'

'I can show you documents, files . . .'

'There's no need. Just tell me what you think he did.'

'It wasn't much. My family paid him to hire reivers who would kidnap Dr Gagarian when your family's ship next reached port. Instead, he reached out to what was left of Sri Hong-Owen's clade, on Enceladus.'

'I don't think it was Tamonash,' Hari said. 'I think it was his friend, Mr D.V. Mussa. Or rather, Mr Mussa's daughter. Another free trader.

My uncle had extensive dealings with her. I think he paid her to recruit reivers and dacoits who could help your family, and she decided instead to look for other people who might be interested in Dr Gagarian. And she found Sri Hong-Owen's daughters, or they found her, and they offered a better price. Or perhaps Mr Mussa's daughter thought that she could be paid twice.'

'However it fell out, my family believed that your uncle was helping them,' said Ioni Robles Nguini. 'Then your ship was hijacked. Your uncle denied that it was anything to do with him. My family threatened him, and threatened his daughter, but he stuck to his story.'

'I don't want to know if his daughter had anything to do with it.'

'I can assure you that she didn't,' Ioni Robles Nguini said. 'My family dealt with your uncle directly.'

'All right.'

'My family was in no position to carry out the threats, of course. They were afraid that their contract with your uncle would be uncovered, and cause a serious diplomatic incident. There was some wild talk about kidnap, assassination, but it came to nothing. There was a truce. A stalemate. And then you released Dr Gagarian's files, and the deal with your uncle no longer mattered.'

Hari thanked the philosopher for his candour; Ioni Robles Nguini said he hoped that the truth wasn't hurtful.

'It is what it is,' Hari said 'One thing I know about the truth, it's hard to destroy it. And it's hard to hide it, too. The only secrets people are able to keep secret aren't worth keeping, usually because they aren't true.'

'My family decided to keep *me* hidden,' Ioni Robles Nguini said. 'They were afraid that Sri Hong-Owen's daughters would find me. They were afraid you would find me. I lived inside the boundary of my mother's estate for many years. I had a partner, but it did not work out. Because my way of life was not natural. Because I was obsessed with my work. It was a shock when he left me. I decided that I could not live as I had been living, and eventually persuaded my mother to allow me to come here. I adopted a new identity. My family own this territory, and I supervise a very large and very successful reclamation and rewilding project. As the ice retreats, we plant out meadows and forests, introduce birds and animals. We recently introduced salmon to the river. We recreated them from gene libraries, and they follow the old patterns of migration. They mature out in the ocean and swim back to the place where they were spawned, fighting their way against the currents to find calm pools where they can spawn a new generation. I was so very proud, so very happy, when they first returned. It was one of the best days of my life.'

Hari thought he understood. 'Sri Hong-Owen and the seraphs gave up on this world. It wasn't good enough for them, or for what they wanted to become, so they went somewhere else. But this world is all we have.'

'If we want to make a difference, we have to work with what we have,' Ioni Robles Nguini said. 'I set aside my work on the Bright Moment because I thought it had no practical value. But now things have changed. Is it the same with you?'

'I gave it up a long time ago,' Hari said.

'You set it free. And by doing so, you set yourself free.'

'Yet here I am.'

'I am glad you came,' Ioni Robles Nguini said. 'Glad that you could hear my confession. Such as it was.'

'We were both used, weren't we?' Hari said. 'Both caught up in family business that reached back through a thousand years of history. Two thousand years.'

'I allowed myself to be used, so that I could pursue knowledge.'

'So did I.'

'And I will continue my work,' Ioni Robles Nguini said. 'But there will be no more secrets. I learned that from you, and I want to thank you.'

'It wasn't my idea,' Hari said, thinking of Riyya. Riyya Lo Minnot. Wondering what she and Rav's son were doing right now, in the garden in the rings of Saturn.

'I'm a trader, from a family of traders,' he told Ioni Robles Nguini. 'I don't know much about philosophy – I can't help you with that. But I think I should introduce you to some people I know.'

ACKNOWLEDGEMENTS

I have the great good luck to be able to thank a whole village of people who saved my life: Mr Austin O'Bichere, his surgical team, and the doctors, nurses and staff of the chemotherapy unit of University College Hospital. My profound gratitude to all of them, and to my partner, Georgina Hawtrey-Woore. If it hadn't been for their treatment, care and support I would not have survived to write this novel.

My thanks also to Simon Spanton and Marcus Gipps for editing suggestions, Nick Austin for his thorough and lucid copy-editing, and Simon Kavanagh at the Mic Cheetham Literary Agency for his help, support, and coffee hit points.

I first read about the epic of Pabuji, and the Story of the She-Camels, in William Dalrymple's *Nine Lives*. The poem 'I shall not coil my tangled hair . . .' is adapted from a traditional song of the Baul minstrels of Bengal. 'On the seashore of endless worlds the children meet with shouts and dances' is a line from Rabindranath Tagore's poem 'On The Seashore'.